"Wena 'Ahote, I am beyond marriageable age by our people's standards, but that is as I want it to be. It somehow seems right to me. Can you understand?"

"Yes, my love. It makes me happy, yet somewhere in the back of my mind I am anxious, for the experience of marriage and having children is what I thought all young girls wanted."

"I am not a young girl. I know what it is that I want, even if it seems different from the normal. How can I convince you?" Moon Fire felt as though she would die if he could not understand.

"You are truly a most unusual woman. Perhaps it is your ability to converse with our big and little brothers that makes you so." Pulling her close to mold her to his body, he added, "I suppose I must give praise to the gods that I have found you." Then he gave a deep throated chuckle. "I am glad Tsoongo and any others are no competition. Knowing this, I will never let you get away unless it is your will."

While lightly tracing his lips with her forefinger, she whispered, "Good. Now the problem is solved. Just love me."

MOON FIRE

JUDITH REDMAN ROBBINS

A SIGNET BOOK

SIGNET
Published by New American Library, a division of
Penguin Putnam Inc., 375 Hudson Street,
New York, New York 10014, U.S.A.
Penguin Books Ltd, 27 Wrights Lane,
London W8 5TZ, England
Penguin Books Australia Ltd,
Ringwood, Victoria, Australia
Penguin Books Canada Ltd, 10 Alcorn Avenue,
Toronto, Ontario, Canada M4V 3B2
Penguin Books (N.Z.) Ltd, 182–190 Wairau Road,
Auckland 10, New Zealand

Penguin Books Ltd, Registered Offices:
Harmondsworth, Middlesex, England

First published by Signet, an imprint of New American Library, a division of Penguin
Putnam Inc.

First Printing, December 2000
10 9 8 7 6 5 4 3 2 1

PUBLISHER'S NOTE
This is a work of fiction. Names, characters, places, and incidents either are the product
of the author's imagination or are used fictitiously, and any resemblance to actual
persons, living or dead, business establishments, events, or locales is entirely
coincidental.

To my soul mate, husband, friend,
and lover, Paul.

ACKNOWLEDGMENTS

Without the support of certain people in my life, the third and final book in the trilogy of Chaco Canyon in New Mexico would never have been the joy it was to complete. First, and foremost, I must acknowledge two of my guardian angels, Charles Breme and Herman Bruns, who watch lovingly over me as I write. Then there is Pat Miller, the wonderful woman who watches over my house when I travel to do research. Last, but not least, I wish to thank Joyce Breasure for guidance and support over many years through many trying times.

PRINCIPAL CHARACTERS AND TRANSLATION OF NAMES WHERE POSSIBLE

Sowiwa (shortest ear of corn), later known as Moon Fire. She is born with six toes and has the ability to speak with all the little brothers, great and small. She is Chakwaina's great-granddaughter.

Wena 'Ahote—A young student aspiring to be a priest due to his love of astronomy and music. He is of Nish 't Ahote's lineage.

Sikyawa (yellow rock), Sowiwa's father, who is a teacher of stone masonry. He has his own ambitions for his three children.

Tupkya (safe place), Sowiwa's mother, housewife, and staunch supporter of her husband, who causes much tension with her thoughtless cutting comments.

Lansa (lance, spear), Sowiwa's older brother, educated but insensitive, materialistic, and manipulative.

Palasiva (copper), Sowiwa's younger brother, who becomes a warrior against the subtle wishes of his parents. He becomes the victim of blackmail.

Leetayo (fox), Sowiwa's cousin who is a student in the holy school and is jealous of Wind Swept Woman's abilities.

Sihu (flower), Wind Swept Woman's best friend. Sihu falls in love with Sowiwa's older brother, Lansa.

Tsoongo (pipe), one of Sowiwa's father's stone mason prodigies, who vies for Sowiwa's attentions as set up by her father and mother.

Tenyam (hard wood), a very narrow-minded elder who came by his name due to the fact that he is always right and does not want to be confused with the facts.

Angwusi (crow), another very verbal self-righteous elder who stands by Tenyam.

Hoohu (arrow), an elder who sees as an arrow straight to the heart of an issue, and always is at loggerheads with Tenyam and Angwusi. He sees the "big picture."

Eykita (he groans), a quiet, reserved elder who spends more time groaning than speaking, and is easily led.

Ruupi Tuuhikya (crystal medicine man), a power-hungry priest who uses a crystal to discern the sicknesses within his people.

Taatawi (songs), sun priest and knower of all songs.

Posaala (blanket), building surveyor, a mild-mannered, quiet man who just does his job and is known for the beauty of his blankets.

Maahu (cicada), architect and expert flutist. Some consider him berdache.

Awta (bow), construction supervisor and expert bow maker who grows increasingly upset as construction comes to a halt.

Iswungwa (Coyote clan member), trade manager and a good hunter in trade.

Teo, leader of the raiders who blackmails Palasiva.

Uta, raider who tries to kill Palasiva.

Kopolvu (tree stump), a sentinel friend to Palasiva.

Masichuvio (gray deer), Anasazi warrior chief.

Tovosi (smooth wood), warrior friend of Palasiva.

Kyaro (parrot), evil elder of an outlier.

Kwahu (eagle), another evil elder of an outlier.

Charisa (elk), an acolyte assisting Ruupi.

Seven Moon, a Mayan-Toltec trader.

Ochata, chief of the raiders and Teo's father.

Mina, young girl of the raiders promised to another.

Nila, Mina's mother.

Ote, Mina's father.

Tachato, good Hohokam elder.

Lumo, Huko, and Pioco, Hohokam elders who favor slavery.

Tosi (Sweet Cornmeal), youngest of Sihu's and Lansa's sons.

Palatala (red light of sunrise), Sihu's and Lansa's oldest son.

Tecpatl (flint knife), Mayan eagle knight.

Chicauaztli (rattle stick), Mayan eagle knight.

PREFACE

Many legends of the Hopi and Pueblo Native Americans speak of their ancestors known as the Anasazi and the fact that they finally arrived at their present homes, migrating from the south to the north. They spent time in many different locations in an effort to find the proper place in the fourth world of today, where they could find resources, peace, and happiness as the Creator had advised them to do. Until around A.D. 900 their villages consisted of pit houses (subterranean homes in the ground). Then suddenly some of the people built "small houses" (one or two rooms made of fitted sandstone with core and rubble inside the walls).

In a canyon called Chaco, located in the four corners region of the Southwest, an unusual thing began to happen, so unusual, that archaeologists called it "The Chaco Phenomenon." The "small house" concept was enlarged upon, and "big houses" began to emerge. In the space of two hundred years eleven "big houses" were built and a very large community developed that included a sophisticated road system. The roads were chiseled out of rock with the primitive tools at hand, and radiated out of Chaco as the central point in all four directions, often leading to other "big houses." It is in this canyon, which to us would seem desolate and uninhabitable, that the Anasazi culture grew.

The largest of the eleven buildings, five stories high and consisting of nearly eight hundred rooms, is known to us today as Pueblo Bonito. This is the home of my character, Sowiwa, and her family. In the concept of "The Chaco Phenomenon" this community of eleven buildings is considered the "Center" of the Anasazi culture. I have used the largest building as a religious school as I also did in *Coyote Woman* and *Sun Priestess,* and even though the story takes place almost seventy years later, it is still a continuation of the saga of the people known as the Anasazi in Chaco Canyon.

In and around A.D. 1130 it is documented that the people began to abandon Chaco Canyon, taking with them only as much as they could carry on their back. Research blames it on a severe drought that lasted almost twenty-five years, but this book attempts to give other explanations. Wandering tribes were constantly raiding the Anasazi for the grain and crops they grew and stored. More migrations from the Mayan-Toltec in Mexico and the Yucatan bombarded the Anasazi with their bloody sacrificial religious rites. Perhaps the most serious problem that has plagued cultures since time began was the decay from within, not unlike what continues to happen in the world today.

In many caves and on many rocks throughout the Southwest today there are petroglyphs and pictographs of human cloaked figures that are thought to be shamans. Many of these have hands with six fingers and feet with six toes. It is thought that this sort of disfigurement was a sign of being gifted. Sowiwa is born with six toes and is truly gifted.

By A.D. 1150 Chaco Canyon was completely abandoned.

PROLOGUE

M y soul soars over the dry, desolate, deserted canyon. Even in death the canyon is an impressive sight. In the half-faded light at the end of Sun Father's journey, the honey-colored sandstone cliffs look soft and alive with the shifting shadows. I float over the area until Sun Father has at last completed his journey and set, filling the western sky with pink, orange, and fiery crimson. The lighting has caused the great houses to take on a pale pink hue like the pink quartz that is so rare to the people.

When I was in my human form, I knew this canyon well, for I was raised by a loving family, and grew to love the people. I was not one of them. Several generations ago, the revered Coyote Woman and sun priestess rescued me as a very small child from the raiders who had killed my parents and left me for dead. All I remembered in that life was the wonderful "people of peace," the Anasazi, who called me Chakwaina. They raised me with unconditional love, yet somehow I wonder if I did my share. You see, I was born with a gift, the gift of having the ability to communicate with animals, birds, insects, and sometimes even plants and rocks. I chose to raise a family rather than pursue that gift, and I now know that I could have given more to the people if I had pursued the gift.

Be that as it may, I made my choice and married a fine man who gave me children. Now it would seem that I passed my gift to my great-granddaughter for she has taken full advantage of it, and it has served her well. Unfortunately the times she lives in were not all like the times I enjoyed. This beautiful canyon in which I was raised was only marginally able to support human life in numbers, but we drew resources from our outlier small houses and great houses where water, timber, and game were more abundant. Ours was a complex culture and this lonely, desolate canyon was the hub of that culture for a time. Our traders traveled far and wide, bringing in a little bit of everything, and many traders traveled to us, for our turquoise was in high demand.

Let my soul quit rambling, but before I move on, I would speak of my great-granddaughter. . . .

CHAPTER 1

A.D. 1116–1119

Pain gripped Tupkya's belly like an angry ice cold hand. It had been a little more than four season cycles since her first baby had torn her apart in agony. The older women had told her that the first child is always the most painful, but she had begun to doubt their wisdom. She had also been told that time would make her forget how bad the last one had been. This child seemed to be trying to crawl through her flesh as she breathed deeply with each pain that was becoming more frequent. At least this time she did not worry as she had before. Having survived one child, she tried to relax into the pain, welcoming the time when the child would arrive and it all would be over.

Wrapping her arms around her belly, she whispered hoarsely to the old woman who assisted, "Laurel tea. Please, laurel tea." She found that she need not have asked, for the woman accommodated her immediately after her request. She straddled the birthing stool, sweat pouring, dealing with each pain that seemed to be closer and closer together.

As the old woman mopped her brow with cool water, she felt a warm surge of fluid, and knew that it would not take much longer if everything was as it should be. The pains became more intense. She fought to keep from screaming, for she had been told that screaming might scare the baby and postpone its delivery. The old woman gave her a piece of leather to bite so that she would not bite into her tongue. At last a searing pain ripped through her as the baby's head entered the fourth world. She bit down on the leather and felt the tiny shoulders slide their way into the harshness of the new reality. The rest was so much easier. She waited anxiously to see if the baby was normal. The old woman cut and tied the cord and cleaned the baby, who let out a hardy cry. She then laid it down and cleaned the afterbirth, putting it and the cord aside to be buried later.

Tupkya asked for the baby. The old woman told her that the child was fine, and was indeed a gifted one.

"Why do you say that is so?" asked Tupkya as she received the precious new bundle in her exhausted arms.

The old one said, "Look her over carefully and you will see."

Tupkya, whose name meant "safe place," wanted to sleep, but she also wanted to know her daughter was normal. She unfolded the soft cotton cloth and checked her little hands that appeared to be perfect. Her body was perfect, but then she noticed her toes. There were not five toes on each of the tiny feet, but six. Tears welled in her eyes as she acknowledged what the old woman had said. It was rare that a child was born with six toes or six fingers, but when that did happen, the child was considered gifted. She wondered what sort of gift her little daughter had received from the Creator, and marveled that she should be the mother of such a child. She knew her people would honor her and settled back into her clean mats and blankets to sleep.

She was named Sowiwa, "shortest ear of corn," due to her size. Her frame was tiny and delicate, but what was most remarkable was the sweetness of her disposition. She was quiet and undemanding. Her older brother had been so much the opposite that Tupkya found that she was enjoying the child more and more. She noticed, however, that Sowiwa was very quiet among humans, and seemed intent on only listening. The child was now nearly three season cycles of age and spoke exceedingly well for one so young. Though her smile was radiant whenever adults were present, her sparkling black eyes reflected an unidentified wisdom. She was great-grandchild to Chakwaina, who had been brought back from the land of the Hohokam by the revered and now-deceased Coyote Woman, who had been sun priestess for most of her life. Stories were still told around the fire of Coyote Woman's abilities and her many journeys. Sowiwa's great-grandmother, Chakwaina, had the gift of speaking to the animals in her youth, but had given up that gift to marry, and to assume the role of motherhood.

Now, as Tupkya observed her daughter playing with a cricket, she wondered if Chakwaina's gift might have been passed on to Sowiwa. The child seemed to be truly enjoying herself. The cricket stood still as stone with Sowiwa lying on her belly, looking directly into the cricket's eyes. Neither of them moved for a very long time. Tupkya marveled that the child made no attempt to touch the insect, but only continued to stare at it while nodding her head.

She felt a soft nudge on her neck as Sikyawa, "yellow rock," her husband, said quietly, "She is so unlike Lansa. He is so blustering and boisterous, much like his name. What a contrast we have in our children. It makes me wonder if there is power in a name. What are your thoughts, my sweet wife?"

Turning to Sikyawa, she threw her arms around him, squeezing him tightly. "Your thoughts are much like mine," she said, "for even now Lansa is out with the other boys practicing his skills as a warrior."

Sikyawa held her tightly. "Tupkya, I have been asked to move from our small outlier home to the holy school, where I shall be an instructor of masonry. I feel it an honor that this has come to pass. Our children will grow up with the best that this world can make available to them, and it is my hope that you will agree," he stated as he traced her lips with his index finger.

"Oh, Sikyawa, you bring truly wonderful news, but look!" she exclaimed.

Sowiwa was now holding the cricket in the palm of her tiny hand. It seemed as though she had put a spell on it, for it moved hardly at all. Even its long sensors were still.

Both parents stared until at last Sikyawa said, "Perhaps I should speak to the elders or our sun priest of what we see happening here."

Tupkya's expression changed from one of wonder to one of concern. "Speak carefully, my husband, for we would not want anyone to think of her as 'pawaka.' Do you not think she is too young to be possessed?"

"Yes, my love, but some might say that age makes no difference. With this in mind I feel that the right person to speak to is Taatawi, the young sun priest in the holy school. I want you to know I cherish the fact that you always stand beside me. Now let us begin our preparations to move into the holy school."

"We can leave when Sun Father next rises, if that is your desire," she said. "I shall call Lansa now to help us." Leaving Sowiwa with her new cricket friend and her father, she went outside calling loudly for Lansa.

The family of four were ushered to their new quarters in the holy school by Tenyam, an elder whose demeanor was reflected in the meaning of his name, "hard wood." He was an average size man whose skin was quite leathery and wrinkled due to years of exposure to the intense rays of Sun Father. His eyes were small black beads that looked sternly at the world under heavy eyelids. Though he did not seem to know how to smile, he welcomed them, telling them to let him know if they were in need of anything. He also stated that their evening meal would be brought to them since they had arrived during the later part of Sun Father's cycle.

After the elder had taken his leave, Tupkya remarked, "Do you suppose that he was afraid his face would crack if he smiled?"

Sikyawa chuckled at her, then replied, "I don't know, little wife, but he certainly is an elder in whom I would not confide. Now let us unpack our belongings and turn our quarters into our new home."

Lansa, who was almost seven season cycles of age, had balked when he learned he must move with his family to the holy school. Even now he said, "I want to go back to our other home. I don't know anyone here and I miss my friends."

"You will make new friends," his father retorted. "In just two more season cycles you will be old enough to attend classes, and there you will have many friends. Now, son, stop your whining and help your mother and me unpack. I am to begin my instructional duties when next Sun Father rises, so let us work together in the short time we have."

Lansa could be heard grumbling to himself as he worked at

unpacking and arranging his belongings. He looked at his little sister, who played quietly with a wooden doll that her father had carved for her, and said, "Why can't Sowiwa help? What good is a little sister? All she does is play. Why couldn't she have been a little brother?"

Tupkya responded in short temper. "When you were almost three season cycles of age, you were no help either. Now cease your prattling or I will give your name to the spirit dancer who punishes."

Lansa's eyes grew wide with terror. "No, my mother, please don't do that. I'll be quiet. I promise." The boy knew that if his name came to the attention of the spirit dancer who punishes bad children, that he would be punished in front of the entire community during a ceremonial and that the embarrassment would be worse than the punishment itself.

Tupkya swept the dirt floors and arranged their sleeping mats. She also cleaned the hearth and arranged her cooking bowls and utensils in a neat row nearby. Sikyawa arranged his hunting weapons and belongings neatly next to Tupkya's, though he knew his hunting days would now be few, due to his instructional duties.

Bowls of rich rabbit stew along with piki bread were brought to them by four acolytes. With weary bones and full stomachs, the little family settled into their new life and a good, sound sleep.

Tupkya made it a practice early in every sun cycle to leave the holy school and take her two children for a walk through the canyon. This was the season of the harvest. Much food had been brought into the granaries, for this had been a season of plenty. There had been no rain for many sun cycles and the vegetation was very dry. Sun Father shone with a warmth that was most welcome to humans but not to plant life. Tupkya was thankful that rain had come when they needed it, and that her people had had an abundant harvest, for she remembered that the previous season cycle had not been good. The rains had not come, and in fact, had not come during the season cycle before that. When her people had appealed for assistance from the Hohokam and the Mogollon tribes, they had learned that they, too, had experienced the same lack of rain. She wondered if the spirit dancers were doing something wrong. Her thoughts ran accordingly when suddenly she noticed her daughter. She listened to the child's tinkling laughter as she approached a hollow log along an arroyo.

Sowiwa's cheeks were pink with excitement. Tupkya watched her little daughter, who squealed in delight. She was glad that Lansa was off pretending to be a great hunter, and she held her silence so she would not disturb what was happening.

The desert mouse had come out of its home beneath a yucca plant and had placed itself squarely in front of Sowiwa. The two of them were as frozen as an icicle and each stared at the other. The mouse had big eyes and ears, and had white socks on his feet. The mouse seemed to sense her rather than see her, yet seemed to feel no threat to its well-being. Its nest was round in shape and the entrance seemed to have a plug or door that could be closed for warmth.

Sowiwa lay on her stomach, parallel to the log, and extended her hand palm down. Though she could hear no sound uttered between the two, Tupkya felt certain there must be some form of communication. The mouse moved slowly and steadily toward Sowiwa's outstretched hand, then climbed on. There it remained for a short time, then finally ran lightly up to the child's shoulder. It seemed almost as if it might have been whispering in her ear, but then, just as quickly, it ran down her arm and back into its hole.

Sowiwa glowed with happiness. "Oh, my mother, the mouse is the mother of a family of five little ones. She says she is most thankful for the seeds, berries, and bark she has stored."

Tupkya sent her daughter a curious look. "She told you that? What else did she say?"

"She said she is worried about her family and their survival. She says that mice have more enemies than any other of Awon-awilona's children and that everyone picks on them. Oh, I am so glad we are not mice."

"And so am I, pumpkin. Now let us return to the complex." She took Sowiwa's little hand in her own.

"You know, Mother," Sowiwa said in a matter-of-fact manner, "mice can show us how to get the big things by working on the little things. That mouse said that we could learn from them."

"And what do you think she meant by that?" Tupkya asked with a surprised look on her face.

"I'm not sure, but maybe when I grow up I will know," she said as she skipped away from her mother, pounding up the desert dust with her yucca sandals. "Oh, Mother, I am so happy, and I love you."

Though Tupkya did not skip and run as Sowiwa wanted her to do, she picked up her speed and sank deep in thought as she watched her gifted little daughter.

When the two children were wrapped in their blankets and enjoying the release of sound sleep, Tupkya, who was wrapped securely in Sikyawa's arms, spoke softly of what had transpired during their walk.

Sikyawa remained silent for a short time after she had finished, as if he were thinking through what she had said. At last he said, "If she says such things now, what will she say when she is grown?"

"I don't know, my husband, but have you found a chance to speak with Taatawi?"

"No, my love, but I will not delay any longer. You can be sure of that. Now let us get some rest. Know that I love you."

When next Sun Father arose, Sikyawa left his family to search out Taatawi. He found him in the healing kiva and as was the custom he waited for him on the roof of the kiva next to the ladder that was used to enter it.

At long last his waiting was over and Taatawi emerged. "Ho," Taatawi exclaimed. "To what do I owe this pleasure?"

"Revered One, I would ask a little of your time, when it suits you, of course."

Taatawi was a striking figure dressed in a flowing white robe. His facial features were bold and handsome. His eyes twinkled under perfectly defined brows and his mouth was wide and generous when he smiled, displaying perfect white teeth. He was young to be sun priest, for he had lived only twenty-four season cycles. He was also knower of all songs. His people loved to hear his warm tenor voice as it soared during ceremonials when certain songs were required. He placed his right hand on Sikyawa's left shoulder in a gesture of friendship and said, "Will we speak in your quarters or in mine?"

Sikyawa replied very quickly, "I would much prefer yours, for there we would have no interruptions." He knew that Tupkya would never disturb them, but Lansa was another story.

They walked silently to Taatawi's quarters. Taatawi spread an additional mat on the earth floor and motioned to Sikyawa to be seated. After sharing the traditional pipe, Taatawi patiently waited for Sikyawa to speak.

After the brief time Sikyawa needed to gather his thoughts, he broke the silence. "My problem is delicate, Revered One. My youngest child is nearly three season cycles of age, and seems to be quite advanced in many ways. She speaks rather eloquently, but only when she is spoken to. Otherwise she is very quiet. Tupkya, my sweet wife, and I have been watching her for some time now, and we have watched her do some most unusual things, or at least we think they are unusual." He paused and waited for Taatawi's reaction.

"Let us speak of these unusual things then," coaxed Taatawi.

Sikyawa cleared his throat and continued. "My daughter, Sowiwa, was born with six toes on each foot, which proved to us from her birth that she would be a gifted child. When she was but two season cycles of age, Tupkya and I watched her playing with a cricket. We noticed it did not jump away from her, but seemed to be in a spell. It almost seemed that my daughter and the cricket were conversing, but of course, not in the language of the people. She had the cricket in the palm of her hand, and well . . ." Sikyawa stopped again to watch Taatawi's face.

Taatawi raised his perfectly etched eyebrows and said, "I am beginning to understand your concern. Is there more?"

"Yes, Revered One, there is. Only recently Tupkya took Sowiwa for a walk, which she does once every sun cycle. Sowiwa made friends with a deer mouse. She lay prostrate on her stomach while the mouse ran up her arm to her shoulder and seemed to be whispering in her ear. On the return trip Sowiwa told my wife that the mouse was concerned for her five young. She also said the mouse has much to teach the people.

Mice can teach us how to get the big things by working on the little things. When my wife asked her what the mouse meant when she said that, Sowiwa laughed and said she did not know, but perhaps she would know when she grew up. Taatawi, I am most concerned. Something says to me that this should not be told to anyone else, for it might be misinterpreted."

"These are my thoughts also, Sikyawa. Some might think her to be 'pawaka' when that may not be the case at all. Does your son know any of this?"

"Not to my knowledge. He is always out playing war with his friends. You are right in that he is not the kind of child to keep secrets. We shall try to keep this from him."

"What is your daughter's lineage? From whom does she descend?"

"My wife is granddaughter to Chakwaina, which makes my daughter her great-granddaughter."

"Ah, and Chakwaina, if the story I remember is correct, had the gift to speak with our brothers, the animals and insects."

"That is correct," replied Sikyawa. "My wife and I have thought that perhaps she may have inherited the gift."

"It may be so, but I would make a suggestion." He delayed further conversation very briefly as if gathering his thoughts. At last he said, "She must be carefully watched. If you find her communicating with owl, or crow, she is 'pawaka.' Let us hope she only has the gift. You may rest assured that none of which we have spoken will leave the confines of these walls. Now let us enjoy another smoke."

The two men sat again in silence as each became lost in their individual thoughts.

When Sikyawa returned to his quarters later during that sun cycle, he found Tupkya stirring a pot of venison seasoned with wild onions and thickened with corn dumplings. She put down her ladle, waiting for his embrace. Sowiwa was playing quietly with her corn husk doll while Lansa was somewhere in the plaza, playing with his newly found friends. Sikyawa folded her in his arms and nibbled on her ear. "My sweet little wife, Awonawilona has blessed us with such a wonderful life. Is the meal ready? Shall we talk now or after we have eaten?"

"As long as I stir the pot occasionally, it can wait. Let us talk now while we have some privacy." She was, of course, referring to the fact that Lansa was absent and Sowiwa probably would not be a problem.

Seating themselves together on a mat, Sikyawa began. "I have spoken to Taatawi, who was most gracious and understanding. He feels that we need to be observant of our little one. He says if she seems to commune with owl, or crow, we may have a problem. Otherwise he feels that due to her lineage with Chakwaina, perhaps she may be gifted." He took Tupkya's hand in his own.

"Oh, Sikyawa, I am glad you did not talk to anyone else. You seem to have chosen the right person." She rose to give the pot a stir.

"Tupkya, the stories in the community and even the outliers are that Taatawi is a just and open-minded person. Truly he has proven that it is so. He did, however, say one other thing."

Tupkya returned to the mat with a curious look on her lovely face. She folded her hands in her lap and asked, "And what is that other thing, my husband?"

"He said that there are those who would prejudge, and well . . ." He seemed hesitant to go on.

"And well, what?" she asked.

"He suggested that our observation of her be done discreetly, which means that even our son Lansa must not know what we are doing, for he may blurt it to his friends."

Tupkya cast him a look of concern. "Then it shall be as he asks, for I must agree that Lansa is loud, and outgoing, and in all probability could not keep a secret."

Sikyawa was once again struck by her unquestionable support, and pulling her to him, he whispered, "I am such a lucky man. You have always supported me in all that I do. Awona-wilona has truly sent me someone who is not of this earth." He trailed his fingers over her lips and down to her shoulders sending a shiver through the core of her being.

"There is something I must tell you," she said. Her obsidian eyes twinkled mischievously as she held herself in check.

"What you have to say is not bad, I hope," he said with sudden tension in his demeanor.

"Oh, my loving husband, I cannot imagine that you would think it so, for you see, we are to have another child."

"Tupkya, my Tupkya," he said with misty eyes. "This is wonderful news. Truly we are blessed, and this is news we need not keep from Lansa. He has wanted a brother for so long."

No sooner had Sikyawa spoken than Lansa came rushing in exclaiming, "My mother, my father, I will be a great warrior someday. All of my friends agree, and oh, I am hungry. Can we eat soon?"

Tupkya rose to stir the pot once more, while Sikyawa said, "Yes, my son, we will eat soon, but first you must sit down, for there is news."

Lansa's face fell. As most children, he was very hungry, and did not want to be put off.

Tupkya gathered Sowiwa in her arms and joined them on the mat. Lansa sat very close to his father, regarding his little sister with jealousy due to the fact that in his mind he felt that Tupkya lavished more attention on Sowiwa than on himself. Sikyawa put his arm around his son, saying, "Lansa, my son, is there not something you have been wishing for lately?"

"Oh yes, my father. I would like a man-size bow and many arrows. I have been practicing with the atlatl, but I must also master the bow and arrow if I am to be a great warrior."

Sikyawa chuckled and hugged his son to him. "No, Lansa, that was not quite what I had in mind. Perhaps this is a good time for me to defer to your mother."

Lansa quickly shifted a questioning expression from Sikyawa to Tupkya, whose smile was soft and knowing. She reached for Lansa's hand and held it tightly. At last she said, "Lansa, Awonawilona has showered his blessings on our little family. We are to enjoy the arrival of another child in the near future. Now I ask you what it is you have been wishing for?"

Lansa jumped off the mat and ran behind his mother, hugging her and burying his face in the sweet sage fragrance of her hair. "A brother! Oh yes, Awonawilona. Let our new baby be a brother!" Again he jumped up and moved to his father, clutching him in a firm hug.

Sikyawa's eyes twinkled as he laughed.-"If I did not know better, I would think my son was related to one of our big-eared rabbits. Lansa, this is truly a special moment. I knew you would be happy. Now let us enjoy your mother's delicious cooking."

Tupkya immediately rose to ladle out the stew in gourd bowls as the family ate heartily and enjoyed feelings of loving warmth and family comradery that had not been felt for some time.

The air was crisp and cool, but Sun Father's rays were still very warm. Shadows were short on the golden sandstone cliffs, for Sun Father still had some time to go before completing his journey across the sky. The blessed rainy season had left the canyon much greener than usual, and the greasewood and four-winged saltbush had become plump and full of vitality. The cottonwoods lining the wash that bisected the canyon swayed in the breeze.

Tupkya and Sowiwa were enjoying their routine walk. Tupkya knew that their sun cycles were numbered, for it would not be long before the cold season would bluster its way in pushing out the gentle season of the harvest. She also knew that when the season of greening arrived she would be too heavy with child to walk any distance.

Sowiwa was skipping merrily at her mother's side, singing her own little song. Her short black hair shining with slightly reddish highlights bounced up and down with each step she took. She was obviously in her element, for she seemed happiest when she was outdoors. When she spotted two small piñon pines growing on either side of a huge rock, she suddenly stopped. Tupkya thought it was as if the child had frozen.

It was then that Tupkya saw the object of Sowiwa's attention. It was standing on its hind legs and rocking to and fro, waving its paws in a strange rhythmic exercise, and looked very much like it was dancing. Its quills lay flat indicating that it was not in the least bit disturbed. The porcupine's color was dark, blackish brown with an overlay of yellowish cast from the guard hairs. Its under fur was soft and grayish brown in color. There was evidence that the young animal had been chewing on the bark of one of the piñon pines. Tupkya's immediate instinct was to seize Sowiwa and run, but the thought was short-lived.

Sowiwa began to sway to and fro, waving her hands in imitation of the young porcupine. Her eyes were closed for a short time, then she opened them and stared at her quilled friend, never ceasing her body motions. It seemed almost as if the two of them were performing an age-old dance long forgotten by humans.

The porcupine's feet never moved from its chosen spot, but it continued its rocking forward and backward along with the waving of its paws. The dance was unlike anything that the spirit dancers did during the many ceremonials of the Anasazi people and seemed to Tupkya like a new rhythm in the dance of life. She looked on in amazement. It also seemed that in some way Sowiwa and her dancing partner had spiritually become as one.

As if on cue, both of them ceased dancing. The porcupine ambled with a waddling gate to the piñon pine, then climbed up and sat in the crotch of the tree. Sowiwa slowly turned and walked toward Tupkya with an enormous smile. She took Tupkya's hand and together they walked back toward the great houses of the community.

Once out of sight of the porcupine, Tupkya stopped and knelt beside Sowiwa, holding her tightly. "Sowiwa," she exclaimed. "Do you not know the dangers of angering that animal?"

"But he was not angry. He was enjoying himself. He told me so," she said. "We talked, but not with words."

"I knew that was what was happening, but it did nothing to assure me that I should not be concerned. Ah, sweet one, you worry me," Tupkya said while pulling Sowiwa's head close to her bosom. "The quills on the porcupine are barbed and cause much pain if they are in your skin. If it had gotten angry and lashed its tail, you would now be one miserable little girl."

"But, Mother, it would not have done so. It, like all of our brothers, can teach us much. One of those things is to learn to enjoy life, and that if you just keep shuffling along, you will still get what you want out of life in spite of the bad things people do to you."

"And did the porcupine say anything else?"

"No, but he did say I would understand everything better when I grow up."

Tupkya did not respond. She was too deep in thought. The two of them walked in silence toward the security of their quarters.

The cold season passed with all the elaborate ceremonials, each lasting sixteen sun cycles. The first was known as "Wuwuchimu," which included the "new fire ceremony," and the reenactment of the emergence of the people from the womb of the earth. It was a supplication for the germination of all forms of life on earth, animal, vegetable, and, of course, mankind. Then came "Soyal,"which honored the winter solstice and assured the people that Sun Father would again return to bring the blessed warmth so necessary for the germination of the crops and, of course, for the relief of the people. Then came "Powamu," where beans are germinated and children are initiated into adulthood. All three ceremonies are interrelated and involve correlative obligations that must function harmoniously for the benefit of all on the one cosmic road of life. All three ceremonies are dramatic interpretations of the "Creator's" plan, which supersedes human will.

Sowiwa's eyes shone brilliantly as she watched the masked spirit dancers. Her little hands clenched in awe when one of them gave her a corn husk doll. Her thoughts were not of fear, which was so typical of most children, but of love and a feeling of being complete. Tupkya had told her that these spirit dancers were necessary for their very survival, but she had not told her why. Again she thought it was a thing she would understand when she grew older.

Tupkya, meanwhile, grew heavier with child as time moved on.

"I am afraid the child is early," whispered an older woman. "She labors as though it is not false labor, but the real thing."

Sowiwa sat quietly listening to the two women who assisted in the birthing process. She watched her mother break out in a sweat as she ground her teeth together to avoid expressing the pain. The child's little body responded in kind to the condition of her beloved mother, feeling her pain as her own.

Suddenly one of the women took notice of her and took her hand. "This little one must wait outside. True she is female, but she is too young."

Sowiwa tried resisting as she turned her head anxiously toward her laboring mother, but there was little she could do. She found herself waiting outside the family's little complex, though she still felt Tupkya's pain. Why was it, she wondered, that she found it so easy to relate to and feel other people's pain? Why was she able to communicate with her "little brothers," the animals? She did not know how long she had sat with such thoughts racing through her mind, when she heard a lusty, but diminutive cry. She ran for Lansa, who was not far away in the plaza, playing with some of his friends. "Lansa, Lansa, the child is here!" she shouted as she tugged on his tunic.

"You must be mistaken," he said. "The child is too early, but then what good is a little sister? Sisters are nothing but a nuisance. Go on! Go! Don't waste my time." With those words he resumed playing with his friends.

Sowiwa turned away once more from the brother who seemed to always reject her. Her heart was broken when she thought about her headstrong brother, who, even with the birth of a sibling, went his own way, making her feel as if she meant nothing to him or even to anyone. Nursing her rejection, she slowly made her way back to their mother, where she waited patiently outside the door.

In her childhood time frame it seemed that perhaps a sun cycle had passed by, when one of the women took her by the hand and gently led her to her mother. Her mother's hair hung in wet strands around her beautiful head, but her smile was one that only a proud mother can give. It seemed to Sowiwa that there was an unearthly glow around Tupkya's head and also around that of the newborn child. The child silently reached to her, saying, "Little sister, I am here." She wondered if she really was hearing correctly, or if it was only because it was what she wanted to hear. Her eyes grew round with love and wonder as she stood at her mother's side.

"Where is Lansa?" whispered Tupkya.

"Mother, I . . ."

"You what, child?"

"He did not believe me when I told him. He said the child is early, and that it could not be." She hung her head as a tear escaped from the corners of her eyes.

"If those are his feelings, then so be it," Tupkya said as she held her little daughter's hand with tight reverence. "I want you to know that you have another brother, and I love you, sweet one."

"Oh, Mother, I hope that this brother is different."

"You need to know that I am aware of your older brother's feelings toward you." She stopped the conversation at the appearance of Sikyawa, who fairly floated across the dirt floor with twinkling eyes and an enormous proud smile that displayed his nearly perfect white teeth.

He took his little daughter's hand, then pulled her into his arms with a firm but tender hug. He continued to hold her as he took Tupkya's hand into his own free hand. "Oh, my loving wife, you have made me a proud father once again . . . a father of two boys and a wonderful little girl. I hope this birth has been easier than the previous ones."

Tupkya squeezed his hand saying, "My husband, this birth was somewhat easier, but maybe that's because he is so tiny."

Sikyawa placed his forefinger into the grasp of his new son's tiny fist. "You are so right," he said. "He is so wrinkled, and his nails are so soft, but his grip is firm and that of a tiny little man. We must consider a name for him." Then suddenly as if coming out of a dream, he inquired, "Where is Lansa? Has he not been sent for?"

Tupkya did not answer. She wanted Sowiwa to repeat her story to her father.

Sowiwa tightened her arms around her father's neck. "My father, I went to Lansa who was playing with his friends. He said he didn't believe I spoke the truth . . . that it was too soon for the baby. He went on playing with his friends." She watched her father clench his teeth to hide his anger.

"Little daughter, go to him again. Tell him I wish to see him immediately."

"I will not be long," she said, and turned on her heels, fairly running as she departed. When she returned well ahead of Lansa, she found her tiny new brother in her father's arms. Tupkya's eyes were closed in an attempt to rest her exhausted body. "He is coming, but I am afraid he is not moving very fast."

Lansa slowly descended the ladder. His face reflected complete surprise as he took in the scene. Seeing the anger in his father's face, he knew better than to speak. He did, however, send a look of hostility toward Sowiwa.

Sikyawa gently placed his son in Tupkya's arms, then turned to Lansa. Taking Lansa's ear in his hand, he slowly twisted it, sending a jolt of pain through the boy. Lansa grimaced, but made a valiant attempt not to show the pain.

"Why did you not come when Sowiwa called you?"

Still Lansa made no comment, for in truth, he had no answer.

His father's anger was inflamed by his silence. Struggling to contain himself, he said, "Your mother is tired. We will not disturb her with our talk. Climb the ladder. We will talk there." He followed Lansa up the ladder.

Sowiwa waited, then climbed the ladder about halfway so they could not see her, but she could hear them. She made herself as comfortable as possible on one of the rungs and listened.

Sikyawa did not raise his voice, for that was not the way of the people. Still she heard a sternness that she hoped she would never hear directed her way. "Lansa!" he said. "Do not ever try me this way again. You have shown us a self-righteous impudence that is totally unacceptable to me and to all the People."

"But, Father, the baby was too early, and I thought it must be a joke," he said in his own defense.

"Lansa, your sister is a bright, intelligent human being. She has no track record of lying. Why would you even think it?"

Once again Lansa made no response, for he could not think of one.

Sikyawa placed his hands firmly on his first son's shoulders. Looking him squarely in the eye, he said, "Hear me well, son! This attitude toward your little sister must stop. Now! We are a family, and members of families should defend each other in times of trouble, and support each other at all times. If you do not understand me, the next time, I swear to Sun Father, I will report you to our punishing spirit dancer. Now go! Oh, no, not back to play with your friends, but to your blankets. There will be no meal for you tonight."

Sowiwa scrambled down the ladder with her father's last words trailing behind her. They found her sitting quietly next to her mother and her new baby brother.

The child was named Palasiva, which means "copper," due to the beautiful deep rich color of his skin.

CHAPTER 2

Six season cycles had passed. Sowiwa had been attending the holy school for the past two season cycles, and had found that she was truly in her element. She enjoyed her teachers, but found she must manage her time efficiently so that she might have time to commune with her winged and four-legged brothers outside the community. She doted on her little brother, whose easygoing disposition was such a contrast to Lansa's. Lansa was now fourteen season cycles of age and as arrogant as ever. Only recently he had gone through his initiation, and was now considered a "man." There were only a few young women in the holy school, but Sowiwa was certain that every one of them had approached her to tell her of their attraction to her older brother. She sighed as she thought of the fact that girls needed no formal initiation, for Earth Mother had provided a natural one with the onset of the womanly cycle. As yet she had not become a woman. She also knew that when the blessed event did occur, she must make the decision . . . to marry or to remain in the holy school. Her mind was so occupied when she heard a familiar voice behind her.

"Sowiwa, what is it that you are thinking?"

She turned to her friend, Sihu, which meant "flower." "Oh, just girl thoughts," she answered. She took in her friend's lovely light copper skin, which sharply contrasted the short lustrous black hair. Since Sihu was two season cycles older than she, her breasts were just beginning to develop and her waist was thinning to accent a subtle flair of her hips. Her eyes were large and luminous with long lashes, and her lower lip was fuller than the upper, displaying a pout that seemed altogether beautiful to Sowiwa.

Sihu sat cross-legged next to Sowiwa. "Do you want to tell me your girl thoughts?" she asked. The girls had been friends for many season cycles despite the difference in age.

"I was just thinking about my two brothers and how very different they are. Lansa is almost impossible to live with since his initiation. Somehow I have never felt that he loved me, but that he only tolerated me as a girl. I thought that when Palasiva was born, things might change, but they have not. At least I know that I have the love of my little brother, and that is some comfort."

Sihu looked into the soft, loving black eyes of her friend, then bowed her head, saying, "I have watched your brother Lansa from afar for a very long time. I wish he would take notice of me."

Sowiwa placed her right hand on her friend's arm. "I consider you the big sister I have never had. I know that most of the girls here in the holy school also have their eye on him. Perhaps he will grow up one day, and realize that without us, girls that is, there would be no babies."

"Do you think that when my body truly becomes that of a woman, he will notice me then?" Sihu asked.

"Sihu, in my opinion, if there is anyone he should notice in the complex, it should be you. You are as lovely as your name. I suppose only time will tell. Have you had your first bleeding?"

"Not yet, but I am certain it will be soon. Maybe then he will begin to see me as a woman."

Sowiwa turned away from her friend, and stood up. "I wonder if anyone will ever look at me?" She looked down at her small feet and the extra toe that grew next to what should have been her little toe. Tupkya had found it necessary to make a custom-designed wider sandal in order to accommodate Sowiwa's six toes.

Sihu rose and took her friend's hand in her own. She had always thought that her friend was beautiful, with her thick shiny head of hair that framed two luminous eyes that somehow seemed to see far beyond that of the average person. "Sowiwa, your feet are special and so are you. I have never heard anyone say anything derogatory about them. Everyone knows that they are the mark that proves you are gifted."

"Even so, I think they are ugly."

"But, Sowiwa, you are so lucky to be able to speak to Sun Father's many children. I wish I had the gift." Even as she spoke, the sweet lilting sound of a flute reached their ears. "Oh that must be Wena 'Ahote. He does play beautifully, doesn't he? I must go now to tend to my studies. We will talk again soon." With that she turned and walked slowly toward her own quarters.

Sowiwa resumed her sitting position and allowed herself to float with the melody of Wena 'Ahote's flute.

Sun Father shone brilliantly in the turquoise cloudless sky. The air was cool in contrast to the intense heat given out by Tawa, also known as Sun Father. Sowiwa walked along what had been a river but was now only a wash. The past season cycles had been unusually dry, which resulted in the fact that the river was now little more than a trickle. Any piñon pines and juniper that had grown along the river, as well as the cottonwoods, had been stripped by her people for fuel during the long cold seasons. It was rumored that the deceased sun priestess, Coyote Woman, had thought that the pines and juniper should never have been removed, and that somehow their removal was responsible for the erosion that had occurred. Now, when it rained, the water was not contained. The fact that it was not contained resulted in almost immediate absorption, which offered little help in watering the crops. In any case, the canyon had become a much drier place than it had been during Coyote Woman's time.

As she enjoyed a long drink of water from her water jug, she looked up and suddenly noticed a ledge among clay red cliff rocks. Intrigued by what might lay beyond that ledge, she carefully made her way through a rocky trail toward what looked more and more like an opening in the rock. She knew caution was needed in case the shelter was occupied by little brothers or even big brothers such as cougars, snakes, bats, and perhaps others. There was one mesquite at the entrance, but that was the only living thing in sight. She found it vacant except for the lichen that covered the three walls of a small room that opened behind the ledge. She also could not help but think that this would be a perfect place for her to visit when she finally began her womanly cycle.

It was then that she saw the wall in the back of the room. Someone had chipped away a cloaked figure with a dog at its side. Or was it a dog? Perhaps, she thought, it was a wolf. Then she knew. This was a coyote, and the figure was . . . ? Her mind raced frantically as she intuitively knew that this artwork was done by the revered Coyote Woman so many sun cycles ago. This was a sacred place, and she knew it must remain her secret. Settling herself in a cross-legged sitting position on the ledge at the entrance, she closed her eyes.

There was a soft fluttering sound in the mesquite tree beside her followed by a song so melodious that she could think of only one person who could make music as well. A vision of Wena 'Ahote flashed through her mind. She opened her eyes to the sight of a small gray bird whose boldness was clearly expressed due to his close proximity to her. It seemed to be singing the calls of every bird that she had ever heard. Sowiwa wondered if it could imitate dogs, and as if in answer to her, the little gray bird proceeded to bark.

The bird and young girl blended their energies as they communed together. She learned that this bird sang day and night and throughout the season cycles. She watched it hop off the mesquite, where it walked along the ground, opening its wings to flash its white patches reflecting the sunlight. This caused alarm to the insects in the area, whose reaction allowed the bird to see them and to snatch them up for a meal. "Yes," she thought, "this little bird can teach us a lot." Then, as if the bird had said and sung all it wanted to say, it took flight.

Wena 'Ahote had seen it all as he watched from behind a huge rock at the bottom of the ledge. He recalled hearing of the girl's gift, and was quite curious, for this bird was one of his totems, sometimes called power animals. He watched her climb down and waited for her to pass his way. When she came close, he said very softly, "I am told you are called Sowiwa."

She turned with eyes wide open in surprise. "Oh, I didn't realize there was anyone here." She blushed as she wondered if he had known she had been thinking of him.

"I am sorry to startle you, but I have been told of your gift. It is a most unusual one, you know."

She looked self-consciously down at her feet, then up into his black liquid eyes fringed with long black lashes. Why, she wondered, did the male species always seem to be more beautiful then the female species? "I—I—I hardly know what to say, for to me it is not unusual, for it has always been a part of me."

"Were you really speaking with the 'chief of all song birds'?" he asked.

"We did not speak. We only exchanged energies, but perhaps it's all the same. Will you walk me back to the holy school?"

"Of course. But while we walk, will you tell me about the 'chief of all songbirds'?"

"What is it you would like to know?" she asked shyly. She had wanted to get to know Wena 'Ahote for a long time, and she could not believe her good fortune. She knew he was four season cycles older, and she felt certain that he would not give her any of his time if it were not for her gift. Her own brother, Lansa, was the same age as Wena 'Ahote, and he never paid her any attention.

"Anything you can tell me," he said.

"Are you curious because the little bird sings as well as you play?" she inquired.

"No, but thank you. I am flattered," he said. He said nothing more as they walked.

At last Sowiwa said, "The 'chief of all songbirds' is a traditional symbol of the South, the direction of heat and sexuality. Its beauty lies in its song. It will live close to humans because it is not afraid. It tells us that songs are to be shared." She paused with the need to organize her thoughts.

"I am told that it sings all the time. Is that so?"

"Yes, it even sings while flying. That is very unusual among birds. It teaches us to sing out our own talents, that people will notice what you do and not your appearance."

Wena 'Ahote scratched his head. "Are you saying that that little bird can help us to realize our inner talents and to sing them forth?"

"Oh, indeed yes. It can help us to find our own sacred song in life which will make our lives more rewarding and more significant. Many people are afraid to act upon their sacred song or life purpose."

They walked for a short time in silence. Then suddenly Wena 'Ahote stopped and turned to her. "I find that for one so young, you are really very old in wisdom. Is there anything else the 'chief of all songbirds' can tell us?"

"Well, yes," she replied. "I do not know if you were close enough to see, but the bird has white patches on its shoulders. The sun reflects on them when it spreads its wings, causing the insects to become startled. When they react, the bird gobbles them up for dinner. It can teach us to flush out injurious insects, perhaps we should say people around us in our life, and to see where and who they are. In doing so, we can then hear the true songs of others and clarify our direction in life."

They continued their walking in silence once again. As they neared their destination, Wena 'Ahote turned once more. "I am honored to have become your friend. You have given me much to think upon. I hope we can have many more occasions such as this."

"That is also my hope," she said ever so softly as they went their separate ways.

Wena 'Ahote summed it up in his mind. "Yes," he thought, "I must sing forth my sacred song in the manner and tone that is most harmonious for me and my life."

Sowiwa, on the other hand, thought, "Yes, and he didn't even say anything about my toes."

Wena 'Ahote hesitated. He had spoken to Taatawi, the sun priest and keeper of songs, of his encounter with Sowiwa. He, in turn, had spoken to Hoohu, the elder, whose name meant "arrow." Hoohu had seen immediately that Sowiwa's talents must be recognized, and had suggested that she attend the next meeting of the elders. Wena 'Ahote was well aware that the occasion would be frightening to one so young, but he knew he must obey orders. Taatawi was the person he most admired. Taatawi seemed to see straight into the heart of anything or anyone, as befitted his name. He was a kind and gentle soul who never prejudged, and who was never gruff. Hoohu was also very even-tempered and nonjudgmental.

Putting all thoughts behind him, he waited beside the ladder on the roof, which gave entrance to Sowiwa's parents' quarters, until someone would notice he was there. Such was the custom of his people. At last Lansa appeared. Wena 'Ahote had no idea where the young man had been, but he seemed to be coming home.

"You wait to see someone in my family?" Lansa asked.

"Yes, I wish to speak with your parents and Sowiwa," he answered.

Without further questioning, Lansa descended. Finally he appeared at the top of the ladder, inviting Wena 'Ahote into his parents' quarters.

When Wena 'Ahote reached the bottom of the ladder, he found Sowiwa grinding corn with her mother. Palasiva was playing with a deer that had been carved from turquoise. He waited patiently until Tupkya asked, "Welcome. What is the occasion?" Both mother and daughter stopped their grinding.

"Your daughter's gift has drawn the attention of many in the community. Only recently I had occasion to speak with your daughter about her conversation with the 'chief of all songbirds.' I was so impressed that I spoke of it to Taatawi. He, in turn, spoke to Hoohu. Your daughter, Sowiwa, has been summoned to attend a meeting tonight. I will come for her shortly after Sun Father has made his descent." Having completed his message, he turned quickly and ascended the ladder.

Tupkya and Sikyawa exchanged uneasy glances. They both knew they could not discuss their concerns in front of the children. Tupkya walked to Sowiwa to give her a big hug of what she hoped would be reassurance for the child, then returned to her grinding.

Lansa, who now threw his broad shoulders back proudly, said, "What in the name of Sun Father is Wena 'Ahote talking about? Why should a silly little girl like my sister be asked to attend a meeting with the elders? It should be me who is asked to attend for I am a man now."

Sikyawa's concern turned from anger to rage. "Lansa! You may think you are a man, but until you still your tongue and learn to listen, you are still a small boy. I have warned you many times before that your attitude toward your sister is unacceptable. Now leave! I do not want you in my sight." He fairly shook to control the urge to strike his oldest son.

Lansa turned very quickly and hastened up the ladder. Seldom had he seen his father so angry.

Sikyawa sat in the corner of the room and lit his pipe to calm his nerves. Again he and Tupkya exchanged looks of mutual understanding and apprehension.

Palasiva, who was now a happy boy six season cycles of age, put down his toy and moved quietly to his sister's side. "Are you afraid?" he asked. "If it was I who was summoned, I would be afraid."

Sowiwa pulled her little brother into her lap. She knew he always thought of her as his "little mother," and she cherished the fact that her relationship with him was so loving. It helped to offset the distance between Lansa and herself. "Palasiva, my sweet little brother who always shows consideration for other people's feelings, you are wonderful." She paused as she held him close, then added, "Yes, I am afraid. I know I need not be, but I think everyone is at least a little afraid of the unknown."

To Sowiwa it seemed like forever before Wena 'Ahote finally came for her. He escorted her quietly across the complex to the kiva in which the meeting was taking place. At the top of the ladder, they paused. He took her hand and assured her that she had nothing to fear. They then climbed down the ladder.

The elders were seated on benches around the perimeter of the round underground room. The two priests, Ruupi the crystal gazer, and Taatawi the keeper of songs, remained standing. Sowiwa had been told that normally there were three priests, but that only very recently one of them had decided to give up the priesthood to raise a family. Now it would be necessary to find another or at least one who might train for the position. A fire burned brightly in the firebox, giving off heat more intense than anything Sowiwa had ever experienced. Her heart pounded so loudly that she felt certain that everyone who was present could hear it.

Wena 'Ahote continued to stand beside her telling her who was who as the meeting progressed. "The man who is speaking now is Tenyam. He is often but not always in charge of the meetings."

Sowiwa listened to him say that there was a child among them with an unusual gift. Her knees knocked together in fear that they would ask her to speak.

Tenyam moved on. "For as long as we knew of her gift, we have watched her. We knew she was born with six toes on each foot, which is usually an indication of some special gift. It seems that she is not bewitched by the evil gods, but understands the characteristics and capabilities of many of our 'big and little brothers.' This, I must admit, is a gift."

Angwusi, another elder whose name meant "crow," responded after realizing that Tenyam had completed his statement. "Tenyam is right. She has not spoken with the owl or crow, at least to our knowledge. Therefore she is not 'pawaka.' Are there any thoughts from our other elders or priests?"

Hoohu immediately stepped in. "Both of my respected elder brothers are correct. The Creator has given us a truly gifted child whose parents are concerned for her welfare. They and those around her say she is not 'pawaka,' and many do not even know of her gift. If you will all remember, her great-grandmother had the gift, but chose to ignore it and have a family instead. Now we are blessed with her great-granddaughter who has inherited the gift. I have had some thoughts." He paused as though he was struggling to gather them together in his mind.

In that time, Eykita, another elder, whose name meant "he groans," gave an audible moan. "Oh, such a bother. I cannot imagine a way to use such a gift." He moved his great bulk on the bench, groaning with every small shift in movement.

It was Tenyam who finally broke the silence. "It is in my mind that we should further observe her, and if there are still unusual reports, be they good or bad, we might think further on this issue."

Hoohu stepped in immediately. In an angry voice, he exclaimed, "Do you realize how you are terrorizing one who is only ten season cycles of age? You claim to use her! You claim to observe her! How can you be so callous? You will do to her what may have been done to her great-grandmother which resulted in her deciding not to use her talents. This is a sacrilege!" He stepped over to Sowiwa and affectionately placed his hand on her shoulder. He had seen her wince more than once during the meeting.

Wena 'Ahote had also seen the fear in Sowiwa's eyes. Somehow he felt he had to protect her, for he knew there could never be any evil in anything she thought or did. He took her hand and squeezed it.

Sowiwa's frightened gaze moved from Hoohu to Wena 'Ahote. She felt somewhat consoled when she caught a slight nod of Wena 'Ahote's head as he attempted to offer her reassurance. Hoohu also gave her a look of fatherly warmth. In the silence that pervaded the kiva she stifled her fear and kept her eyes properly downcast.

At last Angwusi broke the silence. Recognizing the insensitivity of Tenyam's remarks, he turned to Hoohu. "You are right, my fellow elder. We hope you and Sowiwa will accept our apologies. I, personally, feel no need for further observance of the child. If we have found no fault for ten season cycles, I feel certain that we need look no further. It is in my mind that we should ask Sowiwa if she might consider entering the priesthood. We are in need of a third priest, and I feel certain that someone with her gifts would be a boon to the people."

Tenyam sent Angwusi a stony glare. Again there was a pregnant silence as everyone in the kiva evaluated this new idea. It was obvious that Tenyam was wrestling with his thoughts and striving for some sort of reconciliation. When no one seemed willing to break the tension, he, at last, said, "Perhaps you are right, Angwusi." He seemed to be struggling to remain reserved. "Of course, ultimately, it will be up to the child to decide, and, of course, we have other possible candidates."

Now it was Hoohu who took the floor. He still held Sowiwa firmly when he said, "This child is gifted. It would be a terrible injustice to waste such a precious gift. In the season cycles to come, if she is willing, perhaps we might ask her to do some counseling. There are many in our community who are in need. For now, I believe we should allow her to become a woman. She need not be pressured. Those who are given a special talent often do not hold up under intimidation." Having said this, he released Sowiwa, but not before a quick hug.

Wena 'Ahote gave a sigh of relief. Being only four season cycles older than Sowiwa, he knew how he would have felt. Perhaps, he thought, he still might feel the same way. He also had thoughts of entering the priesthood. His gifts were different from Sowiwa's, but were equally important. He was an accomplished dancer, and knew all the ceremonial steps. He had been studying those secretly since he was only four season cycles of age. He also played the flute, and those who heard him said that he was also truly gifted. Taatawi, the sun priest, and singer of all songs, was his idol. He had spent much time listening to Taatawi's songs, and had memorized nearly all of them. He hoped that with Taatawi's influence he might be a candidate for the priesthood, and perhaps with the sun priest's influence, he might reach his heart's desire. Again he clasped Sowiwa's hand to reassure her.

Tenyam rose slowly from the bench with what appeared to be a sigh of relief. "The child is the last point of discussion. If no one has any objections, we will adjourn." He hastily adjusted his robe, and took his leave. Angwusi was not far behind him.

Eykita yawned, and with much effort moved his girth from the bench. He said nothing, but moved almost in slow motion to the ladder. Groaning with every step, he painstakingly took one rung at a time until he was out of sight.

Hoohu smiled broadly at Wena 'Ahote and Sowiwa. "It is over," he said. "Go in peace. Let this not disturb you." Then, he, too, climbed the ladder, leaving the two young ones with the two priests.

Ruupi's expression was one of ice, but he said nothing. Taatawi, however, moved to the two young people, saying, "Have no fear. Whatever will happen will happen, and I, for one, feel certain that it will be good." With that he also took his leave.

Wena 'Ahote took Sowiwa by the hand and led her up the ladder, for he felt the intensity of Ruupi's cold feelings.

Tupkya walked nervously back and forth as she plied Sowiwa with questions. Sikyawa sat quietly on a mat in the corner of his family's quarters, taking a backseat to his nervously excited wife. Lansa, who up to this time had no knowledge of his sister's talent, sat next to his father and listened in amazement at what he was hearing. Palasiva sat alone with eyes downcast, feeling intense pride for his sister.

Tupkya stood with her hands clenched so tightly that her nails dug into her palms. "And you say that there were some who still thought of you as 'pawaka'?"

"Yes, Mother. Tenyam, the leader of the meeting, seemed to think that I should be watched a little more, but then Hoohu stepped in."

"But couldn't they see that you have done nothing in ten season cycles? What is the matter with them?" she hissed.

Sikyawa had heard enough. Glaring hard at Tupkya, he declared, "If you would calm down, woman, and give Sowiwa time to tell us everything, I would be grateful!"

"What?" she said, but she realized that she had been put in her place, and respectfully sat down.

"Now, Sowiwa, you may continue with no interruptions." He cast a long, hard look at Tupkya, who looked as though she had been struck.

Sowiwa took a deep breath. "Tenyam did say that he thought I should be watched, but then Hoohu accused him of scaring me. Angwusi stepped in and said he saw no reason for observing me, but that I should just be allowed to grow up. He also suggested that I be asked to consider entering the priesthood, but that there was no hurry. Hoohu said that maybe when I felt I was ready I might consider counseling those of the people who need it and are interested. He added that gifted people often will refuse to use their gift when intimidated, and then, well, the meeting was adjourned. That was all." She exhaled loudly as she attempted to relieve the pressure she was experiencing.

Sikyawa rose to embrace his daughter. "Our little ear of

corn," he said as he smoothed her short silky black hair. "Truly you have made us proud." Turning to his wife, he added, "You see, Tupkya, there was no reason for concern."

Tears glistened in her eyes as Tupkya rose to join in her husband's and Sowiwa's embrace. For once in her life she seemed to have nothing to say.

Sikyawa beckoned to his two sons to join in the family embrace. Palasiva came willingly and excitedly, but Lansa did not move from the mat. All four turned to look at Lansa curiously.

At last Lansa rose with brows furrowed and teeth grinding. "I cannot handle all this. Girls are only a bother. Why was I not told of this before? Oh, yes, I know. You didn't trust me, or maybe I'm not good enough. Well, if you all feel that way, then I am leaving." Abruptly he hastened up the ladder.

When Sikyawa knew that he was still able to hear them, he said, "When you decide to hear our side of the story, come back, but out of respect, do not be gone too long."

Sowiwa bit her lower lip. Why, she wondered, did there always have to be negativities? Would she and Lansa ever share a true brother-sister relationship?

CHAPTER 3

A.D. *1130*

Sowiwa had been a woman for two season cycles. She was now fifteen season cycles of age, and had flowered into a lovely young woman. In the bloom of young womanhood she began feeling the urge to mate and have a family, yet she also truly enjoyed life as a student and only recently had found herself doing some occasional counseling within the community. When she had experienced her first womanly cycle, she had gone to her small sacred cave and fasted for three days, as was the custom for the females in the school. She could have chosen to remain home in confinement, but then she knew she would not have a chance to commune with her "big and little brothers," the birds, insects, reptiles, and animals. After her first womanly cycle her mother had stopped cropping her hair, and now it had grown well below her shoulders. If she chose to marry, she would begin wearing it in the traditional whorls over her ears. She was still petite and tiny, but her breasts were high and well formed, her waist was small, and her hips were gently flared. Though she was unaware, she drew many appreciative looks from many young men who happened to pass her by.

She worked beside her mother as they ground corn on two metates. "Where is Palasiva, Mother?" she asked.

"He is no doubt out in the plaza playing with some of his friends." Tupkya straightened her back to take a break from her grinding, then turned to Sowiwa. "My sweet daughter, may we talk?"

Sowiwa ceased her work and put both her hands high over

her head to relieve her own back from the drudgery. "Of course, Mother. What is on your mind?"

Tupkya brushed the fine cornmeal from her hands and sat on a nearby mat. "Come join me, child," she said.

"Mother, I am not a child!"

"And that is what I wish to speak of." Her voice faded as she spoke as though she were trying to gather her thoughts. Finally she said, "My daughter, you have grown into a lovely young woman. It is time that you decided what it is that you would do with your life. Five season cycles ago you were asked to consider the priesthood. Have you thought on this?"

"Of course I have, Mother, but I find that making a lifetime decision is not easy."

"I would not dispute you on that issue, but would you share your thoughts with me," she asked with a voice that was almost a whisper.

Sowiwa finally sat cross-legged beside her mother and placed her small delicate hands in her lap. "My thoughts are many," she declared. "The priesthood frightens me for it means I cannot marry. Yet, at this moment, there is no one who interests me, I mean for a husband. I feel that it is not yet the right time for me to make that decision."

"But, Sowiwa, you have passed the age that most young women marry. Does that not concern you?"

"No, it does not." Sowiwa looked at her mother with a blank expression.

"Well, it concerns me, daughter. Our friends are constantly asking me what it is that I think you will do, and I cannot answer them. It is embarrassing."

"I am sorry to embarrass you, but I'm sure you will agree that it is truly my problem. It may be that I will never marry. It may be that there is no one who will ever interest me. If that is the case, then, over a period of time, I will know the priesthood is for me." In the back of her mind she had thoughts of Wena 'Ahote, but she knew she could never share those thoughts with her mother.

Tupkya burst forth. "Ah, you are so frustrating. We do not often live more than forty season cycles, and yet time means nothing to you!"

"Mother, please try to understand. I am very happy with my life as it is right now. There will come a time when I will know, but that is in the hands of Awonawilona."

"There is one who is interested in you," Tupkya said very softly.

Sowiwa made no response.

"Are you not curious to know who has shown an interest in you?"

"Not really, but I am sure you will tell me anyway." Again a vision of Wena 'Ahote flashed through her mind. He was now nineteen season cycles of age and very handsome in her opinion.

"One of your father's most promising students has spoken to your father. His name is Tsoongo. He often speaks of your beauty."

Sowiwa was astounded. She had become very briefly acquainted with Tsoongo during one of their social dances, but she felt nothing toward him. He had struck her as a brash, over-confident young man. It seemed to her that he felt that the whole earth was his for the taking. Yet she knew she should not prejudge. When at last she found her voice, she said, "Have there been any others?"

"No, but I thought you would want to know. You must realize that it is your father's and my wishes that you consider the priesthood. That would truly make us both very proud."

"So I am to understand that your first wish is that I should enter the priesthood, but if I do not want to do that, then the next best alternative is to marry Tsoongo?" she inquired as a clarification of all that they had discussed.

"Yes, my daughter. That is so." Tupkya gave her daughter a hard inquiring look.

Sowiwa refused to look into her mother's eyes. Fear gripped her tightly around her middle. She knew she must consider that which her mother had shared with her, but she really did not want to do so. She almost felt like she was being bullied. She was greatly disturbed, for she knew the value of the family unit. Suddenly she stood up and looked at her mother bravely. "Mother, I wish to remind you that Lansa is nineteen season cycles of age, and you are not pushing him to do anything with his life. Why me?"

"Because you are a woman, my child, and your childbearing years are ahead of you. You should consider that."

"Mother, there are already too many of the people to feed in this season of drought. Why should I hasten to bring into Awonawilona's world one more mouth to feed? Why should I have a child that might starve?"

"Oh," Tupkya said, "you are so opinionated for your age. Let us cease this talk, for it is getting us nowhere."

"Did you expect that it would?" Sowiwa inquired.

They resumed their grinding.

In the early part of Sun Father's journey across the sky, Sowiwa climbed the stairway that was chiseled in stone behind the holy school. It was a direct route to the building in which Iswungwa, the trade supervisor, lived. Goods that traders brought in and out of the community were stored there. It was usually one of the quieter places to be other than her own secret cave where she spent her womanly cycles. When she reached the top of the cliff at the top of the stairs, she turned to take in the view. From her vantage point she could see clearly ten of the eleven buildings in the community. The eleventh was far enough away that it appeared in much less detail. Though all of the buildings were large, the holy school was by far the largest. It was shaped like a half circle with a huge plaza in the center along with a great many kivas of many sizes. The nearly eight hundred rooms were stacked around the perimeter in five levels. The story that was so often told said that her people had begun constructing the sophisticated building almost two hundred season cycles ago. Prior to that time the people had lived in pit houses, which were one-room homes that were half below the ground and half above. Some families still insisted on living in pit houses. As she surveyed the community, she saw quite a number of pit houses as well as many single-family small houses. There was also an enormous kiva almost directly across from the holy school, where many of their most important ceremonials were held. Still other ceremonies were held in the plaza of the holy school due to the fact that it could accom-

modate a much larger audience. During these times many people came from the outlier buildings and small houses that were
scattered in all four directions. The walls of all the buildings in
the community glistened in the heat of Sun Father, reflecting
brilliant gold tones. The thick walls were made of fitted sandstone which the women kept meticulously covered with stucco.
She thought of how truly blessed she and her people were to be
living in such beauty. She only wished the rain gods would be
more sympathetic, for the need for rain was great as the crops
neared the end of their growing cycle and withered in the intense heat of the hot season.

Even now the people had completed preparations for the
Flute Ceremony. The altar had been set up and there had been
much praying. Though she had not seen the altar, her father had
described it as being quite beautiful with the wooden birds
carved to represent parrots, as well as other fetishes represent-
ing tropical birds made out of cornmeal that had been crystal-
lized. He said that in front of the altar were jars of water
symbolic of the water from which the people had emerged into
this the fourth world. Several young men had already been
through their initiation into the Gray and Blue Flute Societies.
When Sun Father reached His zenith the enactment of the
emergence would begin in the hope of pleasing the rain gods.

She closed her eyes while making an attempt to clear her
mind for meditation. Sitting cross-legged on a smooth stone,
she waited. When, after a short time, she found this an impossibility, she realized that she was too excited to meditate. It was
true that she had seen the same ceremony before, but this one
would be different, for it was rumored that Wena 'Ahote would
be playing the sacred flute. This, of course, was because he
played the finest flute in the community and perhaps the best
among all the Anasazi. How lucky she was, she thought, to be
his friend.

After climbing hastily down the ladder, she ran to join her
mother, father, and brothers. They would all watch the ceremony together.

The plaza had been cleared of any refuse. Rooftops and cliff
edges were crowded with people, some who had traveled far
for the occasion. The people would patiently wait until sun-

down for that part of the ceremony that they would be permitted to observe. They waited in reverence for the Gray and Blue
Flute Societies, who were gathered at Flute Spring to pray and
to ready themselves for the colorful part of the ceremony. At
last, when Sun Father had nearly touched the western horizon,
a sudden shout could be heard.

Sowiwa could see them coming from the spring that lay beyond a mesa. There were two groups of about twenty-five men
and twenty-five women, the Gray Flute people in front and the
Blue Flute people behind. Everyone was barefooted and bare-
headed, wearing tufts of tropical bird feathers in their hair and
cloaked in red-banded white blankets. Slowly and regally they
moved along the Great North Road.

Straining her eyes to see, her heart leaped when she spotted
Wena 'Ahote leading the Gray Flute group in front. As they approached, she could see that each person was marked with a
strip of mud running from ear to ear across the chin. The flute
that sang so sweetly due to Wena 'Ahote's expertise was made
from a large reed with a hornlike pumpkin rind cut in the shape
of a squash blossom, painted with flower colors with a paho
(prayer stick) attached. Singing softly to the music of the flute,
the procession stopped at the entrance of the plaza. After offer-
ings of cornmeal, two Flute maidens tossed rings from the rods
they held on to the cornmeal. After carefully picking up the
rings with their rods, the Gray Flute people moved on into the
plaza, where they repeated the performance three more times.
The Blue Flute group followed suit until they all were gathered
at the center of the plaza.

Someone spoke softly in Sowiwa's ear. "Well, what do you
think?"

She turned with a quick little gasp to find Tsoongo by her
side. "It's beautiful!" she breathed. "I have never heard a
sweeter flute."

"Pah! Playing the flute is not man's work. Anyone can learn
to play the flute. It's no different than playing the drum. It
would take me no time at all to learn to play, but I have more
manly activities to attend to. Ask your father. He will tell you
that stone masonry is a man's work. Hunting and trading are
men's work."

Rising to Wena 'Ahote's defense, she declared, "But to play music, one must be sensitive. To lay stones, hunt, or trade does not require any sensitivity, at least not the kind that is required to make music." Her cheeks burned as she thought of Tsoongo's ignorance. She assumed that he would not have dared to speak to her in the presence of her parents if it were not for the music and the low-pitched noise of the crowd that would not permit her parents to hear.

Tsoongo sensed that it would be inappropriate to have a confrontation in front of her parents and disappeared into the crowd.

Sowiwa realized that Tsoongo was deliberately trying to spoil her enjoyment of the proceedings. She could not believe that this was her father's protégé and the young man her mother seemed to think might be suitable for her. He was, in her mind, totally insensitive, and yes, in a way, much like her brother. Though she did not know many of Lansa's friends, she suspected that Tsoongo must be one. They were, after all, about the same age.

Meanwhile the leaders of the Gray and Blue Flute clans moved into their individual kivas to pray in front of their altars. The two groups left in the plaza continued singing the story of the Emergence from the third world to the present fourth world, accompanied by the music of Wena 'Ahote's flute. At the end of each of the four sections of the song, a young man swung his bull-roarer.

Sun Father dipped below the horizon. Shadows reached across the plaza, and the audience shivered a little with the sudden breeze. Sowiwa listened to the restrained voice of the chorus and the hypnotic song of the flute. She hoped that this profoundly simple and yet complex ceremony would please the rain gods.

Then abruptly it was over. The two leaders emerged from the kivas and the song ended. The two groups filed silently out of the darkening plaza.

The following sun cycle found the young people preparing for a picnic. The young men went out first to a prearranged meeting spot, hunting rabbits as they went. Sowiwa, Sihu, and two other young women had baked a traditional corn dish called somoviki, which they would take with them. They also took their little brothers and sisters along. It was an especially exciting occasion due to the fact that there were so few females and so many males.

Sowiwa smiled at Sihu as they walked toward the location for the picnic. "I really enjoy these picnics, don't you?" she inquired. The other three young women followed behind them, carrying on their own private conversation. This meant that there were only five young women in attendance.

"Oh yes, especially when the odds are so favorable for the women," Sihu answered with mischievous twinkling eyes.

"And who will be your choice? I know who will be mine, and it will not be Tsoongo. He is so immature." Sowiwa laughed daintily at her own comment.

Sihu probed gently as she asked, "Then who will it be?"

Sowiwa looked at her younger brother and shook her head. "I cannot say. I will tell you when the time is right."

The girls walked on in silence. Sihu had brought along her younger sister, who was nine season cycles of age. Palasiva, Sowiwa's brother, had now seen eleven season cycles of life. The younger siblings would have a definite role to play during the picnic, but the two older girls did not want them to know too much too soon.

When they had almost reached their destination, Sowiwa whispered, "The odds may be in our favor, but I wonder how many are promised to young women back home?"

"I am afraid there may be many, but even if they are promised, maybe they have changed their minds." Sihu swung her long silky hair over one shoulder.

"I suppose we will soon find out." Sowiwa ceased whispering because they had at last reached the chosen spot, and the young men were busy roasting rabbits and anxiously awaiting the arrival of the women.

Before unpacking their part of the food, Sihu sent her younger sister to invite Lansa, who was the young man of her choice, to join them. Sowiwa was about to send Palasiva for Wena 'Ahote, when she realized that he was not even present.

Sihu saw Sowiwa's happiness fade and in spite of her own

excitement, rushed to her friend's side. "Something is wrong. What is it?"

"My choice is not here." Sowiwa rung her hands in disappointment.

"My sweet friend, if it is Wena 'Ahote you seek, there is something you should know." She paused in her concern for Sowiwa's feelings. "Wena 'Ahote has only recently decided to become a priest, and you know that he cannot marry. Oh, I am so sorry. I thought you knew."

Sowiwa shrugged her shoulders and breathed deeply. "I suppose I should not have been surprised. He will make a wonderful priest."

Their conversation was interrupted with the arrival of Sihu's sister escorting Lansa by her side. Sihu's expression changed instantly to one of joyous surprise. "Would it please you to join us?" she asked. She felt her heart pounding in the hope that he would not refuse. She bowed her head as was the custom of a well-bred woman. Though she could not see him, he looked her up and down as though appraising her value.

"It would be an honor." Then turning his attention to his sister, he said, "And, little sister, will you send Palasiva for someone you favor? You know that there is someone who hopes he will be your choice."

"No," Sowiwa said in a voice that was almost a whisper. "There is no one."

"But what of Tsoongo? He looks on you most favorably."

"Of that I am fully aware, but it just happens that today I do not desire his company." She hoped that Lansa would not press the issue any further, for she did not want to hurt any feelings. She felt certain that her parents would not want to pair her with someone who spoke of others in a derogatory way. She would only speak her mind if it became necessary. Meanwhile she would continue to try to field their comments as she was doing with Lansa now.

Sowiwa rescued her saying, "Come. Let's sit on the blanket and enjoy the somoviki I have brought."

"Oh yes. I am hungry!" exclaimed Palasiva.

Five of them crowded on the blanket while Sihu and Sowiwa served. Lansa unwrapped some rabbit he had caught and cooked and divided it among them. After a short prayer of thanks, little was said as they enjoyed their repast.

When, at last, they had all finished, Lansa spoke softly in Sihu's ear. "Will you walk with me?"

She smiled demurely and with a quick nod of her head, rose from the blanket. With a wink at his sister, Lansa jumped up quickly to follow her.

Sowiwa's emotions were mixed. In one way she was happy that Lansa and Sihu seemed to be pairing off, and that their longtime friendship might continue with the bond of marriage as her sister-in-law. She also knew that she should be glad that Sihu's dreams might come true. Yet, in another way, she was concerned, for she had seen Lansa looking at many other females on many occasions, and was not certain that he was really ready to settle down. There was also the concern that he might treat Sihu as he had treated her for so many season cycles. She knew in her heart that Lansa was probably not in love, but was only looking for someone who would be a mother to his children so that he could prove his virility.

With a quick shake of her head, she put her thoughts behind her. "Come," she said to Palasiva and Sihu's sister. "Let us return to the complex. Lansa will bring Sihu safely home to us."

Wena 'Ahote had informed her that she would be summoned to attend a meeting when Sun Father dipped below the horizon. He had said that its purpose was most likely to invite her to join the priesthood. She found herself quite nervous, but not nearly as nervous as she had been five season cycles earlier. Of course she was now no longer a child, and was aware that the elders were not gods, but people—people who made mistakes as she did. Oddly enough, Sikyawa and Tupkya had not questioned her. She felt certain that they believed she would accept the offer, if indeed that was the purpose of the meeting. In her heart she knew she could not accept. Since her conversation with Sihu at the picnic about Wena 'Ahote's desire to enter the priesthood, she somehow did not feel comfortable with the idea. She could not picture herself never being a mother. In fact she very much wanted someday to have many children of her own. Even if she could not have Wena 'Ahote, she felt certain that she would sometime, somehow, somewhere, meet a man who would father her children. Meanwhile she would continue to help the people through her counseling.

Darkness arrived too soon. Wena 'Ahote escorted her to the kiva where the meeting was to take place. The kiva was as she remembered it. The fire box was burning brightly, giving off an incredible amount of heat. The elders, Tenyam, Angwusi, Hoohu, and Eykita were seated around the perimeter along with Posaala, the building surveyor, Maahu, the architect, and Awta, the construction supervisor. Iswungwa, the trade manager, was not in attendance. When Wena 'Ahote had shown Sowiwa to a seat, he took his place beside Taatawi, sun priest, and Ruupi, crystal medicine man.

As usual, Tenyam raised his hand to signal the beginning of the meeting. In a very short time silence pervaded the kiva. After clearing his throat, Tenyam began. "This meeting has been called as a continuation of one that took place five season cycles ago. As you all can see, our guest of honor is Sowiwa, daughter of Tupkya and Sikyawa. We all know of the gift bestowed upon her by the Creator. She has endeared herself to the people with her talent in counseling through the power animals of her clients, and I'm sure I can speak for you all when I say that I hope she continues to do so in the future." He cast Sowiwa a questioning glance. "As a young woman who is fifteen season cycles of age, you do have some plans for the future, do you not?"

Sowiwa hesitated to speak, taking time to choose her words. Finally she rose from the bench and said, "To be honest I do not, but I assure you that I will be happy to continue counseling, for I enjoy doing it." She turned toward Wena 'Ahote, whose eyes briefly locked with her own.

Several in the kiva, including Tenyam, saw the quick communication between the two young people. He knew that Wena 'Ahote was studying for the priesthood with Taatawi, and that the young man could not marry, but he clearly saw a fondness between the two. "Ahem!" he asserted. "Sowiwa, do you recall that five season cycles ago we asked you in a meeting in this very kiva to consider the priesthood?"

When it seemed to her that Tenyam was not going to continue, she rose again. "I remember it well. I have given it much thought." She took her seat again. Would they truly ask her to enter the priesthood? She was aware that no woman had been part of the priesthood since the revered Coyote Woman, and that she should consider it an honor, but was it the proper thing to do to say no?

Tenyam pressed on. "Then you should know, and I speak for all who are present, that we are officially offering you the opportunity to study for the priesthood. Since Wena 'Ahote is studying with Taatawi, you would be studying with Ruupi, our crystal medicine man. In the role of a priestess, you could continue with your counseling. Many would come to you from the outliers as well as those in our canyon community. We hope you will accept our offer." He resumed his seat.

All eyes were on Sowiwa as she slowly rose from the bench. She reflected her nervousness with a voice that quavered as she spoke the first few words. "To everyone here I must say that I am deeply honored. I am also aware that it is the exception for a woman to be a member of the priesthood." She paused to gather courage, for she knew that this was a turning point in the path she would choose for the rest of her life. "I must, however, in all due respect, decline the offer." As soon as the words were out, she watched most of those who were present drop their jaws in surprise, and so she continued. "I am sorry if I disappoint you, but if I accept, I cannot marry. It is my hope that even when and if I marry, I will be allowed to continue to counsel."

Tenyam rose once more. "Sowiwa, we all wish you to continue your work in whatever capacity you choose, and yes, many of us are disappointed." Then with a twinkle in his eye that did not befit his name (Hard Wood), he asked, "And is there some lucky young man you might favor?"

Sowiwa felt herself burn with embarrassment as she answered, "If there is one I might favor, I cannot tell, for ultimately it is my parents' decision." She cast Wena 'Ahote another imploring glance and sat down.

Tenyam stood and declared, "Then if no one else wishes to speak, we will excuse Sowiwa and go on with the rest of the meeting."

When there was no response, Wena 'Ahote escorted Sowiwa up the ladder. When they were out of earshot, he turned to her. "I am also one who is sorry that you did not accept. Sowiwa, I . . ."

"Do not take it upon yourself to be sorry. It was my decision, and not an easy one. You have a fine path ahead of you. Mine is uncertain, and who knows how the gods will lead us down the 'road of life.' I want you to know that I am truly happy for you." She turned away from him with a heavy heart and climbed down the ladder to the comforts of home.

"You told them what?" her mother screamed.

Sowiwa tried to close her ears as she shuddered at her mother's reaction. She watched the corded muscles in her mother's neck stand out in a fury of tension and anger. She knew her parents fully expected her to accept the offer, but never in her wildest imagination had she thought her mother would react so violently. Although she was glad Lansa and Palasiva were not present, she fervently wished that her father was present. As a teacher of masonry his patience was great, and she was sure his response would have been much more rational.

"Mother, I . . ."

"Don't 'Mother, I' me! Are you not sound in your mind? I have raised a daughter who is truly gifted, and you do not want to make the most of your gift. You are no better than Chakwaina, your great-grandmother, who had the same gift and gave it up. What, in the name of all the gods, possessed you to do such a thing?"

Sowiwa found herself cringing before her irrational mother. Her immediate reaction was to feel guilty, but she knew that this was exactly what her mother wanted her to feel. She also realized that it was useless to make any attempts to communicate with her mother until she had calmed down. For her own protection she imagined that she was encased in a huge crystal that no one could penetrate. Here, within the crystal, she was safe.

When Tupkya realized her daughter was no longer responding, she became even more irate. "Talk, daughter! There must be some insanity in your soul!" She picked up a lovely black-on-white bowl that had been a favorite of hers for years and flung it across the room.

Sowiwa watched it shatter into many small pieces. She knew it was only a bowl, but that it had been special in the family for some time. It was then that her mother picked up a much larger bowl. As she raised it over her head, Sowiwa saw the feet of her father begin to descend the ladder. Still she remained in the protection of her imagined crystal.

Tupkya froze. Sikyawa turned at the bottom of the ladder in surprise. "What is going on here?" he asked.

Slowly Tupkya lowered the bowl and looked at him with fire in her eyes. "I should have cracked it over her head! My husband, you will not believe what she has said to the elders who offered her the opportunity to enter the priesthood. She is not gifted! She is out of her mind! What will our friends say? We expected so much more." She sank to her knees in despair.

Sikyawa shook his head in confusion. Laying a hand on Tupkya's shoulder, he looked at Sowiwa questioningly. "Now, child, what have you said to the elders? Surely it cannot be that bad."

Still visualizing herself within her crystal, she answered simply, "My father, I declined the offer." She watched her father tighten up in disbelief.

Sikyawa took some time to collect his thoughts. At last he said in a stern but rational voice, "What is to become of you then, my child?"

Sowiwa visualized herself only partway out of her crystal as she timidly answered, "I am to continue my counseling for as long as I want. According to the ways of our people I am old enough to make my own decisions except where the approval of marriage might be involved. That, of course, is yours and mother's."

"So am I to understand that you declined the offer because you choose to marry?" Her father's entire demeanor seemed to be changing.

"That is one of the reasons, but there are more I cannot explain for they are only feelings within my heart." She thought of the fact that she would have studied with Ruupi, who did not appeal to her at all, yet she knew not why. There was also, of course, her feelings for Wena 'Ahote. She knew if she became a priestess and he became a priest, either one of them might be sent to any outlier, and that they could not count on remaining within their present living quarters.

Sikyawa pressed on. "Lansa has informed me that you were not interested in Tsoongo at the picnic. If this is so, then there must be someone who has caused you to make such a decision." He said no more but waited for Sowiwa's response.

"Father, please try to understand that there is no one who at this time is of interest to me. I just do not want to be a part of the priesthood. It is as simple as that. I truly love you and mother, but I want to make my own way. When I decide, it will only be with your approval." She bowed her head in resignation.

Sikyawa took her in his arms and said, "By the gods, you are a trying daughter. You must know how you have disappointed your mother and me, but we will always love you. You are our only girl, and a gifted one at that. Let us put this issue aside, and go on with what we should be doing."

Tupkya rose from her kneeling position to resume her grinding.

CHAPTER 4

A.D. *1130*

The little cave looked very inviting to Sowiwa. She actually looked forward to the time of her womanly cycle because she was truly on her own. No studying, no grinding, no pressure from her parents or abuse from Lansa left her with a deep feeling of relief. She only missed Palasiva, Sihu, and Wena 'Ahote. After climbing to the ledge that opened into a small room, she threw down her belongings and gazed at the petroglyph-pictograph on the back wall—the robed person and the coyote. She had brought nothing to eat, as was the custom, but only water, which was at a premium due to the drought conditions that were still going on. There was little else to do but to meditate.

The air was crisp and cool with only a slight breeze that barely disturbed the mesquite tree outside the ledge of her cave. Sun Father was once again making his presence known as the heat intensified. Wrapping a cotton cloth around her head to reflect the heat, she climbed down the ledge and out into the salt amaranth, and wild rice. Only the saltbush seemed to be surviving the drought. The amaranth and wild rice were small and stunted. She had befriended several canyon "brothers" during her regular visits in the last two season cycles, but today she saw no signs of anyone. A level rock next to the dry wash gave her a place to comfortably sit and a place to enjoy her solitude.

Sowiwa sat cross-legged on the ledge of her cave, taking in the beauty all around her. She began relaxing her body, beginning with her feet and toes. She imagined herself undergoing a gentle massage of her muscles. Moving up to the calf of each leg, she repeated the process, and then again with her thighs, the trunk of her body, arms, neck, and head. As she worked up through the body to the head, she found herself pulling her consciousness along with her. Her body felt heavy while her consciousness felt very light. She began to feel that she was dissociated from her physical body.

It was at this point that she directed her attention to her goal, that of finding her "power animal." She found herself spiraling into a tunnel. Down she went until she found herself, surprisingly enough, in a duplicate of where she had been when she had begun the meditation. To her surprise a young rabbit came into her mind. She watched it busily digging its hole within the rather sparse rice grass.

Suddenly the rabbit gave out a harsh cry almost like that of a human baby and bolted into the hole as if it might be life or death. A hawk soared through the air as if it were a god and owned the sky. It did not seem at all interested in the young rabbit, and Sowiwa watched it, wondering what it would be like to have the ability to move through the air, reaching ever upward to the gods.

The hawk dipped and dove and, at last, to Sowiwa's surprise, perched on the mesquite next to the ledge where she sat. As the bird stared at her, they conversed.

Cocking his head to one side, the hawk said, "I know of your ability to speak to your 'little brothers,' but this is the first time we have communicated. I come to speak of that which I can offer you."

Sowiwa was so astounded that she was unable to find words. She watched the magnificent bird fluff out his feathers. Very softly she asked, "Are you my power animal?"

Staring at her without blinking his eyes, he answered, "I would say that it is so."

"Then why have I had to wait so long to find you?" She only hoped the bird would not think her disrespectful.

"Because my tail is red my spirit is tied to the primal life force, the energy source at the base of your spine. I could not enter your life until that energy source had been activated within you. You are a mature young lady now and old enough to understand what I say. Your childhood visions are becoming empowered and fulfilled. This is the stage in your life when you will move toward your soul purpose more dynamically." The hawk preened the red feathers in his tail one at a time while he waited for Sowiwa to gather her thoughts.

She shook her head in amazement, then said, "I wish I had the ability to glide and soar through the air as you do."

"If you are willing, I can teach you to fly to great heights while physically your feet will remain on the ground. You should also know that we hawks are often harassed and attacked by smaller birds. This indicates that there are likely to be attacks by people who won't understand you or the varied uses of your creative energy."

"Will you be my only power animal?" she inquired.

"That may or may not be, but since it is my habit to mate for life, I will be one of your spirit animals throughout your life. I can also assist you in developing your psychic energies. I hold the secret to higher levels of consciousness, and can also teach you the balance necessary to discover your true purpose in life."

"For all of those things I would be most grateful. Is there anything else I might need to know? To my people you are known as the 'red eagle.' The energies of your red tail feathers are used in our healing ceremonies and for bringing the rains and waters so necessary for life. You are also a bearer of our messages to Sun Father."

"Of that, young Sowiwa, I am well aware, for your people of late have been keeping me very busy."

Sowiwa giggled in appreciation at the bird's sense of humor.

"I must go now, but before I do, I would speak further of my red tail." Red Eagle bobbed his head up and down and stuck out his breast. "The feathering of my red tail actually has two phases which are meaningful to you. It is colored lighter during the warm season and darker during the cold season. The lighter is symbolic of joy and social kinds of energies. The darker phase reflects a time to be alone and to withdraw a little. All in all the color phases help us to guard against burning so brightly and intensely that we get burned out." With that he looked to his left, looked to his right, and turned, taking flight. Looking back, he added, "The sky is my realm. Through my communication with humans and the Creator, I awaken your vision and inspire you to a creative life purpose."

Sowiwa was sure that a part of her flew with him. She felt as though she had lost her right arm or some very important part of her. After calling for the white light once more, she slid back into her weakened body. Her eyes fluttered as they once more beheld the empty mesquite tree. Had it all been just a dream, she wondered? Then she looked at the rice grass where the rabbit had dug his hole, but was nowhere to be seen. Had the rabbit really been there? Was the rabbit also one of her totems? She suddenly realized that the rabbit was only the bait for the appearance of "Red Hawk," as she now called him. A sense of wondrous joy filled her so completely that she wanted to sing out. At last she had acquired a spirit animal and she wanted to tell all she knew. This euphoric feeling remained for a good part of the sun cycle, but as she packed her few belongings to return home, she knew that the event had been sacred, and that no one should know.

She was greeted by Sihu as she sat cross-legged next to the ladder that offered entrance to her parents' quarters. Her friend jarred her from her reveries, causing her to jump in surprise.

"Oh, I'm sorry. I did not mean to frighten you," she exclaimed.

"Oh, but you know you did. I had no idea anyone was there."

"May I sit down?" Sihu asked.

"Sihu, you are my friend. You do not need to ask."

"Thank you," she murmured while placing herself opposite Sowiwa.

A short period of silence followed until Sowiwa inquired, "What is on your mind, Sihu?" They both could hear Tupkya singing at the grinding stone in the room below.

"It's about your brother. Is he around?"

"He is not here at this time. He is more than likely out practicing to be a famous fierce warrior. Of course you know he has little use for either me or Palasiva. To him we are only nuisances."

Sihu swung her long hair over one shoulder and lowered the long eyelashes that framed her lovely black eyes. She hesitated again until Sowiwa said, "He did not seem to find you to be a nuisance at the picnic. Have you seen him since?"

Sihu blushed deeply, causing her smooth bronzed face to take on a reddish hue. "Yes, he is often waiting for me at the spring when I go to fetch water. He does not speak, but he stares at me constantly."

Pressing her hands into those of her friend she asked, "How do you feel toward him, or is it foolish of me to ask?"

"Sowiwa, I know you and he do not get along, but I find him, well, quite wonderful. I know I could be happy with him. Perhaps if we were wed, it would be the perfect opportunity for me to awaken him so that he would understand the value of you and me, and women in general. What do you think?"

"It troubles me to say this, my friend, but I do not think Lansa will ever truly learn what he has not learned in the nineteen season cycles he has lived. I know that is not what you wanted to hear, but I speak from the heart."

Sihu frowned, causing creases between her beautifully arched brows. "Perhaps you feel this way because you are his sister, but if I were his wife and bore him a child, I'm sure it would be different."

Not wanting to disturb Sihu any further, Sowiwa said softly, "I hope you are right. My feelings are that he is enchanted with your quiet womanly ways and, of course, your beauty. I am sure he is certain you would not bring him the grief that his sister has for such a long time. Are you sure he is not ogling any others?"

"No, but we both know that here in the holy school there are not very many other females he can ogle." She giggled as she spoke.

"That is very true." She did not want to say that her brother spent a lot of time in the close outliers during the time of light. It was true he was home after dark, but what he did during the time of Sun Father's journey was a mystery.

Again there was a short time when neither of them spoke

until, at last, Sihu asked, "My friend, I am worried about you. You do not seem to be interested in anyone."

Sowiwa responded vehemently. "You sound just like my mother! She says she worries about me, too, and I tell her to let me lead my own life!" Then seeing Sihu's hurtful expression, she backed off. "Oh, Sihu, now I must say I am sorry. It's just that, well, my mother never ceases her prattling. I am just overly sensitive."

Sihu shifted uneasily, feeling that perhaps she should leave. Sowiwa sensed what she felt, and added, "I am hiding my feelings, Sihu. I still have intense feelings for Wena 'Ahote, and there is little I can do about it. Mother has no idea, and she and my father go on and on about Tsoongo."

As if on cue, Tsoongo appeared. If he had heard any of what they had said, he gave no clue. "I am looking for Lansa. Have either of you seen him?" he asked. He looked at Sowiwa in appreciation, then moved on to take in the beauty of Sihu. It was obvious that he was enchanted with both of them.

Sowiwa sensed it all with repulsion. Again she wondered how her parents could want to pair her off with Tsoongo. He had become a nuisance as of late, for he appeared out of nowhere all the time. She was beginning to feel that she had no privacy at all.

Tsoongo strutted about like a turkey. He ran his hand through his long hair as if preening his tail feathers and said, "I am amazed at the beauty around me. The loveliness of you both rivals that of the most exquisite cactus flower. I am sorry that Lansa is not here, for then I would be able to spend more time to enjoy the sight of you both." His eyes traveled between them as he waited for what he hoped would be an invitation to stay. When there was no response, he hastily said, "I shall leave now. Perhaps I shall find Lansa somewhere outside the community." Without further hesitation, he departed.

Heaving a sigh of relief, Sowiwa said, "It almost seems as if he is following me. I am glad he is gone."

Sihu's expression was grim as she looked at her friend. She had not wanted to speak of it, but she could not forget. She stood up to give Sowiwa the signal she was leaving. "I must go now. Perhaps if I follow Tsoongo I will find Lansa," she said.

She did not wait for her friend's reply. Her mind was playing tricks on her as she turned toward the plaza. What is a friend, she thought, if you cannot be honest with each other? Wouldn't she want to be told if she walked in Sowiwa's sandals? She found herself walking slower and slower. Then suddenly she turned and knew what she must do. Returning quickly to Sowiwa, lest she change her mind, she said, "Sowiwa, as your friend, I think there is something you must know. There are times when Lansa is not at the spring. One of those times not long ago, I found Tsoongo staring at me. I did not look at him for I did not want to encourage him. It made no difference to him, for he approached me anyway. I picked up my water jug and walked away. I . . ."

Sowiwa's eyes blazed furiously. "Then my feelings about him have been right all along! Do you want to tell me more?" She had come to her feet and was pacing back and forth on the roof of her parents' quarters.

"No, there is nothing more, but I hope you will not be angry with me. I would not want anyone or anything to spoil our friendship."

"Oh, Sihu, of course we will always be friends. I am glad you have told me. I simply appreciate Wena 'Ahote more than ever. I am certain he would never do such a thing. He knows the spring is sacred, and more than that, I think we both know that it is just not his way."

Sihu took Sowiwa's hand. "Sowiwa, I am happy that your response was what I thought it would be. I am also in complete agreement that such actions would never come from Wena 'Ahote. Now I must truly be gone. We will talk soon again." With those words she departed.

Sowiwa continued to pace. Yes, she thought, she would say nothing of this to anyone, but if her parents persisted, she now could rightly refute them. Tsoongo was no different from Lansa, though her parents would never believe that the two were so similar. She even wondered if the two of them were working together in their womanizing. Surely Tsoongo knew where Lansa was and Lansa knew where Tsoongo was. Her last thought before she climbed down the ladder to assist her mother was, "Men! What will they think of next?"

*   *   *

Sowiwa's cousin and her parents had arrived. Leetayo's father's skill in working with obsidian for weapons was known far and wide. As a result, he was to be a resident and to instruct those young men who were interested in all that he knew, much as Sowiwa's father instructed in stone masonry. Her father would begin teaching when next Sun Father arose. To celebrate their arrival, Tupkya and Sikyawa had prepared a wonderful meal. Two turkeys had been killed from the flock and were roasting along with two rabbits. There were corn dumplings in brine, squash, and corn pudding. The combined aromas were enough to titillate anyone's appetite.

Sowiwa had met her cousin only once at a very young age when she and her family had come to the center for one of the major ceremonials. She remembered little except that Leetayo, which meant "fox," had been a very moody child. Now she no longer saw a child before her, but a young woman whose appearance was very different from anyone she had ever seen. Compared to her own short stature, this woman was tall and lean as a willow tree. Her eyes were shaped almost like those of a fox, like two enormous teardrops with the pointed outer ends lying on her high cheekbones and fringed with long black lashes. Her nose was also sharply pointed, and her ears stuck out a bit. Her lustrous black hair, which hung in a single braid down her back, contained red highlights. Sowiwa judged her to be about her own age, and she marveled at how much the girl really did resemble her name.

Leetayo made no effort to be sociable. It was Sowiwa who finally said, "Greetings, cousin. Welcome to my mother's home." She noticed that Leetayo seemed to be looking past her with glittering eyes, and so she tried again. "We welcome you to the holy school and all that it has to offer."

Leetayo suddenly snapped out of her daze. With intense haughtiness she said, "How can you speak for everyone? Have you no humility?"

"Of course, but I thought . . ." Sowiwa responded in confusion. She then realized that her cousin's moods had not changed over the season cycles, and that she was not sure how to deal with her.

"Of course, you thought! Just because you have lived here for so many season cycles and I have not, do not doubt that my friends will be many in only a short time. You will see!" She turned on her heels and ascended the ladder to the rooftop.

Sowiwa's mind was in a turmoil for she knew the two of them had gotten off to a very bad start, and she did not understand what she had said that so offended her cousin. It occurred to her that perhaps Leetayo had not wanted to leave her former home, and that accounted for her unfriendly comments. She noticed that her parents were so engrossed in conversation with Leetayo's parents that they had apparently not even heard the confrontation between the two of them. With a deep sigh she turned to bring out bowls for the meal ahead.

Leetayo had no intention of returning for the evening meal. She loathed Sowiwa's fine delicate beauty, which so sharply contrasted with her own. She also envied her cousin's quiet serenity and confidence. She fervently hoped that she would not have to be in her presence very often for she had felt herself losing control with just this one visit.

She deliberately changed her thoughts to Lansa, who had nodded politely to her as she reached the top of the ladder. He had continued on his way to enjoy the meal that awaited him below. "Ah," she thought, "if only he were not my cousin." She visualized how he would look without his tunic and breechcloth, the fine square cut of his shoulders, and the narrow waist and hips. As she walked into the plaza, thinking about his other male attributes, she ran headlong into another young man.

"Please excuse me," he said. "You are new here. Allow me to introduce myself. My name is Tsoongo."

Leetayo looked into dark, smoldering, eyes that seemed to bore into her soul. She felt her heart skip a beat as she said, "And mine is Leetayo."

"Ah, and that means 'fox.' Where are you going in such a hurry?" he asked.

"Anywhere," she answered coyly. Here was another young man a little taller than herself with a lean, muscular body, who boasted many of the same features and mannerisms of Lansa. Her parents had told her that there would be many more men than women, and she found herself liking her surroundings more and more.

"Will you follow me? I know a place not far outside the plaza where we can talk," he said as he looked at her provocatively.

Having no wish to return to the meal that her family would be enjoying, and also wanting to avoid Sowiwa, she replied, "Of course, as long as you will protect me."

He took her elbow and guided her out of the plaza. They walked for a short time until they reached an outcropping of rocks. They picked their way through until they came to a flat, open area surrounded by more rocks. Tsoongo spread a blanket with one end touching a huge boulder. He sat down, using the boulder for a backrest. "Will you join me?" he asked with an inviting tone in his voice.

She did not reply, but seated herself next to him and waited.

"When I first saw you, you seemed to be coming from the direction of the house of my favorite teacher. He is proud of my work as a stone mason, and says I will go a long way. Tell me about yourself."

"I am here because my father will be teaching. Like the favorite teacher you mentioned, he is known far and wide for his skills in making arrowheads from obsidian."

"Will you be taking any classes?"

"Probably so. I am most interested in learning to see into the future."

"Then your teacher will be Ruupi, for he is our medicine man who looks into the future with his large crystal. In fact his name means 'crystal medicine man.'"

His hand moved to her leg. When she made no objection, he began kneading and stroking the soft skin of her thigh. He could not help but think that here was a young woman who was free for the taking. In his eyes she was not beautiful, but unusual-looking, perhaps like the macaw, the exotic bird whose plumage was so prized by his people. Certainly her beauty could not compare with Sowiwa's, but why pass up so ripe an opportunity. He heard a quick little gasp as his hand rose higher.

Leetayo's blood was boiling as she turned toward him. She reached for his engorged member, which was stretching the breechcloth to its limits.

He groaned with pleasure as he pulled her to him. While kissing her deeply, he untied the knot on her shoulder that held her tunic in place. He pulled the garment down and around her waist which exposed her breasts. He found them sumptuous, like ripe round squash, and he could not help but compare them with Sowiwa's. Of course he had never seen them uncovered, but he knew they would be delicate and small in proportion to the rest of her body. With one hand he traced feather light circles around one of her nipples, while with the other hand, he removed his breechcloth. Neither of them bothered to remove their sandals. He cupped her backside, drawing her to him, and ground himself against her soft sumptuous breasts. They both sank to the blanket as the world dissolved into nothing more than the two of them.

He loomed over her, rubbing his member back and forth between her legs. She clasped her legs tightly together to create friction as he moved back and forth. Then suddenly, and wantonly, she opened her legs and guided him to her softness. He entered her slowly, then held her fast for several heartbeats. Realizing he could not last much longer, he began with a slow rhythm that very gradually picked up speed. She made little mewling sounds that grew louder and louder. At last he shuddered his fulfillment and held her fast. Sweat glistened from them both in the afterglow.

When, at last, he had begun to cool down, he withdrew, and lay on his back next to her with his arm flung over his forehead. Feeling completely satiated, he said, "It is time we returned to the complex."

"What do you mean? Don't you want to know more about me?" she asked in complete surprise.

"Leetayo, little fox, I must be gone. It has been nice, but Sowiwa's father wishes us to wed. Perhaps we can sneak off again sometime, at least before I am married to Sowiwa." With those words he pulled her to her feet, tied her tunic on her shoulder once more, and donned his breechcloth.

Leetayo followed him numbly as he escorted her back to the holy school. No words passed between them. When he departed, she decided not to return to dinner, but went to her parents' new quarters. She knew she would be admonished by her parents, but she did not care in the least. Her mind worked feverishly in anger and hatred. Sowiwa was her nemesis, her scourge, her curse. Her parents had told her of her cousin's gift, but they had not told her that her cousin was so physically attractive to the opposite sex, nor had they told her of Sowiwa's confidence and grace.

She flung herself on her sleeping mat, hoping that if she slept, she would feel better when she awoke. She found herself unable to sleep. She lay as a carved wooden doll with her fists clenched as tears came to her eyes. She knew she must get past her anger and resentment or she would not be able to think rationally through the problem. She was the "fox," and she was the cunning one. She was the sly one. In time she would decide what her path would be, but for now, she cursed Tsoongo. He had used her, and she had allowed him to do so, but never again. His arrogance was unbearable, and deep in her heart, she hoped that Sowiwa would marry him. Then her nemesis would learn how incorrigible he really was.

More time passed than she had realized, for her parents came down the ladder. "I am not feeling well," she declared.

Neither of them even responded, for they were used to her moods.

Several sun cycles had passed. Leetayo had begun her classes with Ruupi. She had overheard several people speaking admirably of Sowiwa's ability to speak with the animals. The anger in her had festered like an open wound, leaving her short of temper and annoyed with everyone. Something inside her had snapped, leaving her almost irrational. She knew she had to do something, but she knew not what . . . or did she?

She waited until her next class with Ruupi had ended. When the other students had left she lingered behind, folding her hands demurely in her lap.

"You wish to speak with me?" he asked.

"Revered One, I do wish to speak to you." She began to perspire under her arms and beneath her breasts.

Ruupi waited patiently, then said, "Well, what is it?" He could feel her mounting tension.

"There is someone who has entered my life in a terribly negative way, someone who feeds on my energy and consumes me."

"And do you wish to tell me who that person might be?" he asked with increasing curiosity.

"I do, but you must promise that this will remain strictly between you and me." Leetayo's hands were now clutched tightly together.

Ruupi could not help but admire the courage of the young woman before him. Seldom had any other of his students become so personal, and he was beginning to think of her exotic look as rather attractive. In a hushed voice he replied, "You may trust me, Leetayo." He estimated that there might be the difference of ten season cycles in their ages.

"Then I must tell you, Revered One, that it is my cousin."

"You must know that I cannot read your mind. I see the future only in my crystal. Who is your cousin?"

Lifting her liquid brown eyes to his, she declared, "Why Sowiwa, of course."

He reacted as though she had struck him, for he coughed and sputtered. Then gathering his thoughts, he said, "Sowiwa is well loved among the people. She counsels wisely using the wisdom of the animals, birds, and reptiles according to that which is your power animal."

"Oh yes, I know all that, but she is arrogant and abrasive. I am sure she is a witch. If the people knew what she really is, they would agree with me."

Ruupi looked away from her, for he was not quite sure how to respond, and so he threw the problem back into the girl's hands. At last he asked, "What is it you want of me?"

"It is my ardent desire to learn to skry as you do. Will you skry into your crystal to see if I am right?"

"I do not skry when anyone is near. If you wish me to do

this, you must step outside these quarters and give me time. I should not be long."

She immediately turned to go, and whispered, "I am grateful, Revered One."

She waited on the roof at the top of the ladder for what seemed to be forever. She wished she could spy on him to see what he did, but knew that it could never be. He was such an interesting man. True, she thought, he was quite a bit older than she, but he exuded a magnetism that was most distracting. His honey color skin was flawless, and though his body was slight, he seemed well proportioned. He usually wore his hair in three braids, each tied with leather with an inserted eagle feather. His eyes were smolderingly dark and although his mouth was small, he displayed a beautiful set of white teeth on the rare occasion that he smiled. She knew priests never married, but she could not help wonder what he would be like as a lover.

Her thoughts were interrupted, and her heart leaped with the sound of his voice. "I have done as you asked. You may come down now."

She descended the ladder and found him standing with his back to her in a corner of the room. Out of respect she waited, saying nothing.

At last he turned to her as though he was carefully appraising her, as though he were a trader trying to decide her value. "I have found nothing," he said quite simply.

Leetayo felt beaten, and at first as though she had been defeated. She betrayed her feelings with her expression, which Ruupi did not miss. He saw her crestfallen expression, her eyes that already drooped like those of a fox, drooped further, reflecting deep despair. In the back of his mind he wondered if she was rational, but then he himself had no love for Sowiwa, for she was loved by the people and he was not. At least that was his perception. In the back of his mind he wondered how he might use the situation.

After a period of time she said softly, "I thank you, Revered One. I am disappointed."

"I knew you were before you said it. I am sorry my skrying was not in your favor." He placed both hands lightly on her shoulders and drew her to him. Her soft, supple body felt wonderful molded to his, but she kept her head turned in her despondency. When he realized there was no chance of any further intimacies, he let her go saying, "I have other duties now. You must go."

She turned once more and silently climbed the ladder.

CHAPTER 5

A.D. *1130*

Many pahos, prayer sticks, had been made, as many in the community prepared for the pilgrimage to the great canyon, the sipapu or place of emergence of the people into the present fourth world. This would be a long journey, and was the final step in the initiation of the young acolytes into manhood.

Red Hawk, Sowiwa's power animal, had appeared in one of her most recent dreams, telling her that she should go on the pilgrimage. He offered no explanation other than that it was for the good of the people. When she informed her parents that she intended to go, Tupkya was visibly upset.

"There is no reason for a young woman to go," she cried.

"In all due respect, Mother, there is. I have had a dream."

"What kind of dream? You are making up excuses."

"No, Mother, I am not. I cannot disclose the details of the dream, but it is so. You must believe me."

"Then who will help me with my work?" she lamented.

"Who will help you with your work when I am married and living in my own space?"

"That is not the point!" Tupkya's temper was rising.

Sikyawa interceded. "Tupkya, remain calm and listen. What do we really know of our daughter? We know she is gifted. I say she should be respected for it may be that her gift will be needed. Dreams are not meant to be shared unless they might effect others in some way. Lansa is going, so it will be only you, Palasiva, and myself. Surely you can manage the three of us."

Tupkya knew her place and bowed her head in submission. She said no more even though Sowiwa still could feel her angry vibrations.

"I will be fine, Mother. Lansa will be there to protect me. He has been on this journey before when he became a man, and is familiar with the way, and with any dangers that may or may not occur."

In the back of her mind Tupkya was thinking that Sowiwa was all they had. When she married, she would bring them much wealth and many gifts. With the boys, this would not happen. It would be their brides who would receive the gifts. She knew she dared not even hint at what she was thinking, for it was far from spiritual. Realizing that the way of her people was to think positively, she made a concerted effort to put aside her selfish thinking. Finally she said, "Sowiwa, 'littlest ear of corn,' you are precious to us. Come back safe."

"Sun Father will guide us as he always does, Mother." Then turning to her father, she added, "Thank you, Father."

No more words were necessary, for Sikyawa heard the appreciation in his daughter's voice.

They departed when Sun Father next peeped over the horizon. From the grayness of dawn came a soft haze of light, enough to see where they were going. There were seven young men who hoped that this would be the completion of the final step that would make them accepted as men of the community. Wena 'Ahote had agreed to make the journey along with Lansa and Tsoongo. There were several other men who were trained warriors, and of course Taatawi, their revered sun priest. Sowiwa was the only female in the group, but no one questioned her presence. She had spoken to Wena 'Ahote of her dream, and she suspected that he had informed Taatawi. This was why, she was certain, there was no objection to her company.

The west road made the first two sun cycles easy traveling. This was the road that so many of her people used to bring in the huge pine logs from the closest mountain range that were used in the construction of their multistory buildings. In the days when rain was more abundant, and the wash that came from these mountains was full of rushing water, the stories said that the logs had been floated down the wash into the community. Of course recently there had been many season cycles of drought which forced the laborers to haul the logs down on their shoulders.

When darkness was approaching, they camped near the foot of the mountains. It was late in the season of heat, and the temperature dropped rather quickly as Sun Father slowly descended behind the horizon. Several members of the party had gone into the mountains to hunt and had brought down a doe, their main meal of the sun cycle. Everyone enjoyed the meal enormously, for large game of this sort was no longer abundant except in the mountains, where there were still a few springs, and where the clouds left moisture at the peaks.

Sowiwa had no time to communicate with Wena 'Ahote due to the constant close proximity of Lansa and Tsoongo. She hoped that perhaps the two of them would decide to join a hunting party in the sun cycles to follow, which would give her a chance to speak to Wena 'Ahote. After stretching her aching legs, she crawled into her blanket, and fell asleep almost immediately.

It was during the grayness of dawn that she awoke. The full moon still shone brilliantly, almost as if she did not want to relinquish her beauty to Sun Father. Since no one else seemed to be awake, Sowiwa lay very still, taking in the beauty of the colors that were beginning to appear in the east. From the direction of the mountains to the west she could hear the distant roll of thunder, followed by the zig-zagging of lightning. Her nose twitched as it caught the scent of smoke. She quickly arose, for the deep growls of the thunder and the spears of lightning were growing closer. She watched a tree in the far distance explode like a torch sending sparks out in all directions. She screamed as each spark ignited into a new fire.

Now everyone in the camp was awake. "Hurry! There is no time to waste! The fire is moving from west to east! We must turn back!" she screamed as she watched two terrified rabbits scramble from their holes. They ran in circles, unsure of which direction they should take. Sowiwa communicated with them, telling them to go in the direction where Sun Father rose. Two does exploded out of the brush, their eyes rolling in panic. She gave the same message to them, and watched them bound gracefully in the eastern direction.

Blankets were quickly folded, and no one even bothered to dress, for time was precious. A slight breeze had begun quickening the progress of the fire. Sowiwa climbed a large rock and, scrambling to its pinnacle, stared in horror at the approaching firestorm, which threatened to destroy everything in its path with the hot winds that raced toward them.

Confusion seized the little party of travelers. Everyone turned to Sowiwa, who quickly climbed down from the rock. Clasping her few meager belongings, she motioned them to follow her. The breeze became a furious wind, driving the fire relentlessly. The smoke was becoming almost unbearable, and everyone was coated with sweat and a coating of ash. They all knew their only hope was to outrun the fire.

Sowiwa began to cough and wheeze in the thickening smoke. She watched more animals stampede across the desolate land, their eyes glazed with terror. Every so often she waved her hands frantically and yelled, "This way!" for she feared there might be those behind her who could not see her. She hoped that they could reach the toe- and handholds at the edge of the cliff in time. At that point she hoped the fire would have nowhere to go.

It was then that she suffered a misstep and twisted her ankle. When she cried out in pain, Wena 'Ahote rushed to her side to support her. They looked back to see an enormous wall of flame licking greedily at the sky. Disregarding her pain, she yelled, "Run! We are almost there!"

Wena 'Ahote continued to support her with his arm around her waist while they scrambled to the edge of the cliff and down the chiseled ladder that led them to safety at the bottom of the canyon. They did not stop, but continued on as far as their exhausted bodies would permit. At last they turned to see that the fire had reached the tip of the cliff and was dying.

Wena 'Ahote held Sowiwa tightly, rocking her back and forth. He now realized that here was a woman of courage and strength, and one who had saved her people. He knew her story would be told for many generations to come.

*   *   *

Sowiwa was horrified, for she had directed the animals toward the east, never thinking that they could not climb down the toe-and handholds. They had all returned to their Maker at the bottom of the cliff. The carnage was terrible, and her guilt was almost unimaginable. When they had all rested for a short while, she spoke. "I have done evil to our brothers. To honor them, we must return to pray for them, and to take the meat they have to offer for the goodness of our people."

"What is it you are saying?" Lansa asked.

"I am trying to tell you that I communicated with them and told them to move to the east. I did not think about the cliff they would have to encounter." Tears rolled down her ashen black cheeks.

Wena 'Ahote continued to cradle her as she wept. He felt her grief, for he knew of her sensitivity and of her abilities. He gently extricated himself from her and stood tall and proud. "This woman has saved us all from what could have been a terrible death. Her acute senses and her ability to speak with the animals has saved us, but she blames herself. I say she has no reason to take the blame upon herself. The animals instinctively know which way to go in all things, at least when there is a choice. They probably knew that there was no other alternative, and so they followed her lead. Do you agree, Taatawi?"

Taatawi wiped the soot from his eyes as best he could. "Yes, in this I must agree. I feel certain there was no other choice, for to the west are the mountains, much of which has probably burned, and to the north and south is much of the same as we see here with dry grasses and small bushes that would ignite immediately." He uttered a deep sigh, for he was thinking that the loss of wood and green in the mountains in the west was not what his people needed during the season cycles of drought they had been experiencing. Then he added, "I must also agree with Sowiwa in that we must honor the animals and go back. Our people need the nourishment they will provide."

And so it was that a bedraggled party of people covered with ash and soot returned to the complex, bringing all the meat that it was possible for them to carry. Wena 'Ahote had supported

Sowiwa for much of the trip due to the pain in her ankle, with occasional relief from Lansa and Tsoongo.

The community had, of course, known of their return not long after the fire, for scouts were always out and about.

Sowiwa and Lansa accepted their parents' warm welcome with great joy. They both were happy to see the broad smile on Tupkya's face as Lansa handed her their share of the meat. Palasiva and Sikyawa were also beaming.

"We knew what was happening, and we were all three of us very worried," Sikyawa commented. "It is good to have my little family safely together once again. Sun Father surely has blessed us in many ways. We have not seen this much meat at one time for many season cycles."

Tupkya laid the meat on a bench in her cooking area, then turned to ask, "Now please tell us all about it."

Palasiva echoed her enthusiastically. "Oh yes, please tell us! It will not be many more season cycles until I, too, will be old enough to make the journey."

Lansa, of course, took the floor. He began the story truthfully, but when it came to Sowiwa's bravery, he eliminated that part, and said simply that it was obvious to everyone that they should all run toward the east.

"If that is so, my son, then where did all this meat come from?" inquired Sikyawa. "Surely you had no time to hunt in such a short time and in your condition." Then he turned to Sowiwa inquisitively. "Sowiwa, let us hear your version."

"You are right, Father. There was no hunting." She went on to explain how she had seen the exploding tree when Sun Father was just beginning his climb and how beautiful the moon had been. She went on to say that the animals had told her to run to the east. She also told of their climb down the toe- and handholds of the cliff, and of the tragedy of the animals who had rushed to their death at the cliff bottom. She spoke of her feelings of sorrow and guilt, and of how they took the meat of the animals to honor them.

Tupkya watched the temper rising in her eldest son. Very softly she said, "Lansa, you would not make a very good storyteller. You left out the most exciting parts. It sounds as though without Sowiwa, you might not have survived. Is it not so?"

"Mother, she exaggerates. We all knew exactly which way to go. Why do you take her word instead of mine? This happens all the time." He rose from his cross-legged position on the mat to stand at the foot of the ladder.

Sikyawa also rose and walked behind Tupkya, laying his hands on her shoulders. "We do take your word, son, but you eliminated her part. She did not change anything you said. She just added to the events through her own eyes."

Palasiva sat quietly watching his brother's body language. He saw the clenched fists and the flush of anger. He saw his brother's tensed shoulders, and was sure he heard the grinding of his brother's teeth. He was not surprised when he heard Lansa's next comment.

"With all due respect, I must excuse myself. It seems I am always wrong and my sister is always right. I am a great warrior. She is but a counselor. The reason women are here is to procreate, nothing more." He turned and climbed the ladder.

Sikyawa answered furiously, "Go nurse your wounded feelings and act the spoiled child. By your act of refusing to celebrate with us, you are not welcome in this house until you come to your senses."

Tupkya looked up at Sikyawa with tears in her eyes. "Why is it always so?" she whimpered. With a heavy heart she rose to prepare the meat, feeling thankful that she had Sowiwa to assist her.

Lansa did not return.

Just before Sun Father made his descent during the next sun cycle, an acolyte brought a message that Sowiwa was invited to attend a meeting of the elders. The acolyte said he would return to escort her to the meeting shortly after dark.

Sowiwa's heart leaped as she began to prepare herself.

Tupkya continued to grind, but watched her daughter out of the corner of her eye. She wondered which of the two of them felt more anxious and excited, but she did not let on. Her heart was breaking due to Lansa's arrogance and the fact that he had not returned. She wondered what she had done to cause him to be so, but there seemed to be no answers. Of course he had been very spoiled until Sowiwa's birth, but as all mothers do, she felt that somehow she, or perhaps both she and Sikyawa, had somehow been responsible. She swelled with pride when she thought of Sowiwa and the goodness the child bestowed on everyone. In her mind she knew she would always consider her a child in spite of the fact that she was fifteen season cycles of age. And so she kept her vigil and remained silent.

Sowiwa filled a large bowl with some water, which had become so precious a commodity, and rinsed herself thoroughly. Knowing there was not enough time to wash her hair, she coiled it in two large whorls over each ear and inserted a red feather from the red-tailed hawk into the left whorl. She reached for her newest skirt, tied it around her waist, and slipped into her sandals. She gazed at her reflection in a pyrite mirror that she and her mother had only recently begun to share. She applied a bit of charcoal to accent her eyes, and a bit of red ocher to her cheeks. Turning to her mother, she asked, "How do I look?"

Tupkya stopped her grinding with a huge smile. "You look lovely, Sowiwa. You have truly become a lovely young woman."

Sowiwa and Tupkya had no more time for conversation, for the acolyte appeared and beckoned for Sowiwa to follow him. She flung a blanket around her shoulders to protect her from the evening chill.

They walked in silence over the plaza. Though this was the third time Sowiwa had attended one of the elders' meetings, she realized that she was just as nervous as she had been in the first meeting, when she had been only ten season cycles of age.

The fire in the firebox burned brightly in the kiva, heating the room to a temperature almost as hot as that of a sweat bath. All four of the elders were seated on the bench around the perimeter, as well as Posaala, Maahu, Awta, and Iswungwa. Ruupi stood alone with Taatawi and Wena 'Ahote only a short distance away. All eyes were on Sowiwa as she descended the ladder. Taatawi stepped out to escort her to stand between Wena 'Ahote and himself.

Tenyam began by saying, "Sowiwa, daughter of Sikyawa

and Tupkya, we invited you to this meeting to do you honor. Once again you have proven yourself to be a most unusual young woman. At this time I would ask Angwusi to speak." He extended his arm and hand in the other elder's direction.

Angwusi was taller than the other three elders and used his height to his advantage whenever possible. Now he rose, rearranged his robe, and cleared his throat. "Sowiwa, you must be aware that one of the young men traveling with you to the Great Canyon was my son. He has spoken of your bravery along with Awta's son, who was also a part of your group. I wish to speak for both Awta and myself when I tell you that we are deeply indebted to you. We are all well aware that if you had not been awake to see the tree that exploded when it was hit by lightning, it is entirely possible that some, or perhaps all of you, would have perished." He paused to wipe the sweat from his brow, then continued. "If it were in my power to honor you with more than a verbal thank you, I would do so immediately. As of now I can think of nothing, but please do not think that either I or Awta are any less grateful." He quietly took his position once more next to Tenyam.

It was Hoohu who spoke next, for he seemed to have a knack for seeing straight to the heart of an issue, as his name suggested. "From those who have told the story I have learned that Sowiwa rose from her sleep well before the others and that the moon shown brilliantly. Somehow—perhaps it was the vibrations from the animals, who we all know can feel an event before it happens—she awakened. Yet to the west she saw the storm gods strike their vengeful wrath, and awakened the rest of the party. Those who were there say that the moon continued to shine even when Sun Father rose, and under that moon the fire raged. May I suggest to you that the circumstances were most unusual, and may I also suggest to you that we are dealing with a most unusual young lady, one whose humble name is Littlest Ear of Corn. In my opinion her name no longer befits her." He resumed his position on the bench.

"Are you suggesting that we rename her?" inquired the obese elder, Eykita, who groaned when he stood as well as when he sat.

"These are exactly my thoughts," Hoohu answered. "It is in my mind that she surely deserves better."

Sowiwa's heart pounded. Never in her wildest imaginings had she thought she might have any other name. She knew she would always be small, perhaps not the smallest, but nonetheless small. Tupkya had explained that her name was one of endearment, and she had always accepted that as a fact. Now she would be given a new name.

Angwusi proudly rose from the bench. "I would offer a name. Since Sowiwa has so valiantly brought our sons and loved ones safely back to us, let us call her Brushfire Woman."

Eykita groaned as usual, and Hoohu laughingly exclaimed, "So, Eykita, you must think about as much of that name as I do. In fact that name strikes me as funny. I grant you it is a start, but surely we can do better."

Angwusi winced and decided to remain silent.

For a short time everyone sat quietly lost in deep thought. At last Tenyam stood. "I have been thinking that Ember Fire is lovely, and also rather melodic."

"But in my mind it is not strong enough. We should also remember that the moon was full and continued to shine even after Sun Father had risen and completed part of his journey. What do you think of Moon Flame?" Hoohu inquired.

Eykita dragged his girth from the bench, saying, "It's a much better name, but still not strong enough. I suggest Moon Blaze."

Hoohu rose excitedly. "Moon Blaze is good, but Moon Fire is stronger. Perhaps we should ask for Sowiwa's opinion, after all she will be living with the name for the rest of her life."

Sowiwa's eyes sparkled as she stepped forward to speak. "I wish to give thanks to all of you and especially to Awona-wilona, the Creator, who was watching over us all on that occasion. I am also very flattered with the names you suggest, but just the fact that you have invited me here to thank me is quite enough."

Tenyam quickly spoke out. "But this is something we all want to give you. Will you not choose?"

"I cannot, with all humbleness choose, but, with your permission, there is someone here with whom I would wish to speak." She stepped back beside Taatawi and Wena 'Ahote. She did not see the broad smile and fond expression that Wena 'Ahote sent her way.

"Permission is granted," Tenyam answered quickly.

Sowiwa turned to Wena 'Ahote and whispered, "Help me. What is your opinion?"

Wena 'Ahote's startled whispered response was, "In my opinion, Moon Fire is the strongest."

"May Wena 'Ahote have permission to speak?" Sowiwa asked.

"It is granted," answered Tenyam.

Wena 'Ahote stepped forward and said, "Since I was part of the party who escaped the fire unharmed, and I observed Sowiwa's bravery, I believe she deserves the name of Moon Fire."

"It is decided. From this time forward she will be known as Moon Fire." proclaimed Tenyam. "Since this is the last item on our agenda, the council meeting is adjourned."

One by one, as they left the meeting, they stopped to congratulate Moon Fire on her new name.

"Little daughter, your father and I are proud of you. Though Palasiva and Lansa are not here at the moment, I know that Palasiva is also proud, and Lansa, well, who knows about him?" Tupkya pulled her gifted daughter to her bosom, and added, "It will take us all some time to get used to your new name."

"It will take me some time to adjust, too, but it really is a beautiful name, don't you think?"

"Indeed I do agree, but now, Moon Fire, will you take the jug to the spring for some water?"

"Of course. I shall return soon." She placed a cotton ring on top of her head to balance the water jug. Every Anasazi girl learned at a very young age how to walk with perfect posture and how to balance a water jug on her head. They also learned how to balance it in rough terrain or climbing a ladder.

The wash in front of the complex had been dry for some time. Water was a precious commodity, and often very hard to find due to the drought that had been plaguing the people for several sun cycles. Rainwater was normally collected in large cisterns, and there was also a small spring within reasonable walking distance, but it had dried up in just the last season cycle. Of course the terraces, dams, and irrigation canals had also dried. The corn had not developed and the bean pods were nonexistent. Even the wild amaranths, sunflowers, and tansy mustard seed had struggled to live, but had shriveled and died.

Moon Fire's wide sandals crunched as she walked over the parched land. She decided to walk to the spring to see if there might be any sign of moisture. She knew what to do if there was, but then so did all of her people, for they were all trained in survival skills. She prayed to Awonawilona, the Creator, asking that the drought might be broken. When at last she reached the spring, she stood for a short time looking at the ground for signs of dampness. To her relief she found a slightly damp spot not far from the place where the water used to drip out, and knelt down to do her work. She found it necessary to dig down deeper than ever before, but at last water began to collect in the hole. She waited for water to accumulate, then brought out a long, hollow bone and a piece of cotton cloth from a pouch tied around her waist. She wrapped the cloth around one end of the bone tube, then sucked the water up through the tube, spitting the filtered water into the empty jug. It was a long process and required much patience, but water was one of the elements necessary for life, and so she persisted.

Suddenly the small hairs on her arms began to bristle. She stood up, wiping her brow, but saw no one. She thought perhaps it might be a predator, but she saw no signs of one. Placing her hands at the small of her back, she continued to listen. Then she heard from a far distance the sound of a flute that she immediately recognized, for the melody was so smooth and sweet that it could have only been played by Wena 'Ahote. When she realized the sound was getting closer, her heart skipped a beat. Could it really be happening? It was. And so she went on listening even as she continued her work.

Wena 'Ahote had watched her leave the complex with the water jug on her head that made her diminutive figure look so top heavy. Yet there was a gracefulness about her that he found enchanting. Perhaps it was her wisdom with the animals, or maybe it was her bravery, or eloquence in speaking, or her delicate but striking appearance. The truth of it was that it was all of those things that fascinated him. He had grabbed his flute and followed her at what he thought was enough distance. He suspected that she would go toward the spring, and so he waited and watched until she had worked for some time to obtain water. He also knew it would take her some time to get enough water to fill the jug, and he did not want to detain her for very long. When he thought she had probably had enough time to complete the job, he began to play his flute. He continued until he was very close, then stepped out from behind a huge rock. "Please do not let me stop you. May I continue playing while you go on?" he asked.

"Of course, oh yes, of course!" she stammered, then knelt down to continue her work.

He continued to play, weaving a magic around the hard work she was doing. She could hardly believe what was happening, and the work was actually a pleasure. His melodies were hypnotic and she found it difficult to keep her body from swaying to the sensuous rhythms. When at last she had filled the jug, she said, "Thank you for making my work so much easier with your music. What brings you to the spring?" Then lifting the jug to the top of her head, she quickly began to retrace her steps toward the complex.

Wena 'Ahote walked by her side, and when he felt they were far enough away from the spring, he said, "I watched you leave the complex, and I followed. It was you who drew me to the spring." He looked down at his flute and fingered it nervously. "I want you to know you are a very special person in my life. There are many qualities about you that I admire."

Moon Fire gasped and lost her composure. "I—I—I had no idea. I had only hoped. Oh, perhaps I have said too much." She dropped her chin on her chest and lowered her eyes.

"No, Moon Fire, you have not said too much. You have occupied my thoughts since the time long ago when you told me all about one of my spirit animals, the mockingbird. That was when I realized you were a most unusual young woman. Since the fire, you have filled more of my thinking, and I—"

"And you what?" she asked. She was thankful that he had waited to say these words until now, for her people believed that springs were sacred and should never be profaned. They believed that one or more water serpents lived in all springs and carefully watched a person's behavior. If the water serpent became angry he could cause earth tremors by moving his body. Children could not play in the water or bathe in it. There were also several sexual taboos about the serpents in the springs. The people were forbidden to tempt the serpent sexually. Any kind of flirting or lovemaking in or near a source of water was not tolerated, for in doing so a person made himself or herself desirable to the serpent. The worse taboo was the belief that if a female had intercourse at a spring, she would give birth to a snake. Of course the spring had long since dried up, but in her mind she thought it entirely possible that the water serpent might yet be living in the water beneath the ground.

Wena 'Ahote slowed his pace and took her hand. Due to the jug on her head she could not look at him. "I know you cannot move your head," he said. "May we stop and may I help you to remove the jug?"

"Thank you, but I can do it." She lifted the heavy jug from its circular cushion and set it gently on a flat rock nearby, then turned to face him.

"Sowi—, I mean Moon Fire, I have been afraid to express my feelings to you for several reasons. One is that you might rebuff me. Another is that I know Tsoongo has his eyes on you, and I do not know what your feelings are toward him. The third, and perhaps the most important, is that if I am to become a priest, I cannot marry or have children. Priests are, however, allowed to take a lover, but I was afraid that you might find that insulting." He dropped his extended arms to his side while uttering a deep sigh.

Moon Fire felt both surprised and thrilled. "If you would let me, I shall respond to all three of your concerns. First of all, I would have you know that I have been praying to Awonawilona for this to happen, and He has finally answered my prayers. Secondly, I am very aware of Tsoongo, but I have no interest in him. My parents favor him, and are always trying to push me his way. I, personally, consider him much like my brother

Lansa. He is rude and obnoxious. Oh, I know I should not speak of my brother this way, but it is the truth." She paused as she caught sight of a prairie dog.

"But what of my third concern?" he asked.

"Wena 'Ahote, the fact that you cannot marry or have children is of no concern to me. I doubt that my parents will approve, for they remind me endlessly of the fact that I am well past the marriageable age." She turned her head away from him and almost whispered, "It is you I have been watching for many season cycles."

Taking her hand, he pulled her into his embrace. He placed his finger under her chin, lifting her eyes to meet his own. Never in his wildest imaginings did he believe it possible that her answers would be exactly as he had hoped. He brushed her lips with his own, then again more firmly. He wanted to hold her forever.

Moon Fire trembled with excitement and also with the fear that her legs might give out from under her. "Hold me tight. I'm feeling weak," she said "I'm not sure I could even lift the jug off the ground, let alone put it on my head."

He chuckled as he spoke, "Perhaps I should be on my way so you can regain your strength. Before I go, I want you to know you have made me a very happy man. I hope to see you again very soon." With a big smile that displayed his perfect white teeth he let her go and walked toward the complex.

Moon Fire found herself watching his broad shoulders and slender form, which was almost completely hidden by his cotton robe. When and how they would get together again, she had no idea, but for now she fairly floated with happiness. The weight of the water jug seemed like nothing. All she knew was that in her mind she would never have to be concerned with Tsoongo again.

CHAPTER 6

A.D. *1131*

I t was the season of greening again, but nothing was greening. The cold season, which usually saw much snow, had not
been the same. The air had remained, for the most part, very
dry and cold, and the people were beginning to believe that all
their ceremonial efforts to Awonawilona for moisture in any
form had been in vain. A few valiant families were making
preparations to move, where, they were not sure. In the sun cycles where the wind blew, the dust was so intolerable that it ne-
cessitated wearing a cloth over the nose and mouth, and
sometimes even the eyes, to keep out the dust.

Moon Fire made her way to her cave. Fortunately it was a
day of relative calm, and she did not need to take any precautions, or so she thought. As she walked, she noticed fewer animals and birds than before, and wondered what her "little
brothers" were doing for water. She felt certain they were suffering as much, or even more, than were her people. She knew
that many birds and animals were territorial, and she suspected
that many had perished for that reason. Her heart was wrenched
when she allowed herself to even think about it.

A prairie dog lifted its little head to Awonawilona and extended its little hands perpendicular to the earth. Prairie dogs
were the epitome of the idea of community living. They, like
the Anasazi, also lived in towns but theirs was a network of underground tunnels that contained their individual tunnels and
rooms. In addition, the entire town was divided into individual
communities in which the members depended on each other.

What was more startling, and comparable to her own culture, was the fact that each section of the town was inhabited by members of separate "clans." They even had sentinels who sent out alarms in the form of high-pitched yips at the sight of a predator.

Moon Fire froze and shut her eyes in an effort to communicate with the skinny little fellow. She felt his anguish as he, too, begged for moisture. As usual, there were no actual sounds or words between the two of them for their contact was on another level. Her "poor brother" had spent the winter living off what little fat he had accumulated during the last season cycle, and was in desperate need of grasses and plants, which provided him with the nourishment and water he required. She caught the message from him that many of his clan members had perished during the dry, hard cold season, and others were seriously considering moving elsewhere. She marveled at the similarities between these "little brothers" and her own people. When she saw two very skinny prairie dogs kissing and hugging with mouths open, touching their teeth together, she found yet another bond between them and her own people.

At last she came into view of her cave. The mesquite tree next to the entrance looked very bad. Ordinarily there would be tiny leaves beginning to emerge, but when she looked closely, she found none. To obtain warmth during the time when Sun Father was no longer warming the land, she found she had to resort to chopping out dead cactus or whatever she could find. She threw up her arms in supplication, much as the prairie dog had done, begging Awonawilona to send moisture.

When next Sun Father arose, she decided to walk. Her lower back was bothering her and she felt the activity might be of some help. She also knew that she must return to the little cave well before Sun Father reached his zenith, for her water supply was limited. Making her way carefully around a large rock formation, she flushed out a lizard. It scurried a short distance away, then sat very still, feigning sleep. Moon Fire also froze while waiting to communicate with the lizard. This lizard had the usual long tail to help him maintain balance and also had a crested back and a ruff around the neck. It occurred to her that when she was a child, there were always a couple of lizards living in the housing her parents inhabited. She had not seen any at all for the past several season cycles.

"Yes," the lizard said. "It is due to the lack of water. I sit stone still waiting for the subtlest insect movements, but there are almost none. I haven't enough to sustain me, and so I and my family are considering moving elsewhere, but I know not where, or even if we can find an appropriate place."

Again her heart was torn. "Lizard, your situation is no different from that of my people. We are all in difficult straits."

As if her poor "little brother" was too weak to make further communications, it slowly moved away.

Moon Flower made her way back to her cave, wrapped in a deep depression concerning the welfare of her people.

Wena 'Ahote was fully aware that this was the third sun cycle of Moon Fire's womanly cycle. He was uncertain exactly where she spent her time, but it was none of his concern, for her space during that time was sacred. He waited in the same place where he had spoken to her when she had gone for another of her womanly cycles a long time ago, hoping she would return on the same path as she had before. It was not just that he wished to see her, but he was also concerned for her welfare. The raiders had begun attacking again and there was a report that one of the outliers in close proximity had been partially burned out. A young woman alone could have serious problems, and of course in his mind Moon Fire was not just any young woman. It also occurred to him that she might not take the same path especially if she was conversing with one of their "brother animals," birds, insects, or reptiles. He paced as he waited.

At last he spotted her small figure as she rounded a huge rock. Breathing a sigh of relief, he walked toward her. She must have recognized him, for it seemed to him that she picked up speed, or perhaps he did, or in all probability they both did. He wrapped her in his arms and buried his face in her hair. "Sowi—I mean Moon Fire, I am glad you are back safely."

Reveling in the scent of sage that his hair and skin exuded, she asked, "Was there any doubt in your mind that I would not?"

"No—I mean yes, I was worried," he replied, continuing to hold her as if she were an apparition.

"Wena 'Ahote, what ever is wrong? Please don't stop holding me."

Wondering if he was hurting her or holding her too tight, he released her, but firmly held both of her hands. "Only a short time ago, we received word that the raiders attacked an outlier. The outlier was not very large, and our people fought valiantly. Even so, several were killed, and two were captured. Our people were in a weakened condition due to the drought and lack of water, and they could not defend themselves as they normally would. At any rate, the raid took place in and around this area, and I was concerned for your welfare. So here I am."

"I am fine. My new power animal protected me. This was a most unusual womanly cycle. I have much to tell you if you will retain my confidence. Now hold me again, but more tenderly, please."

He placed his forefinger under her chin to tilt her face to meet his. His lips were ever so soft as they met hers with a delicate brush of tenderness. In a husky whisper he said, "I don't know what I would do if anything were to happen to you. I would never want another."

Moon Fire shivered with ecstasy, wondering again if this was really happening to her. "I, too, feel the same. The waiting has seemed forever." She felt dizzy when he placed a hand on her breast, then snapped back into reality. "You say the raiders are in close proximity? Then do you agree that it is wise to return to the complex as quickly as possible?"

He chuckled as he said, "Always the sensible young woman, but yes, I do agree." He took her basket containing her few belongings.

They had not gone far when he stopped and asked her, "Do you want to tell me of your new power animal? I think we are close enough to the complex that we are safe from the raiders."

"Of course I would tell you, but someone approaches."

They watched as a figure slowly became recognizable. It was Tsoongo, and they both breathed a disturbed sigh. It seemed that they were not destined to have any privacy.

Tsoongo said nothing until he stood before them, as if he

was sizing up the situation. His jaw tightened as he said, "Well, isn't this a surprise. I come to escort Moon Fire, and I find our sun priest's assistant by her side."

Moon Fire was immediately inflamed. "Tsoongo, I doubt you came to escort me. I suspect you just wanted to know where I was and if anyone was with me. If it is as you say, why did you come? It seems you are everywhere and know everything."

"That," he retorted angrily, "has nothing to do with why I am here." Then turning to Wena 'Ahote he continued. "Perhaps I should ask why you are here. As the sun priest's assistant, you cannot take a woman. She has no future with you."

"Ah, but you are wrong, Tsoongo," declared Wena 'Ahote. "It is true that I am the sun priest's assistant, but that does not mean I cannot be friends with a woman. It only means that I cannot marry."

"Friends with a woman? You can't be serious!" he exclaimed.

"Well then, it seems that you should look at your reflection in our almost nonexistent water or a pyrite mirror," declared Wena 'Ahote.

Moon Fire marveled that Wena 'Ahote seemed to have such control over his emotions. Her admiration for him was growing immeasurably, but she was also concerned that Tsoongo's temper, which was not so different from Lansa's, might become uncontrollable. Sticking out her chin and standing tall, she said, "Tsoongo, you have avoided the question, and the question is, why are you here?"

"Well, I, uh—"

"Yes, of course. It is because you are watching my every move. Now let me tell you why Wena 'Ahote is here. He was concerned about me. The raiders have been only recently in this area, and he was worried about a woman traveling alone."

"But, of course, that is also why I am here," he whined.

"No, it is not. If that was your purpose, you would have been relieved that I was safe. It should not matter to you who might accompany me, but only that I am unharmed. I see through you, Tsoongo. When will you understand that I do?" She found herself fairly shaking with emotion.

Tsoongo stared at her and backed up. "It is clear that I am unwelcome here." With a haughty turn, he hastily returned in the same direction he had come.

Moon Fire breathed a sigh of relief and turned to Wena 'Ahote, who was staring at her in amazement. He took her hand as they made their way toward the holy school. "It seems," he said, "there is a lot I must learn about our beloved Moon Fire."

Two sun cycles passed with the same unbearable dust. Whenever Moon Fire passed through the plaza she found it necessary to cover her nose and mouth with a cloth. She pitied those who lived in dwellings that were not large and did not face south, for at least in a complex as large as the holy school, with its southern exposure, she did not have to cover her entire face. Even the turkeys and dogs found sheltered corners in their attempt to escape the dust. She had found the time to tell Wena 'Ahote of her conversations with the prairie dog and the lizard, but not to speak of her new animal totem. The people she counseled were growing in number, and almost all of them spoke of the lack of food and of being hungry. She wondered if Awonawilona had forgotten her people, but she could not let any of them know that she had such doubts. She spent time with each passing sun cycle in supplication, asking the gods to send rain.

It was with these same recurring thoughts that suddenly an acolyte descended the ladder to her parents' quarters. He announced another meeting which would take place when next Sun Father had completed his journey and darkness had descended upon them. Moon Fire had no need to ask the reason for the meeting, for she knew in her heart that her people were in a crisis. Still, she was curious to know why they would ask her to attend.

Tupkya was present when the acolyte had arrived and looked at her daughter questioningly. She said nothing, for she had grown to see her daughter in a new light, and was sure that in time Tsoongo would be her daughter's choice.

With Tupkya's assistance, Moon Fire cleansed herself with their precious small amount of water, pinched her cheeks for color, and made her way to the kiva where the meeting was to be held.

* * *

Moon Fire could not help but wonder why, in all the meetings she had attended, the heat was so intense. It did not seem to matter what the season. She thought it might be due to the fact that heat was purifying. Everyone's brow was beaded with perspiration as they passed around the pipe that always preceded a counsel meeting. She quickly noticed that everyone was in attendance except Maahu, the architect. Wena 'Ahote beckoned her to his side.

It was Tenyam, of course, who called the meeting to order. His small beady eyes shone brightly under moist heavy eyelids. It was obvious that he must have been in attendance longer than anyone else due to the perspiration stains on his robe. "It has come to our attention that there are those who are leaving our community. It is only a few at a time, but nonetheless we are losing some of the people. This is the center of our culture. I believe that some of our people do not understand the importance of this. In my mind these people are totally irrational, for in times of hardship, we as a people must remain unified. I bring this before you with a heavy heart."

Moon Fire knew that he truly had spoken from the heart. She also felt that the community was pampered, for food was brought in from all the outliers even though there was some growing within the complex. There were also storage bins that normally supplied the outliers during the cold season and growing season, but there was very little grain in them due to the many season cycles of drought. She waited for someone else to speak.

A period of silence followed until at last Angwusi rose from the bench. "I am in complete agreement with Tenyam, for it is Awonawilona's wish that the people remain in balance, which means that we must remain unified. If we allow these people to abandon us, the people will become fragmented, and we will be even more vulnerable to the raiders. We must issue a warning to our people that they are forbidden to leave. At all cost we must remain unified."

It was Eykita who finally broke the tension. He raised his girth from the bench, groaned, then belched, and said, "I also agree. I see this meeting as a waste of time."

Hoohu bristled in anger, and sprang from the bench. "How can you be so blind? Nowhere in our oral history have I heard of a decree or a warning issued to the people that would forbid them to do anything. Everyone knows that it is negativity that displeases the gods. Is it negative to want to feed your family? They leave with the hope of finding a spot near a large creek or river to use for irrigation. I see that only as the wish to survive this terrible drought we are having."

Eykita suddenly came alive. "Hoohu has made a good point." After an enormous yawn he added, "It is possible that by putting restrictions on the people we would drive them away faster. Instead of walking away proudly, they would sneak away, and perhaps in even greater numbers."

Hoohu was elated to feel that Eykita was siding with him. Rising from the bench, he said, "So we are divided. May I suggest that we hear from our own little Moon Fire? She may be able to enlighten us more."

Tenyam rose with a frown. What, he wondered, could Moon Fire know that they did not already know? Putting aside his feelings, he reluctantly gave his consent.

Moon Fire gathered her courage and stepped forward since she was already standing. "Revered Ones, I would tell you of a very recent encounter with a prairie dog. Prairie dogs have their own little communities as we do. They are also broken down in clans, as we are. They post sentinels to warn their community of impending danger. I encountered one skinny prairie dog who told me that many of his clan had died over the cold season, and that those who still lived were moving on with the hope of finding water and plants that they need for nourishment." She paused to gather her thoughts, then continued. "I also have spoken to a lizard who moved very slowly, saying that, due to the drought, there were very few insects to eat, and that his kind were moving elsewhere." Then plucking up her courage, she quietly added, "Our people are no different." She stepped back to indicate that she had finished what she had to say.

Tenyam took the floor once more. "It is in my mind that Moon Fire has made it very clear that we are not alone in our dilemma. Our little brothers are also troubled. I still maintain that this is the center of our culture, and we must make an effort to keep it intact. How can we permit the people to abandon such a magnificent center? What can we do?"

Angwusi rose with a heavy sigh. "Tenyam, you know I usually stand by you, and I do so now. I have heard what Moon Fire has said, and she has made it very clear that we are not alone. She has also pointed out in her own subtle way that the animals, who are a major source of food for the people, are leaving. I do know that the very large complex north of us is growing. It is surviving because the rivers have not dried up. I would hate to think that at some point in time it would become the cultural center for the people, but if the gods are not favoring us here, is that not an indication?"

Hoohu rose immediately. "How can we place restrictions on the people when all they want to do is to survive? Is it not our duty to represent our people, or are we here to hinder them in their pursuit of life? Are we to become like the Mayans who dictate and manipulate their people? I would turn the floor over to Taatawi, with whom I had a discussion only two sun cycles ago."

Taatawi stepped forward. "I believe this might be the time to report that several of my patients are suffering from lack of food. Many are from the outliers where there is less to eat than here. They complain of severe stomach pains and little to no energy. I cannot tell them that I cannot help them, but I am sure they will sooner or later realize I cannot, and decide to leave in search of better living conditions. It grieves me to have to speak of this."

Tenyam was visibly shaken. He took several deep breaths, then finally spoke in desperation. "Angwusi, can you not see what it is that I do? With a decree that our people may not leave, we will be preserving our cultural center. Why can you all not understand?"

A long silence pervaded the kiva. Moon Fire glanced at Wena 'Ahote. He looked as though he wished to speak, but knew he could not. Her heart ached, for she knew that the welfare of her people had reached a critical point, and she could understand the feelings on both sides.

At last Hoohu declared, "Let us take a vote."

Tenyam stood again. "So be it. If you are in favor of posing a decree, please indicate by extending your right hand."

Hoohu's hand and Eykita's hand remained at their sides. All eyes were on Angwusi, who seemed lost in thought. When, after a time, he did not extend his hand, it was clear that no restrictions would be placed upon the people. Tenyam then adjourned the meeting.

Moon Fire turned to leave, but Wena 'Ahote detained her with a light touch of his hand on her shoulder. The elders slowly climbed the ladder followed by the others in attendance.

"We must not stay long. I would ask you to come to my quarters if you can, but only for a short time. If it is not possible, I will understand."

Moon Fire's heart skipped a beat. She had dreamed of being in his quarters, but never had she thought . . . She nodded, then quickly climbed the ladder. Should she go home first? No, of course not. Tupkya would not want her going out this late, and would also suspect that she might be meeting someone. She was in no mood to speak of her love for Wena 'Ahote as yet. Turning to Wena 'Ahote she said, "I will come now, but you are right. I cannot stay long."

She descended the ladder before him, where she waited until he had stoked the fire. By the light of the fire she could see that his quarters consisted of just one small room that was very sparsely furnished. His sleeping mat was rolled up in one corner and a bench held several robes that were neatly folded. There were two niches in the walls, one that contained his yucca hairbrush along with several different feathers for his braids, and another that housed his pipe and a small pouch containing tobacco. A beautiful clear quartz crystal rested next to his pipe. On one wall he had painted several of the constellations on a dark night sky.

"Oh," she exclaimed, "your wall is beautiful. It makes the room almost magical. I did not know you were interested in tracking the paths of the stars."

"I have always been fascinated with the sky, but it isn't the wall that makes the room magical. It is you," he said.

"I, uh, don't know what to say." Even as she spoke she could feel a burning flush spreading from her neck to her ears and finally to her face.

He walked past her to the corner, where he picked up his mat and unrolled it on the floor. Then taking her hand he led her to the mat, inviting her to join him.

"I must not stay long. I will be expected home and I don't feel like answering any questions," she whispered. She wrung her hands nervously.

"And I will not detain you, Moon Fire. You can relax. I just want to tell you how well you spoke at the council, and also that I think your words are what turned the tide. Without you, I am certain it would have been a draw, Tenyam and Angwusi against Hoohu and Eykita. Or perhaps, even worse, it may have been Tenyam, Angwusi, and Eykita against Hoohu. Everyone knows that the problem is serious, but I also believe that restrictions on the people are wrong, and I suspect you do too."

"If you are asking me, I will tell you that I agree. My ribs may be showing, but I have gotten used to less instead of more," she answered. "It grieves me to think of people slowly dying from lack of food."

"As Taatawi's assistant, I have seen these patients firsthand, and he is right. I also wish there was something I could do or say to them to help them along until the gods finally choose to send us the nourishment that Earth Mother needs." He paused, then with a deep sigh, he added, "I just wish there was some way we could spend some time together."

Moon Fire gazed into his almost black eyes adoringly. She rose from the mat saying, "I really must go now."

He followed her to the base of the ladder. "Are you ignoring my last wish?" He pulled her into his arms, causing her heart to flutter and her nipples to harden.

"No, it's just that I don't know how." She felt his member harden in response to her nipples.

Tilting her chin up so their eyes could meet, he tenderly placed his lips on hers, probing and searching. She shivered with ecstasy as his hand traced her breast and then its nipple. A strange feeling of fullness inflamed her, a feeling she did not yet fully understand, but knew she enjoyed. Again he kissed her, this time more firmly and with more passion. She wondered if she might have even passed on into the fifth world, which was yet to come. Taking one of her small hands in his, he guided it to his excited member. It seemed to her that he was about to burst, and so she caressed him.

With a loud groan he removed her hand and stepped back to look at her. "Moon Fire, I want you and I know that you want me. What can we do?"

"I don't know, but I will agree that it is something we both must work on. At least you have some privacy. I do not, but I will work on the problem."

He kissed her lightly again, then said, "I hope so, for there is no one else." Having said that, he again sighed.

"Wena 'Ahote, I will somehow find a way, but how can I know when I will fit into your busy sun cycle?" Her foot was on the bottom rung of the ladder.

"When you see me, if you need to speak to me, place your hand over your heart and I will know. When Sun Father has descended and completed his journey, come to me. You now know where my quarters are located. I will be waiting." With a huge smile, he hugged her once more.

Moon Flower did not remember climbing the ladder. She only knew that she was so happy she thought her heart would burst.

CHAPTER 7

A.D. *1131*

There was very little food to fill their stomachs. Moon Fire's family sat in silence as they enjoyed what little they had. Everyone in the family was present including Lansa, who seemed fidgety and excited.

Moon Fire knew better than to even speak to him when he was in this mood. She glanced at her parents to see if they were aware of her brother's tension, and then at Palasiva, who looked at her with a knowing smile. Palasiva had learned early on of his brother's impatience.

It was after they had all finished the meal that Lansa spoke. He rose from the mat on which they all sat to stand over them. "There is something wonderful that I must tell you all. At last, after twenty-and-one season cycles, I have decided what it is that I wish to do with the rest of my life."

Sikyawa and Tupkya looked up at him in surprise. "And what is that, my son?" Sikyawa inquired.

"After giving it much thought, it is clear to me that I will make a fine trader," he declared.

Sikyawa's reaction was just as Moon Fire had expected. Her father's facial expression changed from amazement to anger. He clenched his fists in an effort to contain himself and rose to his feet to face his son. "Lansa, my son, your mother and I have always hoped you would choose an occupation of which we could be proud, a craftsman, perhaps, or an artist. It has certainly taken you long enough to discover what you want to be, but why a trader?"

"Because, my father, it, too, is an honorable occupation, and a very lucrative one at that. I will also become acquainted with and deal with other cultures and learn their ways, ways that might be an improvement on some of our people's ways and customs."

Sikyawa lost some of his control and his anger became real. "You dare to suggest that there is something wrong with the ways and customs of the peaceful Anasazi? You blaspheme. Those kinds of disrespectful thoughts will anger the gods even more and they will never bless us with rain. We must live and do in this fourth world exactly as the gods have instructed us through the stories of our ancestors. That is to keep all things in balance. I would tell you now, son, to carefully rethink this whole idea of being a trader, and more than that, beseech the gods for forgiveness. It is people such as yourself who throw the world out of balance, and who are causing this drought that may starve us all."

Moon Fire silently cheered for her father and his wisdom. Frequent family arguments were nothing new to her, and she recalled that most of them started with Lansa and his arrogant attitude. She fervently hoped that he would finally grow up, the sooner the better.

Lansa's eyes blazed fire. He looked as though he might even strike his father. "I wish to remind you that I am more than of age, and old enough to make my own choices. I cannot believe what I am hearing! It seems I have never been able to do anything to suit you and mother."

"And as for a tradesman being an honest profession, I would say this," declared Sikyawa. "A trader is just one step above a thief! It is my opinion that when you deal with a trader, you get at least a little something in return. When you deal with a thief, you get nothing."

Lansa trembled with rage. He could not recall ever being so angry in his life. After stepping hastily to the ladder, he turned and fairly shouted, "I do not need to listen to such irrationalities! Do not expect to see me for a while." Without looking back, he climbed the ladder.

While he was still within hearing distance, Sikyawa yelled, "Go then, son. You have made it very clear that you think very little of us as a family unit. But mark my words! You will need us in the future." Then turning despondently to Tupkya, whose eyes were tearing, he shrugged his shoulders and said, "Tupkya, my wife, we seem to have failed him. What did we do wrong?"

Tupkya threw up her hands. "I don't know that we did anything wrong. Perhaps he was pampered as our firstborn child until Sowiwa, I mean Moon Fire was born, but from that time on, in my opinion, we treated them all the same." Then turning to Palasiva and Moon Fire, she asked, "Did either of you, my children, feel that there was any favoritism?"

Palasiva was the first to respond. "I can speak only for myself, but I felt that you both treated us all the same. Of course, when I came along, we all three caused you both more work, but that happens in any family." He turned adoring eyes to his older sister.

Moon Fire stared at the ladder, lost in her thoughts. At last she said, "Having the gift to speak with our 'big and little brothers' has taught me that they, too, have very different personalities as we do. In my opinion, my revered parents, the things you did or did not do have nothing to do with the problem. The problem rests with Lansa. He is just different, and there is little we can do about that."

Tupkya's tear-stained eyes took in the beauty of her daughter, who sat so serenely and seemingly undisturbed. At least, she thought, she and Sikyawa had raised two beautiful children, and she should rejoice in that knowledge. Rising from the mat, she murmured, "Sweet daughter, there is work to be done."

Lansa was furious. He seethed inwardly, and blamed his parents as he had always done in the past. This was his life! he thought. How could his parents judge what he wanted to do with his life? It was his decision and no one else's. He felt that somehow he walked in the shadow of his sister with the strange feet. Who, he wondered, had decided that if you were born with six toes or six fingers that it was an indication that you were gifted? It was true that his sister had made no comment during the confrontation, but why had he always felt that his parents favored her? To make matters worse, Palasiva seemed to always side with her. He felt like an outcast, and it burned his soul. And so he walked, where, he did not care.

Strangely enough, he walked toward the spring. There was someone there who was struggling to fill her water jug. He hid behind a rock while nursing his anger. The figure at the spring seemed very familiar, and then he recognized Sihu, lovely Sihu. There was something about her that fascinated him. Perhaps it was her eyes fringed with their dark lashes, or the gentle sway of her narrow hips. He had seen quite a few young women outside the complex, but none could compare with Sihu. He had even made love to several of those young women, but now his gaze rested on Sihu, who was until now unobtainable. Yet, here she was, all alone, and vulnerable. Without any more thought, he approached her with a confident swagger.

He was almost upon her when she looked up. "Oh, my! What a surprise to see you here," she declared.

He noticed that she had tucked her dress between her thighs and had her shawl wrapped tightly around her so as not to expose her genitals to the snake god who lived in the water, but he did not care. His need to be consoled was greater than any of the customs of his people.

He was almost within touching distance when she exclaimed, "Lansa, you are disturbed. What is it that is bothering you?"

"I made an announcement to my family of my decision to become a trader, and they rebuked me. I don't know why I came in this direction, but, well, here I am."

"Why did they not approve?" she asked.

"My father claims that a trader is only one step above a thief. He says that when you deal with a thief, the thief gets all, but when you deal with a trader, you might get something. Oh, Sihu, I don't know why my family have always opposed me. It took me a long time to come to my decision, and as excited as I was, they still rebuked me." He wrung his hands and looked at her imploringly.

"If you need someone to listen to your troubles, I am here. But perhaps it would be better if I finished this difficult task of finding an adequate amount of water, then we can meet farther up the path in closer proximity to the complex." Her heart went out to him, for it truly seemed that he did not know how to handle his life at this time, and it flattered her that he had come to her.

He seemed to ignore her suggestion. Moving closer to her, he whispered, "No, my lovely Sihu, I need someone to talk to now. Don't you see? I cannot wait."

Her love and concern for him suddenly turned to anger. It was common knowledge that he was totally ignoring the fact that, according to custom, a man did not flirt with a woman at the spring. Had he not called her "My lovely Sihu"? Was that not flirting? Had he not noticed how she had tucked her skirt between her thighs so as not to excite the water serpent sexually? He stood directly in front of her now. She was so nervous that she could hear the pounding of her own heart.

Lansa took in her loveliness, and could not still the urges of his own personal needs. He reached out to touch her cheek only to find that she recoiled.

Stepping away from him, she hissed, "Lansa, have your needs been so great that you forget that we must not flirt at the spring? If you touch me and seduce me, it will be the water serpent who has intercourse with me, and then I will bloat, burst, and die. If that is as much as you think of me, then I am glad to know it now. Go! I value my life even if you do not!" She seized her water jug and turned away.

Lansa looked at the woman he thought he knew as Sihu in amazement. He thought she adored him, and everyone who knew them said that she did, but who was this woman who abraided him so thoroughly? Admittedly she was right, but he needed her so desperately, now, right now. Yet, here she was, a rock. He turned toward the complex with his head hung low, hoping to hear her speak, hoping that she would weaken.

Sihu watched him walk away. She took in the broad shoulders that narrowed down to a slender waist, and fought the desire that shook her. She knew she must, yes must, stand her ground. Her love for and perhaps her infatuation with him must never stand in the way of rationality. She was only sorry that he had not been interested in meeting her halfway in a place where they could have been free from the influence of the water serpent. With a heavy heart she completed her task and headed for home.

Lansa was completely infatuated. He admired her strength to take a stand for what she believed, and, of course, for what he had forgotten. There had been many young women in his life, but none had ever refused him. It occurred to him that perhaps his anger over the confrontation with his father had precipitated his forgetfulness. He had been thinking only of himself, of his need for consolation and his physical need for her. He thought of himself as a clod of mud, and berated himself accordingly. He was afraid of what she must think of him. To make matters worse, he had been invited to go with a small group of traders sometime before seven more sun cycles were completed, and his heart was with Sihu, not the trip.

He slept badly, but when next Sun Father rose, he walked toward the wash. There he saw her. Her body excited him more than any other female's body ever had as he watched the sway of her hips. It seemed that she was out to gather wood, not water, and his heart soared. He knew he must take the chance and approach her even if he did not know what her reaction would be.

She seemed lost in her own world when he appeared from behind a large rock formation. Her surprise was obvious when she exclaimed, "Oh, it is you! I was not expecting . . ." She turned nervously to resume her task.

"Yes, Sihu, I . . ." He found himself briefly lost for words. He wondered what might be wrong, for he had seldom ever been at loss for something to say. At last he recovered. "Sihu, I was so lost in my own problems that I forgot, and you were right. I should never have approached you at the spring. I . . ."

Dropping the firewood, she ran to him. He folded her tightly into his arms as if she would fly like a butterfly away from him. It was some time before he relaxed his grip, but when he finally did, she looked up at him with unabashed adoration. He brushed his lips lightly over hers, saying, "I care for you, Sihu. You know I do."

Sihu was certain her heart would jump from her breast. She had felt very bad about their last confrontation, but she knew she was right, and that either he had not cared or was not thinking. Whatever the answer, he was here. This was their moment. "And I also care for you," she answered with great exultation. She then added, "I am glad you came to your senses."

He seized her again, but this time his lips met hers in a deep, probing kiss. She felt his excitement rise between them and a deep throbbing of desire that ran rampant throughout her being. More shaken than she could ever remember, she whispered, "Do you wish to come to me during the time of darkness?"

He could not believe what he was hearing. Never would he have believed she would forgive him so quickly. His confidence soared as he realized that he had not lost his touch with young women.

Nocturnal meetings were popular among the young people. The Anasazi were quite accepting of the part sex played during courtship. As was the custom, Lansa wrapped himself with a blanket to conceal his identity from anyone who might be about during the time of darkness, and made his way to Sihu's family quarters. He stealthily climbed down the ladder and made his way to her side, aided by the light of the low fire in the center of the room. He took special care so that he would not awaken anyone, then knelt at her side. He found her awake, but she asked in a very low voice, as was the custom, "Who is it?"

"It is I," he whispered, for she surely would identify him from the sound of his voice.

"Come to me," she said. "I have waited too long." She spoke in only a murmur, for she, too, did not want to awaken any of her family.

He dropped his blanket at his feet, and crawled under her blankets. Her nakedness excited him so intensely that he found himself struggling to contain himself. She lay on her side while he molded himself to her. His engorged member was actually almost painful, but he could not speak of his discomfort due to the close proximity of her family.

Sihu closed her eyes, for this would be her first time. She liked the feel of his skin next to hers, as she had known she would, but she really did not know what to do. As if in answer to her question, he turned on his back and guided her hand to his member. Shyly she touched it, then held it, all the while feeling a wetness between her legs.

Lansa moaned softly, then turned back on his side to place his fingers on her most intimate parts. Very gently he caressed her with all the tenderness that he knew. When at last he could contain himself no longer, he mounted her. She stifled a cry when he penetrated, but nothing else mattered as he enjoyed his own release.

It was then that her father turned over and spoke. The lovers froze until they assumed that her father was talking while sleeping. Breathing a sigh of relief, Lansa turned her to her side and again molded himself to her slender shape. He held her for quite a while, until he whispered, "I must go while our luck holds out. I care for you, Sihu. I will speak to you as soon as I can."

Wrapping his blanket around him once more, he silently stole from her family's quarters and made his way to the quarters of his friend, Tsoongo, the apprentice stone mason.

After several more nocturnal visits, Lansa was convinced that Sihu was the woman of his dreams. After asking her if she would marry him, and warning her of the time he would be away from her due to the fact that he would become a trader, she joyously gave him an affirmative answer. Lansa, of course, returned to his family, asking them to approve of his marital desires.

Sikyawa was very fond of Sihu since Moon Fire had befriended her for so long. He found her as lovely as many others, and considered her a wonderful addition to his family. His only concern was that Lansa had only recently announced that he wished to be a trader, which meant that Sihu would see very little of his son.

"No, my father. She is to be my wife. She can come with me, and if we have children, I will spend as much of my time with my family as I can," Lansa explained.

Sikyawa had his doubts, but put them aside, hoping for the best.

The marriage rites began. Sihu began grinding corn and making piki bread for several days at her mother's home, then going to Lansa's home and spending the next three sun cycles grinding cornmeal from the time Sun Father rose until the time Sun Father set. In this way she was showing her competence, and also compensating Tupkya for the loss of her son's services around the house and fields. Of course she had no idea that Lansa seldom, if ever, had offered his services to his parents.

During the third sun cycle that she was with Tupkya and Sikyawa, several of Lansa's aunts arrived to stage a mock battle. They berated her, and called her stupid and lazy, while moaning that she had stolen their nephew. Of course this was really a good-natured ribbing that indicated that the older women liked the young bride and thought she was making a good choice for a husband.

On the fourth sun cycle, long before Sun Father had risen, Sihu's female kin arrived bringing all the cornmeal and piki bread that Sihu had previously prepared. Lansa's relatives came, too, and both mothers, assisted by their women kin, washed the heads of the newlyweds in one basin, finally twisting the hair of the young couple into one strand which would unite them for life. When their hair had finally dried, Lansa and Sihu climbed Fajada Butte, the butte where a number of their ceremonials were held, to pray to the rising sun.

Moon Fire watched all that was happening as if it must be a dream. She was delighted that she had a new sister, for she had never had a sister before. She was, however, filled with doubts. It had all happened so quickly. She watched her mother's face glowing with a pride that so sharply contrasted with her father's stoic expression. It was the custom of her people to remain reserved even under severe pressure, but this was a festive occasion, a time to show joy, and it was obvious that her father was feeling indifferent. With so many relatives around she knew there was no probability of an opportunity to talk with her father. Her thoughts turned to Wena 'Ahote, whom she had not seen for quite a few sun cycles. Due to preparations for Lansa and Sihu's wedding, she had had no time to search him out and place her hand over her heart, according to their agreement. As she and her family settled down for a much-needed rest, she longed for his company and his touch.

* * *

After the wedding breakfast, Lansa, Sikyawa, and Palasiva descended into a ceremonial kiva to begin to weave Sihu's wedding garments. Only the men did the weaving, and Moon Fire stifled her laughter when she thought of Lansa doing so menial a chore. She thought it might be good for him, and that at last he might learn some respect for something other than hunting, trading, and battle.

The wedding garments consisted of two white wedding robes, one large and one small, along with a long wide belt. White buckskin leggings and moccasins would complete the outfit. While the men were preparing the wedding garments, Sihu remained with Tupkya, industriously grinding cornmeal and doing other housework.

It took a long time for Sihu to grind enough cornmeal to pay for her wedding garments. Two moon cycles passed before she completed the task She counted herself fortunate that she had not become pregnant, for many young women lost their first child due to the excessive amount of grinding they were expected to do. It was, however, most important to have both dresses, for they would be her passport to paradise. The smaller wedding robe would be preserved in a reed case, and tied with the wedding belt. As with all other Anasazi women, when she died, she would be wrapped in the smaller robe, which would serve as wings to carry her soul to the House of the Dead. The belt would guide her in her spiritual flight. She had been told that some young women married simply to get the burial robe, due to their concern for their afterlife.

When she had completed her task, she found that the men had not completed theirs due to the frequent absence of Lansa. No one seemed to know of his whereabouts, but everyone assumed it had to do with the career in trading that he intended to pursue. Sihu was afraid to ask him when he crawled into her blankets. She only hoped that whatever business he was attending to, would be legitimate. She put aside her niggling doubts.

Another moon cycle passed. At last the garments were done. The weaving was finished. Sihu was dressed in the completed garments and allowed herself to be led back to her mother's home. She and Lansa would now take up residence in her mother's household. Later they would establish their own home outside the holy school. Any other couple whose parents lived in their own small home that was not a part of the "great houses" would add a room or two rather than building individually. From this time on, Sihu and her mother would expect Lansa to contribute to the support of the household, which usually meant gathering wood and working in the fields.

They had not lived in her mother's household more than ten sun cycles when Lansa called her aside. "I must make a trip to the Mogollon to trade," he announced to her in a private moment on the roof of her parents' quarters. "I will probably be gone two moon cycles, and I will miss you, my love." He pulled her to him, and wrapped his arms snugly around her.

Sihu felt as if her entire world had turned upside down. She knew when she married him that he was determined to become a trader, but she could not believe he would be leaving so soon. "Why so soon?" she whispered. "What will my family do without your support? Who will chop wood and work the fields? And more than that, why would you want to leave me now when our life together is really just beginning?"

"Sihu, my little flower, I knew you would feel this way, but you knew my trade before you married me. I am sure I was not the only one to tell you that it is a lonely life being married to a trader. We are one now, and I am sorry to say that our life will be apart much of the time." He ran his fingers through her glossy black hair. "Your parents also knew but even they seemed to offer no objection."

"My parents are unusual. Unlike most parents they wanted only what would make me happy. Yes, Mother and I did discuss what my life would probably be like, but we would never have thought that you would leave so soon." A part of her wanted to beg him to stay. As she visualized herself groveling, she grew disgusted with herself. She forcefully withdrew from his embrace, braced her two feet firmly on the ground, and placed her hands on her hips. "Well, husband, if this is your choice, then so be it, but it does not sit well with me."

"I was afraid it would not, but there is little I can do about it," he declared. "I have been asked to join two other traders who will travel to the lands of the Mogollon to see how they are faring due to this drought. It is also possible, depending on what we find there, that we will then travel west to the lands of the Hohokam. I shall be gone for at least three or four moon cycles."

Sihu refused to speak. She was so infuriated that she knew she would only make things worse if she said anything. Why, she wondered, did he have to join the other two traders? Could not the other two traders go without him? She found herself shaking angrily.

"I understand your anger, my love, for your shaking makes it obvious. Please try to understand that there are issues much more important than you realize. Our people are leaving due to the drought. The elders want to know if that is the case with the Mogollon and the Hohokam. They want to know if Sun Father is displeased only with us or also with them. This will be my first journey, and to be quite honest with you, it excites me."

Still she did not respond, but stood her ground staring at him. For an awkward amount of time, they stood, neither daring to speak. At last Lansa broke the coldness with a simple statement. "I will go now. If you had been more understanding, I would have stayed until Sun Father rose." Then he swiftly turned on his heels and disappeared.

Sihu wondered if he would go to Tsoongo's quarters, or if . . . She decided not to think about it.

It was generally known that the traders would not be leaving until Sun Father next began his journey. Sihu had seen the look of concern in her parents' eyes when Lansa did not return to her, but she offered no words of explanation, and to her relief no one asked. She rose well before any light appeared on the horizon, and dressed. Very quietly, so as not to awaken her parents, she climbed the ladder into the darkness.

The traders were assembling in the plaza. As Lansa had said, there were three of them. She hid behind a wall as she watched them ritually smoke, asking the gods for protection on their journey. At last, they hoisted their trade goods in baskets on their backs with trump lines across their foreheads, and took their leave. No one was in the plaza to see them off. Sihu desperately wanted to say good-bye to Lansa, but her pride would not allow her to do so.

When they were out of her sight, she began following them, making sure she was far enough behind that they would not suspect she was there. If they had been warriors, they would have known of her presence, but the traders were respected by all nations, and seldom, if ever, attacked. Their senses were not trained as keenly as those of a warrior, and, of course, they would never imagine that anyone would follow them or that they might be attacked. She made certain that she was hidden behind rocks, or down in an arroyo, but never on the south road.

The traders had cleared the community for only a short time when they came upon a small outlier. It consisted of only two rooms, and a pit for firing pottery, indicating the occupation of one of the Anasazi potters whose black on white pottery was so much in demand. Two dogs barked excitedly when the traders arrived. Sihu made certain she remained downwind from them, lest they give away her presence. She remained at a distance, but not so far that she could not see clearly.

It was then that two young women came out of the outlier, running toward Lansa. They looked to be about the same age, perhaps sisters, but she could not tell from her vantage point. She watched in surprised fascination when one of them reached him before the other and hugged him fiercely. The second young woman was on the first one's heels and also embraced him passionately. Only a few words were spoken, when Lansa sealed whatever had transpired between them with a kiss for each. The girls returned to the outlier, and the traders moved on.

Sihu felt as if her insides had been torn out of her. Doubts about the marriage she had thought would be so perfect welled up inside her. Moreover, she wondered who these girls were and what they meant to him. How many others? Why did he marry her? Could she be happy living the life of the wife of a trader? It also occurred to her that he might be fashioning his life after Kokopelli, the legendary humpback flute player, who never married, but moved from village to village, playing his enchanting flute, and making love to any woman he chose during his travels. Legend said that he was considered the god of fertility, and so he was never denied any woman he wanted. In fact women wanted to couple with him, for then they would have an offspring who was half god and half man. She knew her imagination was carrying her away. She took many deep breaths, counting as she breathed, until she felt a little more relaxed. Finally, she made her way back to her parents' quarters, offering no explanation as to her whereabouts when they asked.

CHAPTER 8

Moon Fire had not spoken to Sihu in quite some time. Neither had she found a way to see Wena 'Ahote, which she found extremely frustrating. She knew Lansa had been gone for almost two moon cycles and she was certain that Sihu must be terribly lonely. She could not imagine why Sihu had kept her distance for such a long time. With these thoughts Moon Fire decided to pay a visit to her longtime friend.

She found Sihu sitting cross-legged in the plaza not far from her parents' quarters, twisting yucca fibers into the sole of a sandal. To her surprise she noticed that the sole was very tiny. "Sihu, my friend, I have missed you. It is in my mind that you have been avoiding me. Can you tell me why? And by the way, that is a very small sandal. Is something wonderful to happen in the not-too-distant future?"

Sihu looked up in surprise, then attempted to smile. "Oh, Moon Fire, it's you. Which question would you have me answer first?"

"Tell me the good news first." She chuckled as she took her position, sitting across from her friend.

"Well, the good news is that I am pregnant. Mother says I am about three moon cycles along. Mother and I have made certain that I refrain from grinding as much as usual so that I do not lose the baby." She lay the tiny sandal by her side, took a deep breath, and stared wistfully at her calloused hands.

"Does Lansa know he is to be a father?" Moon Fire inquired.

"As near as Mother and I can figure, I conceived not more than one moon cycle before he left, and to answer your question, no, he does not know." Her eyes misted as if she were on the edge of tears.

"Sihu, I know you are lonely. Why did you not seek me out. I thought we were the best of friends."

Hearing Moon Fire's words caused Sihu's chin to quiver, while two large tears escaped from the inside corners of her lovely eyes. In a broken voice she said, "I guess I was afraid you would tell me, 'I told you so.'"

"What, in the name of Sun Father, do you mean by that?" Moon Fire's concern for Sihu caused her to move closer, and to take her friend's hands in her own.

"Oh, Moon Fire, I was cross with him when he told me he was leaving so soon after we were finally married. He did not even stay with me in the time before he left. He . . ." She bent her head over Moon Fire's hands, leaving them wet with tears.

Moon Fire waited until Sihu had regained some composure, then asked, "Why did he leave you before time? What did he say?"

Sihu sniffed, then sat up straight. "He said that there were things more important than our marriage. He said that the elders had asked the traders to report back to them how the Mogollon and the Hohokam were handling the drought. When I could think of nothing to say, and when I remained silent, he said he wished I had been more understanding, and he just left. Moon Fire, you were right. He is not easy to live with. He spends much time elsewhere, I know not where, rather than spending time hunting, chopping wood, or tending the fields. Mother does not say so, but I know she is disgruntled."

"These are traits so typical of my brother. He does not think of how others might feel due to his words or actions. But, Sihu, I sense that what you have told me so far is not all. You are too deeply disturbed to be dealing with what you have told me. What is it you are not telling me?"

"I followed him when he and the other two traders left. At an outlier not far south of our community I saw him hug and kiss two young women, speak to them briefly, then turn to go on with the other two traders. Now do you see why I was afraid to come to you?" She gritted her teeth, and looked at the little sandal by her side despondently.

Though Moon Fire knew she could not say anything to Sihu, she thought, "Oh, yes, those two!" Then in concern for her friend and sister-by-law, she said, "Sihu, first please remember that I would never say what you thought I would say. It is one of my most fervent hopes that Lansa will finally grow up. He is not a bad person. He is just insensitive to anyone else's needs. I really believe he thinks that Earth Mother moves around him, and everything she has is his for the taking. It is entirely possible that when he finds himself a father, he will change."

"I hope you are right, sister-by-marriage. I hope you are right."

Moon Fire rose to her feet as she watched Sihu pick up the little yucca sandal to resume her project. "Sihu, family members are meant to support each other. I wish you would remember that I will always support you, and that I love you."

Feeling that no more words were necessary, she departed for her parents' quarters.

Still there was no rain. In desperation the elders had performed the snake dance ceremony, which was one that seldom failed to bring rain. When next Sun Father completed his journey, a social dance was held. Moon Fire scanned the crowd for Wena 'Ahote and Sihu. She felt sorry that Sihu was not in attendance, for she knew there would be many who would dance with her while respecting the fact that she was married. At last she spotted Wena 'Ahote, who seemed to be in an earnest discussion with Ruupi. Even though she was unable to understand what was being said, his body language was tense. She wondered what Ruupi might be saying that would cause the reaction she was seeing in Wena 'Ahote.

Since there were few women and many young men and acolytes in attendance, Moon Fire danced several circle dances while she waited hopefully for a dance with Wena 'Ahote. She had become a very popular and desirable young woman, especially since the prairie fire that had given her her new name. On several occasions she passed Leetayo, who gave her a look each time that could have killed. Her cousin's voluptuous body swayed provocatively to the beat of the drums and the melody of the flute as she flirted outrageously with each of her partners. Moon Fire maintained a stony face even though she felt that it would be wise to guard her back in Leetayo's presence.

She was so lost in thought that she jumped when Wena 'Ahote tapped her on the shoulder to ask her to dance. With a warm chuckle, he took her hand, led her into the circle for dancing, and said, "I did not think your renown with so many males in the community would give me a chance to ask you to dance."

Having watched her cousin so freely offering her attentions to all her dance partners, she recoiled at his comment. "I hope you are not comparing me with Leetayo!"

As they fell into the slow, easy step of the couples' dance, he squeezed her hand, saying, "You know me better than that. There is no comparison."

"Thank you." Moon Fire relaxed and reveled in the wonderful feeling of his hand on hers. When she thought about it, it seemed that his hand emitted a surge of energy through her own.

"I saw Leetayo's expression when she passed you during the last dance. I was waiting on the side to dance with you." After a few more steps, he murmured loud enough that only she could hear, "I have missed your company, little love."

Her heart beat furiously as they approached the end of the dance. She wished it would never end. Even if she could have him only on these public occasions, she thought it would be enough. Her pulse quickened even more when he said, "When the dance is over, follow me."

They made a hasty exit when the last drumbeat sounded. He led her to his quarters, and placed a feather at the top of the ladder to indicate that they were not to be disturbed.

Once again Moon Fire absorbed the magic of the wall that included several of the constellations, then gasped when she saw that the ceiling was also covered the same way, but with additional star clusters.

"Do you like it?" he asked as he stoked the fire that seemed to make the stars dance and twinkle. "When last you were here, you showed so much appreciation for the one wall that I decided there should be more."

Moon Fire clasped her hands together, feeling that perhaps she was standing on the moon and gliding through space. "Oh yes, Wena 'Ahote, I love it. It makes me think you must really love studying the stars and the constellations."

He took her hand in his, guiding her to sit by his side on his mat. Without letting go of her hand, he said, "Besides dancing and playing the flute, and you, that is my next major interest."

"You know just the right words to say, and I thank you." She paused to gather her thoughts. "I know it is none of my business, but I saw you earlier in deep conversation with Ruupi." She hesitated again, then went on. "You seemed most distressed."

"I will tell you honestly that you are right," he replied. "There is something more that you should know about me. I have already told you of my desire to be a priest, but what I have not told you is that someday I hope to be a sun priest. Ruupi knows of my ambition, and thinks I am making a poor choice."

"Why ever would he think that way?" In Moon Fire's mind she thought the position of sun priest to be the most powerful.

"Ruupi, my sweet, says that his position as crystal scrier is much more important. He says that he can foresee everything and anything in the future, but the sun priest only reads the sky, and predicts based on what he sees in the darkness of night. He says I should study with him, not Taatawi. He has led me to believe that he does not like Taatawi though he has never said it, and he resents the fact that Taatawi and I get along so well. He also talks down to me, making me feel insignificant. Oh yes, I know that it is only I who can allow him to make me feel that way, and that is something only I can control." Taking both of her hands in his, he looked at her lovingly. "There you have it."

Moon Fire looked up at him and asked, "Do you have any interest in crystal skrying?"

"No, absolutely not. I have already told you of my true interests, and I know you believe me, but when I speak of this to Ruupi, he does not seem to understand."

"Then that is his problem over which he must gain control, is it not?"

"Yes, my sweet, it is, but it does not make life any easier for me." He gazed wistfully at the stars on the wall that winked with a life of their own. "There is one more thing that does not make life easy for me. Will you listen?"

Moon Fire knew immediately that it must be about her. "Of course," she said. "Would you expect me to say no? What concerns you, concerns me."

Wena 'Ahote's mind worked furiously. He did not want to lose her, but he stumbled on. "Woman of my heart, I do not think I am being fair to you. If I could take you with me and still reach the position of sun priest, you know I would do so, but the rules are what they are, and I may not take a wife. You are so talented, and I know we would compliment each other as a couple, but I cannot offer you marriage, nor can I offer you a child. You are of marriageable age, and deserve better than what I have to offer. Perhaps you should consider another offer, an offer that would give you a normal life and one of happiness."

She recoiled at his words and snatched her hands away from his. Without further thought, she replied, "You are also the man of my heart. Does that mean nothing to you? Do you not recall that we had just such a conversation once before? My answers are still the same. Why can you not understand?" Her lower lip quivered, for she felt herself on the edge of tears.

"Then you are saying for the second time that you do not want marriage with someone else? Perhaps I needed to hear that." He lay on the mat and pulled her toward him.

"Yes, oh yes! You know that is what I am saying." She felt his arms encircle her, comforting her. "Wena 'Ahote, I am beyond marriageable age by our people's standards, but that is as I want it to be. It somehow seems right to me. Can you understand?"

"Yes, my love. It makes me happy, yet somewhere in the back of my mind I am anxious, for the experience of marriage and having children is what I thought all young girls wanted."

"I am not a young girl. I know what it is that I want, even if

it seems different from the normal. How can I convince you?"
She felt as though she would die if he could not understand.

"You are truly a most unusual woman. Perhaps it is your
ability to converse with our 'big' and 'little' brothers that makes
you so." Pulling her close to mold to his body, he added, "I
suppose I must give praise to the gods that I have found you."
Then he gave a deep-throated chuckle. "I am glad Tsoongo and
any others are no competition. Knowing this, I will never let
you get away unless it is your will."

While lightly tracing his lips with her forefinger, she whispered, "Good. Now the problem is solved. Just love me."

He rose to a sitting position beside her and removed his
robe, then finally his breechcloth. He untied the knotted cloth
on her left shoulder and pulled the fabric down to expose her
breasts. He found her nipples peaked and hardened with desire.
He watched her turn her head to observe his hardened member.
He had no doubts that this was her first experience with complete lovemaking, and so he vowed to be as slow and gentle
with her as he knew how. He recalled the classes he had taken
as a younger man that instructed him on how to please a
woman, but that had been a while back and he had had no
women since then. He also knew that she also had had similar
instruction on how to please a man.

After turning these thoughts aside, he caressed her breasts
with his fingertips, tracing circles around the outside, gradually
moving inward toward the nipples. Her breasts were small twin
orbs that vibrated beneath his touch. He used his tongue in the
same fashion, which caused her to moan and call his name. She
whispered huskily, "Yes, yes, I want you to touch me everywhere."

He moved his tongue down to her navel, then over her
pelvic bones, which stood out so prominently beneath her skin,
due to her thinness. His unbound hair swept over her mound of
pleasure, as his people called it. Slowly, he moved his fingers
to her power spot, where he again traced light circles. He found
her very moist as she readied herself for him.

He found the masculine side of his soul fighting the feminine side. A part of him wanted to take her immediately, and another part wanted to make these moments last forever. The

certainty that this was her first time was the deciding factor. He continued touching her with one hand on her breast and the other on her power spot.

Again she moaned and cried out, "Let me touch you."

He guided her hand to his phallus, and moaned loudly when her fingers encircled it. He found it difficult to concentrate on pleasing her due to the pleasure she was now giving him. He placed his lips on hers, slipping his tongue inside to touch hers. "Oh, my sweet love," he said between kisses.

"Come to me now," she said. "Let us become as one."

After positioning his body over hers, he kissed her once again saying, "Little love, if this is the first time for you, it will hurt at first. This you must know."

"Of course I know, but I still cannot wait any longer. Now, please or I will go mad."

Ever so gently he pushed himself into her softness until he reached a thin wall. He hesitated until he heard her say, "Now!"

Without hesitation he gave an exerted push past the wall. He watched her bite her lip, but she did not cry out. His own ecstasy was so great that he wondered how much longer he could contain himself. When he felt her legs lock over his back, he began the age-old rocking rhythm.

Moon Fire threw her head back as ripples of pleasure rushed through her entire being. She wondered if she had died and crossed over to the land of her ancestors where she was told everything was beautiful. It seemed that all the vibrations in her body, all her energy centers had become one. Then without warning she exploded, and clutched Wena 'Ahote possessively.

Almost immediately, he cried out, "Ah, yes, I am here!" His spasms of pleasure faded gradually as did hers. Then finally he rolled off her and lay on his side, looking at her. He noticed several spots of blood on the inside of her thighs as well as on his member. Anxiously he asked, "I hurt you, didn't I?"

"At first, yes, but after that there are no words that could describe the feelings, except that I felt that all my energy centers became one until I exploded. Is that how you felt?"

He chuckled. "I suppose that is an excellent description of what I also felt. You know it will be better the next time."

"I cannot imagine how it could possibly be any better." She

giggled. "But I'm certainly willing to give it a try. Let us hope that we can find more time together."

"There is something I must confess, sweet one." He hesitated, then said softly, "This was my first time too. Oh, and by the way, you must chew this herb to prevent a child. I told Taatawi of my love for you, and he gave me this to give to you."

Moon Fire took the herb and wrinkled her nose at its bitter taste. He offered her water to wash it away, then said, "So that your parents don't wonder why you were gone so long I think we should be going. Here is a bowl of water to cleanse yourself."

After they had both cleansed and clothed themselves and arranged their hair, Moon Fire turned to Wena 'Ahote and said with a wink of her eye, "I know now why Leetayo is such a wanton and a flirt. I did not know what I'd been missing all these many season cycles."

With a hearty laugh he retorted, "Up the ladder, little woman. We both know what we've been missing."

Only once in the next moon cycle were Moon Fire and Wena 'Ahote able to get together. Twice she had placed her hand over her heart to inform him that she was available, but he did not return the signal to indicate that he was also free. Once he signaled her, but she also did not return the signal. On the one occasion they did manage to get together, they had very little time due to other commitments. Moon Fire's heart was heavy.

Tupkya took notice of her daughter's despondency. For many sun cycles she said nothing, but continued to observe Moon Fire's strangeness. It intrigued her that Moon Fire was so moody and restless, and she thought sooner or later the girl would explain herself. Sun cycle after sun cycle remained the same, and at last Tupkya said while the two of them ground corn, "You have been disturbed for quite some time, Moon Fire. You are not yourself."

Moon Fire's hands froze on the mano. "I was hoping I would not be so obvious."

"Well you are, child. Do you wish to speak of that which is troubling you?"

Moon Fire desperately wanted to speak honestly with her mother, but she knew intuitively that her mother would not be happy if she told her the truth. She remained silent.

"Little daughter, if I did not know better, I would say that perhaps you are in love."

Still Moon Fire made no response. Her mother was baiting her, and she did not want to answer.

They both resumed their grinding, but it was not long before Tupkya stopped and rocked back into a sitting position. She made it obvious through her body language that she had no intention of continuing her work until she had some answers. Turning to her daughter, she declared, "You may stop your work. I cannot bear to go on working with you while you are in such a state of mind. We are family, and our duties are demanding. There is work we both must do together, and I cannot go on working with you in the gloomy mood you are in."

Moon Fire was in no mood for another confrontation with her mother, yet a part of her did not care what her mother thought. She was old enough to make her own decisions. She had been experiencing her womanly moon cycles for two season cycles, and according to Anasazi tradition, should have chosen a husband, or a husband should have chosen her long ago. She knew her mother and father were bent on Tsoongo. Why, she wondered, could they not just let her be. Why the rush? Of course she also knew that most of her people did not live more than forty season cycles, which placed the death of the women just at the end of their childbearing years. Therefore time was precious to her people.

Throwing all caution to the wind, she moved into a position facing her mother and defiantly said, "You are right, Mother."

"I am right about what?" Tupkya inquired.

Squaring her shoulders, she declared, "Yes, Mother, I am in love."

"This is wonderful news. Why are you so hesitant to speak of it?" Tupkya's eyes sparkled with the thought that at last her daughter would be married.

Moon Fire again made no response until her mother whispered, "Who is the lucky man?"

It took all the courage she could muster, for she knew she

was about to stir up a pot of chili peppers. "Mother, I know you and Father favor Tsoongo, but it cannot be. My reasons are many, but you must know that I feel nothing for him. I . . ."

"Then who is it, child?"

Very very softly she said, "I love Wena 'Ahote, Mother. I love Wena 'Ahote."

At that moment Sikyawa descended the ladder. He must have felt the tension, for he remained silent, and went to his corner in their quarters to relax on his mat.

Tupkya hoped that what she had heard was not so. "Did you say what I think I heard you say?"

Moon Fire only nodded as she waited for what she knew was sure to be a storm resembling the huge dust devils in the desert that occasionally occurred leaving almost everything in their paths destroyed.

Her mother's hands clenched by her side as she swiftly rose to her feet. Her normally bronze face took on a flaming red hue, and Moon Fire felt sure that if her mother's hair had not been wound into the traditional whorls that married Anasazi women all wore, her hair would certainly have stood on end. She strode over to Sikyawa and glared at him, then back to her errant daughter. "You," she puffed, "you are impossible! You may be gifted in some ways, but you are stupid in others. You are wasting your childbearing years on a man who cannot marry you, due to his ambition to become a priest. There are many who would make you a wonderful husband, but you, you silly child, must choose someone who cannot even honor us by carrying on the family name. What is wrong with you? What is wrong with your thinking?" She crumbled into a heap next to the mano and metate at which she had been working.

Moon Fire softly tried to answer. "Mother, I . . ."

"You what? You shame our name in the community. They offered you the priesthood, and you refused it. They allowed you to go on counseling due to your abilities, but you refuse to nurture your people by carrying on our name. You know it is the women who carry on the heritage, but you are selfish. What is *wrong* with you?" she screamed.

"Mother, there is something you should know. Tsoongo . . ."

Rising again, she shrieked, "Tsoongo, yes Tsoongo! A

young man who definitely favors you. Why, I have no idea, but he does. How you could ever choose Wena 'Ahote over him, I'll never know. Oh, you are so peculiar, so stupid."

Sikyawa had finally heard enough. Rising from what he had hoped would be a short period of rest, he declared, "Enough, woman! I have heard enough. You have not allowed Moon Fire to speak on her own behalf, for you are out of control. You have said things that I am certain that Moon Fire will not forget, and things that, if you were not so caught up within yourself, you would probably never say. Now, cease! I have spoken."

Moon Fire felt destroyed, but she wanted to hail her father, who had, at least to some extent, rallied to her defense. She saw no reason to attempt to explain her side, for her mother's mind was made up, and she did not want to be confused with facts.

At last Sikyawa turned to her. Placing his large hand on her shoulder, he asked, "Do you want to say anything?"

"No, there is no reason." Tears flooded her eyes so that she could not even see her father. She raced up the ladder into the open air and out through the plaza into the beckoning desert.

She found a place of solitude under a huge cottonwood tree whose leaves were small and stunted from lack of water and the blistering sun. Cottonwoods were generally in or near a wash or a creek, for unlike mesquite, palo verde, and many varieties of cactus, these usually magnificent trees needed water. The wash had been dry for so long that everything around it looked fried. She sat very still for quite some time with her arms wrapped around her legs, her chin resting on her knees, waiting for her eyes to clear.

When she finally looked around her, her eyes came to rest almost immediately on a beautiful long red feather. In the distant turquoise sky circled her power animal, the red-tailed hawk. It moved ever closer, then perched at last on the cottonwood above her. Placing the red feather next to her heart, she cried, "Oh, Red Eagle, it is you. You knew of my distress."

The magnificent bird cocked his head to one side to display one prominent beady eye. "Yes, Moon Fire, I am aware of your need. I only wish to remind you that like me, you are likely to be attacked by people who don't understand you, nor do they even wish to understand the varied and different uses of your creative energy. Yours is a creative purpose in life. Do not allow others to attack your ability to soar." Then as suddenly as he had arrived, he departed.

Moon Fire continued to clasp the feather to her bosom, and felt quite comforted.

CHAPTER 9

A.D. *1133*

Palasiva was now fourteen. Much to Sikyawa's and Tupkya's disappointment, he had chosen the way of a warrior and a sentinel. They were unable to understand why all three of their children were so unstable. Palasiva was much more delicate than Lansa. He was not as tall, his shoulders were not as broad, but he was surprisingly sinewy for his age. He knew he had chosen a way of life that probably should have been Lansa's, but his mind was set, and he was determined to succeed. He thought that perhaps a part of his decision had been based on the fact that his sister was often out on her own, as she communicated with her "little brothers," and he was deeply concerned for her safety. He had learned rather too late that he would be assigned wherever he was needed, and now he was guarding the Great North Road.

His training had been extensive, but he knew he was young, and slight of body, and that most were of much more stature than he. He hoped that in the next few season cycles he would develop into a bigger man as Lansa had done. He also thought that the strife and tension in his family had directed him to volunteer as a warrior. It had never been in his mind's eye that his parents would object to his choice of direction in life. He had always felt certain that they would approve and be proud.

He turned to his longtime friend, Kopolvu, whose name meant "tree stump," who was sharing his duty with him on the Great North Road. Sun Father was about to begin his journey, and their duty would soon be done. They both sat with their backs against a large rock not far from the road. "My friend, I am told that the raiders are becoming more ruthless than ever. Have you heard the same?"

"Indeed, you have heard the same as I. At least we are blessed with the fact that, although they have attacked in many other nearby locations, they have not attempted to attack this location." Then, as if having doubts about the power of his words, he offered no further conversation.

They enjoyed only a short time of silence when there was just a hint of commotion behind a rock some distance from them. The rock was surrounded by perhaps twenty yucca trees that elevated their sharp-pointed leaves about four feet, offering some scanty protection to anyone who needed it. Suddenly an arrow whistled so close to Palasiva that its feathers grazed his arm. Both young men knew there was no time for hesitation and threw themselves flat upon the ground. Due to the dust they scarcely knew where they were, or for that matter, where the enemy might be. It was obvious that each man would fight his own battle.

Palasiva had no time to worry about Kopolvu. He seized his obsidian dagger. His bow and arrows were useless due to the poor visibility. A very robust raider, much heavier than himself, stood before him, not more than three hand spans away. He was naked except for a breechcloth, and was oiled from head to foot. Palasiva watched in horror as the raider advanced upon him with a long, keen knife, making a plunge at his breast. He stopped the attack by diverting the raider's right wrist with his left hand, and at the same time lunging his dagger fully toward his opponent's abdomen. The raider caught Palasiva's wrist in his left hand before any damage was done, and for what seemed like a very long time, but really was not, they stood regarding each other. With Palasiva holding the raider's right hand above his head, and the enemy's left retaining his right on a level with his body, the smaller man felt his strength ebbing. He heard a horrible gurgling sound, and prayed that it was not his friend. The fact that the raider was greased gave him a very uncertain hold. Instantaneously he tripped the raider with a sudden violent pass of his right foot, which brought both of them to the ground. Very quickly the savage planted himself firmly on

Palasiva, his right knee on Palasiva's left arm, and his left arm pinioning Palasiva's right to the ground, which left his right arm free. Palasiva knew he was completely at his mercy, for his opponent's strength and weight were greater than his own.

While the raider's eyes boasted triumph and delight, they also showed Palasiva that he was resolved to enjoy his victory. Palasiva's short life passed in review before him in less than several blinks of an eye. The raider's bloodshot eyes gleamed ferociously as he deliberately delayed the death-stroke. Palasiva saw the descending blow of the deadly weapon, and anticipated the force with which it would be driven.

Down came the dagger, aimed at his throat, but he twisted his head and neck to one side to prolong his life as much as possible. The sharp blade passed in dangerous proximity to his throat, burying itself in the dry, crusty earth. The raider's right thumb came within reach of Palasiva's mouth, and he seized it between his teeth. The raider struggled to free himself, but found his efforts in vain. In releasing his grip of Palasiva's right arm, he grabbed his dagger with his left hand, but this resulted in a reverse of the entire affair. Before the raider could extricate his deeply buried weapon with his left hand, and while his right hand was held firmly between his opponent's teeth, Palasiva plunged his dagger twice between his ribs, just under his left arm, while at the same time making a convulsive effort to throw off his weight. Palasiva knew he had been the victor, and enjoyed only a short time of satisfaction seeing his enemy gasping his last breath.

When the dust settled, Palasiva found himself surrounded by five more raiders, who judging from their angry gestures, seemed to be out for his blood. He also realized that Kopolvu was the one whose gurgling sound he had heard, for his friend lay in a pool of blood. Rage surged within his heart, but he knew he had no chance against five raiders. He was certain that this was his time to cross over, to join his ancestors and Awonawilona.

Suddenly a deep commanding voice sliced through the dry desert air. "Leave the boy be!" it commanded.

Palasiva watched the raiders step back in respect, while a large muscular man with eyes that were only slits took command. He could not believe what he was hearing, and wondered what horrible tortures they had in mind for him. Dusty sweat covered his body and trickled into his eyes, making it difficult to see any of the raiders clearly.

The leader of the raiders lost no time in binding Palasiva's wrists together behind his back. Saying no more, he beckoned to one of his men to take charge. The leader led the way, while the other man pushed Palasiva forward with the end of his bow. They moved quickly until Sun Father began to set, then settled in a small canyon that was well hidden and far from any Anasazi homesteads. Only then did they build a fire to offer warmth during the chill of darkness. One of them pulled a rabbit from a pouch, which he skinned, gutted, and mounted on a spit.

Palasiva was far enough from the fire that he could feel no warmth, but the aroma of the roasting rabbit made him salivate, for he had eaten nothing since the previous sun cycle. He also was sure they would not offer him any, due to the fact that, counting him, there were seven, and a rabbit normally fed only three. His mouth was also parched and dry. He hoped they would at least offer him water. His mind worked furiously as he pondered the possibilities of his fate. His wrists were raw from the bindings.

At last the rabbit was removed from the spit and cut into six portions. The raiders ate silently after a silent prayer, supplementing their repast with a kind of cake, made of what, Palasiva could only guess. He offered his own prayer to Awonawilona that they would at least offer him some water. He was no stranger to fasting, for all of his people fasted during parts of many of their major ceremonials. He found himself calling on his newly acquired power animal, the wildcat. During the past season cycle he had had several recurring dreams in which a wild cat had saved him from some eminent danger, and Moon Fire had told him that it was a sign that he had found his power animal. Though he had not asked her for her interpretation, he knew he must do so if he was lucky enough to escape torture or even death. He thought that perhaps if he kept his power animal in the back of his mind, there might be a slight possibility that he might gain some assistance, at least spiritually.

Suddenly the leader spoke to one of his men, who rose and guided Palasiva roughly over to sit next to him. Instructing all but one of his men to bed down for the time of darkness, he waited. When, at last, they were all settled, he turned to Palasiva. Using the hand signs that Palasiva had been told were used by all tribes, he said, "I am called Teo by my people. We are not growers like your people. We consider that soft and something for which we do not want to take the time. What are you called?"

Palasiva was surprised by the casual almost amicable manner of this raider. His power animal whispered to him to be suspicious, while at the same time he counted his blessings that this was as yet no worse. wincing in pain due to his wrists, he answered, "I am called Palasiva by my people." That was all he said, for he was being told to be silent and stealthy.

"You are very young for a sentinel. Why would your people place such a young one as yourself in such a position?" Without another word, Teo rose and walked behind him to loosen his bonds.

"Careful!" his spirit animal screamed into his mind. "I cannot answer that," Palasiva said softly, but not disrespectfully.

"Can it be that your people are leaving your great community, and there are not as many seasoned warriors left to defend your people? Is this why there are two young upstarts such as yourself and your friend defending the outpost?"

Again Palasiva hesitated to respond. No one had given him any information on what Teo was suggesting, but now that he thought about it, he knew it was very likely the truth. He suppressed the rage that once again surfaced when he thought about his deceased friend. At last he said, "No one has informed me of such conditions."

Teo was disturbed, but maintained his composure. "Young man, you obviously want to be of no help to us, and I can honor and respect your reaction. There are, however, some things you should know. There are conditions that will set you free. Are you interested?"

Palasiva's heart leaped with just the thought that they might set him free. Yet, in the back of his mind, his power animal screamed, "Watch! Listen carefully! The conditions will be difficult!" In an attempt to keep any feelings of hope or excitement out of his voice he answered very simply, "Yes."

Teo sat down beside him, once more moving his greasy muscular body closer to Palasiva. After pausing to gather his thoughts and choose his words, he began. "Young man, as you and your people are well aware, we are suffering from a long and terrible drought. Hunting and gathering is no longer providing my people with enough food to survive. Even water is at a premium. In order for my people to survive, we will be forced to do so at the expense of your people, and this is where you will assist us. You will keep us informed of the whereabouts of your people in the small houses to assure us success in our raiding during the harsh cold season that all of us will be forced to face."

Palasiva stared at him disbelievingly. Apparently this raider believed in the survival of the fittest, and possessed no ability to feel compassion for any other human beings but his own. He found it hard to understand any such logic, for to him there seemed to be none. Again his power animal sternly advised him to make no hasty decisions, but to listen carefully and to trust his own senses. He remained stoic and silent.

Teo waited for a response that he was sure would be a definite no, but the young warrior said nothing. He had to admire the young man's self-discipline. It seemed to him that this was one trait that the Anasazi had in common with his own people. Here was a young man, not particularly physically matured, but who was well trained in battle and seemed to be able to hold his own under terribly stressful conditions. Clearing his throat, he continued. "We also know that some of your people are choosing to leave the canyon as well as the outliers to seek better living conditions. If we are to set you free, you must keep us informed of any departures."

Palasiva could contain himself no longer. He knew he must choose his words carefully and so he asked, "Why do you wish me to provide you with such knowledge?"

"There are two reasons. One is that we will then know which outliers to raid so that we may confiscate anything we might need. The other is to capture those who are leaving to trade them as slaves to the Mayan-Toltec pochteca in exchange for food and wealth."

Palasiva felt certain that Teo must be possessed by the most evil of the gods, and could not imagine anyone so callous. His mind raced as he tried to assimilate all that he had heard. The wildcat had told him that the conditions would not be good, but to him that was an understatement. He resolved to remain unruffled in order to think clearly. Suddenly he realized that he could agree to all they asked in order to be set free, but that he would be home safe, and would never have to do what they asked.

As if reading the young warrior's thoughts, Teo added in an ominous deep voice, "If you do not cooperate, you will be traded to the Mayan-Toltec traders for a slave."

Palasiva again made no response. He knew his life was on the line either way. If he wanted freedom, and ignored their demands, he would run the risk of being captured again, as had just happened when he least expected it. It was in his mind that that was fine. If he must gamble his own life to save many lives, so be it. These were the chances a warrior must take. Still he did not respond.

"Once again, Palasiva, you do not answer. There is one more thing I must tell you." He turned to face Palasiva, and stared at him angrily. "Hear me, and hear me well, young man! There is one among you with exceptional talent, talent known even among our people, the Mogollon, and the Hohokam. Among our people, it is common knowledge that this person is often out and about in order to pursue that talent, at times even in places where there is no protection. That person, as you might be suspecting, is your sister, Palasiva. Her life is also at stake if you choose not to cooperate."

Palasiva's stomach churned, and he thought if it was not empty he would surely have lost all that was in it. He felt a sickness overtake him unlike any he could have imagined. At his young age, he thought of Teo as some sort of an evil apparition, for he could not imagine anyone allowing such a curse to happen. Why, he wondered, was it happening to him? He came to an immediate and obvious decision. Raising his eyes to Teo's, he said, "Clearly, you have left me no choice."

"We are agreed then?"

"Yes, I am sorry to say." In the back of his mind he thought that if he still refused, the raiders would have gone their own way regardless, but he could not take the chance.

"We will free you when next Sun Father rises. Do not forget what I have said, for if you do, it will still not go well with your people. My people will survive."

With a heavy heart, Palasiva accepted the blanket Teo offered. It was a long time before he finally got a little sleep.

True to his word, Teo set him free when Sun Father had only given a hint of light on the eastern horizon. Much to his surprise his weapons were also returned to him along with a bladder of water, and some dried venison. Except for his wrists, all outward appearances would have indicated that nothing had happened at all. Inwardly, however, was another story. He thought that perhaps it might have been better if he had joined the land of the ancestors with his friend, Kopolvu. At least then he would have died in battle, which was the most honorable way to die, and which would have assured him a place of honor in the realm of the dead. He prayed aloud to Awonawilona, the Creator, asking why it should be he who should be forced to carry such a burden. Why had they threatened him with the life of his beloved sister? He was now thinking that his parents had been right. He should never have decided to become a warrior. Lansa had chosen wisely, for it was universal law that traders were never attacked. He would also have been safe if he had chosen the life of a craftsman, or even the priesthood. Despair threatened to engulf him, and he found it difficult to keep going.

When Sun Father reached his peak, Palasiva sat down under a small rock overhang for a short rest. He knew he must press on or he would not reach his destination before dark. The dried venison and water seemed especially wonderful to his empty stomach. When he had consumed all that the raiders had given him, he shut his eyes and breathed deeply in an attempt to visualize his power animal, but to no avail. He resolved to ask his sister about his power animal at their earliest convenience. Of course she must not know why he was asking, but he thought she might help him to gain some insight as to how to handle the whole ugly situation. He also decided that he must stop berating himself, for somehow that seemed self-defeating. The problem existed, and there was nothing he could do to change it at this point in time. Therefore he must deal with it like a man. Covering his head with a white cloth for protection in the heat and another shear cloth over his nose and mouth to filter the dust, he trudged on.

Sun Father was just completing his journey when Palasiva approached the holy school. The people in the small houses that dotted the landscape on either side of the Great North Road stared at him as if he were an apparition as he passed by. To his surprise he was greeted by Moon Fire, who stood at the entrance of the plaza. He wrapped her so tightly in his arms that she cried out. Loosening his grip on her, he whispered, "I thank Awonawilona that I have returned."

"I knew you were not dead," she said as huge tears of happiness slid down her cheeks. "Our mother and father did not believe me."

"How did you know, little sister?" He wondered if she might have other abilities about which he was unaware.

Disengaging herself from his embrace, she answered, "Red Eagle told me in a dream." Taking his hand, she added, "Come, let us quickly inform everyone that you are safe."

When they reached the top of the ladder, Moon Fire said with a twinkle in her eye, "Let me go first. You come down behind me." At the bottom of the ladder, while he was still descending, she said, "Look who I have found."

Tupkya's and Sikyawa's faces were amazing to watch as their expressions changed from one of terrible grief to amazement. No words were said as the four of them huddled together in an exalted family embrace.

"How did you know, Moon Fire?" Tupkya asked as they slowly disengaged. "Your father and I did not believe you. We are sorry!"

"I had a dream. I cannot tell you more."

Palasiva immediately said, "I must report to Masichuvio, our warrior chief. He will want to know that I am well."

"But what of your wrists?" Tupkya asked with concern.

"I was captured by the raiders, Mother, but they let me go. Now you must let me go. Don't worry. I will return in a very short time." With those final words, he quickly climbed the ladder.

Masichuvio was a big man with many battle scars on his body. He was old enough to be Palasiva's father, and had a large family of his own. He told Palasiva that runners had informed him of Kopolvu's death and also of the raid. Kopolvu's parents had taken his body to be buried under the corner of their small outlier, and were very much bereaved over their son. He added that many believed that Palasiva must be either dead or captured, and that everyone was deeply concerned.

Palasiva told Masichuvio of his capture, and that he had worked his bonds free during the time of darkness. He added that to his knowledge none of the raiders had followed him, and he was glad to have reached home safely. Though he wanted to expound on his skill in besting the raider who had fought with him, he remained silent with the feeling that the less he said, the better. He was relieved that the interview was over, and politely excused himself.

In the short walk back to his parents' quarters, he could not help but wonder how much Red Eagle, his sister's totem, had seen, and how much he had told her. He was so deep in thought that he was surprised to see Moon Fire waiting at the top of the ladder. "Ho, my sister, are you waiting for a lover?" he inquired.

"Of course no," she retorted. "I am waiting for you. I am so glad you are alive. I have brought water, yucca root, and a healing salve to bind your wrists. Sit down, my brother, and allow me to cleanse your wounds."

"First, little sister, let me hold you. You must know that you are very dear to me."

"And you are dear to me, Palasiva." She found herself enjoying the warmth of his arms, but after a short time she extricated herself from his embrace, signing for him to sit down.

Wordlessly, she cleansed the raw burns around his wrists with water that she had made soapy and sudsy from the yucca root. After applying the salve, she loosely wrapped his wrists with soft, clean cotton cloth. When she had finished, she asked, "Are they painful?"

Again Palasiva was lost in thought and answered, "What?"

"Your wrists, of course. Are they painful?"

Willing himself to gather his thoughts, he said, "Not now. Your attention has taken away the pain." After a brief silence, he turned his deeply concerned attention to Moon Fire. "Little sister, I have never spoken to you of my spirit animal, but it is in my mind that you might enlighten me. Are you willing?"

Moon Fire checked to be certain no one was within close range of hearing, and said, "If you wish to confide in me, you may rest assured I will keep it in my heart. No one will know."

"I am told that if you dream several times over of the same animal, that your power animal is trying to communicate with you." He spoke almost in a whisper as if he could not believe, even though no one was close by, that what he said would not be heard by others. "My power animal has appeared to me in several dreams and has rescued me in various difficult situations. Does that mean I have found my totem?"

Moon Fire chuckled. "Yes, Palasiva, I would say that is so."

"Then I want you to know that my totem is the wildcat," he whispered in an even softer tone. "What can you tell me?"

She wondered as she felt a surging of his energy. It was as if he anticipated some astounding answer, or was suddenly searching with an urgency she could not comprehend. Whatever it was that she felt, she pushed it aside, and began to speak of the wildcat, as her people knew him. "Palasiva, it would seem that the cat is your animal spirit, but you must know that the wildcat is a powerful animal but also a solitary one. I spoke but once to a wildcat, and he told me that coming to terms with learning to be alone without being lonely is difficult and part of what wildcat teaches. Often your friends will share secrets. It is important that you do not break confidences, for there will be strong repercussions which will be found out quickly." She watched his amazed expression as he absorbed what it was that she was saying.

Palasiva's expression changed from amazement to what Moon Fire perceived as depression. He breathed a deep sigh and inquired, "Is there anything more you can tell me about my totem?"

It seemed to Moon Fire that her little brother had changed drastically in the last two sun cycles, yet out of respect she knew she should not question him. At last she said, "Yes, the wildcat told me that he uses the cloud of darkness and secrecy to teach how to project and utilize the life force in silent but powerful ways. His magic, he said, is most powerful when others do not know of it. To speak of it dissipates the power. You must learn when to speak, how much, and to whom it might be essential. Others may see that of which you speak to be distorted or blown out of proportion. What some may see as one way, the wildcat may see as totally different."

Palasiva's expression looked positively dismal when he asked, "There is no more that you can tell me?"

"I can only tell you that if the wildcat is truly your totem, you must look for that which is hidden, for not all is as it would seem to be. Trust your own senses, and if it does not feel right, trust what you feel even if there is no logical reason to think otherwise."

When he remained silent for a short time, Moon Fire looked at him searchingly, thinking that he did not seem to be the same little brother with whom she had grown up. Taking his hand in her own, she gently inquired, "Sweet brother, are you all right?"

Snapping out of his reverie, he hastily answered, "Oh yes, of course. I am fine." Then giving her hand an affectionate squeeze, he added, "Thank you for your enlightening information. My bones are aching. I think it is time I retired for some much needed rest."

Moon Fire withdrew her hand from his and placed the fingertips of her left hand on her forehead. "There is only one more thing I must tell you. The wildcat teaches that there is true power and strength through silence." Then as an afterthought, she added, "Little brother, I care for you. I hope you are all right."

Palasiva could only shake his head, for at that point, his

mind seemed numb. He hugged her briefly and descended the ladder. He felt certain that he would sleep very little.

When seven sun cycles had passed, Masichuvio addressed a group of his warriors, telling them that their numbers were dwindling due to the fact that families had been leaving their homes to seek better living conditions. He said it grieved him that because of this he could not offer those families who were leaving any protection. He added that it was his duty to see that all those who still remained in the community were protected along with the storage bins on the roads.

Palasiva was deeply concerned, for he realized that Teo, the leader of the raiders, had been right, and that Masichuvio had validated his worst fears. He had learned during the previous sun cycle that another of the outlier families would be leaving sometime during the next several sun cycles. His stomach knotted with the thought of what he must do. He was not thinking of himself as much as of the safety of Moon Fire, and he was certain the raiders would not wait indefinitely for what they expected of him. So it was, in a time that he had no duties, he set out to find Teo.

The land was so parched and cracked that it resembled the skin of an old man. In some places on either side of the Great North Road, the land had split into huge fissures with occasional dust devils that seemed to rise out of them. As had become normal routine among all his people, he wore a light cloth over his nose and mouth to filter the dust that blew when the wind gusted. He also found it necessary to keep his eyes lowered most of the time. He left the road when he was no longer in view of the warriors who were now guarding the same storage bins at the site of his attack. He was heading in what he thought was the direction that the raiders had taken him, and the same direction in which he had returned. His uncertainty was due to the fact that he had been so emotionally upset at that time that he had not really taken in his surroundings, as he would have done under almost any other circumstances.

Suddenly, out of the dust, three figures appeared. Teo was flanked by two other warriors, who turned at an angle to escape the direction of the wind that would have blown the dust directly into their faces. Of course Palasiva did the same.

"You have news for us, boy? It's about time we heard from you," Teo blurted out impatiently.

Palasiva hesitated, then said, "Another of our families will be leaving any time now. I know not in which direction they are headed." He hoped there would be no further questions.

"We have waited too long for your response, boy! Where is this family's outlier home?"

Palasiva stifled his anger with what he thought was a cool response. "I have no control over the timing in which the families might be leaving. I can only tell you this family's home is located southwest of our main community buildings."

Teo bristled at the boy's comment and clutched Palasiva's arm. "Don't be impertinent! We will not tolerate any kind of an attitude. How far south are they located?"

"Less than half a sun cycle away from the community." His anger had quickly changed to fear again, for he thought he had covered his anger quite well. He suddenly felt young, small, and insignificant in comparison to his opponents. Though he knew it was wrong, he found himself unable to control his feelings.

Teo released his arm, saying in a voice that nearly snarled, "What you have told us had better be the truth, boy! Now go! Remember, you are under oath to say nothing."

Palasiva turned to go. "Under oath?" he thought. "Under threat is more like it." He hardly knew how to deal with his terribly mixed feelings. Shame, guilt, sorrow, and anger overwhelmed him as he trudged through the wind and dust toward home.

The following sun cycle came ever so slowly for him. His mind was tortured, and he longed to tell someone, anyone, but kept his silence. To his surprise he found himself with no assignment for part of the sun cycle, and took the opportunity to head southwest in the direction the family had chosen. He could not help but wonder what had caused them to decide to head straight into the dry dusty wind, when they might have gone north with the wind behind them. He guessed it was entirely possible that they had decided to go to the land of the Mogollon, but he had heard that even the Mogollon were suffering from the drought.

Sun Father had not yet reached his zenith, but the desert was unbearably hot even so. Beneath the expansive turquoise sky, dust devils danced between the fissures that crisscrossed the dry, barren earth. It was during a lull in the wind that he spotted them in the far distance. He pushed on and picked up speed in an attempt to get closer. At last he was close enough to see that the family consisted of father, mother, and four children. He assumed that the elderly woman, who walked with a slight limp, and who also traveled with them, must be the matron of the family. He could not get close enough to them to hear their words or see their faces. Staying out of sight behind a large boulder, he hoped that their trip would be a safe one, and that the raiders would not find them.

As if on cue, after only a few heartbeats, Teo and his warriors came screaming and ululating out of nowhere. They were upon the travelers in no time. The two women struggled valiantly, but were quickly bound by the raiders along with the children. Meanwhile, the father drew out his knife in an effort to defend his little family. Palasiva knew the man was badly outnumbered, and he admired his courage. The dust became so thick during the skirmish that he could hardly see what was happening. When it finally settled, he saw that they had bound the father's hands behind his back and pushed him in a standing position against a large rock. Heated words that Palasiva could not decipher were spoken between the father and Teo. Teo backed off and gave a signal to one of his men, who stepped up to the father and deftly slit his throat. Blood sprayed heavily at first, but the father made no sound other than the gurgling as he choked on his own blood and crumpled to the ground. The women and children screamed and wailed in horror as they watched the slaughter. Several raiders struck them in an effort to silence them, but to no avail.

Palasiva turned and retched, spewing up the corn mush that he had eaten for breakfast. He clutched at his stomach as it continued to heave. As a young trained warrior, he had not yet taken anyone's life, and now he wondered if he ever could.

With a supreme effort he pulled himself together to resume his watch.

The women and children continued to wail while Teo and his first in command exchanged words. Two of the raiders seized the matron and threw her to the ground. The rest of the party pulled the mother and her children together, tying them with another long rope so that they could walk but could not attempt to escape. With the tip of a blade thrust against the mother's back, they forced her and the children forward, abandoning the older woman.

Palasiva waited until they were out of sight while his mind raced. He desperately wanted to rescue the matron, yet he knew he did not dare She would tell the story and everyone would wonder why he had happened to be there. He knew he had no other choice, but to keep silent at all cost. With a heavy heart, he made his way back home.

CHAPTER 10

A.D. *1133*

M oon Fire sat cross-legged on her mat, enjoying the cool temperature that the thick stone walls of her parents' house offered. She knew that Sun Father was still very high in the sky, and that no one would be out at this time unless it was a necessity. All her people knew that the heat would quickly dissipate when Sun Father had completed his journey, and the temperature would actually become quite cold. She found herself alone, for her mother was on the roof, grinding corn with two other women, and her father was teaching. Palasiva, of late, seldom graced them with his presence, and Lansa . . . well, Lansa was Lansa. It was not often that the opportunity for meditation presented itself, and Moon Fire decided to take advantage of it.

She closed her eyes, taking several deep breaths. After consciously relaxing every part of her body, she found herself offering a prayer to her animal totem, Red Eagle.

"One with graceful wings,
Hear my call.
One with graceful wings,
Hear my voice.
Come share your sky spirit with me.
One with graceful wings,
See my spirit.
One with graceful wings,
See my soul.
Come share your soul with me."

After several repetitions of this prayer, she slipped into a different level of consciousness. The desert surrounded her with its cool air. She found herself waiting in the shade of the cave she knew so well—the cave where she spent her womanly cycle except in the coldest of moon cycles. She waited.

A large bird came into her mind's eye. It circled, then landed squarely in front of her. Neither one of them spoke in words, only in thoughts.

"Red Eagle, it is you," she exclaimed.

"I bring a message," he said, cocking his head to one side as if ready to listen.

Moon Fire's curiosity was piqued as she asked, "And what might this unexpected message be?"

"In my flight during this sun cycle, I saw an elderly woman wandering and babbling in the desert. If she is not found soon she will perish, When last I saw her, she was on the eastern side of the south road, though in truth I do not think she knows where she is."

"How far away from our community is she?"

"I would say, as you people travel, less than a sun cycle away. I thought you would want to know." Having delivered his message, he turned from her and flew away.

Moon Fire shook her head as she pulled herself from her trance. She rose as quickly as she was able to make her way to speak of her vision to someone, anyone, but who? Excusing herself from her mother's presence, she made her way across the plaza. As she turned a corner at the exit of the plaza, she ran headlong into Palasiva, who was conversing with one of his warrior friends.

He reached for her hand, pulling her into his arms. "Ho, little sister, what is your rush? You look like you have just seen an evil spirit."

"Oh, Palasiva, how fortunate I am to run into you. I was not sure to whom I needed to speak, but, yes, you are the one."

"Why me?" he asked.

She pulled him away from his fellow warrior into the shadow of an inside wall. "I must speak privately and softly."

Again he inquired, "Why me?"

When she realized there was no one within hearing distance,

she said, "I have received a message from Red Eagle. He informed me that there is an elderly woman wandering and babbling in the desert to the south of us. He said she would surely die from exposure to Sun Father if she were not rescued. Oh, Palasiva, can you help?"

Palasiva felt the hair at the nape of his neck prickle, for he wondered how much she might not be telling him that her spirit animal had told her. He was also experiencing a conflicting feeling of elation that perhaps he might, after all, be able to rescue the poor woman as he had wanted to do earlier. "Of course, I will help. Leave me, little sister. I will report this to Masichuvio immediately." He hugged her tightly to him, then let her go.

Moon Fire quickly returned to her quarters with the feeling that she had done her part, and could do no more.

Sun Father had more than completed his journey when the woman was brought in. Her lips were dry and cracked due to lack of water, and many were concerned that because of her age and exposure to the sun, she would surely die. She seemed to be hanging on tenaciously with every fiber of her being.

Taatawi directed her rescuers to take the poor bony woman to the healing kiva. They lowered her on a litter with ropes, and placed her gently on a mat that covered a long rectangular stone slab, then respectfully departed. The sun priest was almost immediately joined by Wena 'Ahote as they both tried to make the woman as comfortable as possible. Ruupi was not in attendance, for his skills were that of a crystal scrier rather than a healer.

Wena 'Ahote followed Taatawi's instructions as he coaxed a clean cotton cloth soaked with willow bark tea between the woman's bleeding lips. She gratefully pressed out the liquid more with her gums than her lips, but continued to moan through it all. The two of them checked her over for broken bones, yet they knew that it was her heart that was broken, not her bones. Wena 'Ahote applied cool compresses to her face, hands, and feet to soothe Sun Father's unmerciful burns. Afterward he gently rubbed her burns with sunflower oil. She also managed with much difficulty to take in a very thin liquid made from corn.

At last she slipped into a restless sleep. Taatawi said he would watch her for a while if Wena 'Ahote wanted time for himself, but Wena 'Ahote refused to leave his side out of concern for the woman.

She awoke with a moan, and a cry of anguish. "Gone." She sobbed. "My family is gone! I want to die!"

Taatawi took one of her hands gently in his own while Wena 'Ahote took the other. "Where have they gone, woman? What is your name?" the sun priest inquired.

"The raiders. The raiders!" Again her voice rose in a wail.

"Did they kill your family? Why did they not take you too?"

Wena 'Ahote remained still as he listened to the two of them with a heavy heart.

Between sobs, the woman said, "They only killed my son. He offered resistance, and they, they . . ." Her voice trailed off once more.

Taatawi waited patiently until the woman had regained some composure. Speaking softly, he repeated, "Why did they not take you?"

"They said I was too old. They pushed me to the ground after they cut my son's throat, then bound my son's wife and the four children together and took them away. That is all I know." Her whimpering was pitiful, and enough to tear at the hearts of both who attended her.

"Do you know your name?" Taatawi asked.

"It does not matter, for now I have no family."

"Were you and your family leaving our lands to find better ones?"

"Yes, of course. Why else would we leave? Life has not been easy. We have been hungry for many season cycles. Now will you leave me in peace?" It was obvious that she was becoming extremely annoyed.

"If that is your wish." Taatawi pulled a light blanket over her, and they both took their leave.

At the top of the ladder, Taatawi touched Wena 'Ahote's arm, saying, "I will go no further than this, for I do not know what she might do." He sat down to keep his vigil.

Wena 'Ahote respectfully sat next to him. At last he said, "Revered One, I have so many questions."

"And so do I, and so do I."

"Why do you think the raiders kept the mother and children alive? They cannot even feed their own."

Taatawi's obsidian eyes filled with compassion as he spoke. "I can only speculate. We are living in terrible times. These are times when humans must do what they must do to stay alive. You are correct when you say that they cannot feed their own, but then, neither can we. We are told that the drought is not affecting the Mayan-Toltecs as severely as us. Perhaps . . ." His voice trailed off.

"Perhaps what?" Though Wena 'Ahote's curiosity was piqued, he was almost afraid of what Taatawi's answer might be.

"Well, if you really want to know, I will tell you what I think."

"Of course I want to know, or I would not have asked."

Taatawi cleared his throat, then continued. "You are right when you say that they could not support them as their own. If that is so, then they must be giving them away, or better still, trading them."

Wena 'Ahote immediately knew.

Tovosi, which meant "smooth wood," was a dedicated warrior, and Palasiva's friend. He took his vocation very seriously, never questioning those with authority. He, too, was apprehensive for the malaise of his people, and felt their pain and sadness. He had heard Masichuvio's message about the dwindling number of warriors, and knew that those who chose to leave would be unprotected. In the several sun cycles that had passed since the older woman had been brought in, two other families had attempted to leave. They had headed north to the outlier on the great river, the outlier that was fast becoming a community of great houses that eventually would rival those in the canyon in which he lived. They, too, were attacked by the raiders, bound and led away by them. It seemed very strange to Tovosi that this time none had been killed, and it had been reported that there had been no signs of a struggle. All in the families had simply been whisked away. One of the sentinels guarding the Great North Road had been off duty, and had found footprints and a colorful Anasazi sash that had been nearly buried in the dust.

Tovosi's concern was not just for his people, but for his friend Palasiva, who in his mind, had not been himself recently. The two of them were often given assignments together, and when their duties were completed, they would take time, as friends naturally do, to be together. Of late, he had noticed that his friend was preoccupied, and when off duty would excuse himself, saying he had other things to do. He decided to take it upon himself to follow Palasiva, at least as much as he could to find out why the change in their friendship. He felt certain it must be a girl who interested him. When next they were assigned duty together, he decided to approach his friend.

"Palasiva, you are not yourself lately." He had decided to be gentle with his words.

"What do you mean?"

He noted that his friend seemed, as usual, to be elsewhere. "I mean to say that our comradery has gone. Do you want to tell me why?"

"I'm sorry, but I did not feel that it was so." Palasiva's expression was truly one of surprise.

"My friend, you are not yourself of late. I only wanted you to know I am aware and I care." Knowing he was stepping out of line and should mind his own business, he asked, "Is there a young woman who interests you?"

Palasiva hastily answered, "No, of course not. It's just that other business calls me. Please do not interrogate me, my friend. It's just that . . ." He turned on his heel and added, "Our friendship is still the same."

Tovosi was dumbfounded at Palasiva's brusque response. As he watched his friend walk away, he felt a stab of pain, the pain of being cut off. Now, more than ever, he felt he must find out what his friend was about.

Shortly after being off duty, on two occasions Tovosi watched Palasiva disappear in a northwesterly direction. He did not follow him far, due to the fact that Palasiva seemed to be taking extreme precaution that no one might be following him. Tovosi knew of no small house that might be in the same direction, and so he immediately drew his own conclusions. It was clear to him that there was something very wrong. Normally his friend was willing to share thoughts with him, but something had changed his entire demeanor. The recurring thought that Palasiva might be in danger haunted him as he made his way back to his quarters.

Suddenly he knew what he must do. He rerouted himself to his friend's family quarters, where he was met by Moon Fire, who sat on the roof near the ladder that provided entrance to her parents' home. She was working on a tightly woven waterproof basket and humming quietly to herself. As was the custom, he waited for her to acknowledge him before speaking.

"It seems I have a visitor," she said, looking up at him through her thick black lashes.

"Moon Fire, sister of my friend Palasiva, I wish to speak privately with you. I feel it is of the utmost importance that I air my concerns."

"Come, sit across from me. You must be Tovosi. Palasiva has spoken well of you."

Tovosi assumed a comfortable cross-legged position, and folded his hands in his lap. He was having second thoughts about what he wanted to say. "Perhaps," he thought, "this is really none of my business."

An uncomfortable silence was followed by Moon Fire's quiet interruption. "I am listening," she said.

"I knew you would be more than willing to listen, but now I am wondering if the seriousness of my concerns might be unfounded."

"I was told that when one is in doubt, one should say nothing. Only you can make that decision." She flashed him a curious look, and waited patiently.

Squaring his shoulders, Tovosi began. "Moon Fire, your brother and I have known one another for a long time. I know how easygoing he usually is. He . . ."

"He what?" she urged.

"I am a dedicated warrior as well as a dedicated friend. Palasiva and I usually spend time together when we are off duty, and especially if we have had the same assignment. We have

been assigned duties together on several occasions during the
past six or seven sun cycles, but . . ."

"But what?" she coaxed.

"He does not seem to want the comradery we had only a
short time ago. He always has other things to do. I would not
think much of it, but when I asked him if there was a young
woman who might interest him, he said no, and told me not to
interrogate him. He said he just had business elsewhere."

"Well, perhaps he did," she retorted. "Is there something
more you want me to know?"

Plucking up his courage, he said, "I took the liberty of following him on two occasions. He went toward the northeast,
but I could not follow him very far. He kept looking in all directions as if he might be afraid he was being followed. There
are no small houses or even pit houses in that direction, for the
land, as you probably know, is very barren. It is his safety that
concerns me. You know the raiders are creating a huge problem
for us, and he is out there in those terrible lands alone and un-
guarded. I do not want to make any suggestions, but it seems
coincidental that he should have journeyed into nowhere just
before the last two families disappeared."

Moon Fire stared at him incredulously. Was this young warrior suggesting that her little brother might be a spy? She found
herself unable to interpret his words in any other way. Anger
surged through her so strongly that she bit her tongue. She
wanted to scream at Tovosi's audacity. She wanted to hurl terrible words at him, but training had taught her that nothing was
gained by insults and degradations. She had been taught to val-
idate another's feelings, and to allow herself to walk in their
sandals. And so she struggled to contain herself.

Tovosi watched her, and knew she was wrestling with her
emotions. After all, he had in so many words suggested that
Palasiva was up to no good and might even be a traitor. He
braced himself for what he thought would be emotional harsh
words.

After several deep breaths, Moon Fire sternly said, "Tovosi,
I feel you have overstepped your boundaries. I can understand
your concern, but I am sure there is a simple, rational explanation for these recent events. I cannot say I am thankful for your

visit, but I will certainly think on the information you have offered." Picking up her basket, she descended the ladder into the comfort of her parents' quarters, leaving him standing alone and confused.

Moon Fire thought long and hard on Tovosi's words. As her anger subsided, she began to realize that it was indeed odd that Palasiva would have any business at all in the wastelands to the northeast of them. Those lands were a strange mixture of old logs turned to stone, and weirdly colored spires that covered a vast area. There was no water for irrigation of crops or even for survival. Almost no vegetation grew there and though some had tried, none of her people had ever been able to eke out an existence in the horribly inhospitable land. The other fact that greatly disturbed her was that Palasiva had distanced himself from the family quarters in the very recent past. She had missed him, and wondered why he had not been around. She recalled that they had always been close until now, but then perhaps this was just a man thing, a thing that women would not understand.

She returned to the rooftop when she thought Tovosi was surely gone, to continue with the weaving of her basket. She remembered that for no reason at all, Palasiva had asked her for an interpretation of his spirit animal. She wondered what answers he might be seeking, and why he would suddenly be searching. She had always felt a special closeness with her little brother, and now she simply could not understand what was going on. "I want to believe in him," she pondered, "but somehow I know something is definitely wrong. He is a good person, and always has been—not at all like Lansa. He sits and evaluates what he hears before he responds, and is always compassionate when other people are involved. We have always been so close, but now he is so different. Something must have happened to make this so."

Feeling in her heart that perhaps there might be a grain of truth in what Palasiva's friend had said, she decided to speak to Wena 'Ahote of her concerns. She set her basket aside and moved across the plaza into the close proximity of his quarters. To her delight, she did not have long to wait, for he appeared in the plaza in the company of Taatawi. She placed her hand over her heart to give him the sign that she needed to speak to him.

He saw her at once. Taatawi took his leave after only a few words had passed between them. Walking swiftly to her, he folded her in his arms. "What is it, my little love? It is most unusual that you have come to me at this time. I see in your eyes that you are troubled. Come into my quarters where we can talk." He took her hand as they descended the ladder. Once there they sat on his sleeping mat, but only after a long passionate embrace. "Now what is on your mind?" he gently inquired.

"I have come to ask your help. I know no one else in whom I can confide, and even if I did, you know I would choose you."

"Your eyes are troubled, and full of doubts," he said. He cupped her chin with his hand.

She turned away with a deep sigh, looking wistfully into nowhere. At last she softly spoke. "It's about my brother."

He breathed a deep sigh of relief. "Your brother, Lansa, has always been a problem. What has he done now?"

"No, you do not understand. It is Palasiva, my youngest brother of whom I speak. He, well I think he may be in trouble. I do not know how serious it may be, but then, that is why I came to you."

"But what can I do that you cannot do?"

"You can have him followed. I cannot."

"I what?"

"You heard me, my love. You can find someone who will follow him. I only hope my suspicions are wrong, but why would he suddenly be disappearing into the 'no man's lands' to the northeast of us on a regular basis? Why would he all of a sudden be so distant? And there are the disappearing families to consider. What am I supposed to think?" Tears began to gather in her eyes.

"Stop, sweet one. I will do as you ask. Let us hope there is nothing to be concerned about. Now let me wipe away your tears, and offer you consolation."

Without another word he moved his hand to her breast and circled her nipple. Bending over her, he softly found all her sensitive spots, while the world stopped all around them.

*   *   *

She tossed and turned in her sleep. It was not long before
Sun Father would rise when she finally found respite, and fell
into a sound sleep. At one point she awakened to find herself
drenched in perspiration. Gulping some of the precious water,
she returned to her sleeping mat. This time she dreamed. She
dreamed of several different animals, as though they might be
trying to reach her for some reason that was not made clear.
When all seemed to be complete, she fell into another light
sleep. The light sleep turned into a deeper one that allowed her
to swirl through a tunnel into a deep canyon. The canyon was
filled with the precious water that her people needed. The rocks
sang with the sound of the river as it rushed to its destination.
The land was filled with lush juniper, piñon pine, and even
some tall grandfather pines. There was sage, yucca, and even
agave, as well as other abounding edible plants. The scent of
mint that grew at the edge of the water almost overwhelmed
her. She lay down next to it to revel in the odor.

A bird loomed in the distance. Very gradually it came closer
and closer until she realized that it was Red Eagle who was approaching. He perched silently on a lower branch of the nearest grandfather pine and waited.

Moon Fire shaded her eyes with her hand as she watched her
spirit animal in all his glory. She intuitively knew his message
must be important. Not daring to let him out of her sight, she
silently said, "Red Eagle, I am honored to be in your presence."

"And I also am honored," he replied, "but the tidings I bear
are not good ones."

She caught her breath, for she knew in her heart what he was
probably going to say. He had the ability to fly far and wide,
and she was certain he was going to speak to her of what he had
seen. She made no comment.

At last, after cocking his head first to one side, then to another, he said, "I cover vast areas in search of food. Just this last
sun cycle, I flew toward the northeast to the edge of what your
people call 'no man's land.' There I saw your younger brother,
Palasiva, heading into the strangely colored area. I followed
him. He finally was greeted by several raiders, and conversation followed. My hearing is acute, but not good enough to hear

what was being said. In only a short time, he turned and came back in the direction of your community. I thought you would want to know." He paused to pull several long feathers through his beak, then continued. "There is more. I also witnessed the raiders' capture of the last two families, and followed them to watch the pochteca take them away."

She struggled to withhold the tears that threatened her, and said, "Oh, Red Eagle, you have just confirmed my worst suspicions. When next Sun Father rises, someone will be assigned to follow Palasiva. This was at my request. It was something I did not want to do, but felt I must."

"I am glad you did. I also did not want to have to bear this message, but I knew it was necessary, for it does not appear that any good can come from what your brother is doing."

"Should I try to talk to him, Red Eagle?" she asked with a little choke in her voice.

"I would think not," he answered. "I must go now, but keep in mind that you must do what is right for the good of the people. You have my support and also that of Wena 'Ahote. Perhaps your brother also must do what he must do. May Awonawilona watch over us all." With those words of wisdom, he thrust out his chest, flapped his wings, and flew away.

Moon Fire awoke to find herself sobbing. Tupkya sent her a look of concern, but knew better than to speak. It was customary not to awaken someone suddenly, for it was believed that the spirit wandered during sleep, and might not return to the body if such were to happen.

CHAPTER 11

The following sun cycle Wena 'Ahote was to be inducted into the priesthood. He awoke and washed with yucca soap and warm water, then rubbed his body down with sage. He fashioned his lustrous ebony hair into a single fat braid down his back, and laced a single eagle feather through the braid at the base of his skull. After wrapping himself in his usual drab robe and tying a large piece of turquoise on a leather thong around his neck, he sat down on his mat to await his summons. This was his day, the day he had longed for. He wondered how many other priests over the generations had had the same anxious feelings he was now experiencing. Taatawi had assured him that there was nothing that should concern him. He had composed his songs, and felt that he was as ready as he would ever be.

At last an acolyte descended his ladder to tell him it was his time, and he emerged above to find the plaza swarmed with people, many more than usual. The elders were formed in a group behind Taatawi and Ruupi while others had arranged themselves on both sides. A group of musicians—drummers, singers, and flutists—followed him with a hypnotic song as he marched slowly toward the center of activity. Taatawi handed him a basket of cornmeal, and he walked first to the east (the direction of birth), then to the north (direction of the gods), west (direction of death), and finally to the south (direction of warmth and fertility). In each direction he sprinkled cornmeal and quietly recited a prayer. He noticed the proud, loving smile on Moon Fire's face when he walked toward the east. "How appropriate," he thought, "that she should be standing in the east (the direction of their new love affair)." Following that, he made his entrance into the kiva along with the elders and the two priests.

There were more musicians softly chanting in the kiva. The air was hot and dry due to the brilliantly burning fire in the fire pit. The elders gathered on the west side, Ruupi at the south side, and Taatawi on the east side, for he was the sun priest, and the sun rose in the east. The chants were low and sublime, but as Wena 'Ahote took his place beside Taatawi and Ruupi, the chanting became gradually louder. Many generations had seen these same events as priests were inducted into the Anasazi culture. Each elder chanted his own prayer, followed by Ruupi and Taatawi. Tenyam passed around a pipe, and the smoke wafted toward the entrance of the kiva to purify all who were within it.

When the smoking was completed, several women arrived for the washing of Wena 'Ahote's hair. After drying his hair, they again braided it in a single braid, then replaced the eagle feather and added a large chunk of turquoise. This completed, they took their leave. The soft chanting had gone on through the entire occasion.

At this point the music became more intense. Tenyam and Angwusi guided him to the rectangular stone slab in the center of the kiva, and lay him on his back. Taatawi began to dance, and the music became louder and faster. When Taatawi's dance was complete, Tenyam presented the sun priest with a basket of cornmeal. He accepted it lovingly and sang a prayer over it. Taatawi moved reverently toward Wena 'Ahote and parted his robe to leave his body exposed to all in the kiva. Taking some of the cornmeal sacrament, he traced a line of it over Wena 'Ahote's right side, left side, and over his chest. The musicians stopped. Taatawi began chanting and traced another line of cornmeal from his neck to his male member, which indicated the sacredness of the four directions. Still chanting, he threw cornmeal into the air and on the ground to complete six of the seven sacred directions. He then gave Wena 'Ahote a mouthful of cornmeal to chew, which completed the sacred seven directions. At this point the musicians resumed.

After their song, Taatawi touched Wena 'Ahote's shoulder to inform him that it was his turn. He played songs of the six directions, and a final one that bared his soul. His flute was so sweet that it brought tears to the eyes of several in attendance, especially the musicians.

Angwusi then led him to a large feathered hoop that lay in the center of the kiva. Wena 'Ahote stepped into it, and the musicians began once more. The four elders stood around it in each of the sacred four directions. A song of purification began, while the elders slowly raised the hoop from head to toe to symbolically cleanse him. The newly ordained priest remained inside the hoop until the music had ended.

From a cache in the kiva, Taatawi withdrew a perfect eagle feather, and tied it into Wena 'Ahote's braid. He then withdrew a cape made of a wondrous combination of feathers that reflected many colors and hues, and tied it around his shoulders. He then took Wena 'Ahote's hand and directed him to ascend the ladder to the plaza. Everyone else followed him.

As usual a large crowd had gathered. When everyone had assembled from the inside of the kiva, a shell horn blasted, and Wena 'Ahote was given a basket of cornmeal. With Taatawi and Ruupi behind him, he walked first to the east to sprinkle sacred cornmeal, then to the south, west, and finally to the north. At each direction, prayers were recited by either Taatawi or Ruupi. When all was completed, the crowd returned to the warmth of their quarters. Thus was completed the induction of the new priest.

Four people did not return to their quarters. Moon Fire waited and watched from afar as Wena 'Ahote turned to the other three standing alone in the shadow of a massive wall. She could only assume that this was his family, for one was an older man and woman, and one woman was somewhat younger. They communicated for a short time after affectionate embraces, then went on their way to their quarters.

Wena 'Ahote's parents and his cousin left when next Sun Father arose. After seeing them off, he chanced to meet Hoohu, who greeted him warmly. Wena 'Ahote returned the greeting with a smile.

Hoohu did not seem in a particular hurry, so as they walked a short way, he said, "How does it feel to finally be a revered priest?"

"Somehow I must say I do not feel any different, but I understand that now I belong to the people, and I must never forget that it is so. I thank you, revered elder, for your friendship."

Hoohu stopped and touched the young priest's elbow. "It seems we are alone and that is good. There is some information I would share with you if that is your desire."

Wena 'Ahote stopped and answered, "Of course it is my desire." He was suddenly aware that in the past he had learned most of what he knew from Taatawi, and now with his new position, Hoohu was apparently feeling free to open his heart.

"Before your induction into the priesthood, a council was held. This is nothing unusual, of course, for we must approve any candidate for the priesthood. When it came to the vote to ordain you as a priest, the vote was closely divided. Ruupi saw to it that it was so."

Wena 'Ahote's confidence in himself began to burst as he hesitantly asked, "Tell me what you know, revered elder."

Hoohu cleared his throat, then continued. "In the meeting Tenyam and Angwusi sided against you, while Eykita and I supported you. Because the vote was tied, Posaala, Maahu, Awta, and Iswungwa broke the tie. Three of them voted their support, and while I do not wish to mention names, one of them did not."

"Then," exclaimed Wena 'Ahote in surprise, "I have been made priest as a result of voting that was far from unanimous."

"That is so. I thought you would want to know." Hoohu's demeanor seemed as though he was casually indifferent.

Wena 'Ahote's head was spinning, but he knew that Hoohu's indifference was typical of his people's appearance, and that, in fact, they worked very hard to make it so. He knew that if Hoohu did not care, he would not have attempted to befriend him. And so he asked, "What of Ruupi? You said he did not support me."

"That is true. He did not."

"What does Ruupi have against me?"

Hoohu shook his head despondently. "Revered priest, he

seemed to think you too young for such a position. He also tried to convince the council that you should marry your present lover, Moon Fire, for he says she is your obsession."

Wena 'Ahote swallowed hard in response to Hoohu's words. "But that is all speculation. Other priests have taken lovers, and other priests have been ordained at a much younger age. What is really the problem?"

"That is exactly the rationale that I used, and that convinced enough of the others that they should support you. I am not sure what the root of the problem is as yet, but I feel certain we will know very soon."

Wena 'Ahote clearly sensed that Hoohu had told him as much as he knew. He felt that he should not press him any further, and said, "Hoohu, I thank you for your confidence. I wonder if anyone else would have informed me as you have. You have given me much to think on."

Hoohu grasped the young priest's shoulder, saying, "I, for one, sense nothing but good in you. You have never shown anyone otherwise. I go now." He immediately turned away, leaving Wena 'Ahote with the feeling that his new position might be tenuous.

"Leetayo, you are my most promising student. I find you a most interesting young woman," declared Ruupi as his mind worked furiously. He knew of her animosity toward Moon Fire and thought perhaps he might use that as a way to accomplish his own goals.

She lowered her thick lashes in false modesty as she said, "Revered One, I find that you also fascinate me."

Running his hands over her shiny black hair, he felt his pulse quicken. Was it possible that this young woman might desire him sexually? He was quite a bit older than she, but there was always the possibility that age was not an issue. Placing a finger beneath her chin and lifting her interesting face to his, he softly asked, "Can it be that you and I could be more than friends?"

Her heart quickened, for she had had this in mind for some time. Looking him straight in the eye, she said, "It is a possibility." She thought that she might use him to achieve her own goal, which, of course, was to destroy Moon Fire. The fact that Moon Fire's feet were so ugly with a disgusting extra toe did not seem to repel masculine attention. In her mind her cousin seemed to attract only the most desirable of young men. Now, here was Ruupi, begging for her attentions. Due to his position as a priest, was he not the most desirable of men? It was true that he could not marry, but was that so important?

Ruupi pulled her toward him with his arm around her waist, cradling her against his chest. He knew she probably could hear the pounding of his beating heart, but he did not care. She was his chance. She was his ally. Here was someone he could use to his own advantage. At last he said, "Leetayo, there is something we must discuss. Something that could give you the revenge you want against your cousin, and something that could help me to achieve my own goals."

"And what is that, Revered One?" she asked.

"We will speak of it later. Now is not the time." He continued to hold her until, at last, he lifted her face to his own, and sealed their new relationship with a tender kiss.

The following sun cycle found the two of them in deep conversation with Tenyam and Angwusi. The two elders were listening intently as Ruupi said, "In the best interest of the people, we feel that there is something you should know. It pertains to our newly ordained priest."

Tenyam spoke for himself and his fellow elder. "You have our full attention."

Ruupi said, "I thank you both for giving me the opportunity to speak." After clearing his throat, he continued, "This young woman is called Leetayo. She was out gathering herbs on a particular day, and she wants you to know what she saw. I will let her tell the rest."

Leetayo's voice shook, not because of what she had to say, but because she had never spoken with any of the elders. Ruupi had told her that these two had not supported Wena 'Ahote as their choice for the priesthood, and on that she gained quite a bit of confidence. Gathering her thoughts together, she said, "I was out gathering herbs during the earliest part of Sun Father's journey not long ago. I found it necessary to go for quite some distance on the south road for what I needed. Then I moved away from the road to the east. As I was finishing my duties, I thought I heard voices. There was a large rock formation between me and the voices. One of the voices sounded familiar, and so I hid myself behind the rocks, and peeked around to see who it was." She hesitated while lowering her long lashes demurely.

Angwusi took a step toward her in order to hear her better, for they were in the plaza where people were conversing and passing by. "Well, young one, what did you see? What did you hear?" he asked in a most curious manner. Tenyam also stepped closer.

Leetayo was thrilled. She had her captive audience she so adored, and a most important one at that. "I was surprised to see our own Wena 'Ahote conversing with strange-looking people, dirty, and unkempt. I could not get close enough to hear what they were saying, but I thought the people must be the raiders."

"This is very interesting," exclaimed Tenyam. "Can you tell us exactly when this took place?"

Ruupi was thrilled. Everything was going exactly as they had hoped it would. Now Wena 'Ahote, who was Taatawi's protégé, would be out of the picture, and his competition for the position of sun priest would be gone. His admiration for Leetayo knew no bounds.

Leetayo was at last feeling comfortable with her newly gained power over the elders. Lifting her chin valiantly, she answered. "The time was the very earliest part of the sun cycle that the old woman was brought in. That is all I can tell you."

Angwusi sent Ruupi a somewhat doubtful look, and asked, "Who is this young woman? We know of her lineage, but how can we know of her honesty?"

Ruupi quickly responded, "She has been one of my most outstanding students for quite some time, and has always been most sincere. I could not doubt her. That is why we came to you. I know this is a most serious accusation, and that perhaps there is a simple explanation. There is nothing more I can say."

Tenyam and Angwusi exchanged serious looks. Then Tenyam finished the conversation. "This will be brought up in our next council meeting. I think it would be wise if we all sleep on what Leetayo says has transpired." He spoke for himself and Angwusi when he said, "We will retire now to consider what you have said." The two elders turned with a swish of their robes and made their way to their usual kiva.

Ruupi sent Leetayo a triumphant look, and they discreetly went their separate ways.

Moon Fire had been in contact with Wena 'Ahote several times during the next sun cycle. News traveled quickly in the community, and they knew that something critical was happening. She felt an undercurrent of dissension that she could not explain. An emergency meeting had been called to take place when next Sun Father set, and she knew it must pertain to Wena 'Ahote. Her heart went out to him due to his tenuous position as priest. She only knew she wished there might be some way she could be of assistance. She had seen him during the time of darkness, and he had spoken of his dilemma. Taatawi had told him there would be a meeting, but the sun priest would not divulge any other information. She knew how close Taatawi and Wena 'Ahote were, and she could not understand Taatawi's reservations.

Suddenly Wena 'Ahote frantically signaled her, his hand over his heart. She saw him searching for a private spot for them both to talk, and when they could find none, he beckoned her to his quarters. She moved hastily across the plaza and down the ladder.

He took her in his arms and held her fiercely. He knew he must tell her the news, but the words stuck in his throat. He almost wished that Tovosi had never returned, or at least had never found out who the traitor was.

She sensed his tension, and gently extricating herself from his embrace, she inquired, "You are greatly disturbed. Will you tell me the reason?"

He continued to hold her hands while gazing up at the hole in the roof of his quarters as if he wished he could escape what it was he must say. At last he said, "Moon Fire, my love. What I have to say will not be easy on you, but it must be said." He hesitated.

"Wena 'Ahote, in the name of Awonawilona, just tell me what you must. Don't keep me waiting. Do you want me to guess?"

"No, my sweet. Just let me hold you as I speak."

She silently moved back into his embrace. In her mind she already knew what he would say due to the visitation of Red Eagle in her dream.

"I have done what you asked me to do. I asked Tovosi to follow Palasiva, and he reported to me not long ago, telling me that it is Palasiva who is secretly meeting with the raiders. Their meeting place is in the useless lands to the northeast of us, probably because almost no one goes there, and it is unlikely that he would be caught. Oh, Moon Fire, you have no idea how it grieves my heart to tell you this. I almost wish it was me rather than your little brother, for I know how close you are to him."

Moon Fire could not fight the small sob that escaped her, but she valiantly checked herself, saying, "Red Eagle told me. I know."

Pushing her away from him and holding her shoulders in his hands, he stared at her in amazement. He breathed a small sigh of relief and said, "Then you have had some time to prepare yourself."

"That is so. That does not make it easier, but yes, that is so." She could not help but think of her parents, and how they would probably react when they learned of this turn of events. "I am also wondering who will inform our parents. I suppose it should be me." Another soft sob escaped her.

"No, my sweet, it should not be you. You and your parents are at odds because of us, and I do not think it advisable that it should be you."

"Then who?"

"It is in my mind that it should be Tovosi. He can inform your father, and your father can inform your mother. That will insure your neutrality."

Her heart ached as she thought about what he had said. It was true that her parents were disappointed in Lansa and his choice of a career, and in her as well, for she had not yet married to carry on the family line as was the role of the female in the Anasazi way. Now Palasiva had committed a most heinous crime, one that threatened the very survival of the people. She only hoped that her parents would not be completely destroyed. "You are right, and I thank you. I cannot bring this news to my parents, for they would look upon me with even more disapproval."

"There is one more thing," he said. "A meeting of the council has been called when Sun Father sets. I have asked Taatawi what it is about, but he avoids the question. Of course I must attend. I have an ominous feeling that it concerns me. I say that because Hoohu has told me that Ruupi disapproves of my becoming a priest due to the fact that I am too young, and that you are an obsession to me. I suppose he thinks that we should have married instead."

During their conversation they spontaneously sat down facing each other on his sleeping mat. In both of their minds, their problems seemed insurmountable, yet they both knew they must deal with them in the best way they knew.

"Do you suppose," she asked, "that it has always been this way? Were the problems always the same in the past?"

"As a priest, I am told that in the not-so-distant past there was a greater effort to remain unified as a people, but that may be due to the fact that our ancestors were not experiencing the prolonged drought as we are at this time. I am also told that the raiders have always been a threat, but the relations between the Mayan-Toltecs were much better than they are now. Our own grandmother, Coyote Woman, was sent as an emissary to the lands of the Mayan-Toltecs, and was successful in her efforts, at least for a couple of generations, to improve trading relations with them."

A period of quiet followed. Moon Fire moved once more into the warmth of his arms, and he felt the power she exuded as they became one spiritually. Neither one wanted to break the soothing calm of their embrace.

Feeling that she could not ask for more in a relationship, and wondering if her parents shared the same, she said, "I must go now. It is not my choice, but there is much to be done both by you and me. Know that I love you."

He voluntarily let her go, for he knew she was right. There was much to be done.

Wena 'Ahote, as usual stood on Taatawi's left with Ruupi at his right, as the members of the council meeting gradually assembled in the dry heat of the kiva. The fire burned unmercifully, sending its smoke through the hole in the ceiling where the ladder rested. The new young priest's nerves stood on edge while being even further aggravated by the negative energy that pervaded the kiva. He watched the four elders take their places on the bench at the north side of the kiva. It was believed that wisdom came from the north. Posaala, Maahu, Awta, and Iswungwa sat on the south side, because the south is the place of warmth and physical energy. The priests, of course, were on the east side due to the fact that east is the direction of rebirth and innovation. He also watched Tenyam's beady eyes dart nervously around the kiva, finally coming to rest on himself. He tensed even more. He had spoken to no one as yet about Palasiva, and dreaded the fact that he must do so. He had asked Moon Fire to try to have her brother close by in case there was a need for his presence, though he had also told her he fervently hoped that would not be necessary.

At last when all were seated, Tenyam opened the meeting. Attempting to make his average size seem taller, he strutted, and cleared his throat. "It has come to the attention of some of us that we must deal with a most hideous situation that has developed among the people. As many of you know, there is one among us, who is obviously an informer, a traitor, and one who is costing lives among the people who are moving on in search of more comfortable living conditions. Until now, there was no reason to meet, for we had no evidence as to who that person might be." He paused and beckoned toward Ruupi. "I would ask all who are in attendance to listen to Ruupi, our crystal scrier, and listen well. Ruupi?" He stepped aside, allowing his heavy eyelids to almost completely conceal his vision.

All eyes were turned toward Ruupi, who proudly stepped forward to speak. In a very low voice, he began. "Sometimes there are those among us who in all outward appearances seem devoted and humble. There are those who are not what they seem. It has come to my attention through one of my students that we may have finally identified the traitor among us. I would ask that she have permission to speak."

Tenyam responded perhaps too quickly, saying, "By all means. Are there any objections?" When no one responded, he stated, "Have an acolyte summon that student."

In no time at all Leetayo descended the ladder and took her place beside Ruupi. She stared at Wena 'Ahote haughtily, and with Ruupi's cue, began her story. "I thank you for the opportunity to speak." She told them exactly what she had told Tenyam and Angwusi, gaining confidence with each sentence she uttered. When in her last sentence she said it was Wena 'Ahote she had seen, her speech was stopped with loud exclamations from all in attendance.

Wena 'Ahote gasped in surprise at the accusations. Immediately he understood the hatred Leetayo and Ruupi had for both Moon Fire and himself, though he shuddered to think about it. He knew now how immature Leetayo really was, but he could not understand Ruupi. Here was a grown man who also hated both of them. What, he wondered, was the reason? What did the man really want? His mind worked furiously, and he knew that if he did not summon Palasiva, his own life was at stake. He decided instead to send for Tovosi, but he knew he must wait for them to ask him to speak.

When, at last, the kiva finally grew silent, Tenyam said, "In all due respect to our new young priest, we must hear from him. You have our permission to speak."

Everyone in the kiva could see that Wena 'Ahote was visibly shaken, but he stepped forward valiantly, saying, "To everyone in attendance, I must say that there has been a terrible mistake. I ask permission to send for Tovosi, a young warrior who may be able to clear any misjudgments. I believe he is not on duty, and should be easily found."

Tenyam said impatiently, "You have it."

Tovosi was escorted in by an acolyte, and seemed quite disturbed by the almost hostile energy that pervaded the kiva. He glanced at Wena 'Ahote wishing he could tell him that he had not had the chance to inform Palasiva and Moon Fire's parents as he had been asked.

Tenyam began again. "Tovosi, young warrior, Wena 'Ahote has sent for you to share with us what you know. He has been accused of being the informant to the raiders, and has asked for you to speak."

Tovosi's voice quavered as he began. "I have a friend warrior who suddenly, after many moons of good times, began to avoid me and treat me differently. I could not understand what was going on, so I asked his sister about him, and spoke of my suspicions. She only said that he had also been distant with her family, but that she was sure there must be an explanation."

Tenyam interrupted impatiently. "Come to the point. What is it you are trying to say?"

Tovosi turned to him. "If you will hear me out, you will soon know." He then realized his disrespect due to his nervousness, and apologized. Tenyam grunted, then said, "Continue."

"I have been avoiding names, but it seems an impossibility. It was Moon Fire to whom I spoke, and Wena 'Ahote who sent me to follow Palasiva. I did so and found that it was as we had hoped would not be so, but was as we had suspected. Palasiva was in contact with the raiders." He stopped abruptly to squeeze his eyes in pain, then added, "Palasiva is my friend. I cannot believe this is happening."

In truth, no one in the kiva could believe the turn of events. Again there were loud protests and cries of frustration. Many thought that everything was out of balance. What was happening was surely displeasing to the gods, and many were sure that such negativities would only prolong the drought. They all knew something must be done, and quickly.

Tenyam broke the commotion. "My fellow elders, priests, and respected representatives. It seems that our only recourse is to summon Palasiva, but I suggest that his family also be present, for they may be able to offer verification that others could not. I feel somewhat certain that our own priest and crystal scrier would not lie, but since there is now a shadow of doubt, let them be summoned."

The kiva was filled with a deathly silence as they awaited the appearance of Palasiva's family. Everyone knew that when the traitor was identified, he would be put to death, and that few exceptions had ever been made. The love in the community for

Moon Fire and her family was little short of devotion. None could imagine that her younger brother could be guilty. To everyone, Moon Fire was a wise counselor, her brother, Lansa, a respected trader, and her father, a devoted teacher of masonry. They all saw Tupkya, her mother, as a devoted mother and a valuable asset to the community.

In silence they descended the ladder, all but Lansa, who was away of course. All but Moon Fire were visibly shaken. Wena 'Ahote beckoned to them, and they moved to his side. Palasiva averted his eyes from everyone in shame. Tupkya's brown eyes were full of fear and awe, for this was the first time she had ever been in attendance in a council meeting. Sikyawa maintained a stony expression that was impossible to read, for such was the way of Anasazi. Moon Fire, of course, remained calm, for she knew that she and her family would not have been summoned unless something unforeseen had happened, but she could not understand the presence of her cousin, Leetayo.

Tenyam began. "As you know, the present circumstances are most unusual. There are two conflicting stories we are told. One is, of course, correct, and one is not. I would have Leetayo, Ruupi's student, speak of what she claims to be true." He resumed his position on the bench with the other elders.

Leetayo stepped forward to speak with a sultry sway of her hips. She reiterated her accusations and what she had seen. She seemed to glow with delight as she watched the amazed expressions on Moon Fire's family's faces. She felt very confident that she had finally destroyed Moon Fire and Wena 'Ahote in the eyes of the people. A feeling of deep satisfaction filled her being.

When Leetayo had repeated her story, Tenyam called upon Tovosi. Tovosi sent a beseeching look at Palasiva, who simply lowered his eyes in response, for he knew what his friend would say. Tovosi told his story once more, then ended by saying, "This is not the way I ever expected it to be. I value my friendship with Palasiva, and I cannot begin to express the agony that fills my heart." Tovosi still held a feeble hope that what he had reported was somehow easily explained, and that his friend could not possibly be a traitor. He only knew that it was not Wena 'Ahote he had seen, but then he thought that there might be a chance that they were both involved. What would become of Moon Fire's credibility if that were so?

Tenyam turned to Palasiva. "Palasiva, it is time for you to speak." At this time, even he was beginning to think that perhaps both Wena 'Ahote and Palasiva were traitors. Everyone knew that Moon Fire was Wena 'Ahote's obsession, and Palasiva was her favorite brother. He also thought that the world was terribly out of balance.

Palasiva stepped forward on legs that he thought might not support him, so great was his trembling. He glanced at his mother, father, and sister, and suddenly knew what he must do. The road of life had become very clear. "Elders, revered priests, and to all who honor us with their attendance, I must confess. Circumstances presented themselves that were unavoidable. To clear our revered priest, Wena 'Ahote, and my sister's name, I want you to know that Tovosi's story is the one you should believe. I, and I alone, am the traitor. I cannot divulge any reasons for my behavior for they are too complex." He moved another step forward, extending his hands in supplication. "Do with me what you must do. I am glad to be rid of this problem."

Tupkya wailed and clawed at Sikyawa. Moans and gasps came from everyone in attendance, including Wena 'Ahote and Moon Fire. Even though Moon Fire had known of his guilt, she was proud of the valiant bravery her brother had displayed. She was concerned for her mother, for Tupkya was plainly hysterical, so much so that she even attacked Sikyawa, who had always supported her. Taatawi took her mother by the arm and with Sikyawa following behind, led her to the ladder and out of the kiva.

Much time passed before Tenyam could pull everyone together to go on with the meeting. He cleared his throat loudly several times before anyone took notice. Finally he said, "It is my suggestion that we adjourn the meeting to consider all that has passed. When next Sun Father has completed his journey we will meet again to decide what must be done."

Hoohu rose quickly from the bench. "I am in complete agreement, but it would seem to me that we should place

Ruupi, Leetayo, and Palasiva in confinement until the time of the next meeting."

A brief silence was ended when Angwusi said, "My heart is heavy, but I am in agreement. It would not do for any of the three to suddenly disappear. I say let them be confined, and yes, we need time to sort out all that has happened."

"If there is no objection, then so be it," declared Tenyam.

The meeting was over. Moon Fire caught Wena 'Ahote's eyes, and held them lovingly with her own. Her heart rejoiced in that Wena 'Ahote had been innocent, but was broken at the loss of her brother. Everyone knew that the penalty would be death.

She spent only a very short time with Wena 'Ahote after the meeting. Though she felt relief that he was no longer the accused, she knew that she would undoubtedly have trouble with her parents. So it was that she crept on silent feet down the ladder into her parents' quarters. Her eyes burned with the tears she had shed when she thought no one was looking. She felt her grip on the road of life was now more tenacious than Wena 'Ahote's, and dreaded the encounter with her parents. Now, as she descended the ladder, she tried to brush away any evidence that she might have been disturbed, and made her way to her sleeping mat, hoping that no one would notice her.

She had barely lain down when she heard her mother weeping. Sikyawa was holding her in his arms in an effort to soothe her. Moon Fire was not even sure that Tupkya knew she was nearby, for she heard her mother say, "My children are dead. Oh, Sikyawa, my children are dead. What are we to do?"

"Tupkya, our children are not dead. How can you say that?"

"Because it is so. Lansa has pursued a road of life that is little better than a thief, and he mistreats Sihu who expects his child. Moon Fire does not want an honorable marriage to carry on the family name, and now, Palasiva. Oh, my husband, what are we to do?"

"Tupkya, my mind tells me that there is not much we can do. Of our three children, it seems to me that we can only try to speak to Moon Fire, and try to discourage her in her relationship with Wena 'Ahote."

"Then that is as it shall be, my husband. At least we might convince her that she should marry and carry on the family name. Now I am exhausted, and shall try to get some sleep." She fell much more heavily into his arms, and closed her eyes, immediately falling into a deep sleep.

Sikyawa lay awake for some time, trying to decide where they had gone wrong as parents. Yet a part of him thought as he looked back on his own youth, that perhaps it was truly the right of everyone, even the young, to make their own choices. With those muddling thoughts, he also drifted into sleep.

Moon Fire had heard their discourse, and felt like a trapped animal. She had heard her parents' dialogue which warned her that she was the only one left, and that they would make a concerted effort to disrupt her happiness. In the emotional state she was in, she thanked Awonawilona that her parents did not realize she was there, and she, too, drifted off into a restless sleep.

CHAPTER 12

A.D. *1133*

Tenyam called the meeting to order when next Sun Father set. All who were in attendance during the former sun cycle were in attendance now, including Leetayo, Ruupi, and Palasiva and his family. A strange combination of sorrow and hostility pervaded the kiva. Everyone was certain that Palasiva's fate would be death in a most horrifying manner, but what of Ruupi and Leetayo? They had caused no deaths among the people, but they had, in effect, tried to bring about Wena 'Ahote's death. Hoohu was one of the more sensitive persons in attendance who knew the world was terribly out of balance. He wondered how many others felt the same.

Moon Fire had slept very little and was wondering if she would be able to handle the fact that Palasiva would surely be put to death. She knew her parents could not, but would she be strong enough?

Wena 'Ahote also looked her way with great concern, for she did not seem to be handling things well. There were circles under her eyes, and she did not exude the stability that was usually her trademark. He had an urgent desire to take her in his arms to shelter her from the outcome of the meeting. Her parents looked even worse. Tupkya's eyes were swollen and red, and Sikyawa's were glazed with pain. He watched Moon Fire as she looked at her mother and reached for her with a trembling hand. The pain he was feeling for her as well as her family was acute, and he was not sure even he could bear it.

"Having had a full sun cycle to confer and discuss the issues at hand, we elders have decided that those who were confined should be questioned individually." Tenyam stroked his chin thoughtfully as he spoke. "We would ask Sikyawa, Tupkya, and Moon Fire to leave. Ruupi and Leetayo will return to confinement until it is their turn for questioning. We will send for you and your family, Sikyawa, when the questioning is completed."

Moon Fire could not hide the disappointment on her face, for she had desperately wanted to learn why Palasiva would have done such a thing. She guessed that she would have to learn the details from Wena 'Ahote at a later time. She also thought her parents deserved to know, but it occurred to her that perhaps the elders thought Palasiva might say nothing with his family present. She followed Sikyawa and Tupkya up the ladder, but did not return home with them. Instead she sat quietly near the opening at the top of the kiva, but far enough away that she could not hear what was being said below.

Palasiva visibly trembled as all eyes turned to him. He kept his eyes downcast, hoping that by doing so, his fear would not show. He knew that Tenyam would be his inquisitor. Tenyam, whose mind was usually already made up and did not want to be confused with the facts, would undoubtedly be harsh. Palasiva uttered a little prayer to Awonawilona that such might not be the case.

Tenyam coughed and cleared his throat, then said at last, "Palasiva, you are the youngest and quietest in Sikyawa's family. None of us would have thought that you, of all people, could commit such a heinous crime. We feel, in all fairness, that you should be allowed to speak on your own behalf, and we hope you will use the opportunity well."

Palasiva made no response.

Tenyam found himself growing impatient and tried to fight the urge to shake the young warrior in an effort to make him wake up. "Palasiva," he said gruffly, "if you say nothing, your sentence will be the worse for you."

For a short time, Palasiva still did not respond, but continued to hang his head. Then, as if having second thoughts, he murmured, "What is it you would like to know?"

Tenyam began by sternly asking, "How is it that you know the raiders?"

"I was captured by them while my friend, Kopolvu, was killed. We both had been assigned to guard the Great North Road."

"Who is the leader of the raiders with whom you were acquainted?"

"Their leader is Teo. He . . ."

"He what, Palasiva?"

"He, he . . ." Palasiva squared his shoulders and looked Tenyam straight in the eye. "He has an agreement with the Mayan-Toltecs. He provides the captives that they want for sacrifice, and they provide food and wealth to the raiders. They threatened to kill me if I did not cooperate. I was surprised when they let me go."

"I, too, am surprised that they did not kill you, and that they would let you go. It is in my mind, however, that you could have made your promise to them and not fulfilled it. You could have informed us, and we would have protected you and the others to the best of our ability. Is that not so?"

"That is so," Palasiva answered.

"Then why, Palasiva? Why did you not do that?"

Again the young warrior murmured, "There was more."

"More?"

"Yes, more. They threatened my sister, Moon Fire. They know she is out and about speaking with the animals, and they . . . Well, now you know."

Affirmations of understanding resounded from everyone in the kiva. Wena 'Ahote's heart was overwhelmed with the realization of the great love that Palasiva had for his sister. He only hoped that the elders would see that Palasiva had been forced into his actions. Surely their love for Moon Fire and her counseling would have some influence on what they decided the young man's fate would be.

Tenyam eyed the young warrior shrewdly. "It seems that you had little choice in what you did?"

"I knew not what else to do " Palasiva said sadly. "I could not allow them to harm my sister."

With a heavy sigh, Tenyam said, "Are there any questions from any of my fellow elders?"

Angwusi rose. "Palasiva, it is in my mind that if you had informed us, we could have asked Moon Fire to temporarily refrain from her communication with our 'brothers.' Did you not think of that?"

"I did, but I know how much she helps our people with her counseling, and I felt I could not interfere with her gift. It is all she has."

Many turned their eyes to Wena 'Ahote. Angwusi said softly, "No, young man, that is not all she has." He resumed his seat on the bench.

Tenyam waited to see if there would be any others who might question, but when there was no response, he said, "Palasiva, you are to return to confinement so that we may question Ruupi and Leetayo."

Palasiva rose without hesitation, for he just wanted to put everything behind him even if his escape must be to meet his maker, Awonawilona.

Leetayo climbed down the ladder. Her heart pounded in fear for in her mind she had resolved to say nothing, and she had no idea what punishment she would receive. She only knew that she would not be able to withstand physical punishment. Her fascination with Ruupi, and of course his position as priest, bound her to him, not out of love, but out of status and what she could gain from him. She stood among them and waited.

Tenyam took the floor as usual. He took the time to truly look at her, and she knew he was coming to his own conclusions as to what she was about. She tried valiantly to conceal her nervousness, but found she was totally unsuccessful. At last he said, "Leetayo, what would you like to tell us?" When she did not respond, he added in a deep, threatening voice, "What you have done is inexcusable. You must know that."

Still she did not respond, for she knew he was right.

"Leetayo, you are but a student. Do you not know that making an attempt to destroy another is no different from witch-craft, and witchcraft is punishable by death? You have commit-ted a terrible crime that could have cost another person his life. Speak to us, child, or your future is already determined." Tenyam felt it was not necessary to say more.

Leetayo was frightened, truly frightened, and wished things might have turned out as Ruupi had predicted. She shuddered when she realized that she must go against Ruupi, but still she hesitated.

Tenyam said with much frustration, "Girl, if you do not speak, we must assume . . ."

She could not contain herself any longer. She wondered if her confession would make a difference in her punishment, and so she began. "What is it you would like to know?"

Tenyam said assertively that all in attendance wanted to know what exactly had caused the untruths, and that if she did not speak of what really happened, she could expect the worst punishment.

Leetayo saw herself being dismembered, and quietly bowed her head. "I hate my cousin, Moon Fire. She is all that I would like to be. She is in love with Wena 'Ahote, who I admire from a distance, but cannot reach." She paused in an attempt to gather her thoughts.

"And what was your motive then, for doing what you did? You acted as an accomplice to Ruupi. Why would you do such a thing? What are his motives?" Tenyam straightened his robe and scratched his head.

"He thought," she said softly, "that we could undermine Wena 'Ahote's position as a new priest to benefit Ruupi's posi-tion in the future, and at the same time separate Wena 'Ahote from Moon Fire for my benefit. Also Ruupi already objects to Wena 'Ahote's position due to his youth and devotion to Moon Fire. I know nothing else. I only did as he commanded for I was only his student."

Hoohu stood to bring the attention to himself. In his usual authoritative, stern manner of speaking, he asked, "Who is Ruupi to you? I am sorry, but I must be blunt. Is he your lover?"

Leetayo felt her entire body quaking. She asked, "Does it matter?"

"No, it does not, for you have already answered my question." He resumed his position on the bench.

Once again the silence was deafening, until Tenyam stood and said, "Leetayo, you are dismissed. You will return to confinement."

She obediently rose and climbed the ladder, wondering what terrible punishments her confessions might bring.

Ruupi had been summoned and stood obediently awaiting his questioning. He felt certain that since they had kept him waiting for so long, they must have already questioned Palasiva or Leetayo, or both, and he knew he must be careful in his responses. He also felt confident that two young people, no matter what they said, could never outwit him. Leetayo had given her promise that she would say nothing. He had assured her that if she cooperated with him, the elders might even be convinced that Wena 'Ahote and Palasiva might be working together. To his surprise it was not Tenyam, but Hoohu, who began his interrogation.

"Ruupi, devoted priest, Ruupi, who works for the good of the people and not for the destruction of the people, why did you so unjustly try to implicate Wena 'Ahote as traitor to his people?" Hoohu had asked Tenyam if he might be chief interrogator, for he had no love for Ruupi. In his mind Ruupi had always seemed sneaky and sly, yet, until now, he had never had any concrete reason to believe that it was so.

Ruupi responded slowly and deliberately after giving Wena 'Ahote a hostile stare. "In all due respect, everyone, I felt and still feel that Wena 'Ahote is too young for a position in the priesthood."

"That is strange, for Taatawi, our sun priest, does not think so."

"I know that our revered sun priest thinks of him as his protégé, but I ask you, as I ask myself, if such a young one has the wisdom?" He almost choked as he mentioned Taatawi, the revered sun priest.

"I seem to recall in our oral history that there have been

many priests and priestesses who have been much younger than Wena 'Ahote at the time of their induction. I might mention our legendary Coyote Woman, who was but fifteen sun cycles of age, but very gifted, and an exceptional woman for one so young." Hoohu found himself fighting the impatience that threatened to overwhelm him.

Ruupi knew it would be wise to discontinue any further conversation on the issue of Wena 'Ahote's youth. He folded his arms and waited.

Gathering his countenance, Hoohu continued. "I speak for all of us when I say that your reason for your actions is small, silly, and shallow. Are there any other reasons?"

"Yes, there is another. A priest's duty is to his people. Our young Wena 'Ahote is so besotted by his lover, Moon Fire, that he neglects his duties."

"Neglects his duties? It seems you are the only one who thinks so. None of the people have had anything but good to say about him. Come, there must be more of which you could speak."

In a final effort, Ruupi declared, "A priest cannot wholly fulfill his or her duties when they are so distracted with a love affair."

Hoohu was valiantly trying to control his temper. "Oh yes," he said, "such answers are an insult to all our intelligences. Many of our priests have and have had lovers. They thus become more complete, and do not have to fight the frustrations of celibacy. If that is what you are advocating, why then do you have a lover?"

Ruupi suddenly knew that Leetayo had not kept her promise. He wished he knew how much she had divulged, and knew that the very principles on which he stood had been destroyed. He sent a hostile, angry glance to everyone in attendance, which culminated with a particularly evil one to Wena 'Ahote. He folded his hands over his chest, and decided to say no more.

Hoohu knew that he had delivered a killing blow, but went on to say, "We know now exactly what happened, when it happened, where it happened, how it happened, but we still do not really know why. Your answers are weak, Ruupi. There is more to the story than you are telling us. Do you wish to add anything more?"

"There is no more. Do with me as you will."

Hoohu turned to those in attendance and asked as was customary, "Does anyone else have a question?"

When there was no response, Hoohu threw up his hands in disgust. "Why are we plagued with such ridiculous problems, when our very real problems are starvation and the welfare of the people? We are losing people from our community, and it seems that there are those among us who are actually working to add to our problems, rather than help. I am sorry. I have said enough." With those final words, it was obvious that he had turned the meeting over to Tenyam.

Tenyam was visibly shaken at what had transpired. He had little to say except to tell Ruupi to return to confinement. The interrogation was over.

Decisions were finally made, and Ruupi, Leetayo, Palasiva, and his family were brought back into the kiva. The tension was so thick that it seemed possible to slice it with a dagger. Expressions on the faces of all four of the elders were drawn and haggard, betraying their dread of what they inevitably had decided must be done.

Palasiva kept his eyes downcast, but inwardly he knew that he was as good as dead. He had cost the lives of some of his people, which was unforgivable. He did not dare to steal even a short glance toward Moon Fire or his parents, for his shame very nearly overwhelmed him.

Moon Fire kept looking from her beloved brother to Wena 'Ahote. Though she never made eye contact with Palasiva, Wena 'Ahote seemed to be sending her strong messages of love and support. In her heart, Moon Fire also knew that her little brother was as good as dead, and she dreaded the reaction and interaction with her parents when it was over. It was very obvious that Tupkya was on the edge of hysteria.

Tenyam, of course, began by saying, "We elders and officials in attendance have reached a decision, but not without pain. I would ask Leetayo to step forward first."

Leetayo also looked almost fanatical, but she lowered her eyes, and obediently did as she was told.

"Leetayo," he said, "you are young, but old enough to know that you were an accomplice in an attempt that might have destroyed an innocent life. It is our decision that you will be banished from the holy school for two season cycles. If you wish to return when the two season cycles are over, you may do so, but think well on what you have done during that time. You have but one sun cycle to pack what you wish and leave our community." He allowed a deep sigh to escape him, which indicated his reluctance to go further. At last he said, "Ruupi, step forward."

Ruupi did so while exuding much more confidence than he really felt. He wished the elders had chosen to interrogate him first instead of Palasiva and Leetayo, for he felt certain the outcome would have been different. If they had interrogated him first, he could have paved the way for Leetayo, making it easy for her to keep her promise to say nothing. Then it would have seemed that both Palasiva and Wena 'Ahote were in collaboration, and everything would have worked out perfectly.

Tenyam interrupted his thoughts, saying, "Ruupi, our once-revered priest, your first duty is to work for the good of the people. Wena 'Ahote is one of the people just as we all are. Were you working for the good of the people when you worked to put the blame on someone that might have cost him his life? We think not." He paused to clear his throat. "It is our unanimous decision that we trade you." He paused to watch Ruupi's response, which was one of stark fear. He chuckled when he thought that perhaps Ruupi was fearful that they might trade him to the Mayan-Toltecs or to the raiders, and so he played with him for a short amount of time. At last he continued. "You will go to the outlier north of us on the great river for two season cycles. You may return at that time if the priest who comes to us during that time wishes to return to the same outlier. If he does not, well, so be it. In those two season cycles, think well on what you have done. You also have one sun cycle to leave our community."

Ruupi's chin dropped in amazement, but he quickly cast his eyes to the floor of the kiva.

Again Tenyam paused. Even in his "hard wood" heart, he felt sorry that Palasiva had been placed in such a situation that he felt it necessary to betray his people. He wondered what he would have done if, in his youth, if he had been placed under the same circumstances. His voice, which normally boomed, softened as he spoke. "Palasiva, you did not make it easy for us to come to a decision, but we have done so. Though we know that your life, and the life of your sister was threatened, you did cost the lives of several of our people, and maybe more."

Moon Fire audibly gasped as she grappled with what Tenyam had said. So Palasiva had been defending her as well as himself. Her heart seemed to be bleeding big drops of love for him as she listened further.

"The traditional punishment for a traitor is death by dismembering, but in your case, and since there was no hostility toward the people on your part, it is our decision to banish you. You also have one sun cycle to depart. May Awonawilona go with you to protect you."

Tenyam's speech was broken by a piercing wail. Tupkya crumbled to the floor, scratching her arms and drawing blood with her fingernails. Sikyawa promptly lifted her and helped her up the ladder, for he knew he must watch her carefully to keep her from truly harming herself. Tears spilled unbidden from Moon Fire's eyes until she could not see anyone in the kiva. Then whimpering silently, she slowly climbed the ladder, her destination unknown.

"The meeting is adjourned, and I might say, I hope there will never be any others like it."

Palasiva left before any others. He knew he was as good as dead.

Moon Fire reluctantly returned to her parents' quarters. Her insides felt knotted with apprehension mixed with concern for her hysterical mother. She was sure that Tupkya would be uncontrollable in her grief, and a part of her wanted to steer clear, yet another wanted desperately to offer support. Such were her feelings as she quietly descended the ladder.

She found Sikyawa lying next to Tupkya on their sleeping mat. He was on his side with his body molded to her mother's body, running his fingers through her hacked off hair in an effort to soothe her. It was customary for women to cut their hair short, sometimes even to the scalp, if there was a death in the family, and Tupkya had done a mediocre job, probably because Sikyawa had sustained her to some degree. Tupkya had ceased her wailing, and was now only moaning. Moon Fire could not help but wonder what her father was made of, for he remained the rock, never letting on how deeply he might feel.

While trying to reach her own sleeping mat without being noticed, she stumbled over a pot that Tupkya had carelessly left in an inappropriate position. Her clumsiness aroused both of her parents, much to her chagrin. Both of them sat up instantly.

The fire that burned low cast shadows and eerie reflections everywhere. Suddenly Tupkya burst into loud wailing once more. It seemed that the sight of her own daughter was more than she could handle. Glaring at Moon Fire through her hysteria, she shrieked, "So you are so infatuated with that priest that you could not come home where you belong to comfort your own parents. What is wrong with you? *What is wrong with you?* There is not a tender feeling in your person. I wish it was you, not he . . ."

Sikyawa put his hand over her mouth to silence her, for he knew she had gone too far. He himself was careful not to place his fingers in a position where she might be able to bite him, for he knew she was not in control of herself. He cast his daughter an angry, distraught expression, and pulled Tupkya down on the mat once more. It was clear to Moon Fire that her father supported her mother.

Moon Fire was devastated. She only hoped Palasiva would come for his belongings while their parents slept, yet she knew that even if he did, he, too, would be subjugated to his mother's wrath. She decided to overlook her mother's irrationality once more, and crawled under her blankets to try to block out the world.

Palasiva, meanwhile, had decided that since he was as good as dead, he had no need for material things. Therefore he did not return to his parents' quarters. His feelings were so numb that he wished he was already dead, and if he wasn't, perhaps this was the way one felt when dead. He thought of his friend, Kopolvu, and wished that his death would be as swift as his friend's. He wandered aimlessly into the darkness of night with nothing to ward off the sinister cold, for in truth, he did not care. He was not feeling. He heard the coyotes howl at the moon, with an occasional hooting of an owl as it searched out its prey by night. The moon cast shadows that played tricks with his eyesight, and the stars were brilliant. His sandals walked, but he knew not where, for he truly felt he was already dead. He spent the time of darkness reclining as best he could against a smooth rock.

Dawn was just breaking when he heard a bird call. He waited, and then the same bird call came from another direction. He was so dispirited that he gave it no thought until suddenly, a raider appeared holding his atlatl ready to strike. Even then he did not care, for he knew he was already a dead man. Something, or someone seemed to prevent the raider from closing in on his prey.

"Stop! He is one of us," declared a familiar voice. "This is our informer."

Palasiva's guts were wrenched in guilt. He thought he might lose what little was left in his stomach, and he did not even care. Here were the people who had ruined his life, and they were saying he was one of them? How could they possibly think he was one of them? It was with this new twist of events that he suddenly had thoughts of a direction and new possibilities. What if he asked if he could join them. At least it might offer survival. If they turned him down, it did not matter. He was already a dead man, and he knew he probably would not survive the cold season alone.

When he did not respond, Teo approached him confidently. "Well, what have you to tell us?"

Palasiva made no response. Teo was visibly shaken, saying, "What is wrong with you, young one? Are you saying you are here and have nothing to tell us?" It was obvious that he was losing his patience.

Palasiva decided to be straightforward. "Teo, I have been found out. Someone followed me. I am a dead man."

Teo stared at him with pity. "You were careless. You are young and maybe stupid. Why did you not cover your tracks?"

"I did, but one of my warrior friends began to suspect. Then my sister had a dream. That is all I can tell you," he answered despondently. "I guess I am a dead man."

Teo shook his head and asked, "Do you want to die?"

"No, of course not, but I cannot survive the cold season without my people."

"You could live as we do. It is not always comfortable, but we survive," Teo suggested.

Now Palasiva was completely baffled. He wondered if Teo actually had a heart. He had thought Teo would walk away, or even just finish him off. Yet, here was an opportunity. Perhaps he was only partially dead. Plucking up his courage, he asked, "Are you suggesting that I become one of your people?"

Teo squinted his eyes due to the glare of Sun Father. "If you wish. You will find it a hard life compared to what you are used to, but it is survival. If what you say is true, what do you have to lose?"

Palasiva was slow to respond for he was faced with a great decision. A part of him wanted to die and a part of him wanted to live. It was a struggle to determine which was stronger. Suddenly his survival instinct overruled his death wish, and he answered, "I will try to live your way, but I cannot yet thank you, for I truly wanted to die."

At a later time and in retrospect, Palasiva would be thankful to Awonawilona that his survival instincts had been stronger than his death wish.

The small war party with Palasiva accompanying them made their way in a northwesterly direction. Much of what Palasiva was seeing was new to him, and in many ways strikingly beautiful. The raiders seemed to know exactly where any outliers might be, and took great care to go around them. Palasiva found that they did not have to travel far before the terrain would become different, sometimes in stark contrast. As a young Anasazi warrior, who spent his time traditionally defending his people, he had not had any opportunity to see much more than one could travel in a sun cycle beyond his own canyon community.

They traveled through rugged mountains with piñon pines and juniper at the lower altitude, and tall pines as they climbed higher. Rock formations jutted here and there, some that closely resembled animals and birds. Water was not plentiful until they came to a sizable river that cut its way through the rocks and mountains. Here, because of the availability of water, game was still plentiful. They dined at last on something larger than desert rabbits when Teo brought down a four-point buck. Palasiva thought he had never tasted anything so good.

At last they came to an area where the ground leveled out with a line of cottonwoods in the distance. From afar Palasiva saw perhaps fifty lodges made of what he supposed were hides that had been placed in parallel lines in close proximity to each other. As they drew closer, he saw that one lodge of red painted buffalo skins was much larger than the rest, and was tattooed with mystic totems that he supposed might be those of the chief or the medicine men. Upon closer scrutiny, he saw that from the center lodge, two medicine men, attired in the skins of wolves and bears, and bearing long peeled wands of wood in their hands, occasionally emerged to attend a small fire. He also saw that before each lodge was a tripod of spears supporting the arms and shields of the people, and on some of them smoke-dried scalps rattled in the wind. Palasiva shuddered to think that one of them might be Anasazi.

Both men and women decorated their bodies and clothing with paints. He saw that the people wore mostly tanned skin clothing, for their only means of attaining cotton was in trade. Some of the women wore red earth for rouge while others had painted their faces with red clay mixed with animal fat to protect their skin from the sun and wind. The men were tattooed on the forehead with an oval design, a cross, or a semicircle, while many of the women had a circle on the forehead, a semicircle over each eyebrow, and horizontal lines across their cheeks. The women's hair was parted in the middle and worn loose, while the men's was also parted the same way, but drawn into two thick braids that lay on each shoulder. A few had wrapped their braids with skins in which they attached feathers or shells. Palasiva's fascination was suddenly replaced with the acute observation of the many differences between his own people and this strange new group of people.

From the largest lodge a short robust figure emerged who was obviously not one of the medicine men, but one of high status. He wore an enormous cape made of buffalo hide with only a breechcloth beneath. His eyes were piercing, his nose wide and flattened, and his mouth was unusually wide. Around his neck was a shell choker necklace spaced intermittently with small turquoise beads, and his waist-length braids were completely crisscrossed with thin leather strips through which were inserted two eagle feathers.

The warrior at last stood before him. With his right hand he gripped Teo's shoulder in what almost looked like an affectionate grin. "My son, I rejoice that you have returned. You have brought us another slave?"

"No, Father, I have not." Teo went on to explain everything to his father, then added that Palasiva wished to become one of them.

Palasiva understood only bits and pieces of their language, but he knew that Teo must be telling this man, who must be the chief, all about him. He found himself becoming very nervous at the thought that this man might reject him or perhaps even have him killed. Somehow his death wish was not as strong as it had been.

At last the chief disappeared into his lodge. Teo excused his warriors, and turned to Palasiva. Using sign language and words, he explained, "That man is my father, and the chief of this tribe. His name is Ochata. He thought I had brought you as a captive and a slave. When I explained your story, he very reluctantly said you could stay, but only if you hunted and supported yourself. We have no lodge to offer you. You will have to provide your own lodge by hunting, and you will stay a short distance outside the camp, not among us. It is in my mind that if you prove that you are a contribution to our people, perhaps conditions will change. For now, I will provide you with a blanket and skin under which you can sleep, and water to last you a sun cycle or two. Beyond that, I can do no more."

Palasiva thanked Teo, then Awonawilona, that at least he might survive.

Tupkya had given Moon Fire so much grief that she found herself wishing she could speak to her father alone. At least he seemed to know when her mother had gone too far, and he appeared to be much more in control of himself. It was with these thoughts that she descended the ladder. She had finished her counseling for this sun cycle, and was looking for a reprieve.

Tupkya sent her a hostile look, and began. "Palasiva did not even return for his belongings. My dead son did not even return to say good-bye. It's your fault! Your gift has endeared you to the community, yet, even with this gift, you could not even counsel your brother. What is wrong with you? You are so strange!"

She watched Sikyawa seize her mother to try to restrain her, but it was obvious that Tupkya was irrational with grief. Quietly she said, "Mother, I cannot counsel those who do not ask."

Tupkya wrenched herself from Sikyawa's grasp, and hissed, "You can do anything you want to. You could have saved Palasiva! You are nothing more than dog dung! You would split this family apart because of your so-called gift. Lansa is gone, and now Palasiva is dead! My daughter, who should be carrying on the family name, is also gone, and even makes no attempt to help her brothers when they need it. You are vile! *Vile!*" She collapsed in Sikyawa's arms.

"You are irrational, Tupkya," Sikyawa said quietly. "You need sleep."

"I am not irrational!" she screamed. "I do not wish to have a daughter any longer!"

"Well, I do! Now I have had enough! Cease your useless insults, woman!" He guided her to their sleeping mat, but she was so distraught she would not lie down. She continued to glare at Moon Fire as though her own daughter were a stranger.

Moon Fire's heart had broken into more pieces than she could count, but she knew what she must do. She packed her few belongings, and left.

With what little she possessed, she made her way to Sihu. She knew Lansa was away, and perhaps she could stay with her for at least a little while.

Sihu was overjoyed. "Oh yes," she said. "Lansa is never here, and I cannot think of anyone else's company I could enjoy more."

With those encouraging words, Moon Fire relaxed a little and put down her burdens. She found that Sihu asked few questions, for she already had been informed by others in the community of Palasiva's dilemma, and understood her friend's situation with her parents well enough that she remained quiet.

Sihu made Moon Fire comfortable, and went about her daily chores methodically. The child within her was growing, and she seemed to be in perfect health, as though she was truly meant to have children.

Moon Fire felt both joy and envy for her friend. She wished she could have the experience of motherhood, yet another part of her did not want it unless everything was just right, and she could not imagine bringing a child into such a world of suffering. Pushing these thoughts from her mind, she set out to find Wena 'Ahote. She found him, at last, and signaled him with her hand over her heart.

He walked by her saying, "Tonight, my love."

She thought Sun Father would never set. Her stomach fluttered as she at last descended the ladder into his quarters. He was the only person she had for her family life and most of her world seemed to be shattered. She fell into his arms.

He held her close, moving his hand firmly up and down her spine in an effort to relax her. He buried his face in her hair, inhaling its pungent sage perfume that was so typically her. If there had been any way to alleviate her pain, or to take some and share it, he would have been more than willing.

At last she looked up at him with a tearstained face. "I need a place to live," she whispered. "I cannot live with Sihu long, for Lansa will return, and . . ."

"Yes, I know, little love. I am sure there are accommodations available, for many have left the community. You may not be accommodated in the holy school, but certainly it will be close by. I will do what I can when next Sun Father rises."

She clung to him as he led her to his mats. With a cool cloth he wiped away her tears, eased away any further tension with a back massage, and then with a tenderness he did not know he had, he made love to her.

CHAPTER 13

Moon Fire had been living in her own quarters for two sea-son cycles. Fortunately for her, Wena 'Ahote had found quarters for her in the holy school, but on the opposite side from her parents. He did not want her far from his side, and had searched diligently for a place in which she could be in close proximity. She seldom saw her parents, and when she did, they ignored her. During the first season cycle, she thought she would never heal, but with Wena 'Ahote's undying love, she gradually accepted the inevitable, and the inevitable was that her parents had disowned her. As time passed she watched Tup-kya and Sikyawa gain many more facial lines along with much graying of the hair. Their vitality was gone, to be replaced with a slowing of their motions, and almost never a smile. Of course, she thought perhaps they might only appear this way to her, but when she asked Wena 'Ahote, he confirmed that everyone saw them that way. Lansa was seldom at home, and she had re-newed her close friendship with Sihu, who had only recently delivered another child. She and Lansa now had two beautiful boys who were eighteen moon cycles apart in age. No one knew if Palasiva was alive or dead, and as was the custom, no one spoke his name, for they assumed he had crossed over to join the ancestors. Awonawilona had still not seen fit to send them any amount of rain, and the people were suffering more and more. Even in the season of growing, which was usually their rainy season, there had been little rain. It seemed to Moon Fire that there was not a single overweight person in the area.

Most were gaunt and drawn, and some even appeared emaciated. More and more people were leaving the community with little more than they could carry on their backs. The traditional winter ceremonials had lost enthusiasm, for Awonawilona seemed not to listen. There was little to do but to wonder why the gods had obviously forsaken the people.

Her love for Wena 'Ahote had grown immeasurably, and she knew she would never love another as she did him. Even though she was now nineteen season cycles of age, she still felt no different than when she had experienced her first menses. She worried about Sihu and her two boys, for Lansa was never there to hunt, and she knew Sihu depended on Sikyawa, or whoever else might share their rare small bounty with her. She was so lost in these thoughts that she was surprised when she suddenly looked up to see Wena 'Ahote standing at the bottom of her ladder.

"I was unsure if I should interrupt your privacy, but I thought you would want to know of the latest developments within one of the outliers," he said. His face was etched with lines of worry.

Moon Fire was quick to notice his concern, and invited him to join her on her mat. Time had passed and she had gotten used to the feeling of being entirely on her own, and having no contact with her parents. In fact, she rather liked the peace, solitude, and privacy that she had acquired. "What is it that has you so concerned?" she inquired.

He kissed her lightly on the lips, then went on to say, "Runners have reported that there is cannibalism in one of our outliers far to the north."

"Have there not been other reports in the past?"

"Yes, of course, but this one is the most abominable. It seems that as many as six hands of people have been sacrificed and ritually eaten. Truly, my love, this is the ugliest. Our world is out of balance, and Awonawilona is no longer with us." He shook his head and clutched her hand.

"You must know, my love, why things are as they are. The people are hungry. There is little game to be found, and they . . ."

"No, that is not the case. They are not that hungry, at least not as hungry as many other outliers are, and even ourselves, for there is a river in close proximity. They have water, far more water than we have. The problem is once again the Mayan-Toltecs. It is the general belief of the elders and others that the Mayan-Toltec faction of immigrants are using the drought as a way to convince our people that Awonawilona has forsaken us, and that their gods are going to provide the answer."

"But our people are weak if they believe such nonsense," she exclaimed. "Wouldn't it be better to just move to a more fertile location as many of our people are doing?"

Wena 'Ahote pulled her closer to him and ran his fingers lovingly through her hair. "Moon Fire, you surely must know that people who are established, and who have grown to love the land of their ancestors, are reluctant to move. Even we, here in this community, are desperately trying to hold on to what we have. Need I say more?"

"No, I suppose you are right, but somehow I sense that there is more you wish to tell me."

"If I did not know better, I would call you 'pawaka.' How do you read people as you do?"

"I could not begin to answer that. Perhaps it is the gift that I sometimes wish I did not have, or it may be that I just let my mind flow. I don't know."

"And that is just one of the reasons I love you." He placed his thumb and forefinger at the bridge of his nose, and continued. "The elders have decided there is little we can do about it, but the problem is amplified by the fact that the Mayan-Toltec are demanding slaves instead of turquoise. Our turquoise miners are at a minimal number due to malnutrition, along with families who have left us, which has reduced our production of turquoise to a fraction of what it has been in the past. The Mayan-Toltec are demanding slaves as a substitute for turquoise."

"Awonawilona, help us!" she cried. "What have the elders decided?"

"There is unanimous agreement that what the Mayan-Toltec pochteca ask cannot be granted. The lives of our people are at stake."

"If all that you say is so, then what are our southern neighbors doing?"

He heaved a despondent sigh and said, "The Mogollon and the Hohokam are also suffering so severely that they are offering to trade their own as slaves."

Moon Fire was horrified. She clutched Wena 'Ahote desperately, for she wondered how much longer her people could go on. In fact she could find nothing more to say. She sat quietly, almost in a stupor, squeezing Wena 'Ahote's hand. She was hungry, and she knew he was hungry. There was only enough to eat to prevent their stomachs from growling, and they had grown used to it. At last she rallied and said, "Wena 'Ahote, my love, can you arrange for me to speak with the elders and those who are superior?"

He seemed surprised at her request, and he asked her what she had in mind. When she avoided the question, he said no more, but began to make sweet love to her. It was after their lovemaking that he informed her that Ruupi had returned from the same outlier where the cannibalism had taken place.

She descended the kiva to find all who should be there in attendance, including Ruupi. Ignoring him and taking her place next to Wena 'Ahote, she waited patiently for the meeting to begin. There seemed to be so much talk about the horror of the cannibalism in the northern outlier that she and Wena 'Ahote both wondered if Tenyam would ever call the meeting to order.

At long last he did. "Our purpose in this meeting is to decide what to do about the demise of our northern outlier. I feel certain everyone here knows of the grizzly events, but in case any of you do not, we are faced with ritualistic sacrifice and human consumption of at least thirty of our people." A groan was heard from all in attendance. "We must air our feelings, and try to decide what, if anything, we can do." He resumed his seat on the bench.

A period of silence followed until Angwusi rose to speak. "I am shocked to think that our people would stoop so low. What has happened is abominable! There is no other word to describe it. We, the proud, peaceful Anasazi, have committed the ultimate sin. If this has been going on for a while, it is no wonder that Awonawilona has deserted us." He glanced nervously about the kiva before seating himself.

Fat Eykita rose with his usual groan. "I must agree with all you both have said, but"—and he heaved a great sigh—"if they wish to choose this terrible road of life, then why should we bother? Let them do what they want."

Hoohu shot straight up, as his name would have indicated. "Eykita, do you wear blinders? Do you not see that if we permit this, then other outliers will do the same. We here, in this canyon, are the center of government for the Anasazi nation. It would be an outrage if we did not do something, for by doing nothing we are giving our permission. Come now, don't you see how crucial this issue is to our very survival as a people?"

Stillness pervaded the kiva with tension that could hardly have gone unnoticed by anyone. Tendrils of smoke slowly worked their way toward the hole in the ceiling, wrapping themselves around the ladder, then out into the darkness. It seemed that everyone was deep in thought.

At last Tenyam spoke. "Moon Fire, our revered counselor, has asked to speak. I am told that she asks you to listen, for she has had some thoughts on the issue at hand." Turning toward her, he added, "Moon Fire?"

Her heart skipped a beat as she gracefully rose to take the floor. She drew on the support of Wena 'Ahote as she squared her shoulders and began to speak. "I thank you elders and others for giving me this opportunity to speak. It is my understanding that we are a nonaggressive people, a people of peace. I think it is important that we all realize that there are two different realities in which we all live, and that we, the Anasazi, are an exception. Please stop me if I am wrong." She waited, but hearing no objection, continued. "I would like to elaborate on what I have already said. There are those who are people of power, people who must control, defeat, counter, manipulate, and intimidate others. It is true that you are the governing power over our people, but your control is for the welfare of our people, and our religious beliefs are woven into your governing. Our 'road of life' is not to control, defeat, or manipulate others, but to just provide the defense system so that others will leave us alone. We do not involve ourselves with other peoples except for trading purposes. We are not out to divide and conquer." She paused to gather her thoughts as she twisted her hands together. "Rumor has it, and it is also my belief, that the Mayan-Toltec are master manipulators. They have convinced the people that Awonawilona has forsaken us, and with this manipulation, they have led our people into the most abominable of actions. As Hoohu has told you, we must do something, or other outliers will be drawn into the same situation. It is in my mind that none of this would have happened if it had not been approved by the elders of that outlier."

A gasp was heard from everyone, which to Moon Fire indicated that few, if any, had thought of what she had just disclosed, and so she continued. "I would ask this question. If it were possible to single out the elders who voted in favor of such an abomination, could we not punish them in some way? If we do not, the seed will germinate, and there will be more of the same. I want to add that it is not my nature to be vindictive, but I see no other way. I believe we are not being vindictive, but are only trying to protect our own." She glanced quickly at Wena 'Ahote, who stared at her in amazement, then stepped back to resume her position next to him.

Iswungwa, the trade manager, was the first to rise. He rearranged his robe, and placed the palm of his right hand on his forehead. "I am horrified that we must deal with such an abomination. I must say that I am in complete agreement with Moon Fire, and I am thankful that she is in attendance and has spoken her mind. The elders who voted in favor of such an action must be identified, and in my opinion, must be put to death publicly. Those who have not been converted will then see that they must maintain the old ways."

When Iswungwa had resumed his position on the bench, Hoohu rose. "I am in complete agreement with both Moon Fire and Iswungwa. We must find someone who can go to that community and find out who they are, but first I would ask Ruupi what he can tell us since he has only recently returned from that same outlier."

Ruupi simply declared, "This event happened after I had left. I know nothing."

"Then if that is the case, I would suggest that Wena 'Ahote

go. He could go on the pretense that he might be the one to assume the position of the terminally ill old priest who has little time to live." Hoohu stepped back and resumed his position on the bench as though he believed he had found a solution to the problem.

Moon Fire audibly gasped. She was sorry that she had spoken, for never would she have thought that Wena 'Ahote would be their choice. She immediately could see the dangers he might face.

Tenyam, who had taken a backseat for a while, finally asserted himself. "I would sooner think that the person we send should be one who would not be noticed, but rather someone whose face is not a new one to that outlier." He paused to run his fingers through his graying long hair. "Yes," he said, "I know you are thinking as I am. Who might that person be? I believe that the reason for Wena 'Ahote to be the one, is weak. We need someone who is a familiar face for this assignment— someone who will not raise any suspicions."

Moon Fire's heart rejoiced, and for the first time in her life she wanted to throw her arms around Tenyam's neck to thank him. Perhaps, she thought, there was some good in this hard, usually narrow-minded elder.

Again there was no sound in the kiva. At last Eykita groaned as he rose from the bench. He groaned several more times, then at last cleared his throat to speak. "There is one among us who is a frequent visitor due to his position. It would not be unusual for him to be there for a time, and no one would question his presence. It is my suggestion that it be Lansa, for the outlier is on his trade route on a regular basis."

Moon Fire was elated that they might not send Wena 'Ahote, but she also felt sympathy for Sihu, who seemingly never had a husband. If they chose Lansa, even though it was for the good of the people, he would still be gone for an indefinite amount of time or until he learned what he must know. It was apparent that the world was completely out of balance.

Tenyam took the floor, saying, "Eykita, you are a marvel. Your groans are stimulating your brain. I believe you are right. Lansa would be the appropriate choice, and he would never be questioned. Does anyone here have any objections?" When he heard none, he adjourned the meeting, after which everyone gradually went their own way.

Moon Fire and Wena 'Ahote walked slowly across the plaza toward his quarters under the brilliance of the full moon. Neither said much, for they were too lost in their own thoughts.

Sihu was terribly upset when Lansa left, but said nothing. She did confide in Moon Fire, telling her of her long-term feeling of abandonment. Moon Fire hardly knew what to say, for she knew her friend and sister had an absolute right to her feelings. She validated her friend to the best of her ability, and offered her support. Beyond that she knew she could do nothing.

He had been gone for ten sun cycles, and when he returned, Sihu had placed his belongings outside their dwelling, which indicated that she had had enough and was divorcing him.

Lansa was enraged. He bellowed his anger when she refused to come out from their dwelling. "What is the matter with you? You are crazy!" he screeched. "I have been on a mission for the good of our people, and you . . . *you* are crazy! Why can't you see things my way? Why does it always have to be your way?"

Though he continued to vent his rage on her, she remained inside with the two children, who were too young to understand what was going on. She had no intention of coming out until she felt he was more in control of himself. The children whimpered, indicating that they felt the tension. The youngest began to cry, and she pinched his nose to stop his wailing. She hated to use the technique, but she knew it worked, and that her people used it if they did not want the enemy to know of their presence. "Yes, I am acting as if he is the enemy." Her heart was broken, but she knew she must press on.

At long last she felt she had heard the last of his ravings. The children were asleep, and she climbed the ladder to face him.

He turned when he saw her, and told her he was not in control of his own emotions. "*What* are you doing? Have you lost your senses? You know I love you."

Gathering her resolve, she answered, "Lansa, we have been married for almost three season cycles, and during that time, you have offered little or no support to your loving wife and two children. In the time we have been married, I have been graced with your company for little more than four moon cycles. How else would you expect me to react, and you call this a marriage? At times you are gone for so long that I forget what you look like."

"I would expect you to know that I am a trader, and cannot be at home. I have done a service to the community and even to our people, and you have no appreciation of what is going on. In fact you do not care what is going on around you. You are a heartless woman, and one I cannot understand. You are not the same woman I married, not the same gentle mild-mannered woman, when we met. What is wrong with you? What is *wrong with you?*" He strutted around as though his reality was the only one that mattered.

"Lansa, in your reality the world revolves around you. Be aware that I am no longer the doormat that you thought you knew. You don't seem to understand that the world, as we know it, revolves around starvation and malnutrition. Because you are a trader, you are always comfortably welcome wherever you go, and you are fed and treated as royalty. In the real world, as our people know it, we are sickly, hungry, thirsty, and in real trouble. Look at your scrawny children. See them as they really are. We, as a nation, are in real trouble, and you don't seem to see it. Oh, yes, occasionally you bring us some little trinket that does nothing to correct the basic situation." She turned her back on him in disgust and seemed unwilling to offer any more words.

He came up behind her to stroke her hair. She recoiled angrily, saying, "Get out, and don't come back. You live in your world and your children and I will live in ours."

"You can't mean that. You know that I love you and the children."

"Oh yes, I do mean that. I have also heard through many, that you have lovers in many of the stops you make along the way. You have no respect for me or for your children, and least of all for the marriage you made. You are not Anasazi. You are Lansa, and only Lansa, and you have a strange way of loving." Without another word she returned to the children in the comfort of what had been his home.

Lansa knew he could not enter, for that was the way of the

people. He was enraged, but somewhere inside, he knew that she was right. He consoled himself with the realization that there were many women who awaited his attentions.

Moon Fire knew the vibrations were not right. She had been counseling for many season cycles, and felt that Sihu needed her. She had been aware for quite a while that Sihu was deeply unhappy with Lansa. She had known when they had married that Lansa was not a man with any intention of truly settling down, and that Sihu had not wanted to hear of it. Her more recent visits had shown her that her sister-by-law was losing weight and looking terribly despondent. In all probability Sihu was probably giving much of what little food she had to her two children. It was with these thoughts that Moon Fire found herself at the top of the ladder that provided entry to Lansa and Sihu's quarters. She knelt down listening to what she thought were whimpers, and said, "Sister, may I enter?"

"Of course. You do not have to ask. You know you are always welcome in my house."

Saying nothing, she climbed down the ladder, then turned to face her sister. Nothing could have prepared her for what she saw. The children were asleep, but Sihu sat cross-legged on her sleeping mat, whimpering softly as tears poured from her lovely eyes.

In two swift strides Moon Fire was at her side, gathering her into her arms. "Oh, sister, what, in the name of Awonawilona, is wrong?"

"He is gone, and never coming back." Sihu choked.

"Lansa is gone? But why? He has always returned before, hasn't he?"

"Yes, but . . ." Sihu broke into tears once more.

Moon Fire waited for her grieving sister to calm, then gently inquired, "But what?"

"I did it. It's my fault that he will never return. I threw him out. We are no longer married, and I am a failure. There must be something terribly wrong with me."

"Sihu, we have known each other for many season cycles, and I must tell you now that there is nothing wrong with you.

Everyone who knows you is aware that you are a very lonely wife and mother. I am sure you told him of your loneliness."

"Yes, but he said that I am no longer the sweet woman he married, and he shouted that there was something *wrong* with me. It seemed that no matter what I said, I could not find the right words to explain so that he could understand me. I guess there really is something wrong with me." She reached for an old piece of cotton cloth to blow her nose.

"Listen to me, Sihu. Please just listen, and don't interrupt. As a counselor I have come across many similar situations with a wide variety of couples. Unlike the animals, insects, and birds, we humans harbor an enormously wide variety of behavioral traits. Over the season cycles I have found that those I counsel, in general, fall into one of two groups in relation to reality. Most of them fall under the 'power over' reality view of life. That is to say that they must have power over other people in order to maintain their ego and self-esteem. They must control, manipulate, verbally abuse, and sometimes even physically abuse those around them. In short, they cannot be wrong. They must feel superior. Sihu, Lansa is one of those people. On the other hand, there are those whose reality is not 'power over,' but 'personal power.' The 'personal power' reality is one in which people live in mutuality, and cocreativeness in order to solve their problems. You, Sihu, are one of those people. To put it in a few words, you and Lansa do not live in the same realities. Your worlds are different. He has no concept of mutually solving a problem, and so he blames others. I grew up with him. I should know. You must not blame yourself. You were only reaching out to someone who does not have the ability to understand you due to the two different realities in which you both live."

"But, Moon Fire, he did not deny that he has lovers in many locations. Do you suppose he treats them the same way?"

"No, probably not. You are the only one he feels the compulsion to control because of your two children. I know my brother well, and I can almost assure you that it will never end, for he has a very strange way of loving."

Sihu was visibly shaken by Moon Fire's words. Shaking her head in despair, she murmured, "I hope you are wrong. I just want to find a life of my own with the children, of course. I only wish he would leave me alone."

"You know, Sihu, you could look at it from the bright side. At least he is a trader, and is gone most of the time. If he had chosen any other kind of work, he might be badgering you all the time." She took her sister's hand and gave it a gentle squeeze.

"Leave it to you to look for the up side. I am indeed lucky to have such a warm, loving sister. I cannot tell you how I appreciate all you have said to console me. I only wish we could spend more time together."

"I see no reason why we can't," Moon Fire answered. "That would be good for both of us, and also give me the opportunity to get to know my two little nephews better. I must go now, but you know it is my hope that you and the two boys will also visit me anytime." She turned to ascend the ladder.

"We shall see that it is so. Thank you for being you," Sihu whispered.

Wena 'Ahote was in attendance when the two elders who had been identified by Lansa were brought in. There were none who were absent, due to the critical importance of recent events. The two elders from the outlier gave the appearance of being harmless, though one seemed to constantly shift his beady black eyes from person to person in obvious apprehension. One of them was short and slender of body, while the other was stocky and round.

Tenyam rose from the bench on which most everyone except the priests were seated to indicate that the meeting was to begin. It took only a very short time for everyone to quiet. "We are here to attend to a most horribly unpleasant problem that has arisen among our people. After learning that thirty or more people were cannabalistically sacrificed and eaten, we have further learned from our own sources that the two elders who stand before you approved of the act. Of the three who govern the outlier, these two were in agreement and one was not. Allow me to introduce you to Kyaro and Kwahu. In time we will allow them to speak for themselves, but for now I would ask if any of you have any comments?"

Only Hoohu spoke. Everyone else seemed lost in the horror of the responsibility they knew they must assume. He shook his head, and cleared his throat. "It seems to me that we are dealing with a problem that is no different than how we deal with the blaspheming of the roads in our most sacred winter ceremonials. These men have given their approval for an act that is totally opposite of what we, as a people, are about. Yes, I agree that we are hungry, but still there is no excuse. To partake of another's flesh is evil, and enough to disturb Awonawilona who normally supports us with abundance. I ask you, all who are here, how long this has been going on, but perhaps on a smaller scale, and if it has been going on for a long time, perhaps that is why Awonawilona is angered and the drought is upon us." He turned to Kyaro and Kwahu as he added to his concerns. "Why would the two of you give your consent to such an abominable thing?"

When no one else seemed willing to take the floor, Tenyam said, "Would either of you care to speak on your behalf?"

Kwahu stepped forward. "Kyaro and I were put in such a position that we hardly knew what to do. Our people are hungry as everyone is, and we knew times were very difficult. We felt we had no other choice."

"Are there no dogs left in your community?" Tenyam inquired.

"There are a few, but most have been consumed by us for meat, and we knew not what else to do. I answer your questions as I speak for my fellow elder and friend, Kyaro. We made our decision based on the fact that we all must survive."

Hoohu was immediately up once more. "You must be aware that there are other outliers who have not resorted to such atrocities. Many have simply moved away to places where there is a more dependable water supply, and because of that fact, there would be more game and fertile soil. What I cannot understand is the fact that your outlier has a reasonably dependable water supply, yet you do what you consider logical, but to us is not."

Kwahu spent a short bit of time in silence, then finally responded, "To Kyaro and I"—he gestured toward his friend— "we had no other choice." He seemed resolved to say no more.

Suddenly Tenyam broke in. "It would seem to me that you

are avoiding the question. Your friend, Kyaro, acts as his name indicates. He is as a parrot, and he is 'ayawamat,' or one who follows orders. He is no better than you. Now let me tell you what we know has happened. The Mayan-Toltec faction got to the people, telling them that Awonawilona has deserted them and they must do as the Mayan-Toltecs tell them to do. Do not say that it is not so, for we know that it is true. The Mayan-Toltecs have always been a thorn in the side of our people, and now we are plagued by them once more. What have you to say to this?" He resumed his seat with an angry swirl of his robe.

"I say you are assuming," retorted Kwahu. "You are only assuming, yet really know nothing." His face was turning bright red in rage.

Hoohu quickly took the floor with his fists clenched, and lips pressed tightly together. "No, it is you who are assuming, Kwahu, that we have no way of knowing, yet I declare to you, we do have our ways of knowing. You are assuming that we are naive and perhaps idiots. I must assure you that we are not. We have taken the necessary steps to find out what the truth is. The truth is ugly, and we know we must do what we must do."

Kwahu continued to maintain an air of indignance, but made no further comment. In his mind he knew he was beaten, and could only await the consequences.

Once more silence pervaded the kiva. Wena 'Ahote was so depressed that he found himself looking forward to the culmination of the meeting when he could find solace in Moon Fire's arms. They had both agreed that the world was terribly out of balance, and as the season cycles pressed on, continued to appear more and more that way.

Angwusi broke the stillness, saying, "It would seem to me that we are dealing with not only a blaspheming of our religious ways, but worse than that, an undermining of our people. In our ceremonials to Awonawilona and all our other gods, we punish those who have the audacity to interfere with what is sacred by dismembering them and scattering their body parts in the four directions. Are these two priests not doing the same thing?"

"Indeed, you are right," exclaimed Hoohu. "I would be in favor of treating them as you suggest."

Tenyam rose and waited. When he heard no objection from any others in attendance, he declared, "I am in total agreement, but it is my suggestion that this punishment be inflicted in the presence of those in the outlier from which these elders came. Perhaps it will set an example for them."

An audible gasp escaped the lips of both Kwahu and Kyaro as they absorbed their demise. The priests had advised them, and they had listened. In their minds they had had no other choice, yet they knew the decision had probably been made even before their arrival in the holy school.

After a short period of time, Tenyam declared the meeting over. Warriors came in to escort Kwahu and Kyaro to their confinement, and almost everyone in the meeting made a hasty retreat to find whatever peace might be available to them.

CHAPTER 14

A.D. *1133*

Leetayo had gone to her parents' outlier, where she remained for two season cycles. She had withstood the abuse and judgment of her parents when she had so surprisingly arrived back home, and had resolved that she would return to the holy school as soon as possible. Women's duties did nothing for her, and she wanted no part of them, even though she begrudgingly did what was necessary during the time that was her sentence. She only hoped that Ruupi would also return, and that his relationship with her would not change. Her hatred for Moon Fire and Wena 'Ahote were more fired than ever, and she wished them dead. Of course, during her time at home, she had had several sexual relations, but none of them could possibly compare with Ruupi, who was so experienced. At one point Lansa had stopped by on his trading route, and she had come on to him, but he had apparently not realized what she was doing, or had just not been interested in responding. She preferred to think that the first reason was the apparent one, and decided to think no more about it. Her parents continued to remind her that she should be married, and that she would soon be beyond the marriageable age, but she parried their occasional approaches. Though she was certain she would never marry, she knew she could never tell them.

So it was that she returned to the holy school, and was given a room with another student, who seemed to be into a different reality than her own. The young woman who shared her accommodations was much younger than she, and exuded an enthusiasm in her studies that Leetayo found difficult to swallow. Her roommate's exuberance disgusted her, and yet reflected in her own mind that she probably should never have attended the holy school in the first place. Again she threw all such thought over her shoulder, and began to look for Ruupi.

At last she found him. Traders from the far south had arrived, and everyone who found it convenient was in attendance. He was really not very far away from her, so she chose to casually come to his side, pretending not to notice him. The traders had laid out a display of beautiful wings of very large birds along with gems, honey, shells with beautiful inlay work, and many other fascinating things.

It seemed forever before he noticed her. Her heart beat with uncertainty, for in her mind he was the only reason she had resumed her role as a student. A gentle nudge proved to her that he was aware of her presence. She stepped back in pretended surprise. "Oh, Revered One, I . . ."

He whispered in a husky voice, "When Sun Father sets, meet me in the plaza." He immediately removed himself from her presence to mingle with the rest of the people.

Since she was unable to keep her mind on anything else but what he had said, she withdrew to her own quarters. Her roommate was not there, and for that she was thankful. She just wanted to be left alone with her own joyous thoughts and anticipations.

Though time seemed to crawl like a turtle, at last Sun Father set. She had cleansed herself as best she could, and dusted her cheeks with red ocher. After taking several deep breaths, she entered the plaza. Would he really be there? Replacing her doubts with positive thoughts, she walked confidently, finally stopping in a dark corner. As yet she had not seen him, and she began to wonder if she had imagined what he had said.

As if materializing out of nowhere, someone took her elbow, steering her toward a darker corner not far away. "Leetayo? I somehow did not think you would return."

"Why would you think such a thing?" she retorted.

"Allow me to lead you to my quarters where we can have more privacy." He guided her, making sure to stay in the shadow of the thick stone walls until they entered a ground floor dwelling that was obviously his own.

His quarters were rather barren, as if he had no real interest in making them his home. A shelf with a couple of robes and a pipe was all that the room had to offer. Of course his sleeping mat was spread out not far from the fire. Taking her hand, he led her to sit next to him on the mat.

Running his hand lightly over her cheek, he said, "I repeat. I am surprised you are here. I was sure that some young upstart would have been more than happy to grab you."

Leetayo's mind flashed over the several young men with whom she had had sexual relations, then smiled as she said very simply, "There was no one who could compare."

Ruupi was overjoyed. It seemed to him as though time had stood still for two season cycles. Here she was again, just as if nothing had ever happened. "Of course you don't expect me to believe that," he stated in a matter-of-fact way.

"You will believe what you will believe. I cannot change that."

Taking her into his arms, he clutched her to him. "I have no choice but to believe you. Let me make love to you."

"I would go out of my mind if you did not," she declared.

He touched her in ways he had never touched her before. He seemed to be searching for all her little secret spots, and when he found them, he glorified in them. She, in turn, treated him the same way until he almost shouted in ecstasy. They culminated their foreplay with a joining that was like none other that either of them had experienced.

At last, basking in the afterglow, he turned to her and said, "Are you happier since you returned?"

"With you? Of course."

"But what of those who caused our exile?"

The afterglow disappeared to be replaced with a consuming hateful anger. "Revered One, I must tell you honestly that I detest Moon Fire and Wena 'Ahote more than ever. Our exile only fanned the flames."

"Then it is Wena 'Ahote you really want?" he asked.

"If you mean sexually, absolutely no. If you mean dead, absolutely yes."

"Little woman, you mince no words."

"In that you are right. But what of your true feelings?" she inquired.

"I will tell you truly what is in my heart. I also feel more fervently than ever that I would like to see Wena 'Ahote dead. Moon Fire is also a threat to what I wish to accomplish. There is little more I can say. Shall we agree to find a way to those ends, little woman?"

"Nothing would delight me more."

He pulled her into his arms again. "Then so it shall be."

The cold season arrived early. A light snow covered the ground, offering very little water to the parched earth. An almost eerie quiet had settled over the canyon. The people were hungry, with many only marginally surviving. People were spending more time in fervent prayer, desperately hoping Awonawilona would hear their pleas. Everywhere there was tension, sometimes mixed with hope, and at times with desperation as the struggle for survival continued. There was little fat left on anyone in the community, and Moon Fire could not help but wonder how the other outliers were faring. She never saw Lansa, and could only rely on what Wena 'Ahote told her when he said that the rivers were drying up, and that everyone seemed to be in the same predicament. Her people had already been through the New Fire ceremony, and were preparing for the Powamu ceremony, though rather despondently. Everyone truly thought they were doing the right things to please the gods, and that they must continue to do so. There was no more news from the northern outlier where the two priests had been put to death, but a dark somberness had settled over the entire community.

Moon Fire was walking the east road when she heard the rumblings. At first she thought it was thunder, but she knew that in the cold season that would be highly unusual. She saw no lightning, and she realized that the rumblings were not coming from the sky, but from the earth. The very ground she stood upon was lightly trembling. A skinny little desert rabbit scuttled frantically in front of her. Other than that she saw no other sign of animal life, for she knew they had all left to seek greener and riper land. Then she saw an arch of fire split the sky with a horrible growling sound. The ground continued to tremble while she hastily made her way back to the holy school and to her quarters. Upon arriving, she changed her course to Wena 'Ahote's quarters. He was immediately aware of her arrival, and beckoned her to join him.

"I have seen and felt strange things," she excitedly exclaimed. "Have you felt anything here?"

"Yes, my love, I, too, have felt the slight trembling of the ground. What is it that you have seen?"

"When the rumblings began I saw an unbelievable streak of fire cross the sky to the west of us. Do you think that this is the end of the fourth world?"

"No, I think not. Taatawi has told me that such an event happened during the time of Coyote Woman, and that the fire had no effect on our community at that time. He spoke of a mountain that decided to express its rage, and that it breathed terrible danger to those in close proximity, but not to those far away. There is even a story that Coyote Woman and some of our acolytes who make the journey periodically to the huge canyon or sipapu of the earth, had to abort a trip due to the anger of that same mountain. Taatawi is certain that it is the same mountain that still vents its anger."

"I hope he is correct. Things have been so out of balance for so long that I hardly know what to think anymore."

"I must say that I agree with you. From all the stories passed down from generation to generation, I have never heard any that revealed such hardships such as we endure. Just know that our love will never be changed no matter what happens." He drew her into his arms and reined little kisses around her ears and throat to speak of his love. They joined as one as the earth shivered much as Moon Fire did due to Wena 'Ahote's loving touch.

The time for the winter solstice ceremony had arrived. It was the time when Sun Father spent the least amount of time in the sky, and it was time to call him back. In Moon Fire's mind, she wondered if it was wise to call him back, for he had already done so much irreparable damage. A small part of her thought that if he did not return, then they might have rain for a very long time, but that was definitely against the belief of her people, and she chose to quell what she rationalized to be a ridiculous thought.

The earth was very cold and still in the early part of the sun cycle. The robes made of feathers and various skins of animals were very comforting. As everyone did, she covered her feet with soft socks of animal skins with yucca sandals tied around the socks. This was the part of the ceremony where the governing body climbed to the top of the butte, using toe- and handholds to meet a young girl who was already at the top awaiting them. A deep sensuous drumbeat accompanied them as they climbed laboriously to the top. At the bottom of the butte everyone sang praises. This was one of the most sacred of the rituals of the people.

When everyone had reached the top of the butte, Taatawi escorted the young girl to a fire pit that spit and sparkled flaming fury. The young girl was led to sit next to the fire pit, where she waited. Seeds and prayer sticks surrounded her. Her hair had been washed and hung loosely on her shoulders. It was here she would remain, for she was symbolically hatching the seeds upon which she sat. She had been chosen after four season cycles for a special sacrifice, not physically, but mentally, for she represented the rebirth of life, and life must be paid for with life. She would die to insure rebirth like a seed periodically dies to be born fresh again. In the mind of the Anasazi, all was a great cycle. Everyone knew that the girl would die within the next four season cycles. No one would physically or mentally harm her, but it would happen.

To Moon Fire the ceremony was beautiful, but she wondered why there needed to be any kind of sacrifice. Were her people any better than the Mayan-Toltecs? Those despicable people sacrificed immediately, yet her people still did the same on a small scale. Where was the need to sacrifice, she wondered.

As if in answer to her thoughts, the sky lit up with a display of fire unequaled by anything any of her people had seen. Colorful balls of fire lit the sky, and the ground shook once more as the mountain to the west of them declared its fury. It seemed to Moon Fire as if Mother Earth was declaring her last eulogy, and that all the ground under them might dissolve instantaneously. She could not imagine what it would be like if she saw it during darkness. Again the ground convulsed, sending a tremor that seemed to last forever.

Stark fear was reflected on everyone's face. The ceremony was immediately halted, and without any words everyone in attendance climbed nervously down the butte to return to their own quarters. Moon Fire had been with the crowd below the butte and could not reach Wena 'Ahote. She was concerned for his safety, for she knew he would be one of the last to reach his quarters, along with the Taatawi and the elders. Ruupi never even entered her mind. She knew that just such an event had occurred during the revered Coyote Woman's life, and that the people had adjusted to the many changes caused by Earth Mother's ragings. She uttered a prayer to Awonawilona that such would be the case now.

She stumbled down her ladder into the security of her quarters, and sat on her mat in contemplation. Somewhere in the back of her mind she wondered if Awonawilona really was angry with her people because of the fact that, in a sense, her people still sacrificed. She tried without success to still her mind.

It was then that Wena 'Ahote descended her ladder, saying, "My love, I need your company. You are all I need."

She rose immediately to say, "Is there some way we can lose ourselves in some other reality?"

"If that is what you wish, I want you to know that that is also my wish." He took her in his arms, relishing the soft scent of yucca with which she had washed. Her soft, shiny hair fell like a veil over her shoulders and down her back as he unwound the thick shiny braid. Clasping her to him with his left hand at the small of her back, he twined his right hand in her hair, and lightly brushed his lips over hers. In a voice husky with desire he said, "Ah, my love, all through the ceremony all I wanted was to hold you. Then when the fire lit the sky, I was sick with worry about your safety. Let us put the world aside. Even if it ends, we can still celebrate life together at this moment and forever."

Moon Fire quivered with delight at his touch, and her heart soared with happiness at his words. "Touch me. Love me," she whispered.

After removing their clothes they lay entwined on her mat. She did not know where her roommate might be and did not care. Throwing all caution to the wind, she nibbled at his ear while her hand traced little circles over his chest.

Suddenly he turned her on her back and placed himself over her. He began by caressing her breasts with his tongue, easing her nipples into little hardened knots. He then moved his tongue like a delicate feather, making a trail from each of her breasts to her navel. Her sighs encouraged him to move on to the dusky area of her sex. He guided her into a position that enabled him to rest his head between the sleek columns of her upper legs. When at last she had voluntarily parted her legs, and her sweet scent surrounded him, he placed his lips about halfway down on the inside of her thigh, and closed his teeth gently over the skin, sucking until her skin reddened. She moaned again while he continued several more times, all the while massaging her power spot until she softly screamed, "Now, my love, *now!*"

He found he could wait no longer, for she had amplified his need. After running his engorged member once more over her power spot, he slowly entered her, taking care to control his overwhelming desire to immediately satiate his own needs.

Moon Fire felt as if she were teetering on the edge of a cliff. As she felt his intense desire within her, she finally let out a cry as the cliff no longer seemed to exist and she found herself flying. She and Wena 'Ahote were the only two people who existed, and she even wondered if she had become a part of eternity rather than a part of the world of her people as she heard Wena 'Ahote groan with pleasure well spent.

They lay entwined in each other's arms for some time after.

As was her custom whenever she could, she walked, often not on any of the roads, but following animal trails when she could find them. Two sun cycles after the great mountain had shot such intense flames into the sky, she found herself west of the community. The air was dry as usual, there was no breeze, and the sun warmed the cold air. She had wrapped her feet and legs with skins as well as her body, and was enjoying her solitude. Much to her surprise, a small bird soared over her head. It landed on another rock close by and cocked its head to one side. The songs it sang identified it as the most vocal of all birds. Moon Fire had not seen a mockingbird in some time due to the drought, but here it was in all its splendor. Knowing it was Wena 'Ahote's spirit animal, she stopped in her tracks to pay her respects. It opened its wings, flashing its white patches, which reflected the sunlight. Since it was unable to alarm any insects in the area due to the drought, it stopped to preen its feathers. Suddenly she received a message from the remarkable little songbird. "I am here to tell you that there are those around you who are like injurious insects surrounding you, as well as Wena 'Ahote. Look carefully to recognize who they are and what they are about. Listen to the true song of those about you." Flashing its wings once more, it disappeared into the horizon.

Moon Fire closed her eyes as she absorbed what she had heard, keeping perfectly still lest she disturb the magic. When she opened them, she beheld a long-eared rabbit far in the distance followed by a coyote with his tail slinking between his hind legs in pursuit. Closing her eyes once more, she marveled at the fact that it had been several season cycles since she had seen any animals with whom she might commune, and wondered why she was seeing so many now. A soft scuttling sound brought her eyes wide open. A desert mouse stopped to look her in the eye and ask her a question. "I have appeared at this time to tell you that it is time to pay attention to details that will be shown to you. Open your soul and you will know how to focus and pay attention to what is going on around you."

The mouse quickly disappeared, leaving Moon Fire marveling at the number of animals she had been privileged to witness. It seemed to her almost as it had been when she was a child, and the long prevailing drought had not yet taken such a terrible toll on her people. A bobcat appeared instantaneously from behind one large rock, then disappeared behind another rock formation. She knew that the bobcat was a solitary animal, as was she, and taught that one must learn to be alone without being lonely. She was amazed at the number of animal contacts she was making, as she tried to make sense out of all their messages.

At last she decided to stop trying. Closing her eyes once more, she shut out the world, and waited. She opened her eyes and a large bird appeared far away on the horizon. It soared high in the sky in magnificent circles as it drew closer. Moon Fire knew immediately that it was Red Eagle, and waited for him to finally reach her. She had not spoken to him for some time, and found herself hardly breathing lest she spoil the time at hand.

Red Eagle took his time dipping and soaring until he decided to land on a large rock nearby. After preening his feathers and settling himself, he spoke. "I come to explain to you that the many 'little brothers' you have seen and to whom you have spoken are here to escape the anger of Earth Mother as she belches forth fire. They will be here only temporarily. It is important that your people understand this."

Moon Fire could only feel joy and awe as her spirit animal graced her with his company once more. Shaking herself out of her reverie, she replied, "From what you are saying, I must assume that our little brothers are only passing through, for there is nothing to offer them here. We have no water, and most everything has died out."

Red Eagle stared in another direction for a short time, then said, "For a short time your people will have food, but you must warn them that they must use it wisely. Make them aware that it will not last."

"But what if they will not believe me?"

"There will be attacks by people who do not understand you, but you must try to convince them that balance will teach the true purpose in life. You must take special care in how you express yourself." Then abruptly saying no more, he flapped his great wings and soared once more out of sight.

Moon Fire felt the cold air seeping into her bones, and returned to her quarters to think on what she had heard.

*   *   *

It was bitter cold. The celebration of Powamu was at hand. At this time the people celebrated when plant life made its first appearance, and mankind, as children, were initiated by a host of spirit dancers, and the "road of life" was purified. All is interrelated in a web that must function harmoniously for the perpetuation of everyone on that "road of life." As was the usual in all the winter ceremonials, there were eight days of preparation, and eight days of celebration, which in the past had culminated with unabashed feasting.

Moon Fire had spoken with Wena 'Ahote, telling him of her time of seeing and communing with so many animals. She also had told him what Red Hawk had told her, and that the abundance of game was only temporary. She did not speak of the fact that Red Eagle had told her that there would be people who would not understand her. She felt he already knew that it was so.

"My love, I feel it is once again imperative that you speak before the council to at least give them whatever information you can. Perhaps it will not be as your Red Eagle says it will be. It is my hope that they will listen to you as they have in the past."

And so it was that Moon Fire once again found herself in the kiva of meetings with a fire so voracious that it might have dried the hairs on her head. She wondered if the intense heat and smoke might be a method, due to the lack of water, of ridding oneself of any possibility of head lice.

The meeting, as usual, was called to order by Tenyam. Several small items of business were discussed and settled accordingly. There seemed to be very little tension in the kiva due to the fact that Awonawilona had at last provided them with an abundance of meat for the feasting, prepared by the parents of the initiated children in honor of the newly selected parent-by-the-gods.

Angwusi rose from the bench with a belch. "It is in my mind that we should return to the true traditions given to us by our ancestors. Since Awonawilona has seemingly answered our prayers, I would suggest that we once again end our sixteen sun cycles of purification with a feast in the Creator's honor."

Many grunts of agreement resounded until Tenyam rose to

say, "I am in complete agreement. If there is no objection, so it shall be." After waiting and hearing nothing, he continued. "As you all see, Moon Fire has once again asked to speak to this council. Are we all in agreement that we should hear what she has to say?" Again grunts of agreement were heard, and Tenyam took his seat on the bench to give Moon Fire the stage.

She stepped forward to speak. "As you all know, my gift is that I speak with our 'big' and 'little brothers.' Until very recently there has been little opportunity to speak with any of them due to the fact that there are just not any in close proximity to our community. Not long ago, after the eruption of Earth Mother to the west of us, I spoke with several of our brothers, including my own spirit animal. I am here to speak of their message." She paused and nervously clenched her hands together in front of her. "They have informed me that their sudden return is only temporary. The drought is not over. They are only passing through in search of better living conditions, and will soon be gone. They also advised me to suggest to you that we should be considering doing the same. To the south of us is Mogollon country where at least in some locations there is more water. To the east of us is a great river, not so great right now, but nonetheless a reliable water supply, and to the north of us are other rivers that have not dried up. They are headed in these directions and will soon be gone. I have listened to your agreement to have an enormous feast to honor Awonawilona, but based on what our brothers are telling us, it is my suggestion that we feast only moderately or perhaps even meagerly as we have had to do in recent times. Would it not be better to hunt while the hunting is good, and dry and store the meat for the lean times that will surely come again?"

Angwusi waited until he was certain that Moon Fire was finished, then shot from the bench as though a fire ant had bitten him. "This is an outrage!" he shouted. "Are we to believe that Awonawilona has returned to us only temporarily? Are we to listen to the babblings of a mere mortal woman who claims she speaks to our little brothers? We have been praying to Awonawilona for many many season cycles, knowing we would not be deserted. Now here we have a woman who tells us that Awonawilona will desert us again? This is rubbish, and more than that, it is disgusting." He turned on his heel to resume his place on the bench.

Tenyam was also clearly shaken. "I must say that I agree with Angwusi. No mere mortal, male or female, can know what Awonawilona will do or not do. It is my suggestion that we go on as we have planned to honor the joy we all feel that things are returning to normal. I feel that Moon Fire has stepped out of her boundaries."

Eykita slowly raised his girth from the bench and passed wind as he groaned. "I say let's get on with what we had planned."

Moon Fire felt sick at heart at their lack of foresight and logic. She wondered if there might not have been some other way she could have stated her case to be more convincing. Red Eagle had said they would probably not listen, and even Wena 'Ahote had voiced his doubts. She knew there was little she could do or say that would change their minds.

Tenyam rose to adjourn the meeting, but before he had said two words, Hoohu rose. "Let us not adjourn yet, my brothers, for I also wish to speak." He looked up and shut his eyes briefly as if in prayer. "As I see it, the problem comes down to Moon Fire's credibility. We all know her record, and that it is honorable and good. Why, I ask, should we so verbally abuse her for what our 'little brothers' have told her? Let us look at the logic of the situation. It is a given that Earth Mother is even at this moment belching fire from her loins to the west of us. It is also a given that the animals would run from such fury probably in all four directions. Those who are running east in our direction will most certainly not want to remain here unless Awonawilona finally blesses us with rain. At this time we have still seen no rain. It is still another given that our brothers will seek a reliable water supply as Moon Fire has suggested, and they do not have what they require for survival here. I say she is logically correct, and that as the gods have always told us, we should use moderation in all that we do. This would indicate to me that a very moderate feast is in order, and that any other abundance be carefully saved just in case Awonawilona still does not send us rain or snow, and our 'big' and 'little' brothers do choose to move on. I would ask you to think on what I have said." He turned to sit down.

Moon Fire cast him a grateful glance, then lowered her eyes once more.

Silence pervaded the kiva again. No one seemed to want to speak, so Tenyam rose, saying, "Should I assume we are at an impasse?"

Angwusi responded quickly. "In my mind there is no impasse. I do not agree with Hoohu, and Eykita has sent me his special groan that indicates that he also does not agree. We will feast in full abundance in honor of Awonawilona."

Hoohu cast a despondent look at Moon Fire, then said to all in attendance, "So it shall be, but there will come a time when you will remember my words."

"The meeting is adjourned," Tenyam said with a stamp of his right foot.

CHAPTER 15

A.D. *1134*

Awonawilona had still not sent any substantial amount of rain. One season cycle had passed with so little precipitation that once again the people were sure they were forgotten. The drought had continued and the animals who had migrated into the area had long since vanished in their search of water and better living conditions. In what normally would be the season of greening, nothing was turning green, and the people were frightened. The winter had been unusually cold with little snow, and the people had experienced a shortage of firewood, for the only available wood was three sun cycles walking distance in the mountains to the west of the community. Many old people had died from exposure to the cold, and many more had sickened. Fewer and fewer were happy in the area, and many were leaving. The population was very quickly dwindling. There had been talk of performing an antiquated ceremony called the Ladder Dance, but as yet no decision had been made. The three major cold season ceremonials had been completed, and still it seemed that Awonawilona had not heard. The spirits had abandoned them.

Wena 'Ahote was readying himself for the social dance that was intended to lift the spirits of the people. His thoughts were on Moon Fire and the fact that her bones protruded more than ever, and he wondered how long any of his people could go on. True to Hoohu's word, the people were sorry that they had not been frugal with the abundance of meat bestowed upon them by Aniline, for now there was nothing. Times seemed worse than ever before. He was certain that Awonawilona had tested them, and they had miserably failed the test.

He entered the plaza to find many people socializing and making a major effort to enjoy themselves. The drums beat hypnotically, and had times been different, he would have joined in with his flute. He spotted Moon Fire sitting with Sihu, and sent her a loving smile. Before he could reach her, he found himself intercepted by Taatawi, who informed him that it was now almost a given that the Ladder Dance would be performed in the near future. It was only a matter of the elders' approval.

The drummers changed their cadence, indicating that the social dancing had begun. Wena 'Ahote excused himself to ask Moon Fire to dance, but before he could reach her, Leetayo stepped in front of him and touched his arm, asking him without words if he would dance with her. He noticed that she had matured into a fully developed woman with wide hips, small waist, and almost pendulous breasts. He could not help but contrast her raw, overly developed beauty with the delicate nubile beauty of his beloved Moon Fire. He politely took Leetayo by the elbow and steered her toward the circle where the people were dancing around an enormous fire. They danced silently until the song had ended. Wena 'Ahote took his leave of her with only a few words, and quickly made his way to Moon Fire's side. Now it was the men's turn to ask someone to dance, and he wanted no one to intercept him.

The time passed happily for him, with Leetayo asking him to dance only twice more. He danced with Moon Fire most of the time, and only occasionally with Sihu, who had found no one as yet who interested her. Everyone danced in the normal manner, decorously, with their feet shuffling, and their knees relaxed, taking small steps. Their heels lifted and dropped, while the balls of their feet slid across the ground as they danced in a circle in the direction of the path of Sun Father.

It was toward the end of the dancing when Leetayo approached him once again. Her foxy downturned eyes with their long lashes looked at him imploringly as she said, "I must speak with you privately. It is important."

He was so surprised that he found himself at a loss for words. While wondering what, in the name of Awonawilona, she might want to say, he allowed her to steer him away from the dancing, around several corners, and into the shadows.

She stood hesitantly and silently for only a very short time. Squaring her shoulders, she looked at him and took his right hand in hers. "I have missed the sound of your beautiful flute, and I was also admiring the precision of your dancing. I hoped to dance with you more often, but certain people were in the way." With those words she placed his right hand on one of her breasts, then moved it to the other.

In a flash, he knew what she wanted, and decided to go along with her. He removed the hand of hers that controlled his, and moved close to her, keeping his right hand on her breast, cupping it and running his thumb over her nipple, which was hardening with his touch. Why, he wondered, would she be doing this when both he and Moon Fire knew that she hated them both. Could her feelings really have changed in three season cycles? He doubted that it was possible, but for now, he thought it wise to go along with her.

She moaned at his touch, then moved his hand to her other breast. He cupped it in the same manner and backed her against the massive stuccoed wall, pressing his body urgently against hers. She lifted her face to his to accept his kiss, which began with a gentle touch only to become more inflamed. No words were spoken.

Leetayo slowly brought her hand to his member. The breechcloth that covered it was greatly swollen, and she rejoiced, for she was sure he would surely soon succumb to her advances. Her other hand reached around to draw his buttocks closer to her until she could feel his member rubbing against her mound of pleasure. His lips continued to cover her own, and she felt her own pleasure rising to an uncontrollable level. Of course it was compounded with the fact that she hated Moon Fire, and she hoped to destroy both his and Moon Fire's credibility among the people. This would be just one step toward making it happen. She was beginning to feel so victorious that she whispered huskily, "Now, Revered One, now! I want it now!"

He pulled her even more tightly against him, while raining

little kisses on her neck and shoulders. "Now? Are you sure you are ready?" he asked.

"Yes, oh yes!" she hissed. "I cannot wait! It must be now!" He had driven her to distraction along with the need to be victorious.

Abruptly he stepped away from her, placing both hands on her shoulders to keep her against the wall. "Leetayo, since you are ready now, I will take my leave. I have never desired anyone but Moon Fire, and you must know that I will not change. I go now." Saying no more, he turned and walked toward what she thought seemed to be his own quarters, but was really an alcove just around the corner.

She burst into tears, and it was only several breaths when Ruupi and Taatawi walked her way. When she spied them, her tears turned to hysteria. She collapsed on her knees and held her temples with the palms of her hands as she wept uncontrollably. Her body shook and her chest heaved as she wailed.

Taatawi was astounded at the sight, and could not imagine what might be the cause of her hysteria. He watched in surprise as Ruupi walked quickly to her, and held her in his sympathetic arms.

Ruupi turned to Taatawi, saying, "I will walk her to her quarters. She needs her own space in order to gain control of herself. Please excuse me."

Taatawi watched them with curiosity as they left him. He could not understand the cause of her anguish, and so he returned to his own quarters.

Wena 'Ahote quietly returned to Moon Fire's quarters and the comfort of her arms.

Before Sun Father rose, Wena 'Ahote went to join Taatawi, who was beginning to teach him how to chart the heavens, and the responsibilities of the sun priest. He tried very hard to keep his mind on the instruction, but found his mind wandering to Moon Fire. When he had returned to her after his encounter with Leetayo, he had told her all, holding nothing back. After she had heard all that he had to say, she had shaken her lovely head and declared that it all sounded strange to her. "Why," she had said, "would Leetayo want to seduce him when she and

Ruupi had tried to destroy him not so long ago?" She had said it made no sense. Then before he had departed for Taatawi's quarters to chart the sunrise, she had said, "Why did Ruupi and Taatawi just happen to walk by at that moment? Speak of this to the sun priest, my love. There are too many questions." And so here he was, trying desperately to concentrate on what Taatawi was saying, but finding much difficulty in his efforts.

Taatawi turned to him suddenly. "Wena 'Ahote, somehow I do not feel you are absorbing my instruction as you usually do. What is it that is bothering you?"

Wena 'Ahote looked as if he had been stricken. Shaking his head and emitting a deep sigh, he said, "Taatawi, I must speak to you about your encounter with Leetayo during the last sun cycle."

Taatawi immediately responded, "Yes, that was a most curious incident, but how could you know of it?"

"Revered One, I was responsible for her hysteria. She said she needed to talk to me, and drew me into the shadows. Then she proceeded to seduce me with her charms, of which she has many. I led her up to a point, then stepped out of her way, telling her that Moon Fire was my only love. I hid behind the closest alcove and listened, though she thought I had returned to my quarters. I cannot understand what was happening."

"It seems to me that she should hate you, young priest, for it was you who caused her banishment. Perhaps she only meant to cause Moon Fire grief, and she failed. That could account for her behavior." He stroked his stomach area with his right hand for a time, then said, "But why did Ruupi almost command me to walk with him during your time with her? Did he lead me to you, perhaps for a reason?"

Realization dawned on Wena 'Ahote, but he did not want to believe it. "Taatawi, you and Moon Fire are my only confidants. I feel I can be truthful to you and you will honor my truth without telling others. It is my feeling that Ruupi wanted to discredit me, for whatever was his purpose. He set up her encounter with me, hoping I would succumb. When it did not happen he was shaken and disappeared with her for whatever his reasons might be. I don't understand. I am baffled."

Taatawi scratched his head, then said, "Wena 'Ahote, you

know that Ruupi and I are not close. I'm sure you have noticed that he keeps his distance. He caught me off guard when he insisted that we needed to talk. I saw no reason why we could not have talked in the plaza, for there were few people remaining. He fairly pushed me in the direction he wanted us to take, leaving me no choice but to follow. He remained silent until we found Leetayo, who was terribly upset. You may or may not be right about it being set up, but until we know, if we ever find out, we must remain quiet and on guard."

Wena 'Ahote shook his head in agreement, then disclosed his innermost feelings with a question. "When the council decided to exile Ruupi and Leetayo for two season cycles, what did they expect that act to accomplish? Did they think Ruupi and Leetayo would change?"

"I'm not sure," Taatawi replied. "I imagine they thought perhaps it might be so. I don't think they ever thought that by allowing him to return to the community that things might become worse. It is very possible that the exile only fanned their hatred. Only time will tell."

"Well, clearly we can prove nothing. We must wait and see." The young priest shrugged his shoulders and added, "I would like to share with you something my parents always told me. They told me that people do not change. They only become who they really are over a period of time. You are right when you say only time will tell."

Taatawi sent him a knowing grin and said, "Now, let us get on with more instruction."

Preparations for the Ladder Dance were under way. To the east of the large community was a clearing pinched out to a narrow, rocky ledge running along the edge of a high cliff. In it were four holes spaced well apart that had been chipped deep into the solid rock. The holes were round and nearly a foot in diameter, just large enough and deep enough to hold securely the trunks of four pine trees. The two pine trees to the east had been stripped of branches and bark, but protruding ends of some of the limbs had been left to enable a man to climb to the top. At the top of these two poles were secured crossbars, and attached to those were long buckskin thongs wound around the poles. At the time of the ceremony four men would perform incredible acrobatic feats, using the thongs for their daredevil acts. The four pine trees were lying on the ground, awaiting the acrobats who would perform when next Sun Father rose.

Ruupi had taken Leetayo back to his own quarters, and after listening to what had taken place, had made love to her, and returned her to her quarters. He did not reprimand her, for indeed in his mind she did not deserve it. He knew she had done her best. He only knew that he must take a different path, and that path would be more extreme. He wanted the position of sun priest more passionately than ever, and had reached a point where he was ready to do anything necessary to achieve that goal. Desperation clouded his every thought. Then he knew.

He summoned a young acolyte who admired him, and had always done many favors for him whenever he asked. "Charisa," he said, "I have summoned you to ask a favor. I know you are aspiring to become a priest. If you will do what I bid you to do, your path toward the priesthood will be much faster, perhaps even faster than you could imagine." He thought about the fact that Taatawi had been selected to be one of the four performers, and ground his teeth as he spoke. He also knew that he was one of the few who really knew who the acrobats would be. Putting on a false smile, he continued. "You are free to say no if you wish, but this is what I would bid you to do. The poles are ready to be righted when Sun Father begins his next journey. Under the cloak of darkness I would like you to weaken all the thongs by slicing halfway through each one of them. Let no one see you, for you would be killed on the spot. It is a dangerous mission, and again, I repeat, you are free to say no." He had no doubt that the young acolyte would agree, for his desire to become a priest would be foremost in his young mind.

"Revered One, I do not like the danger of what you are requesting, but for you I will do it." Charisa, whose name meant "Elk," bowed to Ruupi in obedience.

"So be it, and I give you thanks," Ruupi declared.

Charisa took his leave, while Ruupi thought through what he knew he must do.

*   *   *

Charisa was very tense as he rose during the darkest time of Sun Father's trip to the other side of the world. He wrapped himself in a dark blanket so that it would be less likely he would be seen. He also allowed his long black hair to hang loose even over his face to further conceal himself. His knife was securely wrapped in its sheath beneath his blanket. In truth he was terrified, but as an acolyte aspiring to be a priest, he felt he had no choice but to obey the revered one, for surely he knew best. He crept silently into the night.

The canyon was unusually quiet. Moon Mother was brilliant as she cast her shadows and lit the way. There was no wind, and no dust, so he did not have to conceal his face. When at last he reached the area where the Ladder Dance would be performed, he quickly surveyed the area for signs that anyone else might be present. He finally decided that there should be no problem, and slunk to the first of the poles, where he quickly placed a generous slice in the buckskin ropes. Counting himself in luck, he went on to do the same as Ruupi had requested. His mind was turbulent because he knew he was desecrating a most holy ceremonial, and it was not a deed he really would ever have wanted to do. Yet here he was, and the deed was accomplished. Wrapping his blanket tightly around himself, he decided that it would be best to leave as quickly as possible.

He was not far from his own quarters when out of nowhere a dark-cloaked figure stepped in front of him. He was afraid to cry out and only wrapped his blanket more tightly around him. Suddenly the hand of the cloaked figure shot out from the darkness, striking him in the head, and he lost consciousness as he fell to the ground on his back. His predator then withdrew an obsidian knife and deftly stabbed his chest, leaving him gurgling in his own blood. Charisa never knew who, and never even realized that his spirit was leaving his body.

As an evil spirit would do, the killer quickly and silently took his leave.

Moon Fire's sleep was restless. She tossed and turned wondering why sleep was evading her. Suddenly she heard the sound of a long, desperate agonizing howl followed by whimpering. She sat bolt upright on her mat, shaking her head as she listened again. She knew what she had heard was not the howl of a coyote, but that of a dog. She rose and tied a skirt around her waist followed by a tunic. She wrapped her feet in leather and climbed the ladder out of her quarters into the plaza. The plaza was absolutely still. Moon Mother was perhaps one sun cycle from being full, and the beltway of stars shone with a milky brilliance. Seeing nothing out of the ordinary in the plaza, she stopped to listen once more. Hearing soft whimpering from outside the complex, she followed the sound to just a short distance to the right.

Moon Mother lit her way until she saw a figure lying on the ground with a scrawny yellow dog resting his head on the legs of the body, crying softly all the while. Without words she communed with the dog, saying that she only came to help if possible. The dog did not seem to object when she bent down next to the body of the young man to check for a pulse. Finding none and seeing the chest wound and the pool of blood in which the young man lay, her heart went out to both the deceased and the dog, who was obviously mourning the passing of his master. She reached for the dog, hugging it to her to offer her warmth and sympathy. Then after a short time, she left the dog to guard his master, returned to the plaza, and finally to Wena 'Ahote's quarters.

He was sleeping lightly as usual, and heard the soft leather on the rungs of his ladder as she descended. "Is there something wrong, my love? I am surprised that you are awake."

"Yes, Revered One. I awoke to hear the pitiful howling of a dog, then whimpering that would not cease. I followed the sound to a space just outside our complex, and found a young man's body most recently stabbed in the chest. His dog's head was resting on the young man's legs as he mourned the death of his master."

Wena 'Ahote was already up and donning his robes. "Did you check for a pulse?"

"Yes, yes, of course. There was none. He was lying in a pool of blood around his head and chest."

"Come, Little Fire. We must hurry," he exclaimed as he grabbed her hand to send her up the ladder.

They ran quickly across the plaza to the sight of the murder.

After Wena 'Ahote had also checked the young man over, he turned to Moon Fire, saying, "This young man is an acolyte aspiring to be a priest. His name is Charisa, and to my knowledge, he has never caused any trouble." He watched the tenderness between the dog and Moon Fire as she held the bereaving animal in her arms against her bosom. "I believe our next step is to inform Taatawi. Will you come with me?"

"No, my love. I will stay to comfort Charisa's dog until you return."

Wena 'Ahote's eyebrows shot up with concern. "Moon Fire, I would not leave you here at the scene of the crime. What if the murderer is still close by. I would not want to live if you became his next victim."

Without a word, she replaced the dog next to his master's legs, and hooked her arm in his. She knew that her empathy with the sorrow of the dog, had clouded her good judgment, while at the same time she reveled in Wena 'Ahote's love, logic, and understanding.

Taatawi was also sleeping lightly, for he rose from sleep earlier than anyone else in the community to trace the path of Sun Father. He also heard padded footsteps on his ladder as he pulled himself to a sitting position. "This is a surprise," he exclaimed. "Has anything happened? Are you both all right?"

"Yes, yes, Revered One," Wena 'Ahote replied excitedly. "Well, I mean we are both all right, but there has been a murder. You must come quickly."

Taatawi said nothing. He wrapped his feet, threw on a blanket, and climbed the ladder behind them.

They were there very quickly. Taatawi also bent to check for a pulse, while Moon Fire held the dog in her arms. Then he slowly rose and stared at Moon Mother briefly. "This event has desecrated our Ladder Dance due to the fact that this murder has been committed at this holy time. Who, in the name of Awonawilona, would ever do such evil?"

Wena 'Ahote gulped as he realized that he had been too caught up in the emergency of the murder to think of the double significance of what had happened. Not only was there a murdering witch among the people, but by that very act, the witch had profaned their holy ceremony. Suddenly he turned to

Moon Fire with a question he had not thought to ask. "Moon Fire, you were the one who discovered Charisa's body. Did you see anyone at all when you first entered the area?"

"No, I did not," she answered. "I only know that I never expected to find anything such as this, and I only checked because of this sweet yellow dog."

"Then it will be necessary to report this to Ruupi and the elders." Taatawi scratched his head, then drew his cloak closer around him. "I have another thought. Why would Charisa have been out here at such a time? What was his purpose?"

Moon Fire interrupted them excitedly. "This little yellow dog is trying to tell me that we should follow him." She set the dog on the ground, and without further conversation, the three of them trailed behind.

To their surprise they were led to the stage area of the Ladder Dance. Nothing appeared out of place until Moon Fire reported, "I am getting a feeling from this dog that something is not right in the arrangements for the Ladder Dance."

Taatawi said, "Wena 'Ahote, you look over that side of the ladders, and I will check this side."

The two priests ran their hands over the poles finding nothing. Suddenly Wena 'Ahote silently brought Taatawi's attention to the buckskin ropes he held in his hand. "Look, Revered One, these lifelines are sliced partially through. It is obvious that the intention was to weaken them."

After scrutinizing the situation, Taatawi exclaimed, "It would seem that someone is bent on the death of one of our dancers. I wonder which one and why?"

"I think we should waste no more time informing the elders and Ruupi. What do you think?" Wena 'Ahote asked.

Taatawi did not hesitate. "I believe you are right. I would ask you to speak to them, for my duties as sun priest are about to begin. I must go now." He turned on his heels to return to his quarters.

Moon Fire set the dog next to his master's legs, and went with Wena 'Ahote to break the news.

It had been decided that the Ladder Dance would go on, and a meeting would be called after the occasion. There was no time to do otherwise, for the ceremony was performed when Moon Mother was at her fullest. Charisa's body would be held in state until the ceremonial was concluded. The buckskin ropes had been replaced, and everything was ready. Since this was not a ceremony that was performed except in time of emergency, and the people were definitely in such a circumstance, the rituals began.

Sun Father was at his zenith, and though Moon Mother was not visible, she was at her fullest. The timing was right, but the world was not. Everyone hoped that this last desperate occasion would solve all their problems, and so they waited.

Two performers stood next to the poles located at the edge of the canyon wall. There were also two other performers standing next to the other two poles. One of these performers was Taatawi. It was true that he was getting old and some felt that he should not be a part of the ceremony, but even at five hands and four season cycles, he was still as agile as he had been as a youth. He knew that most of his people did not live beyond eight hands of season cycles, and he felt truly blessed that, even in spite of the drought, he was doing as well as he was. This was a ceremony he had done only once before when he was truly young, but he remembered it, and had taught the other three performers all about it. He had trained them in the acrobatics that would be necessary.

The ceremony began with music as usual. Taatawi and the other three had been ritually prepared, and their naked bodies had been painted for death, while each of them wore hawk and eagle feathers in their hair. The performers and a chorus of old men were accompanied by a drummer, and of course, Wena 'Ahote, the flutist. When their music was concluded, the two performers at the east began climbing the poles. They faced each other in a precariously upright position when they reached the crossbars on top. Tenyam gave the signal with a blow through a conch shell, and immediately the performers jumped forward and passed each other in midair, grabbing the opposite crossbar to swing out over the edge of the precipice.

Taatawi was awaiting his chance. In less than a blinking of an eye, he and his other very young partner leaped forward to the western poles, grabbed a leather thong secured at the top of the crossbar, and swung out in a wide arc over the land below, flying as an eagle as the thong unwound around the pole. This was of course, a death jump, for any miscalculation or faltering of strength or skill would have hurtled any performer to the rocks below, and to the death for which he had been ritually prepared.

The audience was gasping and cheering, for they were well aware of the danger their loved ones were challenging. Moon Fire and Wena 'Ahote were clutching each other's hands as they watched. Wena 'Ahote was clearly admiring Taatawi's agility, and hoped he might be in such fitness when he reached his age. He decided to ask Taatawi to begin instructing him for this ceremony if it was not too late. The other three performers were much younger, probably less than four hands of season cycles.

The acrobats repeated this same cycle four times as they defied the laws of the universe. It was over very quickly. The people knew they must remain pure of heart, and that no negativities must be allowed into their minds, for such would defeat the purpose of the ceremonial. As everyone left to return to their own quarters or outliers, they all continued to marvel at the skill of the performers.

The council meeting began after the Ladder Dance and when Sun Father had completed his journey. Everyone who should be there was in attendance including Moon Fire. Lines of fatigue and anxiety were etched on many faces, indicating the seriousness of the problem at hand. Everyone had become bony, even gaunt, for no one was getting enough to eat. Even the once-fat Eykita was now a shadow of his former rotund self. Taatawi looked particularly exhausted, which was understandable, since he had been the dancer who had shown the most skill and also been the most daring.

Moon Fire observed Ruupi out of the corner of her eye. He seemed almost bored with what was about to occur, and pressed his lips together, giving an expression that she thought smug and altogether disturbing. She wished she could speak to him as she spoke to the animals, but he was human and had put up a wall of defense ever since returning from his exile.

Tenyam, as usual, called the meeting to order. "I am sure by now that word has reached all of you informing you that there is one who is 'pawaka' among us. The Ladder Dance was profaned with the brutal murder of one of our young acolytes. It is not clear whether he or his murderer sliced the leather thongs to make them weak. At any rate the deeds were done, and I call you here to ask if any of you know anything more?" He heaved an audible discomforting sigh, and sat down to indicate that any who desired to speak might do so.

Angwusi rose from the bench. After rubbing his hands over the bags under his eyes, he said, "It has come to our attention that Moon Fire was the one to discover the body. In my mind this would suggest that she also might be a suspect, though I cannot see what motive she might have to do such an evil deed."

Moon Fire gasped aloud. She had not given a thought to the fact that she might be suspected just because she had known something was wrong and found the acolyte. Her body trembled in fear, for she knew what her people did to those who were witches.

Wena 'Ahote clasped her hand and squeezed it slightly to let her know of his support. He, too, was taken by surprise that any of his people could even consider Moon Fire as a possible suspect in the crime. He knew he would not be able to defend her due to his position and because he was her lover, and he prayed silently to Awonawilona that someone would exoreate her as quickly as possible.

As if in answer to his prayers Hoohu rose to speak. "In my mind, I am disappointed that anyone would even think of pointing a finger at our beloved gifted counselor. Moon Fire has done nothing but good for our people, and will surely continue to do so in the future. Perhaps we should let her speak for herself."

When no one objected, Moon Fire took the floor. She shut her eyes for a brief time to gather her thoughts together, took several deep breaths, stepped forward, and began. "I slept restlessly before the sun cycle of the Ladder Dance. After tossing and turning for a very long time, I dozed, then awoke to the sound of a desolate howl. I knew it was not that of a coyote, and I somehow knew immediately something was not right. I threw a blanket around me and followed the sound of the howling and whimpering until I came upon a body and a yellow dog who was still whimpering. The dog had laid his head over the legs of the young acolyte, and could not be consoled no matter how hard I tried. He told me the acolyte was his master. I went to Wena 'Ahote to speak of what I had found, and he went to Taatawi, and you know the rest. I want you all to know that this is the truth. Awonawilona knows that it is so." She stepped back again into the protective aura of Wena 'Ahote. For some intuitive reason she stole a glance at Ruupi, whose face still showed only boredom, but his body language was tense and fidgety, offering a most unusual and startling contrast. Moon Fire had no time to reflect on her observation, for another speaker stood.

Eykita rose with almost a spring in his step. Whether it was due to his loss of weight, no one knew, but he was no longer the same heavy, lethargic Eykita. "I have been thinking through the problem, and I have some thoughts to share. First, I do not think it wise that we try to place the blame when we don't have all the facts. There are too many unknowns and we should not be hasty. To Moon Fire, I would like to say, I believe you. You have never done anything but good for any of our people, and I cannot believe anyone would even begin to question her validity. It is my suggestion that we adjourn to further research the problem, for without solid evidence we have no case."

Moon Fire was so taken back by Eykita's support, she found herself unable to speak, even if she had been asked to do so. She felt Wena 'Ahote's hand gently squeeze her own, and she rejoiced.

When no one else seemed to wish to speak, Tenyam rose. "There is something more that has come to my attention that you should know." He sighed heavily and seemed to hesitate to go on. "It is not good news, but traders have given me the information I give you now. The large outlier to the north of us at the end of the Great North Road is growing fast, and is surviving the drought better than we are due to a major river that runs adjacent to it. The river is slightly more than a trickle, but one can dig down and get more than they need. As a result hunting is better, and growing crops on a small scale is possible. It grieves me to say this, but it is beginning to seem that our northern outlier may be becoming the new center of trade for our people."

Those in attendance were so exhausted that only a low groan escaped from their lips. It seemed that their world was falling into ruin, and there was nothing anyone could do about it. It was the consensus of opinion that it was definitely a "world out of balance."

The meeting adjourned.

CHAPTER 16

A.D. *1136*

Two more season cycles had passed. Even with the Ladder Dance Awonawilona had not seen fit to offer a break in the terrible drought that was now not only costing lives because of malnutrition, but also was sending many people out of the canyon to seek better living conditions elsewhere. Many were in such a weakened state that they were unable to fight any predator, human or otherwise, who came upon them. Only the most staunch supporters of the canyon valiantly remained behind, leaving little more than one out of five persons who had formerly occupied the community. There was little trading except with the northern outlier, and everything seemed to be a ghost of what had been. No one any longer had a bit of fat on their bones.

The landscape was arid and sun-baked. The once-flowing creek had been dry for many season cycles, and even the plant life that normally grew along the edges, reaching down for water, was long since dead. When, on rare occasions, Awonawilona chose to send rain, the people gathered it in huge clay cisterns or bowls, treating it with more respect than they had ever imagined, for even then there was very little. Even most cactus were dried up, true indication of bad times. The people had been given something of a reprieve with grain they had received from the northern-most outlier, and also from new outliers even farther north, but it was not enough. They lacked protein and greens.

Moon Fire had been watching all this, and could not blame

her people for leaving. She was now four hands and one season cycle of age, though at times she felt she must be an old woman before her time. She had grown so used to the gnawing twinges in her stomach that she was beginning to think that it was normal, and that there had never been a time when she might have felt different. All in all, she, too, was growing despondent. When she saw her parents, who were so emaciated and lacking in spirit, she grieved. When she thought of Sihu and her nephews, and the fact that Lansa was robust and thriving because of his trading, she felt saddened, but it was Palasiva who concerned her the most. She intuitively felt he was still alive. After all he was a wanderer, and could go where there was water and game, but she still could not understand why he had done such a terrible deed to his people. She found it very difficult to keep her mind from negativities which violated the foundation of her people's beliefs. It was with these thoughts that she looked up to see her beloved Wena 'Ahote descend the ladder to her own quarters.

She gave him a huge smile to show her delight that he would seek her out. She chuckled to herself as she realized that he often asked for her advice, yet each time he did it, she was amazed. He was a priest, and somewhere in the back of her mind it still surprised her that he would need to speak to her of his problems. Perhaps, she thought, he did not really need to speak to her, but wanted to share his life with her, and she was overjoyed. "What has brought you to my side, my love?" she inquired.

He sat down on her mat in his usual cross-legged position, and said, "Times are not good. Not only are we experiencing starvation, but as I have suggested to you before, there is unrest between Ruupi, Taatawi, and me. I needed a sympathetic ear, and I knew I could trust in you, Little Fire. May I speak?"

"You do not have to ask. In a relationship such as ours, it is expected. You know that," she responded in her usual soft, gentle voice.

Without hesitation, he began. "It's Ruupi. He, well . . ."

"He what, my love?" She placed her small hand on his crossed knee as she urged him to continue.

Wena 'Ahote placed the palm of his right hand on his fore-head. "At times Ruupi seems to completely ignore me, which makes me think he is bored with my company or perhaps it is condescending on his part to speak to me. I am a fully ordained priest as he is, but I am younger and as yet do not have a spe-cialty. Someday I hope to be sun priest, but I still have much to learn from Taatawi, and I would never do anything to usurp his position. I never feel uncomfortable when I am around Taatawi, but Ruupi is entirely different." He paused as if he was await-ing her validation.

"I know you will someday make a fine sun priest. You are already the finest dancer and flutist among our people. You know you are well loved and respected by the people."

"Of that I am aware. I am sorry there are so few of our peo-ple left in the canyon, and often that alone depresses me, but when Ruupi behaves as oddly as he does, I am at a loss to un-derstand why. Sometimes when we are talking, he even goes so far as to refute what he misconstrues I have said. I want to lash out and tell him to stop, but he is my senior and as such should deserve my respect."

Moon Fire stopped him, saying, "What you are describing to me appears to me an invasion of your boundaries. Go on."

"Sometimes he discounts me by telling me I am jumping to conclusions or I'm blowing everything out of proportion. It's as though he thinks he knows it all, and I know nothing."

"Are you saying that it's as if he has taken up residence in your mind and swept away your experiences? Does he seem to be replacing those with his own ideas?" she inquired.

"Indeed it is so, sweet one. How is it you know and under-stand so well?" Then shaking his head with a chuckle, he said, "Of course that was a silly question to ask. I forget that you are a superb counselor, and how the people adore you. Anyway, he also often accuses me of thinking wrong, telling me that I am looking at things the wrong way. I know our people are sup-posed to be 'people of peace,' but sometimes I want to punch him in the nose."

"Again I remind you that he is invading your mind through manipulations, making up a story about your motives, and telling it to you. He has no right to do that," she exclaimed.

"As if that were not enough, he occasionally tells me I don't know what I am doing, which makes me feel so small, and again makes me want to scream at him. He also sometimes orders me around, and will tell me I never said something that I know I said. All in all he is driving me crazy with confusion. Oh, Little Fire, is there anything I can do short of becoming violent?"

Moon Fire heaved an audible sigh. "Let us take the last two problems in hand. You say he tells you you don't know what you are doing. First you must realize that his judgments and criticisms are lies about your personal qualities and performance even though his reasons for doing so are unknown to us. Lies, yes lies. He has no right to judge you or criticize you. No one should try to define someone else, for that is also a violation of your boundaries. Secondly, if he orders you around, he has forgotten that you are a separate person with the right to life, and that you are a free person. Perhaps you could respond with a comment to him such as, 'Can you ask me to do this politely?' and when he is judging you, you could say, 'Stop judging me,' or 'Stop the criticism.' The next time he tells you you did not say what you clearly remember you said, tell him, 'I know what I said. Stop trying to make me think I am crazy. Is your hearing selective?' "

"But wouldn't such responses be disrespectful? I think I should speak to Taatawi of what you suggest."

"Perhaps you should, but you must impress upon him that Ruupi is constantly violating your boundaries, and after discussing the situation with me, we have come to the conclusion that there is no other choice but to speak out to defend your own person. Also remind him that you are not the cause of Ruupi's irritation. Ruupi's problems are his own. You do not have to take his abuse, you are a worthwhile person, and deserve to be treated with respect. Meanwhile, my love, know that you are my world and my salvation in these miserable times in which we both are living. If you have no immediate obligations, I would enjoy some attention. I think we both need it."

Wena 'Ahote drew her to him as they stretched out on the

mat together and planted a searching kiss on her full lips. When he moved to nibble her ear, she stopped him.

"There is one more thing I want to say, my love, before we are too intoxicated with each other to want to make any sense." He looked at her curiously and waited. "Ruupi, as you know, does not like us, and especially you. He was exiled because of his efforts to ruin you along with Leetayo who hates me and who is, I am sure, his lover. He has not changed. The elders, in my opinion, were foolish to think that a two-season cycle exile would change him and his ways. He is still an evil man. I would not want you to speak of what I say now to Taatawi, but I feel in my soul that it is so. He still would ruin both of us if he could. All he has done is to attack you covertly instead of overtly, but the attack is still there. I am sure you would agree. Be careful, my love. He is still treacherous. Now, enough. Kiss me again."

He kissed her lingeringly on the lips, moving to her shoulder, and drawing her close, feeling the warmth of her small breasts on his chest. When they drew apart, she loosened the wood-carved pins that held the braids in her hair, letting her hair fall below her waist in a thick black cloud covering her breasts and part of her back. Seductively she removed her skirt while she watched him remove his robe, for she knew he wore no breechcloth beneath it.

She giggled and asked him, "Do you ever wonder why I am different and have six toes on each foot?"

"No, I look at your lush body and never get that far down. Do you think I should?"

"Oh, no. Please don't. I don't think I have any sexual feelings in my toes."

"Then let me continue," he said passionately as he continued kissing her in long, slow, sweeping kisses, until he had ignited her to such a frenzy that she dug her nails into his back.

When he had made her ready, he buried himself between her legs bringing her to such a climax that she had to stuff her unbound hair into her mouth to keep from being heard with her screaming. Moon Fire never thought of herself as a woman who might scream with pleasure, but after they were both sat-

isfied, she laughed as she lay in his arms, and he had to quiet
her with more kisses.

They lay together for some time, reveling in each other and
the wonder of love.

Taatawi shook his head as he listened to Wena 'Ahote's
words. They were seated on his mat next to one of the white-
washed walls in his quarters. At thirty-one season cycles of age
he felt old beyond his years. His hair was still very black,
streaked with gray only at his temples. In his role as priest it
was necessary to fast for sometimes many days at least once
every moon cycle, and compounded with the shortage of food,
he struggled to remain active, for the life span of his people was
on an average only forty season cycles. At times it was an effort to maintain his image.

His back was already up against the wall, and now he leaned
his head back for support and gazed up the ladder as if wanting
to escape the world. Yet escape, he knew he could not. He only
felt tired. At last he turned to Wena 'Ahote, who was many season cycles his junior, and said, "As you know, Ruupi is a hot-
head, and thinks he can do no wrong. Since his return from his
exile, we cannot prove he has done anything wrong, even
though we suspect it might be so. He, too, is suffering along
with the rest of us. Perhaps you should consider that before you
respond to him as you would like to do."

"But, Taatawi, Revered One, he does not show the signs of
hunger. He is not fat, but he is not skinny. Does that not raise a
question in your mind? Likewise, Leetayo also is not fat, but
not skinny. I ask you. What is going on here?"

He heaved a deep sigh, then turned to Wena 'Ahote. "You
are very observant. I also have noticed and wondered, but
due to the dilemma of our people have chosen to ignore it. I
assure you there are many suspicions in my mind, but there
have been so many other problems to deal with to protect the
few who still insist on remaining in the canyon that I feel that
it is not the time for another crisis, especially one we might
avoid."

Wena 'Ahote covered his mouth with his right hand and
thought for a time. At last he said, "Taatawi, I fully understand

what you are saying, but my life has been miserable since Ruupi returned from his exile. Oh, at first it was not so bad, but as time has gone on, it has steadily gotten worse. I have only you and Moon Fire who support me, and yes, of course the people. I was sure you would understand."

"Of course I understand," he retorted, "but we must consider the complexity of the situation. The people are hungry and many are sickly and weak. You and I both know that Ruupi would not hesitate to make an enormous mountain out of an anthill, for such is his disposition. It is my honest opinion that Ruupi is a very unhappy, ambitious man, who may even be out to destroy us both. We cannot allow such a thing to happen, not only for our own sakes, but for the sake of the people. We need to stand firmly together if we and the people are to survive." His eyes held Wena 'Ahote's sympathetically.

"I suppose you are right. I will try harder to ignore him for the sake of the people, but I must tell you honestly that what you ask of me will not make me happy, for he is constantly trying to undermine my self-esteem. He is also trying to make me crazy." Then rising from the mat, he added, "I guess I should take my leave. I thank you for listening."

Taatawi heaved a great sigh, then said, "May Awona-wilona give us strength. My father used to tell me that Awona-awilona would not give us more to handle than we are able, but sometimes I wonder." He watched Wena 'Ahote despondently climb the ladder.

When Sun Father had finally set, he did not wait for Moon Fire to come to him. He went to her.

She looked up in surprise and rose from her mat to embrace him. "I read you well, she said. "Things did not go as you hoped."

"No, Little Fire, they did not. Taatawi advised me to remain quiet for the sake of the people. He said that my responding to Ruupi as you have suggested would inflame his temper, and Taatawi has no doubts that Ruupi would not hesitate to make a mountain out of an anthill, He also said that he honestly thinks that Ruupi is an unhappy, ambitious man, and may be out to destroy us both. He says for the sake of the people he and I must stand firm for the sake of unity." He stroked her back as he held her close.

After a short period of silence, she extricated herself from his embrace, beckoning him to sit with her on her mat. When he had made himself comfortable, she offered him some thin corn gruel, but he refused. She knelt beside him, taking his hand in her own and clasping it to her breast. "It must be very difficult to be in such a position as you are in. Taatawi says you must put your life aside for the sake of the people? That is hard to believe."

"Unfortunately, my love, he is right. The life of a truly devoted priest is not his own. Everything is, or should be, for the good of the people. I am blessed to have you and your understanding, but I must tell you something that has been on my mind for some time now. No one else must know, but things are at such a point that I must speak of my innermost feelings." He paused as if trying to gather courage.

"You know what we speak of will never leave this room," she whispered.

"I know," he answered. "I am only human, and I have my boundaries. Ruupi is, I feel, taking great joy in invading my boundaries. I don't think I can take any more. I am thinking of resigning my position in the priesthood."

Moon Fire gasped in surprise. "Wena 'Ahote, my love, you must not be serious. I cannot believe he has gotten you to go so far as to consider resignation."

"He has. Oh, he has. I do not want to listen to him anymore. He is trying to destroy me mentally, and I cannot stand by and allow him to do it." He squeezed her hand tightly. "Don't you understand?"

"Oh yes, of course. I do understand, but now I want you to hear me out. Will you do that? I know you are distraught."

He closed his eyes briefly, then sighed deeply. "Yes, go on."

"Wena 'Ahote, love of my life, I am sorry I advised you as I did. I treated you as an ordinary one of the people. I did not take your position as priest into consideration. I know that you promised when you were ordained, to let the people's welfare always come first, for that is the role of a devoted priest. I also know that the times we are living through are miserable, and

the people are shaky and nervous as well as sickly and hungry.
If they ever needed you, they need you now. You are younger
than Taatawi and Ruupi, and are likely to be around longer. You
know that the people adore you. They would not believe anything bad about you, but I agree with Taatawi. Why put them
through any more hardships than they are already experiencing? I also adore you, and will always offer you my support and
love." She took both his hands in her own and clutched them
tightly, then added, "Are you saying that Ruupi has a stronger
will than you do?"

"Absolutely not! Yet if I resigned, we could become man
and wife. We could live a normal life, well, as normal as starvation would allow." His warm black eyes were moist as he
spoke.

Moon Fire valiantly struggled to compose herself, then said,
"There is nothing I would like more, but do we want to bring
more strife to the people? In season cycles to come, if you were
to resign, would you be able to live with yourself?"

Wena 'Ahote struggled within himself for a short period of
time. After thinking on her words, he finally said with a deep
sigh, "Perhaps that is how it must be. I shall do my best to remain neutral when I am in Ruupi's company."

Breathing a sigh of relief, she drew him into her arms and
buried her head in the hollow of his shoulder.

The community was in a flurry of excitement, for sentries
had warned them that Mayan-Toltec traders were approaching
from the south road. It had been decided that Tenyam would
greet the visitors when they arrived in the plaza of the holy
school. Those who remained in the other great houses clamored
to see what demands the traders would make. There was much
bustle and fuss, for everyone knew that nothing good could
come of this visit.

Moon Fire watched the steady stream of visitors as they
drew closer to their destination, and felt a great sense of evil en-
veloping the community. She could not explain why. She only
knew she must honor her feelings, and so she watched.

Tenyam moved out to speak with the traders, but even as he
did, Moon Fire noticed that there were two warriors with the

two traders. The traders were dressed in their simple fine cotton robes, with their hair loose and flowing. The warriors wore their long hair gathered in a plait, and wore only a loincloth and sandals made from maguey fibers, with a spear and knife strapped on their shoulders. They also each carried a bow with many arrows in a quiver of leather strapped on their backs. The backs of both the warriors' and the traders' heads were flattened from much time in the cradle board, while their foreheads had been flattened so that their heads appeared pointed on top. The elder trader had a yellow topaz inserted in one side of his nose with his two upper front teeth inlaid with the green stone called jade. He also wore bones inserted through his earlobes. It seemed strange to Moon Fire that the traders would need warriors to protect them, for it was understood everywhere that traders were neutral and should not be attacked. Surely, she thought, this did not seem like an ordinary trading visit.

Tenyam approached the one who seemed in charge of the party, greeting him in friendship. "we are surprised to see such a trading party, for we are in the midst of a terrible drought and famine, and we have nothing to offer in trade. We are, however, honored to have you with us, and offer whatever hospitality is possible in our miserable conditions."

The trader who seemed to be in charge of the small party stepped forward. "My name is Seven Moon, for that is when I was born. I am here to trade with your people. I am aware you are experiencing difficult times, but I still offer you any exchanges you might have."

Moon Fire knew that no good could come from what she heard, but she remained still and anxious as the bantering continued.

"Seven Moon, I hear you and respect you, but there is really nothing we have to trade. We are a destitute people trying to survive if only marginally, and that is the way of it," Tenyam replied.

Seven Moon shook his head and adjusted his robe. "No," he declared, "you do have a commodity that we have always traded for in the past, and hopefully will trade for in the future."

"And what is that?" Tenyam asked, though he knew the answer would be turquoise.

"I cannot believe you would even ask such a question," answered Seven Moon as he began to bristle under the evasion of Tenyam's response.

"Then you must answer me," Tenyam replied.

Seven Moon began to feel that Tenyam was putting him on, and he responded somewhat angrily, "Come now. Your people are the protectors of the most lucrative turquoise mines in the area. We covet those gems, and wish to secure more." He tried to abate his anger, which seemed to be rising.

"The season cycles in the past have been very hard on our people. We have not given these mines the attention they need due to the lack of workers to keep them functioning. I would hope you can understand what I am saying." Tenyam was beginning to feel desperate, yet he knew not why.

Seven Moon fingered his robe, cleared his throat, and said, "Then it seems obvious that we must make a trade of a different kind." His eyes became cold and hard as he went on to his next statement. "If your people cannot supply us with turquoise, then there is an alternative."

"And what is that?" asked Tenyam.

Thrusting his chest out proudly, Seven Moon's voice rose to a high pitch. "Then we would trade for your people."

Tenyam's anger immediately was aroused. Clenching his fists at his sides, he declared, "My people are not for sale, never have been, and never will be. We know that you want us only to appease your bloodthirsty gods, and this we will not condone. I would advise you not to push the issue any further."

Seven Moon's eyes glittered with hatred as he fought to contain his temper. "Your people, known as 'People of Peace,' are spineless. If you would offer your gods the ultimate gift, that of human blood, you would not be in the miserable condition you are experiencing now. I would suggest you give what I am saying some consideration, for you are a dying people. I can offer you bags of corn, quetzal feathers, and even cocoa beans to put your people out of their misery. Give me ten hands of your people, no old ones mind you, and the rest of you will gain a respite from your miseries."

At this point Hoohu stepped into the conversation. "You don't seem to understand the meaning of *no*. Tenyam has told you and I also will tell you, there can be no bargaining, for our people will not be traded. What we say is what we mean." He turned to Angwusi, for he knew that it was useless to ask Eykita for support, and that Angwusi almost always agreed with Tenyam.

Angwusi stepped forward, saying, "There can be no bargaining, for what you are asking for is impossible for us to give."

Seven Moon turned away to briefly confer with the younger trader. Whipping his robe angrily around his lean body, he turned back to the elders, and snarled, "Since your brains are made of stone, you may be assured that we will never return to your canyon. From this time on, our trading will be done only with your fast-growing northern outlier. They, at least, are reasonable people."

"Of course they are reasonable. They have a source of water, meager though it may be. We do not. Four out of five of all the people who used to live in this community have left due to the drought, and according to our informers, many of them have been captured by your people along the way. Go! Go, I say! Trade with them. Just leave us alone." Tenyam was growing weary and turned away from them all.

Seven Moon fairly boiled with rage. Spittle flew from his mouth as he hissed, "All right. Have it your way. You will be the ones to suffer. In your weakened condition, it would be easy for my people to send an army to forcibly take you all into slavery. In fact when I return to Tula, I may just make that suggestion."

Dead silence pervaded the plaza. Moon Fire knew the confrontation was over when Seven Moon, the younger trader, and the two warriors turned abruptly and left the plaza, heading for the Great North Road.

CHAPTER 17

A.D. *1137*

Palasiva had lived with the raiders, and remained alive for more time than he ever thought would have been possible. He had never been fully accepted by the raiders, and his allegiance was, and always would be, with his own people. He thought that Teo sensed his unhappiness. Yet, in spite of everything, he had developed a grudging respect for the "mountain people," as they called themselves. Their constant quest for survival kept them in top physical condition. There were no paunchy elders as there were occasionally among his own people. Though many did not reach maturity due to the hard life they led, the ones who did were masters of their environment and well equipped to provide support for their families. These were a tough people, tougher than his own, but he still found it very difficult to condone some of their ways, especially their war-faring ways.

Time had passed, and now the band of raiders had expanded to twenty hands of lodges that were, as usual, erected in two parallel lines that covered a large space of level prairie. The center or the space between the lines was occupied by the large lodge of red painted buffalo skins, tattooed with the mystic totems of the "medicine" peculiar to the people. The medicine men who occupied this lodge seemed particularly busy as the arms, shields, and smoke-dried scalps clattered in the wind.

Palasiva found many of their customs strange, and perhaps that is why he longed to return to his own people. Stealing from others was considered a necessary thing, but their belief was that one should never steal from a guest who was visiting, or from another of the "mountain people." Theft among their own people was an unpardonable crime, and one who was caught lost all his or her possessions. A man and his entire family could be dismissed from the band, while a woman might be beaten and turned out of the village alone. This was only one of many of the strange customs these people practiced.

Another custom, very different from his own people, was the frequent violence shown among estranged married couples. Adultery, of course, was condemned, but a jealous wife was often seen taking aggressive action against her rival. Palasiva had only recently watched a wrestling match between two females, only to learn that the victor would win the man. There were other ways to get even, such as taking the rival's possessions, cutting her hair, or even physically assaulting her. He had also watched a husband trying to physically remove his wife from another man's presence, which resulted in a tug of war with the woman caught in the middle. The rival might take the husband's possessions, thus making certain that the husband could not reclaim his wife. To Palasiva violence seemed a way of life to the raiders.

One other thing was very different from his own "people of peace." Several families would be organized into one band. Each band had one or more leaders. Leaders or chiefs were usually older members who were respected for their deeds, and wisdom. Whenever bands joined together, one principal chief would be elected who was the most powerful. Often there would be a war chief and a hunting leader. Palasiva knew of one band where one man handled all the responsibilities. The strangest thing was that there was always a council of elders who would discuss issues of concern, but ultimately the principal chief made the final decision, and no one questioned his decision. If anyone did, they were free to leave and form their own band. There was no vote taken, no unanimous decision, which was totally different from the Anasazi.

Palasiva's life was filled with chores, sometimes those of the women, and he struggled with himself when he watched the deriding expressions on the faces of the people. There was one young woman, however, who looked at him with sympathy in her large doe eyes. He knew she was interested in him, though he could not imagine why. True enough, he was lean and muscular, and taller than almost all of the "mountain people," but in his mind he stood out like a sore thumb. She was small and dainty, and reminded him of Moon Fire. Her hair was so long that it fell below her hips, and her body was well proportioned. He enjoyed watching her, as he knew she enjoyed watching him, but due to the fact that he was a nobody to the raiders, he knew there was no chance. He struggled with his own physical desires, and valiantly put them aside. He was biding his time until he could break away from them. In his mind a long-range plan was shaping up.

A sentry came into the camp, informing Teo and his father that ten Anasazi, very weak and bedraggled, had left the canyon, heading northeast toward one of the great rivers that had not yet completely dried up. Ochata, the chief of the raiding band of people, and Teo's father, simply nodded to his son, giving him instructions without words. Palasiva watched Teo, who was war chief, rise immediately to rally his warriors.

Once again Palasiva's heart was wrenched from his chest at the thought that his people might die or be given to the Mayan-Toltecs into slavery. Here was yet another reason for him to find a way to leave these bloodthirsty people who seemed to place no value on human life unless, of course, it was of their own people. He vowed he would escape even if he could not return to his own people.

He watched as Teo's warriors prepared for warfare, though he thought it was ridiculous to consider attacking innocent people as warfare. He waited and watched as Teo and his men painted themselves as though they were sure death was awaiting them. They smoked, and trance-danced as though there would surely be a major battle. When they finished, they set out with screams and yips.

Palasiva followed them, keeping his distance so they would not learn of his presence. He wondered why he felt the compulsion to watch such a heartbreaking event when there was nothing he could do to help that would not mean certain death. In the recesses of his mind, he had formulated a long-range plan that would be of no use to him or his people if he chose to die now. Since he had been forced to live some distance from the lodges of the "mountain people," he had found ample time to maintain his warrior skills. Because he had only a makeshift lodge and no real belongings except for a single blanket, he had become as tough, or perhaps tougher than Teo and his band of warriors. He also had secretly been making arrows to fit his newly made bow, and had also made himself an obsidian knife and a tomahawk which he was keeping carefully hidden.

From his vantage point he watched. Ten bedraggled figures were coming toward a deep rock passage. Their faces were covered to filter out the dust that blew in occasional gusts, and they all carried bifurcated baskets on their backs, held in place by soft leather straps across their foreheads. The baskets held the basic necessities and anything that was meaningful to them. Their heads were covered, and their bodies were wrapped with at least two blankets. Their feet were wrapped with cloth and bound within yucca sandals. They had covered themselves so completely that there was no way to identify any of them. The little group trudged on slowly toward the passage.

Palasiva wanted to scream as he watched Teo and his warriors silently waiting for them at the far side of the passage. As far as he could see, his people stood no chance, for none of them seemed to be armed. Suddenly the group of travelers decided to stop to rest. Though they had just entered the passage, they removed their baskets, and sat down to rest their aching legs and feet.

Teo immediately signaled his warriors, who crept silently halfway through the passage, then raised their voices in hideous screams, yips, and howls declaring their war cries.

The travelers were on their feet immediately. Throwing off their blankets, they revealed themselves as warriors who were fully armed.

Palasiva's heart skipped a beat with the realization that it all had been a trap. Though he was overjoyed with the cleverness of his people, he still saw that they were slightly outnumbered. The ten Anasazi warriors were outnumbered by just one hand of raiding warriors. He felt sure that due to their weakened state and way of life in general, they would be an easy win for the raiders.

The raiders continued on with their horrendous war cries and noise that was intended to frighten the enemy until they were within shooting range of the ten waiting warriors. As they raised their bows to shoot, the ten warriors surged silently forward to meet them in battle. Palasiva wondered why his people's warriors did not raise their own war cry, but he had not long to wait for the answer, for from the rear of the raiders came a new sound. War hoots and trills, screams and animal noises erupted from behind the raiders. Anasazi warriors lunged from their hiding places in the pass, six on either side. The odds were now on their side unless their weakened physical health proved detrimental. Palasiva grew hopeful.

The battle raged. The ten who had been disguised moved smoothly into range of the raiders, but the raiders were confused and caught by surprise by the additional twelve who were behind them. Arrows flew, and where close contact was made, knives and spears sometimes found their mark. As far as Palasiva could see, his people were holding their own.

Teo and his fifteen had been reduced to eight. He frantically gave the signal to retreat to the side of the pass they had entered. He and his warriors defended themselves as best they could in their closed-in conditions, but two more raiders were down by the time they returned to the entrance through which they came.

Then, much to Teo's amazement, additional war cries were heard from either side, and twelve more Anasazi warriors ran from either side of the entrance again behind the raiders. He was now badly outnumbered, and even without his signal his men were retreating as quickly as possible. The shields of his remaining six men offered little protection to the onslaught of new arrows. Three more of his fifteen warriors were felled, leaving only three including himself. The two who still stood beside him had been grazed by arrows in several places, and one of his warriors was bleeding rather profusely from his right arm.

At long last, with one desperate effort, Teo and his two remaining warriors broke free, making a run for their lives. Teo knew when he was beaten and thoroughly beaten. He was filled with shame to think of returning to his father and admitting his defeat.

Palasiva, on the other hand, was filled with happiness that his people had defended their own and been triumphant. As far as he could tell from his vantage point, the Anasazi had lost perhaps two warriors. He watched silently as his people gathered the wounded and dead to return to their community. A piece of his heart went with them, for they had, at last, delivered a significant blow to the raiders, and one the raiders would not forget.

He was so engrossed in his own thoughts of happiness for his people that he did not consider the seriousness of his own situation for a short time. Clearly the entire battle had been a setup by his own people. How would they have known that raiders would attack? Then, quite suddenly, he realized that he must return to the "mountain people," and be there before Teo and his warriors arrived. If he was not, Teo and his father might suspect him of being the informant, and he did not want to even think about what those consequences might be. He only knew his very life might be at stake.

Palasiva's heart thundered in his chest as he made his way silently back the way he had come, never stopping to rest, but pushing himself at top speed to reach his destination. In the back of his mind, he thought Teo and the two remaining warriors would travel more slowly than he, due to the shoulder wound of the one warrior, but he could not count on that, so he flew.

He finally reached close proximity to his own lodge, and slowed to regain his breath. As far as he could see, Teo had not yet returned, and for that he was thankful. His heart filled with pride when he thought of the way his people had defended their own. Now, he hoped, and he was sure that they did, too, the raiders would think again before they attacked Anasazi who were seemingly leaving the community to seek better living conditions. He marveled at the tenacity and courage of his people, and his heart swelled with pride. Perhaps, he thought, this was as Awonawilona intended to show him how tough he could be as he continued to lay out the plan for his own future.

*   *   *

Women shrieked and wailed due to the loss of their loved ones. No one gave Palasiva a second thought, for which he was most grateful. In some strange sense of the word he felt some sympathy for Teo, who would have to face the wrath of his father when he broke the news. Now, it seemed, the hard part for Teo was over, for he rallied more warriors to bring back the bodies of those they had lost. Only a few warriors were left behind in case of an attack on their own lodges by other marauding tribes.

Palasiva found everything to be very quiet. Women and old people were temporarily the primary occupants, though there were still a number of warriors whose main concern was to protect the village. He worked diligently on the cache of weapons he was accumulating and enjoyed the solitude. As he worked, he thought of the dead who would be brought in, and realized that his own people and the "mountain people" had a few things in common, for their burial customs were similar. He had lived with them long enough to know that their burials were pit burials, with the bodies placed in a flexed position as was also the custom of his own people. The male burials were accompanied by projectile points, bows and arrows, scrapers, and any other tools associated with hunting. Females were usually buried with manos, metates, hammer stones, choppers, and other bone tools having to do with food gathering and processing. Infants' and young children's burials were usually accompanied by more ornamental items, such as shell and bone beads or pendants. The differences between his people and the "mountain people's" burials were only two. One was that his own people were buried under a cornerstone of the house in which they had lived, while the raiders buried theirs in pits in the ground, and occasionally in a cave. The other was that a person of high importance among his own people might be buried flat on his or her back while this was not a custom among the raiders.

He had reached a point in his work where he no longer could remain hunched over, for his upper neck and back were giving him grief. After relieving himself behind his lodge, he decided to walk toward the water. Sun Father had warmed the air comfortably, while puffy clouds filled the sky. He picked his way through the mesquite and various kinds of cactus, reveling in the beauty that Awonawilona had bestowed on everyone. Cottonwoods lined the narrow river, offering their shade and intimacy, beckoning him to stretch out on his back to ease his stiffness. Sighing deeply, he closed his eyes.

Just before sleep overtook him he thought he heard someone singing. Curiosity got the best of him as he raised himself up on one elbow to listen more intently. The sound was of a young woman who could not be very far away. Moving stealthily and silently toward the owner of the voice, he peeped around several mesquite and a cottonwood to see the young woman who often looked at him with interest. He did not know what to do. She was washing clothes in the water, and humming and singing in a sweet melodious voice. Her hair almost completely hid her face, but her body with its delicate sweet curves were most familiar to him. Still he did not move.

She continued to sing for a short time, then stopped, looking in his direction. "I know you are there," she whispered softly.

He still did not move, though he was enjoying the beautiful view.

She squeezed the last piece of cotton and piled it on a rock with all the rest, and moved sensuously through the mesquite to his side. They stared at each other for some time before she finally said, "I have watched you from afar for some time."

"And I have also watched you," he answered.

"I am called Mina. You are so different from my own people. You are taller but just as broad of shoulder," she said.

"You remind me of my sister. She is small and delicate like you, and carries herself in much the same way."

"Is that what compelled you to watch me?" she inquired. She lowered her black lashes, then looked up again into his own obsidian eyes.

"No, you are lovely in your own right. But, yes, I did find it amusing to compare both the differences and the similarities."

"My people do not trust you, you know," she declared. "I cannot imagine why, for I have seen you do nothing that is contrary to the ways of our people."

"I am very much aware of that, but at least I am surviving

during this terrible drought that has caused so much misery and even death. That is a gift your people have given to me." He shifted nervously from one foot to another.

"That may be so," she said, "but I do not think they will ever accept you as one of our people." In a hushed voice she added, "I wish they would."

He stared at her in amazement. "You know we should not be talking. There are still people in the camp who might be watching. I have heard you are promised to another."

"I am, and you are right. We are both taking a risk, and though I don't wish to leave, I guess I must." She reached out and laid her hand on his arm, then turned and departed.

His mind was in a turmoil. Both desire and common sense were fighting within him. He had never had a woman before, and here, of all the inopportune places, was his chance. She was so small and delicate, and moved with a feminine grace few women he had observed possessed. It was not easy, but he willed himself to stop thinking about her. He searched within himself for a space of nothingness, of a void. At last he relaxed, and plodded slowly back to his own meager lodge. Regardless of this lovely young woman, he knew he must continue to plan his own future.

Teo and his chosen men had returned with the bodies. Once again the women and children wailed and shrieked, releasing their grief. Gone was the peace and solitude that Palasiva had enjoyed while they were away. Though Sun Father shone brilliantly in the sky, it seemed that black clouds shrouded the village. Some women cut off all their hair, and some inflicted cuts on their arms and legs to offer the ultimate gift of blood to their deceased loved ones.

Palasiva watched it all from afar, thinking of Tupkya and Sikyawa, the parents he adored in spite of the shame he had brought upon them. He wondered if they were even still alive, and if they were, would they, like so many of his people, have the stamina to move on in search of better living conditions. When he had left the community he knew they had been upset with Lansa, and Moon Fire. He had been their only hope, and with his exile, he had destroyed even that. Guilt flooded through him, sending a chill up his back. He could only hope that they were not allowing negativities to eat them alive, but knowing his parents as well as he did, he suspected that it was so. It seemed imperative that he carry through his plans as soon as possible.

Two sun cycles passed while the village buried their dead. Teo had walked by, giving him an evil eye, which he could not understand. Surely, he thought, the raiders could not think that he had informed his people of the expected raid. He hastily put the thought from his mind, and began to ponder whether he should leave during Sun Father's journey or the time of darkness. If he left during the time of darkness and was followed and killed, he would suffer an afterlife of eternal torment, for such were the beliefs of his people. Leaving during the time of light also seemed unwise, for he would be easily spotted.

Then it happened. Teo arrived again, but this time telling him to report immediately to Ochata. Palasiva did not dare to ask why, but was overcome with feelings of uncertainty and dread that he could not explain. He thought they surely must be considering him to be the informer.

Lifting the hide flap of Ochata's lodge, which was larger than all others except the central lodge, he was surprised to see not just Ochata and Teo, but Mina with an older man on her right side and an older woman on her left. Mina was trembling, with eyes red and rimmed with tears. Palasiva was at first puzzled, but suddenly in a flash as bold as lightning, he knew.

Ochata and Teo frowned at him, their brows furrowed angrily. At last Ochata spoke. "Palasiva, the Anasazi. You have been summoned here to hear Ote, Mina's father, speak. Hear his words well or it will not go well for you."

Ote rose to his feet and beat his chest with his two fists. "The scum that lives outside our village has defiled my daughter. During the time our warriors were gone to bring back the dead, this piece of buffalo dung tried to seduce my daughter who is promised to another. My wife, Nila, saw their encounter. What is worse she says that you, you who spread evil as does the skunk, even touched my daughter. I ask that you be duly punished as befits the crime." Then turning to Ochata, he said, "Let justice be done."

Though it was not acceptable for a woman to speak without being given permission, Mina rose nervously to her feet. "I know I do not have permission to speak, but speak I must." She turned to glance at Palasiva, then back to Ochata. "I know I am promised to another and that I should not have had conversation with this man, but I also know that my respected mother, Nila, has not spoken the truth. He did not touch me. I touched him. Yes, I touched him on the arm just before we parted. Do not blame him. He was minding his own business when I approached him. I am the one who is at fault. I beg you, please. Punish me, not him."

Ochatals eyebrows rose high above his small black eyes in surprise. "Answer truthfully, girl. Are you saying that Palasiva is not the seducer, but that you are the wanton?"

Mina grimaced as she answered him with her shoulders squared. "You have said it."

Ote and Nila gasped as the meaning of what she had said became clear to them. Nila shut her eyes in grief, for she had been trying to cover for her daughter, and had failed. She knew that the outcome of this meeting would never favor her daughter, and might even destroy her in the eyes of her people. Even if Mina was not physically punished, it was entirely possible that she might be disowned by her future husband, which would shame her forever in the eyes of her people. She would be forced to live with her mental anguish for the rest of her days.

Palasiva was visibly shaken. The customs of the "mountain people" were so strange to him. Here it was apparent that you must not even communicate or touch someone unless you were betrothed to that person. His own people accepted flirtation and touching as a part of growing up. Even if you were promised to someone, you were still allowed friends of the opposite sex. He was horrified that he had unknowingly violated one of their customs, and was equally concerned about the outcome. Mina's eyes met his only briefly.

Ochata rose, and cleared his throat. "Since this is a decision I alone must make, I must say that the situation is not as I thought it was. Palasiva is not one of our people, and does not know all of our ways. As such, I suggest no physical punishment for him. He will have to live with himself in the season cycles to come. Mina, however, is another story." He turned to Nila. "Whether you are covering for your daughter, or your daughter is covering for Palasiva, is not my concern for I may never know the truth. Regardless punishment is due." He stopped speaking, feeling the power that was his and only his. At last he continued. "Mina, daughter of Nila and Ote. If you are telling me the truth, you will receive three lashes for your transgression. Speak now, daughter, or receive your punishment."

Mila made no response, for she had spoken the truth, and would have to live with herself for the rest of her days if she changed her story. She simply bowed her head and waited.

Ochata said softly, "She shall receive her punishment immediately." He gave a nod to Teo.

Mina stood her ground proudly, but her parents wailed and sputtered as she was led out into the central part of the village where she was stripped to the waist and her hands were bound tightly in front of her. She bent forward allowing her long lustrous hair to cover her small proud breasts. Her eyes met Palasiva's only long enough to convey her sorrow.

People were coming from every corner of the village in wonder to watch the occasion. Palasiva could not help but think how barbaric these people were as they gathered in droves to watch the torture. Didn't they realize they were only adding to the humiliation that he knew Mina must be feeling? Why did the sight of pain, blood, and torture inflame the "mountain people"? Again the difference between their ways and the ways of his people tore at his heartstrings and reinforced his ardent desire to leave this madness and return to his own people.

When everyone seemed assembled, Ochata raised his hand high, which caused an immediate hush among the villagers. "Mina, daughter of Nila and Ote, has shamed her family and the customs of our people. She has openly admitted flirting with Palasiva of the 'stone house people,' even though she is promised to another. Her punishment shall be three lashes of the whip, which will be delivered by our war chief and my son, Teo. Let the punishment begin." He stepped back to the edge of the crowd, allowing Teo and Mina to become the central attraction.

Teo picked up the whip, a long, thin piece of buckskin with two mesquite thorns attached to the end. Palasiva cringed when he saw it for he knew it would double the pain, and that Mina would probably have scars on her now flawless back for the rest of her life. When she refused to beg for reconsideration, he marveled at her fortitude even though he knew she must be terribly frightened. He also wondered if the man to whom she was promised was present.

The crowd almost in unison chanted, "Hey, hey, hey," and stamped their feet. The whip whistled through the air, landing squarely on Mina's back, causing a long welt of blood ending with two deep cuts. She winced, but did not cry out.

Palasiva stifled the urge to shield her with his own body. He knew now he must leave as soon as possible, and thought of taking her with him. He had no idea, however, what her promised husband might do, or in fact what the entire village might do, or even if she would want to accompany him, so he watched as Teo delivered the second and the third blow, pausing dramatically between each one as if savoring the job at hand.

His feelings for Teo were confused. He knew Teo had never really trusted him, and also had prevented his acceptance by the people. Thus up until now this had presented him with no problem, for if it had not been for Teo, he would have long since been dead. Though his life had been lonely these past season cycles, at least he was alive and had survived. On the other hand, Teo was the man who had blackmailed him and caused him to deceive his people. Now he saw a man with an expression of near ecstasy as he wielded the whip and delivered needless pain to such a lovely young girl. Somewhere down deep he hoped Teo would never marry the young girl who was promised to him, for there seemed to be a side of the young war chief that was sadistic.

The three lashes were delivered, and Mina was led by Nila back to their lodge, where he assumed she would be cared for. The crowd gradually dispersed, with much talk of the wrong she had done. Palasiva returned to his own dwelling, trying to deal with his own guilt.

He rekindled the dying fire, and curled into his blanket,

wishing that sleep would overtake him. Such was not Awon-awilona's intention, for he lay awake long into the time of darkness, tossing and turning, in sympathy for Mina and the desire to escape these people.

CHAPTER 18

←————————→

Palasiva awoke with the gray dawn, completely unnerved. His power animal, the mountain lion, had appeared to him in a dream, beckoning him to climb one rock formation after another. He knew the big cat was instructing him to leave the "mountain people" as quickly as possible. He recalled what Moon Fire had told him in her analysis of his power animal. She had said that the cat was a solitary animal and a very powerful one. He now knew that if he left, he would have to learn to be alone without being lonely as was the nature of his totem. She had also said that his magic would be most powerful when others did not know it, and that he should trust his own senses and feelings no matter how ridiculous they seemed. All in all it was now crystal clear to him that now was the time to begin pursuing his plan.

He sat up on his mat to praise Awonawilona for the blessing of a new sun cycle after which the realization came to him that he must be gone before Sun Father began his next journey. He had been taught by his people that death was not a fearful thing so long as torture was not accompanied by it. It was imperative that death come upon him at once, for his people knew of no atonement after dying. They believed all sins or crimes were punished in this life, and when the soul was released from the body, it simply went to Sipapu, where there was eternal dancing and feasting. In Sipapu everything happened as in this life, but with less pain, care, anguish, and danger. There was no reason to shun death, and with these thoughts he rose to ready himself for the rest of his life.

After spending some additional time in prayer, he made ready all that he would need to survive while living alone for quite a while. Often his thoughts shifted to Mina. He knew in his aching heart that he probably would not see her before he left. He only hoped that her mother was attending her wounds, and that the man to whom she was promised would not be offended by what she admitted she had done. He felt powerless and miserable whenever he thought of her. It was in his mind that at some point in time he might return for her, but he knew it would not be in the immediate future, for he had much to do to make things right in his life before he could consider returning for her. Then again, it could be that her life would be a happy one anyway.

When Sun Father had completed his journey, he prayed to Awonawilona again, stretched out on his sleeping mat, and fell into a sound sleep.

He awoke well before Sun Father began his journey. Shouldering his bow and quiver of arrows, the hunting knife of obsidian he had so painstakingly made, and the small amount of food he had put aside over the last several moon cycles, he left the village. He had taken the time to smoke his moccasins, clothing, and body before Sun Father had set to conceal his human smell. Stealing quietly into the darkness, he allowed his night vision to gradually take over.

Once he had cleared the village area he stayed on rocky ground as much as was possible. Fortunately, the terrain consisted of great numbers of huge rock formations, some that would defy even the best climber. He had deliberately chosen the rocky route to avoid leaving footprints whenever possible. He had to travel slowly so he would not lose his footing on some of the massive rocks. He had no idea when Teo and the village would discover his absence, but he knew he must make the most of the time before the inevitable happened. He spent some time backtracking and wherever possible he jumped ravines, thus enabling him to leave a confusing path.

Sun Father had barely begun his journey when he sensed he

was being followed. He had not seen anyone, but due to the events of the previous two sun cycles, he had no doubt that eyes would be checking on him. Despite the fact that he sensed the danger he was in, he could not help but appreciate the vast, awesome beauty of the massive rock formations in this wilderness. Colors of pink and orange reflected on the rock monoliths. Occasionally he took only a heartbeat of time to thank Awonawilona for the creation of such an unpredictably wondrous Mother Earth on which his people lived.

He continued on as carefully and quickly as he could. At one point, he had just left a flat area to climb over more rock when he saw several warriors tracking him. His rock precipice was higher than theirs, which was much to his advantage for it offered him much better vision than those who pursued him. Again he backtracked, hoping to confuse them. He moved on, assuming they had not seen him, and that they would finally give up his trail. Again he backtracked, and saw no sign of the raiders.

Sun Father was beginning his descent. Palasiva was bone tired, but he pushed on relentlessly. He noticed a cave facing south, and doubled his efforts to get there. He knew if he did not build a fire, he would probably be safe. Moving slowly in exhaustion, he climbed to the cave site, lowered his gear, and spread his blanket and mat out for the night. Fortunately, the night was mild, and he was not uncomfortable. His spirit animal had led him to his temporary destination, and all was well.

After remaining for two sun cycles in close proximity to his cave, he decided to move out. His location was only two sun cycles of walking from the mountain range that separated him from his own people, and he knew he would need to continue to be alert for the presence of any raiders. Since he had only a small portion of food left, he knew it was imperative to reach the mountains where there was water, and hopefully still some game to be hunted. Earth Mother was also well into the season of greening, which should offer him some greens and flowers to eat.

Moon Mother was bright and full, enabling him to travel during the time of darkness. Though the "mountain people" did not usually travel in the darkness, he still kept a sharp vigil. He slept during Sun Father's journey, though very lightly, and moved swiftly under Moon Mother's light. His journey proved uneventful except for a brief encounter from afar with his animal totem, the mountain lion. His spirit animal was sitting on his haunches, enjoying a haunch of meat, licking his chops while seemingly savoring the flavor. Palasiva decided that the appearance of the big cat was a good omen.

When, at last, he reached the mountains, he began the steep climb. Here, he felt quite safe, for he not only had the protection of large and small canyons, but also of foliage that he had not had before. This was familiar territory to him, for some of his warrior training had taken place within this mountain range. Most of the grandfather pine and spruce that was so necessary for the support of the massive buildings in his home community had come from these mountains. It was exhilarating to be so close to home, yet frustrating that he could not return to his family.

As Sun Father once more began to rise, he found a small canyon with a very small cave, and decided to take advantage of its warm southern exposure. He lay his blanket down in full view of Sun Father's warming rays, and fell sound asleep.

Sun Father was more than halfway through his journey when he awoke. His stomach was rumbling and his food provisions were long since gone. Water, however, was his first priority. Picking up his belongings, he moved higher into the mountains. He moved silently, stopping periodically to listen. A small hissing, bubbling sound made him turn completely around as he searched for its source.

The canyon was rocky, very rocky, with sheer drop-off on either side. He walked along a plateau thickly covered with juniper, piñon pine, and occasional grandfather pines. At the bottom of the canyon were cottonwoods, indicating the presence of water. At last he found a path, probably an animal path, that led to the bottom, and hastily descended to the rocks below. To his delight, though most all of the rocks were dry, there was one small area where they were moist. The hissing, bubbling sound became louder as he neared the source, where he found a small but constant trickle of water gurgling and sputtering through the rocks. He wasted no time filling his water bags.

Sun Father was nearing the end of his journey. Palasiva found a lovely flat area at the top of the canyon, backing up to a solid rock wall. There, for the first time since he had left the raiders, he decided to build a fire. His stomach was growling from hunger, but he ignored it, for he had water and warmth from the fire. There was nothing to do but listen to the song of the coyotes as they sang their praises to Mother Moon. He fell asleep with thoughts of Mina, followed by the good omen of the appearance of the mountain lion.

When Sun Father again appeared to warm the canyon, he awoke and stretched like his power animal, the great cat. He arose to the direction of the rumblings of his empty stomach. He did not even bother to dress, for the canyon had warmed considerably from the night chill. Knowing that there was water in the canyon, however meager it might be, he grabbed his knife and bow and arrow, and stealthily climbed down toward the bottom. To his delight he spotted a long-eared rabbit sitting warily not far from the spring. Hiding behind a large four-wing saltbush, he notched his arrow in the bow, aiming it at the rabbit through the bush. The arrow rang true to its mark, throwing the rabbit on its back.

Palasiva wanted to shout, but contained himself as he quickly retrieved the rabbit, and climbed back to the plateau. He removed the head and entrails while thanking Awonawilona for this bounteous gift. He had watched his mother prepare small game as he was about to do, and felt his mouth salivate at the thought of the finished product. He covered the rabbit with well-worked clay that was two fingers thick, making certain that not even a bit of hair stuck out. Before he had gone down into the canyon he had stoked the fire, which now was burning hot with embers. He spread the embers apart and nestled the rabbit into them, making sure it was completely covered. He then built another fire over the embers. It was not long before he removed the roasted rabbit from the fire, and broke the clay with a stick. As he pulled off the clay, the fur came with it, leaving a wonderful moist meat with the finest taste.

Having eaten his fill, he decided that a shelter was next in order. Within the canyon was an abundance of willow. He used willow because of its pliability to make a small rounded frame up against the rock wall on the plateau. Over that he wove branches of anything he could find, then covered them with mud, leaving a hole in the center through which smoke could escape. He took no great pains with the construction, for he had no intentions of remaining in the mountains for any length of time. His long-range plans were in the back of his mind.

When he had completed his shelter, he warmed the rabbit, and ate his fill once more before retiring for the time of darkness.

During the next several sun cycles he spent the first half of each one in meditation, and the second half gathering edible leaves and flowers to complement his diet. At sundown he made it a point to be at the spring, knowing that this would be the last stop for any game in the area. As luck would have it, he found a variety of small game, and even killed a hen turkey, which lasted him for three sun cycles. Since his animal totem, the mountain lion, had appeared so very recently, he decided to try to think like the great cat. In his meditations, he actually imagined himself as a cat as he recalled the facial movements, and the feline body language.

On one such a sun cycle he had a revelation that came out of his meditations. He decided to dance his animal totem, and marked off a sacred space in front of his dwelling. The only dance step he knew was the simple toe-heel that was easy to perform. He decided to move clockwise in a wide circle, focusing his attention on his power animal in the center of the spiral. In his mind he heard a slow hypnotic drum that sounded almost like the beating of his heart. He shuffled very slowly toward the center, where he knew he would meet his animal totem. When he reached the center, he saw himself as the animal and felt the cat's energy alive within him. He spent some time imitating the animal, then danced in a counterclockwise direction, slowly spiraling out to the perimeter of the circle. Upon his arrival he found himself still feeling the energy of the lion, then slowly danced in a wider circle to dissipate some of its energy.

He found himself so exhilarated that for the first time in a long while, he wished there were someone in whom he could confide. Yet he somehow knew that if he were to do so, some of the power would be lost. Of course there was really no danger of losing his power, so he continued. With the passing of each sun cycle he felt more and more like a mountain lion, with all the stealth and wiliness that accompanied the cat's personality. As time went on, he came to appreciate and to absorb the fact that the cat could teach how to project and utilize the life force of darkness and secrecy in silent but powerful ways. These were the very forces he would need to use to implement his long-range plan, and so he continued for almost two moon cycles until he truly felt he owned the personality and abilities of the cat.

Before he had left the raiders, he had overheard conversations about the Hohokam, who were ordinarily a people of peace, as were his own people. It seemed that the drought and marginal living conditions were such that the Hohokam had begun trading their own people to the Mayan-Toltec in exchange for food. Some said that the exchange was not really necessary, for there were still rivers that flowed at least to some extent, and the people could certainly move to take advantage of the source. He had also heard that there were three elders in a large center who had agreed to the slave trade. No one seemed sure how many elders there were, but the number three was consistent. It may have been that he wanted to assuage his own guilt, but he had long ago decided to destroy any who would trade for slaves.

At the end of one particular sun cycle, he prepared to leave. When Sun Father again shed his glorious light on the mountains, he filled his water skins and left. Coming out of the mountains, he bypassed one of his own people's communities, where most of them were living in huge caves. In the center of the area was a tall pointed stone which some called sacred. Again he felt the strong urge to stop for at least one sun cycle, but refrained from doing so. He had no idea if this community would or would not know of his exile.

He moved on through terrain that was mostly rock formations and no mountain ranges of any size. Water was scarce, and he was glad he had filled the several water skins he had. He drank sparingly. Once he found cottonwoods along a dry wash, and dug down to find water, which he strained through a small piece of cloth he happened to still have since his exile. He gave thanks to Awonawilona.

After many sun cycles he realized he was climbing. Since he had left his comfortable place in the higher mountains, food had been more than scarce. He had resorted to eating bugs, rats, anything he could find along the way, including budding flowers of some cactus and occasional greens. Now as he climbed, he noticed that the higher he went, the cooler it became. Sun Father did not beat down so unmercifully, and the time of darkness was quite chilly, but not as chilly as the place of his people. He knew he was heading south.

The rest of his trip was over rugged mountain terrain that would have challenged the best of warriors, but presented no problem to him, as he thought of his animal totem. The mountains were really no different from those that were next to his own people, and were filled with unexpected game and spring water. He marveled at the vastness of Earth Mother, and also of her beauty.

At last he rounded a mountain and stared at the enormous bowl that stretched out before him. There seemed to be little in it, but the temperature had definitely risen. The more he moved down into the bowl or valley, the warmer it became, until he found himself sweating profusely. He sat down to rest in the shade of a tree that was all green, including the trunk. In no time at all, he was dry, and so he moved on. He had not moved very far when he sat down once more, and so it went until he was well into the valley and out of the mountains. Still he viewed the valley from above. The trees and plants were so different from those that were familiar to him. He thought perhaps he might have stepped into another world.

Something caught his eye deep in the center of the valley. It appeared very small in the distance, but was nevertheless outstanding among the strange foliage. He saw a large town with residential areas consisting of numerous clusters of houses, each enclosed by a rectangular compound wall made of mud. These houses were clustered around at least two hands of platform mounds that were also enclosed by a wall. A small temple stood on top of each mound. Palasiva shook his head in amazement, for he remembered tales of Coyote Woman's visit where, not so long ago, people lived in pit houses, as many of his own people still insisted on doing. He knew that the Mayan-Toltecs also built enormous pyramids, but they certainly did not resemble these. Or did they? He also wondered if they had turned to any of the bloodthirsty religious rites of their southern neighbors. He felt sure that this was the right community for which he was searching, for he had been told that in most other communities there were far less mounds.

Now that he had reached his destination, he decided to return to a small cave back in the mountains and make that his temporary quarters. He felt it was far enough away from the population, and somewhat hidden from any Hohokam scouts. The weather was very warm during the time of darkness, and he had little need for a fire. After a meal of cold desert rabbit left over from the last sun cycle, he settled in for some much-needed rest.

Hearing the raiders speaking among themselves, he had learned that the Hohokam were also trading their own people to the Mayan-Toltecs in exchange for food, though some said the rich were trading for more riches. In such desperate times, he felt a deep hatred toward the rich, if this were so, and even if it wasn't, the entire concept was abhorrent to him, as it was to his own people. He knew he must somehow mingle with the people, but he knew not how.

For two sun cycles he thought and meditated when he was not searching for food. He had grown almost desperate and was beginning to give up when he saw several figures approaching the area not far from his dwelling. At first he thought they must surely be warriors who had learned of his location, and he hastily made ready to depart. As they got closer, he realized they were not warriors, for they bore no weapons. They seemed heavily laden with goods, which told him they were traders. As they drew closer, he saw what he thought seemed to be a familiar face, and as they drew even closer, he recognized his brother.

Plucking up his courage, he stepped out unarmed from his

hiding place. When they were close enough to hear him, he cried, "Lansa, you are Lansa the trader. I recognize you."

The party of three stopped. None of them were armed, for as traders it was not necessary according to universal law. Lansa looked confused, but did not put down the burden of trading goods. "Who are you?" he asked.

"You do not recognize your own kin?" Palasiva noticed that his older brother had survived the devastating drought conditions with seemingly no effect. He, on the other hand, had lived so harshly that he was certain that he must look emaciated.

Lansa walked closer and squared his shoulders. Shaking his head, he said, "What do you mean, my own kin?"

"Your own kin is exactly what I mean, brother," Palasiva said with such authority that Lansa stared at him with disbelief. "Yes, brother, it is I. I have survived the past four season cycles, but marginally. I suppose that is why you do not recognize me. Of course, you probably assumed I had crossed over."

Lansa's doe-shaped eyes opened wide in amazement. "But you are a man now. Is it really you, Palasiva?" He viewed Palasiva as if he were looking at a ghost.

Palasiva made no response. His still childish grin was enough to cause Lansa to let down his guard. Walking hastily toward his brother, he said, "Awonawilona be praised! Is this person before me an apparition?"

"No, brother, I am flesh and blood as you are. May we talk?"

"Of course, of course." He hastily dismissed his other two traveling companions while the two of them sat down, taking in the sight of each other as if it might be the last. Palasiva waited.

At last Lansa said, "All that has happened is in the past, brother, and we need not discuss the injustice of it. I am overjoyed to see that you are alive and well. I know it has not been easy for you. I trade with everyone, and I know the different customs of many. I still cannot believe you are alive." He looked at his little brother with a respect that never would have been there before. Then he added, "It would seem that you have grown into a hardened, experienced warrior."

"That may or may not be so, brother, but I would ask you a favor."

"And what might that be?"

"I would ask that you allow me to accompany you into the village you are approaching."

Lansa gave his brother a hard look, then placed his hands on his brother's shoulders and sighed. "You are my brother and I am glad you are still alive. If this will help you in any way, I would be glad to say yes to your request. I will ask no questions, for there is not enough time to answer them all. Come, join us."

After Lansa had introduced him to the trading party, which consisted of a young apprentice to Lansa, and a Mogollon trader they had picked up along the way, they clothed him in more appropriate attire to fit in with their party. They then moved on toward their destination.

The little trading party arrived in the Hohokam town and were welcomed as any trading party would be. Palasiva stared in amazement, for the community was quite large, with many adobe buildings, ramadas used for shade when working outdoors, and three platforms that he assumed must be for ceremonial purposes. The entire village was surrounded by a sturdy adobe wall.

Among those who welcomed them were two elders who introduced themselves as Tachato and Lumo. Palasiva noticed that Tachato's face was etched with laugh lines and his eyes twinkled, while the lines on Lumo's face were drawn and serious, with eyes that would turn anyone to stone. Palasiva could not help but wonder if Tachato was the elder who had voted against trading his people as slaves.

The Mogollon trader, Palasiva, and Lansa, and the apprentice spread out their wares. Lansa had given Palasiva some of his wares so that he would appear to be a trader. Some of the trade items were pottery of various sizes and shapes, hawk and eagle feathers, obsidian arrow head points, and a limited amount of turquoise. Not one Hohokam made any comments about the meager amount of turquoise, for they, too, were in the midst of the terrible drought. They did, however, have their own pottery, shell beads, etched shells, small clay trays, effigies, and figurines. The one thing that was most desired by

Palasiva's people were the copper bells that the Hohokam aquired from the Mayan-Toltecs on a much more regular basis than his own people, due to their closer relations and proximity.

The trading went on until Sun Father set, and no one could see any of the goods for which they were trading. The two elders showed them to the quarters reserved for traders, and told Lansa that they were welcome to stay as long as they wished. After Lansa built a fire and food was brought to them, they settled in for some much-earned sleep.

Over the season cycles that he had been a trader, Lansa had learned enough of the different languages of the Hohokam, Mogollon, and even the Mayan-Toltec to make his desires known. When he found the need, he sought out someone who could translate, but that was very rare now due to his many season cycles of experience. He had explained to Tachato and Lumo, that Palasiva was also a novice, and had much to learn. So it was that over the two sun cycles that Lansa remained, Palasiva learned much and was offered a translator whenever he needed one.

Palasiva had always been a good listener, and now he bent his ear to try to absorb any and all that he heard. From Lansa he learned that Tachato was indeed the one who had voted against the human trading issue, and that the two other elders besides Lumo were called Hoko and Pioco. He also learned the location of their quarters, and began watching them to learn their routine, if there was one.

They were fed royally or perhaps as well as was possible during the drought they all endured. Palasiva enjoyed his time with his brother, especially since there was no opportunity to discuss any of their own personal problems. He could not help but think that brothers and sisters could certainly be closer, if they did not allow their personal problems to become an obstacle. He was grateful that Lansa had accepted him for who he was, and had asked no questions.

After two sun cycles, Lansa, his apprentice, and the Mogollon trader left. Palasiva stayed on, saying that he was intending to move south, and just needed more time before facing the rugged desert terrain. No one questioned him, and he remained in the same quarters. He knew he had very little time to remain with the Hohokam, but he gleaned as much information as he could for his purpose.

Two sun cycles after Lansa had left, Palasiva also left. He had acquired the information he needed. The village thought he was heading south, and he did for a short time. Then he turned north, for he knew that was where he wanted to be. The elders he sought lived on the north side of the community. He had mentally made note of their daily habits, and knew that Lumo normally came out of his lodging to relieve himself well before Sun Father rose.

Moving silently to the north side of the complex, he waited. Sun Father was only halfway through the time of darkness when Lumo left his quarters, walked out of the village to the spot on the northside where the people normally emptied their slop pots, and relieved themselves. Palasiva visualized himself as his power animal and stealthily crept up behind Lumo. Lumo was completely unaware that anyone was behind him until it was too late. Palasiva had seized him and instantaneously severed the jugular vein in his neck. Only a low moan and a gurgling sound could be heard from Lumo, as he fell. Palasiva hastily moved away toward the other end of the north wall.

To his amazement he saw Hoko approaching. Realizing there was no time to hide, he waited. Hoko was making his way to the same location when he stopped, trying to make out who he was talking to. "Oh, Palasiva, it is you. What are you doing here? I thought you had left."

Palasiva thought quickly, saying, "I forgot something." Without another word, he whipped out his knife and severed the throat of the unsuspecting elder.

Time was at a premium. There was nothing else to do but to make his escape as quickly as possible. He mentally assumed his mountain lion identity, and left the area with padded feet, leaving not a trace behind him. He felt himself fortunate that he had managed to rid the community of two out of three of the evil elders, and thanked Awonawilona that he was alive and well.

Palasiva would not know until much later that when the bodies had been found with no footprints to follow, the people had been aroused to a point of feeling that witchcraft had somehow been responsible for the death of their elders. They also questioned why these two elders had been singled out, though many assumed that the slavery issue might be the answer. It did not take many sun cycles for the people to rise up, declaring that the killings had been an omen, and the fact that the people were in a severe drought was not an excuse for the exchange of goods to support the elite in exchange for slavery of the people.

Pioco, the third elder, felt the will of the people who had become hostile toward him. He had lost his support with the death of Lumo and Hoko, and knew that he probably never would regain their respect. In fact he feared for his life.

The entire community appeared just before Sun Father set, gathering around one of the three mounds that ordinarily was the setting for ceremonial purposes. Now the people were angered. The fact that they chose to gather around a mound was a blasphemy to the gods. Pioco was caught up in the anger of his people and knew not what to do.

As they gathered in anger, he returned to his quarters, and packed his belongings. Rounding the corner of the north wall where Lumo and Hoko had been killed, he set out for the comfort of his children to the south. He knew he would be resigning his position as elder of the community, for he saw no other alternative.

When the village people found no one to turn on, they backed off to mourn their loved ones, and to rejoice with the realization that perhaps there would be no more slave trade, and that they would have the opportunity to elect new leadership.

Moon Fire had gone to her cave for her womanly cycle. She actually enjoyed the three sun cycles she was free, but she missed Wena 'Ahote. When she was in the cave she felt vibrations different from any other place she had ever been. She had always thought perhaps it was because this was the cave of the famous Coyote Woman, who had found such balance in life. At least that was what the stories told that had been passed down for several generations. During the many season cycles she had been coming to this special spot, she had added to the picture in the back of the cave. Next to the shaman figure, she had added her own handprint and a spiral indicating the circle of life in which all her people were bound. Now she settled down for a period of quiet, away from the troubles she and her people endured. Food was not a problem, for there was none. This was her time to just drink the precious water she had brought with her and meditate.

The second sun cycle of her three arrived, and with it the same blistering sun that was so normal to her people. She drank sparingly of the water, and except for attending to her own physical needs, she attempted to conserve her energy. She sat on the ledge at the mouth of her small cave, wishing she had the energy to climb down and to communicate with any living creature that might still be in the vicinity. Then far in the distance a speck that looked like it might be a human seemed to be coming toward her. She watched it with interest, wondering who would be traveling in such heat. The figure grew larger as it gradually moved closer. She found herself hypnotized and fascinated, though she knew she should probably go into her cave so she would not be found.

The figure pressed on, looming larger and larger. As she watched, she suddenly felt a tug of familiarity with the way the person carried himself and the way he walked. She could only assume that the figure must be a male, for what female would leave the confines of her lodging to wander outside the canyon. She knew she had been seen, but it did not seem to matter. Since she had been without food for more than a sun cycle, and was experiencing a buzz, she waited and watched.

The features of the person became larger as he approached. When at last he was close enough that she could see him, she said, "Who are you? If there was not something familiar about you, I would say you were probably out to kill me."

Palasiva looked at her tenderly. "Little sister, I would never harm you. I have missed you."

Tears sprang unbidden from her eyes as she rose to acknowledge him. She hastily climbed down from the ledge of her cave and flew into his arms. They remained in an embrace for some time as she wept, and he soothed her.

At last she whimpered, "I cannot tell you how happy I am, but is it not dangerous for you to be in such close proximity to the community?"

"Of course it is, but I had to see you, little sister, and tell you what has happened during the four season cycles that I have been gone."

Wiping her tears, she said, "Oh yes, please tell me. You are right. I want to know. You know, of course, that it is bad luck for a man to be with a woman during her womanly cycle. Perhaps you should go. At least I know you are alive. May I tell our parents?"

"I would rather you not, but let us think about it. The fact that you are in your womanly cycle means nothing to me. May I join you?"

And so he stayed. Sun Father set, and they talked long into the time of darkness. He spoke of the two elders he had killed due to the fact that they were trading their own for slavery, and said to her that perhaps he was repaying a debt. She spoke of the hardship that all the people were experiencing, physical, and psychological, and that four out of five had left the community to seek better living conditions. She also told him that the people were in a period of terrible unbalance, and that she had no idea what to expect at any time.

Palasiva told her of his plans to do the same to the Mogollon as he had done to the Hohokam, for they, too, were trading their people off to stay alive, yet they had better resources than the Hohokam. They had much more mountain runoff, and also many more active available creeks and rivers.

When Sun Father had barely begun his journey, Palasiva was awake and preparing to leave. Moon Fire was awake, awaiting his departure. Her heart was in a turmoil as she thought of the danger that would be awaiting her little brother.

He was ready to leave almost immediately, for he had very little baggage. "I wish I could offer you food for your journey. It grieves me that I can't," she whispered.

"I will catch what I can, and if I can't, little sister, it will be no different than what you are going through now." He took her into his sinewy arms and again held her for some time. Finally he said, "I would like to meet you here again two moon cycles from now. By then, I can probably tell you of the outcome of my efforts with the Mogollon."

"Oh, Palasiva, I shall look forward to your return, and ask Awonawilona for your protection. May I confide in Wena 'Ahote?" she asked reluctantly.

"To that question I would say yes, for Wena 'Ahote is also your confidant and would dare do you no harm." Releasing her, he turned to go.

"Little brother, I love you, and I always have. I will pray that no harm may come upon you." Her lower lip quivered in her attempt to curtail her tears.

"I will accept any prayers you may offer. We will meet two moon cycles from now." He walked toward the west toward the mountain range where the people obtained their wood for building purposes.

When he turned to wave his last farewell, he was close enough that she thought she saw tears in his eyes.

CHAPTER 19

A.D. *1137*

Teo was furious when he learned of Palasiva's desertion. In his mind, Palasiva had not just left his people, but had deserted the mouth that had fed him for the four season cycles of his stay. He was also angry because Palasiva had been clever enough to elude his trackers and warriors and to manage to escape into the unknown. It would never have occurred to him that during the four season cycles Palasiva had been with them, he had never offered to adopt him as one of his people. He never thought about the fact that Palasiva had been treated as an outcast with less than the basics with which to live, and that anyone would no doubt become discouraged under those conditions. He had faced his father's anger and survived, which only made his anger fester even more. Teo had also only recently discovered a new side to his personality. He realized that he had actually enjoyed whipping Mina and had become sexually excited by what had happened. Palasiva was the catalyst who had caused the scene, and now was no longer present for any hope of a replay. He decided to approach his father once more.

He approached Ochata with an earnest attempt to appear calm, but his father smiled knowingly. "Father, I come to you to ask your permission to speak."

"You have it, Teo, but you cannot hide your feelings from me."

Dropping his guard, he squared his shoulders and said, "Father, the Anasazi have bested us once more, and . . ."

"What do you mean, once more?"

"I mean that we were beaten back when their warriors disguised themselves as travelers leaving the canyon, and now we have allowed one solitary Anasazi warrior to best us and escape undetected into the wilderness."

"Well, these things happen," replied Ochata with a face as stoic as a rock.

Teo began to lose his temper and fought to keep it under control. "Father, have you no pride? The Anasazi are not a warring people. Their warriors are not trained as ours are, and more than that they are weak from malnutrition. It is in my mind, with your approval of course, that we should launch an all-out attack on the main community and the main building. I think we should wipe them out once and for all."

Ochata's face showed no emotion. After a brief amount of time he finally said, "Teo, the Anasazi are our enemies. They are our lifeline to survival, for they provide us with slaves to trade for food and other necessary items for our survival. If we wipe them out, who will replace them? Shall we find new enemies, and if so, where do we find them?"

"Father, these are probably wise words, but I am sure we will be able to find other enemies. We may just have to relocate in order to do so."

"That may be so, but you must keep in mind that to relocate is not easy with drought conditions to consider."

Teo was beside himself and trying not to show it. In desperation he begged, "Will you give me permission to launch an all-out attack in order to save our pride as a people?"

Ochata leaned back into his blankets. Heaving a great sigh, he answered, "Oh, how well I remember how hotheaded I was in my youth. If that is your desire, Teo, and you can rally substantial forces, so be it."

Teo rose immediately, thanked his father, then backed out of the lodge with excitement abounding in his heart. He knew his work was cut out for him, and he sent out his scouts.

Palasiva shifted mentally into his mountain lion mode. The mountain lion was alert and aware, and could sense things happening for great distances. Sun Father had just completed his

journey, and the human smell was faint, but definitely there. He
followed it on padded feet with his ears laid back which indicated he was in pursuit of his prey. The human scent became
much stronger, when at last he was close enough to be within
voice range of the humans who were gathered around a fire.
Hiding behind a rock, he waited with ears forward to better his
hearing.

There were three scouts, raider scouts. One of them was
turning a rabbit on a spit, which made Palasiva salivate, but he
kept his vigil. One was saying, "The land is relatively flat there.
It should not be a problem. I think the south side would be the
best approach."

"I think I agree with you. The other advantage is that there
are no major outliers along the south road. We can work around
that easily," declared the second scout.

The third scout with a distinctly low voice added, "Then
we will take this information back to Teo, who will be delighted with our efforts. Here, my friend, have a back leg and
enjoy."

Palasiva silently moved away. He had heard enough and
smelled enough, and was salivating uncontrollably. When he
was far enough away to feel comfortable, he knew it was imperative to get information to his people. He knew what he
must do.

Moon Fire was in deep meditation several sun cycles later.
She had willed herself to fly over the great canyon to the
west of the community that was six walking sun cycles away.
Several of her clients, including Palasiva, had described it to
her. In order to complete the initiation into manhood, all
young men had to take the journey, and Palasiva and Lansa
had both done so. As she flew, she took in the wondrous variety of colors that reflected from the deep canyon walls. She
had been told there were people, not her people, but another
people who lived at the bottom of this unbelievably deep
canyon, and she had always wondered what it might be like
to live there.

Her heart was light as she dipped and soared over the
canyon, much as Red Eagle would do. She continued to marvel

at the wonderful feeling until she saw in the far distance a speck in the brilliant turquoise sky moving toward her. She in turn moved in the direction of the oncoming speck.

Almost instantaneously she recognized Red Eagle. They circled each other with the lightness of a single feather. She waited until he was close enough, then spoke. "Red Eagle, we meet again."

"Indeed, Moon Fire, it is so. I bring a message from your brother, and a very important one. In fact it is so important that you must find him immediately, for the welfare of many may be at stake."

Circling each other once more, Moon Fire said, "But where shall I find him?"

Red Eagle flew in the direction of her cave, saying in a fading voice, "There is only one logical place he might hope to find you. Think . . . think . . ." He faded from view.

Moon Fire immediately landed, and worked herself out of her meditative state. When her consciousness was again fully aware, she knew that the only place would be where they had last met, and so she made haste toward her cave. She was not far from the ledge before the entrance when she saw a familiar figure not very far away. "Palasiva," she said, "I know it is you. Red Eagle told me it would be so."

Palasiva again moved into her embrace, but only briefly. "Little sister, you must carry a message to your people. I overheard raider scouts who from their discussion made it apparent that they had scoped out the four directions surrounding our eleven great houses, and I also heard them mention Teo's name, and that he would be very pleased. They spoke of the south road and south entrance as being the most advantageous due to the fact that there were no other great houses in close proximity. They are planning an attack. You must warn the people."

She stared at him incredulously. "But our people are weak. It would be difficult for them to fight."

"The raiders are very aware of that fact and are counting on it. However, if our people are warned far enough ahead, and use a little strategy, perhaps the raiders can be outsmarted." He seized her by her shoulders, saying, "I must go now. Time is running out. You must also make haste."

She turned to leave and so did he, but as if their minds were one, they both turned back at the same time for one more short embrace.

Moon Fire fairly flew back to Wena 'Ahote, and was fortunate to find her beloved in discussion with Taatawi in the plaza. She gave him the old signal by placing her hand over her heart. He easily cut his conversation short with Taatawi, for they both saw the damp tendrils of hair and body perspiration that was so unusual for Moon Fire.

Wena 'Ahote took her hand, leading her down the ladder and into his quarters. "What is it, my love? Your eyes are wild, and you almost look as though you are possessed."

Moon Fire spoke of her astral traveling and her encounter with Red Eagle. She told him also that Red Eagle had directed her to Palasiva, and what Palasiva had told her. The words came out so fast that Wena 'Ahote stood back and asked her to slow down. When she had repeated herself, he said, "This must be reported to Hoohu. Come, Little Fire. We must hurry." Seizing her hand, he pulled her toward the ladder.

They ran swiftly to Hoohu's quarters. After rapping on the ladder to let him know of their presence, a soft feminine voice invited them down. Hoohu's daughter informed them that he was in the men's social kiva. Giving her a mumbled thank you, they climbed out of his quarters and ran to the men's kiva. When they reached the top of the ladder, Wena 'Ahote stopped Moon Fire. "My love, allow me to descend the ladder. I will bring him to you."

Moon Fire said nothing as she waited for them both to make their appearance at the top of the ladder. She watched the tendrils of smoke rise through the hole on the roof where the ladder rested. When time is of the essence, two hands of heartbeats can seem like forever. At last they were both before her, and she reiterated her story once again.

Hoohu stared at her incredulously for only several blinks of an eye, then said, "I will consult with Tenyam, Angwusi, and Eykita. I can assure you that scouts will be sent out immediately." Then placing his hands on Moon Fire's shoulders, he added, "Little Moon Fire, you are a blessing to your people." With that he turned on his heels and returned to the men's social kiva.

Wena 'Ahote put his arm around Moon Fire's shoulders and kissed her on the forehead, telling her that Tenyam and Angwusi were in the men's kiva, and that the only one who needed to be found was Eykita. He also chuckled and said, "Little Fire, it seems it is your destiny to always be trying to save your people. Let us go. We have done all we can."

So it was that scouts were sent out almost immediately in all directions.

When Sun Father next made his appearance on the eastern horizon, the scouts from the south returned. They reported seeing a very large group of raiders who were perhaps two walking sun cycles away. When they were asked how many, they threw up their hands, saying that they could not get close enough to count, but that the number was great, and that the warriors were painted for war, and well armed.

All four elders were in complete agreement that every able-bodied Anasazi warrior must be rallied. Tenyam summoned Tovosi, who had become war chief, telling him to make ready for a counterattack. Tovosi turned on his heel to do their bidding.

Hoohu ordered the women, children, and old people to vacate their dwellings and to go to the large building complex that was in the east, and well away from the rest of the buildings in the canyon. He ordered Taatawi, Ruupi, and Wena 'Ahote to accompany them. They were to depart immediately.

Moon Fire thanked Awonawilona that the priests would go with them. Priests were not warriors, and would have been cut down in battle immediately. She caught Wena 'Ahote's eyes and flashed him a brave smile.

So it was that two out of three people left the canyon and hurried to safety.

Meanwhile, Palasiva, whose sinewy muscles allowed him to run as much distance in a sun cycle as a walker could cover in three, arrived at a large northern outlier. Disguising himself as a trader, he entered the community without incident. He was apologizing to an elder due to his extremely limited amount of trade goods when he felt a hand close over his shoulder. He turned, and to his amazement he found Lansa.

Lansa smiled broadly saying, "So, my trading friend, we meet again. My pleasure."

Palasiva was at a loss for words for a few heartbeats, then rallied himself. "My friend, I must have a private word with you immediately."

Lansa's eyebrows rose in curiosity, but he drew his brother away from the small group of people gathered around them into a quiet corner. "It is obvious you are not yourself, my friend. What is it that is troubling you?"

"Lansa, all our loved ones are in mortal danger. We must do something immediately before it is too late. There will be an attack!"

Lansa gripped Palasiva by the shoulders and said, "Wait, brother! Begin at the beginning. I want to make sense of what you are saying."

"I'm sorry, brother, you are right." Palasiva regained his composure and began at the beginning, telling Lansa of the scouts he had overheard, of his meeting with Moon Fire, and her vision and discussion with her spirit animal.

Lansa's tension mounted the more he heard. He thought of Sihu and his two boys, and also of Tupkya, Sikyawa, and Moon Fire. The thought of any of them being the targets of raiding warriors shook him to the bone. When Palasiva had finished his story, he beckoned him to follow him. Due to his travels for so many season cycles, Lansa knew who was who in most of the outliers and even in villages of the Hohokam and Mogollon.

They approached a man whose face was deeply etched with wrinkles from the heat of Sun Father. The two of them told him their story, and he immediately rose to summon the other elder. Everyone knew that traders often overheard confidential information, and the elder moved quickly. Within a very short time, they were informed that warriors were being rallied to move south immediately.

*   *   *

Two sun cycles later the large raiding party was seen nearing the south entrance of the plaza of the holy school. They were dressed as the scouts had seen them, in full war paint and fully armed. Teo was their leader, and he led them confidently on toward their destination. At the opening of the plaza, they watched many people scatter in defense. Teo was certain that there would be no problem, and that the people would easily fall into his hands. He led his warriors on.

They entered the plaza of the holy school with the utmost confidence, for they knew they were hardened warriors who had the advantage of moving to good water sources as well as game sources. Here, Teo thought, were people softened by relying on their growing of crops that had failed miserably for so many season cycles of drought, and who would probably show no strength at all. His warriors moved into the center of the plaza.

When they were in the heart of the plaza, they were met with such a heavy shower of arrows from Anasazi warriors in four directions, that they were taken totally by surprise. Teo watched in horror as one out of three of his warriors were either killed or wounded so that they could no longer function. Only one Anasazi warrior, who had been much too bold and stood within range of his raider warriors was taken. He gave his men the signal for a swift retreat, for he was completely disoriented. They made a hasty retreat back to their camp in the south from where they had come.

Their camp was far enough away that travel was slow, for the warriors who were wounded slowed their progress. The camp was located on the south side of several small hills. Teo kept his mind on his warriors as they traveled, and until the last possible heartbeat, did not see the smoke rising from what was very probably the camp location. He bellowed orders to his men as they rushed into what was left of their camp.

The camp was in total disarray. Sentries lay dead. Extra weapons and food were gone. He found himself unable to believe what he saw, and was beginning to have second thoughts about pursuing the attack any further. His warriors looked at him discouragingly, and he felt a sudden responsibility for all who had so faithfully followed him. His patience grew thin, for he knew someone must have informed the Anasazi, and it was in his mind that he would kill anyone who might be even a suspect.

This thought had only fleetingly crossed his mind when he heard horrific war cries coming from the hills next to the camp. Knowing they could only be the cries of enemy warriors, he turned toward the sound and saw a sizable number of Anasazi warriors screaming and attacking. They came into his charred campsite as though they were demons. Though they were noticeably leaner than his own warriors, they were relentless as they swooped down to attack. Teo screamed an order for retreat, but the Anasazi warriors were upon them in no time. Apparently some of the enemy warriors had not been a part of the defending warriors at the great holy school, but had done their work while Teo and his raiders were in the plaza doing battle.

The battle was ferocious as Anasazi warriors, bent on protecting their own, fought the raiders with a long-established vengeance. Many were slain on both sides, and much blood was shed. Again Teo shouted to his warriors to retreat to the north, for now his troops had been reduced to only half their original number. Those who heard him turned to follow, but had not gone far when to the north they were blocked by Anasazi warriors out of nowhere.

Teo's heart nearly leaped into his throat. To his surprise one of the oncoming warriors in the front lines was no other than Lansa, the trader, and the brother of Palasiva. Here, he thought, would be his opportunity to gain his revenge. He knew that traders were not usually trained warriors, and he was absolutely certain he now had the upper hand.

Hand-to-hand combat began. Teo was amazed that the scrawny Anasazi fought as fiercely and as well as they did. He dodged several of them and came face-to-face with Lansa. Screaming his death cry, he shouted, "Scum brother to Palasiva! Now you die!"

Lansa was doing his best to remember his training prior to becoming a trader, but his reflexes were slow. He only knew he must fight for the honor of his people, his family, and of course his brother.

The two of them rolled, then rolled some more, crashing into several other warriors in the heat of battle. Each time they rolled, Teo tried to plunge his deadly knife into Lansa. Twice Teo had stabbed Lansa's arm as he had tried to block the raider's attack. They rolled hard over sharp pieces of rock that opened cuts and bruises on their chests and backs.

Teo seemed to be everywhere at once. He brought his elbows into Lansa's face, kneed him in his groin, thrusting, and clubbed him again with his obsidian knife. Lansa realized he could not last much longer, and was losing strength fast. He was even having thoughts that he might as well just give up and realize that this was a good day to die.

Suddenly Lansa heard a mighty bellow. Though he could not see who it was, due to the fact that he was on the bottom, a warrior was on top of Teo, pulling them apart. Lansa shut his eyes in relief as Palasiva screamed, "Today *you* will die, not my brother!!" With a single swipe of his blade, Palasiva brought his free hand around to plunge his blade into his opponent's chest.

Teo's eyes began to glaze as he crumbled to the ground on his back, with his lifeblood oozing in great quantity from his wound. In moments he realized that his men had been fighting an enemy whose spiritual force overcame their physical weakness. Looking up at Palasiva, he wheezed, "I've underestimated you. You are indeed a great warrior."

Those few raiders who were able, upon seeing the death of their leader, turned and ran in any direction that seemed safe.

Lansa rose weakly to thank his brother, but was unable to find him. Had he been dreaming or hallucinating due to his wounds? He knew his brother's voice, and was sure he heard him tell his attacker that it was not a good day for him to die.

The battle seemed to be over. As the remaining Anasazi warriors gathered their dead, several of them spoke to Lansa, telling him that they had seen his brother come to his rescue. Everyone declared that he was indeed a great warrior.

*   *   *

The return to the canyon community was a mixture of joy and sadness for everyone. By the time the first round of dead and wounded were brought in, the women, children, elders, and priests had returned to the great houses. Much wailing was heard as the news of those who had crossed over reached their loved ones. Although there was a feeling of relief that the raiders would not be bothering them for a long while due to the valiant efforts of their warriors, there was also an undercurrent of total despair. Awonawilona seemed to be delivering one blow after another to destroy the people.

Moon Fire was having similar thoughts about the world being out of balance, when Lansa asked permission to enter her quarters. "Of course you may enter, brother," she answered in surprise. She could not remember a time when Lansa had wanted to be in her company. "Come seat yourself on my mat."

After making himself comfortable opposite her, he began. "Moon Fire, little sister, I come to you with news of our brother, Palasiva." He went on to tell her of Palasiva's bravery in rescuing him, and of how he had helped Palasiva masquerade as a trader so that he could glean information concerning the Hohokam. He told her of his and Palasiva's involvement with the northern outlier in order to rally additional warriors. He admitted that he was not a warrior, but that he could not stand by and watch his people slaughtered. To end his speech he added, "Little sister, I am sorry. I have never given you credit for the talents you have. I know now, that if it were not for you, many of our people would have died on at least two occasions." He reached across the mat to rest his big hand on her small one.

She stared at him with wide eyes, hardly able to believe what she had heard. Had these past events finally enabled him to find compassion? Had he finally seen how selfish he had been in the past? Was this a real change or only a temporary condition? Was he becoming the person that Awonawilona intended him to be? She supposed only time would tell. Finally she said, "Lansa, my brother, the brother I hardly know. Do you realize that this is the first time that we three children have truly worked together toward a common goal?"

"Yes, Moon Fire, you are right. Our family has never truly been a family unit, and much of it was my fault. Will you come with me now to visit our parents, Tupkya and Sikyawa?"

She squeezed his hand as her eyes brimmed with tears. "Of course I will come." She rose first to dash away the liquid that filled her eyes.

Tupkya and Sikyawa were sleeping when they arrived. When no one answered their request to descend the ladder, the two of them crept down anyway out of concern for their parents' well-being. Neither said a word for a short time as they took in the emaciated appearance of the old couple. Tupkya's tangled hair had turned completely white, her face was cracked much like the parched earth, and her bones had become very gnarled. Sikyawa's hair was gray and unkempt, his mouth had lost its jovial look, and had turned down in a permanent scowl. They seemed like two people just waiting to die.

Lansa and Moon Fire knelt on either side of them while gently touching their hands. Their eyes widened in surprise as they beheld their two children. Sikyawa was the first to speak. "What? Ho! What is going on here?" Tupkya kept her vigil.

Lansa was first to speak. "My beloved parents, we wish to bring you the news. We know you are exhausted from the trip to and from the outlier with all the others, but we want to speak to you."

"Then stop wasting time," Sikyawa snapped.

Lansa began with his meeting with Palasiva in the village of the Hohokam. He explained how he had tried to assist him, and had asked no questions. He then spoke of Palasiva's deed that destroyed the elders who were responsible for trading their own people for slaves to the Mayan-Toltec. He watched both of their faces brighten.

Sikyawa asked anxiously, "Then it is true? He is still alive?"

"Yes, my father, he has become a hardened warrior. I am sure he has led a miserable life during the time he has been gone, but he has survived."

Tupkya's eyes filled with tears of happiness. Still she said nothing.

"But there is more to the story."

"Go on, son. Go on." Though it took him a while, Sikyawa finally assumed a sitting position.

Lansa looked at Moon Fire. "Little sister, will you take over?"

Moon Fire smiled, then proceeded to narrate the story of her meeting with Palasiva due to her vision with her animal totem, and how Palasiva had sent her to warn her people of the upcoming invasion. "From this point on, I must ask Lansa to resume the tale, for indeed he is the one who lived it."

Lansa finished the tale of the battle, and of his rescue, as he applauded Palasiva's bravery. He explained to them that he realized he would have crossed over if Palasiva had not been there. He also added that somewhere inside he felt that he did not deserve the rescue, for he had never really made any effort to have any kind of relationship with his brother.

Tupkya struggled to a sitting position with more tears in her eyes. "Son, we are none of us perfect. I am proud of you, proud of Moon Fire, and proud of Palasiva. I suppose that we would probably not be here if it were not for the three of you."

Suddenly a loud rap came from the top of the roof. After gaining permission to descend, a young acolyte entered with an expression of sadness and concern. "It is without pleasure that I must tell you, Tupkya and Sikyawa, grandparents of Sihu's children, that the youngest of her two boys is very critically ill and in fact may cross over any time. Sihu has requested your presence." Pressing his lips together, with furrowed brows the young acolyte turned immediately and made his way up the ladder.

Moon Fire saw the shock in the faces of her parents and Lansa. She had known for some time that the small child had become sickly and had not been doing well. Lansa seized his parents' hands, helping them to a standing position, then over to the ladder. It took more time than was normal for Tupkya and Sikyawa to make their way up the ladder, but at last all four of them were on the roof of Sihu's quarters. After several taps on the ladder, Taatawi's voice invited them down.

Sihu's beauty had taken on a gaunt, almost haunted look.

There were dark circles under her eyes as she lay her hand on the forehead of her son, Tosi. She did not even look up, because she knew her son might be taken from her any time. Tosi, whose name meant "sweet cornmeal," was well named. He never caused any disturbance, and had an easygoing temperament that was the opposite of his brother's. She had sent Palatala, her oldest, to stay with her aunt. She and Lansa had named their first son Palatala because it meant "Red Light of Sunrise." His disposition was almost as fiery as the sun. She knew that her youngest had been small at birth, and due to the shortage of food, had always been hungry. She had given him all she could give, at times even at her own expense, but Taatawi had said it was not enough, and that there was little he could do. She knew Awonawilona was the only answer, but also that if it was her son's time to cross over to the land of the ancestors, there was little she could do.

Moon Fire knelt beside Sihu, and as she placed her hand on Sihu's shoulder, she saw that Tosi's breathing had become very shallow. His frail body was almost still. Suddenly he opened his eyes, and whispered, "Mother, I . . ." His little body gave a small final spasm, and he was still.

Sihu flung her body over her son with a wrenching cry. Moon Fire looked at Taatawi in desperation, silently asking for help. He gently shook his head, for they both knew it was over.

It was then that Sihu's parents descended the ladder. Everyone was finally there to offer their support. Since it was not the custom for one clan to embrace another, and in this case really was not necessary, they all remained where they were except for Moon Fire, who sat close to Sihu, waiting for her to rise.

Taatawi was the one who finally pulled Sihu from her son. She fell into Moon Fire's arms with a wrenching sob. Moon Fire held her sweet friend close as she fought back her own tears. She glanced at Tupkya, whose eyes were also red with emotion. Sikyawa remained stoic, but Moon Fire knew he was only covering his true emotions. Sihu's parents were also similarly showing their grief, but Lansa was the one who most concerned her.

Lansa's grief-stricken eyes opened, then closed, opened, then closed, wishing he knew what to do. His fists were clenched at his side. Taatawi saw his pain and beckoned him to kneel beside his son. He placed a hand on Tosi's chest as if he could not believe that he was really gone, then knelt down with his mouth next to Tosi's ear, saying, "I am sorry, my son. I am the fool."

Whether Sihu heard him or not, no one could tell, for suddenly she opened her eyes wide and twisted out of Moon Fire's embrace. She raced for a knife, intending to do harm to herself and hack off her waist length hair as was the custom. Everyone present watched as she sawed off her hair at different lengths close to her head. She also slashed her arms in several places. When she began to slice at her chest, Moon Fire and Taatawi together stopped her, knocking the knife from her hand and holding her close. They could not allow her to go on.

Moon Fire whispered into her friend's ear, "Enough, Sihu. You have another son who needs you."

With those words, Sihu gave up and her body grew limp. She did not even seem to be in the fourth world. She only whimpered her continued grief. It was at this point that Lansa took her from Moon Fire's and Taatawi's arms and held her close.

At last Taatawi signaled everyone to leave, for he knew he must begin the preparation of Tosi's body immediately. He did, however, ask Moon Fire to stay. Reluctantly everyone left. He had asked Moon Fire to remain with him in case Sihu decided to do something desperate. And so he prepared the small boy's body for burial.

Lansa was beside himself after his son had been interred under a corner of the room that he and Sihu had shared and called home. He was having nightmares in which he was constantly berating himself for the fool he was. Life had taken a turn that was terribly depressing, and at the same time new to him. He realized that he had not really been a father to his children, and as painful as it was, that had been his choice. Now, because of that choice, he had lost a son, and it was due to his neglect. He had been away most of the time, and when he returned it was to bring goods that had little to do with the needs of his family. Taatawi had told him that Tosi had died from malnutrition, and he hated himself for trading for material wealth instead of food to sustain his family. Now seven sun cycles had passed, and he felt worse. So much had happened in so short a time that he thought perhaps Awonawilona was punishing him. The image of Sihu torn with grief haunted him whether he was awake or asleep. It was true that she had thrown him out, but he now knew he had deserved his fate.

Suddenly he knew what he must do. Walking slowly to the top of Sihu's ladder, he rapped softly. Palatala, who was now six season cycles of age, said in his funny little childish voice, "You are permitted to enter."

Lansa climbed hesitantly down the ladder, and found Palatala playing with a small bow that he had made. It grieved him to think that one of Sihu's uncles had instructed the child when it should have been him. Sihu was working on a sandal for Palatala, and did not even look up.

He stood silently watching her, taking in her quiet loveliness, which was only marred by her hair, which was chopped in varying lengths on her head. Her arms were bare, displaying the scabs from the slashes she had inflicted upon herself in the grieving process. He suppressed the urge to take her into his arms to share the grief and shame he was feeling so deeply.

At last, after what seemed to Lansa like an eternity, she said without looking up, "I know it is you, Lansa. I still recognize the sound of the weight of your footsteps on the ladder. Why are you here?"

Lansa swallowed hard, then said, "Would you rather I go?"

"If that is your wish," she answered coldly.

"It is not my wish, Sihu. May I take a bit of your time?"

"If that is your wish," she repeated.

"This is not easy for me, and you are not making it any easier." He paused to gather his thoughts and remained standing tensely in front of her.

"Why should I make it easy for you? Life has not been easy for me or for your two children. You must know that."

"Sihu, what I have come to say, you may or may not believe, but I would ask that you at least listen." When she made no response, he continued. "So much has happened so quickly in my life. You know I am not a trained warrior. I am but a simple trader. Yet, not many sun cycles ago I could not stand by and watch our people killed by the raiders, and so I fought at the side of our best warriors. I watched many who were killed, and as you probably also know, I was rescued by my brother, Palasiva, who killed the leader of the raiders. I owe him my life, but more than that, I also owe Moon Fire my life, for she brought the word of the attack to our people. Sihu, it was the first time my sister, brother, and I ever did anything cooperatively."

She made no reply, but continued with her work.

Lansa continued. "That experience has taught me much about the importance of family. When I returned with all the other warriors, I found my entire family in the throws of intense grief for our child. Sihu, I have not been able to sleep because your sweet face continues to appear in my dreams. I have been a very selfish, self-centered person, and done nothing for you or our boys. Awonawilona has seen to it that I suffer the ultimate punishment. If you can find it in your heart, I am asking to make it up to you. You are a good mother and a wonderful person, and I have horribly mistreated you. Will you allow me a second chance?" He held his breath while waiting for her reply.

At last she looked up with her beautiful doe-shaped eyes brimming with tears. "Are you proposing to change your way of life for Palatala and me? Indeed this is very hard to believe."

Feeling encouraged by finally getting a response from her, he declared, "Yes, I want to make many changes, and I need your help. I cannot stop being a trader, but I can limit my time away, and more than that, I would trade for food rather than material goods. I want to be a father to Palatala, and if you will have me, a husband and provider for you."

Palatala looked at Lansa curiously, for he had no real memory of having a father, and now this man had said indirectly that he was his father, and wanted to be with them again. He wondered why his mother had never spoken to him of his father.

Sihu lowered her eyes and resumed her work. "This is all so sudden. I will need some time to think."

Lansa was overjoyed that she had not thrown him out again. Again he felt the need to take her into his arms just to hold her, but he did not want to push his luck. "You may take all the time you want. I will wait." He turned to climb the ladder, then added, "I still love you, Sihu. I was just stupid and irresponsible."

When he was out of sight, Sihu called Palatala to her side. Very softly she said, "My son, now you know."

CHAPTER 20

A.D. *1137*

Two more hands of sun cycles had gone by. Sihu had consulted with Moon Fire several times before making up her mind to give Lansa a second chance, if only for Palatala's sake. Lansa remained close to home, making every effort to make friends with his son. When he was not at home it was only to go out hunting, but like everyone else, he brought little meat, for there was very little available. He told Sihu in an intimate moment that he thought he should go out once more as a trader, but that this time he would trade for food, if there was any to be had. She agreed, and he left, promising that he would not be gone long.

Sikyawa and Tupkya had regained some of their hope for the family they had raised, and talked intimately to each other with the hope of regaining what they had lost in the past. It was with the culmination of one of those discussions that together they decided on a course of action.

Ignoring the pain in many of her joints, Tupkya ascended the ladder of her lodge and made her way to Moon Fire's quarters. She waited at the top of the ladder after rapping on it persistently. No one answered, and because she had no energy for another round trip, she waited.

She had fallen asleep when Moon Fire finally knelt by her side. "Uh, oh, I guess I am getting old," she said.

"Revered Mother, I am sorry to be so late arriving at my quarters, but there were those who needed counseling."

"I know you are busy, daughter, but may we talk?" Tupkya asked with a yawn.

"Of course. Let me help you to my quarters."

Tupkya declared that she would not be helped, but that Moon Fire should just let her take her time. She descended the ladder slowly and laboriously as Moon Fire patiently waited for her. Moon Fire invited her mother to sit beside her on her mat, and Tupkya accepted and took almost as much time assuming a sitting position as she had in descending the ladder.

Moon Fire wanted to say so many things, but she remained silent. Her past experience with her mother had taught her that she must not share her feelings, for they would be discounted. She had never met her parents' expectations, and she had no reason to believe that they should be any different now.

At last Tupkya had made herself comfortable, and looked around at her daughter's surroundings. She saw the ladder with blankets hung on the rungs, and the alcoves with her daughter's personal belongings. There was a mano and metate with vestiges of corn remaining in it, and a broom made of yucca in one corner. Several bowls of various sizes and shapes were neatly piled in another corner. Feathers hung from the ladder, some that were so brilliantly colored that she was certain that they must have come from the Mayan-Toltec country. She supposed that Wena 'Ahote had probably given them to her. What attracted her attention the most was the fact that Moon Fire had painted animals, birds, and insects all over one stuccoed wall, which gave her quarters a personal touch.

At last Moon Fire said simply, "Welcome to my quarters, Revered Mother."

Tupkya immediately gave her attention to her daughter. "Moon Fire, your home is lovely. This is the first time I have been here, and I hope it is not the last." She stopped to look searchingly at her daughter.

Moon Fire's nerves began to feel taut. She wanted to say, "Whatever has kept you away need never have been," but she bit her tongue, and remained silent.

"Moon Fire, your father and I have been talking, and we want you to know we have made some serious mistakes—misjudgments may be the more accurate word. What is worse, we have allowed these misjudgments to consume us, which has aged us prematurely, and given us health problems we might not have otherwise had. For many season cycles your father and I allowed our world to fall apart, and we are sorry. As you know, Lansa disappointed your father, but we now realize that Lansa's role as a trader was most fortunate in recent circumstances. He has also achieved growth and maturity, for he has shouldered responsibility, at last, for Sihu and Palatala. Palasiva broke our hearts, but has also grown into maturity, and shown his allegiance to family and his people through his recent deeds. You also have made us proud, for without you working with Palasiva, and Palasiva working with Lansa, I am afraid that most of our people would be dead. In short, my lovely daughter, your father and I would like you to return to live with us. We are proud of you."

Moon Fire could only stare at her mother in shock. Never, in her wildest dreams, did she imagine that she would ever hear what she had just heard. She found herself unable to speak.

Tupkya smiled with a twinkle in her eyes. "You do not believe me, do you."

"No, no, uh," she stammered.

"Little daughter, your father and I also have done some growing. We know your childhood was not the happiest. We remember how Lansa picked on you because you were a girl, and we know that when Palasiva came along, Lansa was too old to understand his little brother. Your father was much better than I when it came to mediating between the three of you, but we now know we should have made more of an effort in our parenting. I have been a problem due to my lack of patience, and I have promised myself that I will do better." She stopped to wait for a response from her daughter.

At last Moon Fire gathered her wits together. "Sweet Mother, for now I am too shocked to give an answer. Will you allow me some time to think on all that you have said?"

"Of course, child, but remember not to wait too long, for your father and I are not young anymore. Time is running short."

She realized that her mother was, without knowing what she was doing, trying to make her feel guilty, and using her age to force her to hasten her decision. She doubted that her mother would ever truly change. Plucking up her courage, she said, "Well since, as you say, time is short, I will tell you that I am honored that you have invited me back, but I must decline the offer. This is my home, and I have been here for so long that I know no other, and I am happy here. This has nothing to do with my feelings for you. You are both my parents, and I love you regardless of anything that has happened, and always will."

Tupkya's jaw dropped in disappointment, but she smiled, saying, "You know, child, you have given us the answer we suspected you would. We also love you, and hope you will feel free to visit any time."

"I want you to know, Mother, that I feel the same way. You and Father may come to visit me whenever you wish."

"We will," Tupkya mumbled. "Now help an old lady to her feet and up the ladder." When she was only halfway up the ladder, she stopped and asked, "Do you think we will ever see Palasiva again?"

Moon Fire, who was only three steps behind her mother on the ladder, stopped, but continued to keep her hand on her mother's back to steady her. She gave the only answer she knew. "Who can say, Mother? There is always a possibility."

When Tupkya had finally disappeared from her sight, she sighed and sat down heavily next to the top of her ladder. Her usual buoyant spirit was gone, and in its place a sense of futility had overcome her. She knew she should feel proud that at last her family seemed to be accepting her way of life, and yet she felt depressed. She had missed her last womanly cycle, and was not feeling well when she arose to watch Sun Father peep over the eastern horizon. Her nausea did not last long, but she knew the symptoms well. She vaguely remembered her mother speaking of nausea when Palasiva was on his way, and of course, she also knew because all Anasazi girls were taught all the facts of life shortly before they experienced their first womanly cycle. She had also begun to thicken around the waist, which she knew would sharply contrast with her almost emaciated body, and she wondered when Wena 'Ahote would take notice. She did not want to speak to Wena 'Ahote of her condition until she was absolutely sure. Her thoughts returned to

Tupkya, and she thanked Awonawilona that her mother had not noticed. Of course her loose clothing concealed her well. She considered confiding in Sihu, but knew there was little chance, for Lansa was usually home now, and she was thankful for her friend. Finally, sighing despondently, she shouldered what she would need for the trip to her cave for her womanly cycle that should have been happening.

She arrived at her cave just as Sun Father began to make his descent in the west. There had been very little harvested due to the lack of rain and the drought conditions that seemed to go on and on, while the sun cycles were gradually becoming shorter. When Sun Father dipped below the horizon, the air immediately became chilled and quickly turned cold during the time of darkness. She found her cave unoccupied and very dusty. In better times she would have wondered each time she returned if any of her animal, reptile, or bird friends might have chosen to occupy the cave during her absence. She swept it out with a yucca broom that she had made those many season cycles ago when she had had her first womanly cycle, then hastily built a fire. When the fire had taken hold and the flames were burning brightly, she sat cross-legged in front of it, basking in its warmth. Fire, she thought, could be such a friend if it was cared for, and such an enemy when neglected, much like human beings. Finally she rolled into her blankets to sleep.

She found that sleep eluded her. Her mind was still awake, but her body was tired. Her thoughts turned to Palasiva, and she wondered if he was even still alive. Ever since he had told her of his mission in the land of the Mogollon, she knew that he was placing himself in great danger. The next couple of sun cycles would tell her if he was dead or alive. She also pondered on how Tupkya and Sikyawa would respond if he had crossed over. They both seemed to have regained hope for the family, and were walking with a bit more bounce in their steps. Of course her thoughts also turned to Wena 'Ahote, who did not know he was to be a father. In his role as a priest, she wondered what, if any, repercussions might occur. Finally, she wondered about herself and the child. A child could not survive without proper nutrition, and she was not getting what she needed. She could only pray to Awonawilona that she and the child would survive. It was with these prayers that she fell into a deep, exhausted sleep.

She awoke at the first glow of sunrise with a feeling of nausea, and stoked the fire, which had almost burned itself out. After relieving herself, and enjoying a long drink of water, she decided to take a walk. The air was still cold even though Sun Father was struggling to warm Earth Mother to the best of His ability. She wrapped her legs and feet in leather, and wrapped her body in her warmest blanket, and set out.

There was no wind, and the land was more desolate than ever. Even the many varieties of cactus were no longer healthy-looking. In most cases the mother plant had died off, leaving the new shoots to struggle for survival. As she thought of her own pregnancy, and the parallels between herself and the condition of the cactus, she found herself becoming nauseous again. She knew she must stop such thoughts, but it was too late. She wretched, but there was nothing to bring up. She wretched again, then heard a voice behind her.

"Little sister, you are sick! Let me hold you." Palasiva held her until she quieted.

"No, Palasiva, I am not sick. I am pregnant"—she wheezed—"and I thank Awonawilona you are alive. I am as fine as is possible considering my condition, but tell me of your mission with the Mogollon. How did it go?"

Smiling with a confidence that was so different from his childhood, he declared, "Oh, it was much easier than with the Hohokam. Lansa had left me with the clothing of a trader and a few items to trade. Lansa had informed me of the village and its location where slave trading was taking place. I stayed in that village long enough to learn the habits of the two elders who had supported such an abomination, then I departed. I returned only long enough to do what was necessary. You see, the people were terribly upset with the thought that they might be next to be traded. I can only hope that they will appoint elders who are less corrupt."

Moon Fire was experiencing conflicting emotions. She was proud of her brother, yet horrified that he had found such a need to prove to himself that he could kill. A part of her wondered if killing was ever justified.

Palasiva seemed to read her thoughts as he added, "I know our people are a people of peace, and fight only to defend themselves, but what about the forces of evil that are inevitable? If the Mayan-Toltecs are a threat to the welfare of any group of innocent people, should we not respond?"

Moon Fire was not in agreement, for it was in her mind that what happened to other people, was not the business of her people, and her people should not interfere. She remained silent. This was Palasiva's mission, which she could understand, and there was no reason to speak.

Palasiva realized that her lack of response must mean that she disagreed with him, so he said, "I am sorry that you disagree with what I had to do, but I understand why it is so. Please remember that anything I have done has not changed my love for you. You are my sister, and at this time the love of my life." Pulling her into his embrace, he asked, "How are our parents?"

Laying her head against his shoulder, she answered, "Tupkya and Sikyawa are better than they were. Tupkya asked me if I would live in their quarters once again. I answered no, for I am happy where I am. They said they were proud of Lansa, for he has gone back to live with Sihu, and Palatala. Their youngest son crossed over recently, but Lansa seems to have become the provider he should have been all along." She suggested they both sit down.

It was no problem to find comfortable rocks on which to sit. Palasiva asked, "What are their feelings toward me?"

"Palasiva, they are proud of you, and have asked me if they might ever see you again. I could only answer that there might be a possibility, for I did not want to disappoint them."

The wind had picked up just a little, and both of them had to cover their noses and mouths with cotton cloths. Palasiva looked away as if he were in another world, then turned back and said, "Moon Fire, I would very much like to return to our people. Do you think there is a chance?" He removed his cotton face cloth, and looked at her imploringly.

"Little brother, I could not even begin to guess. I do know that it would make our parents very happy. If you would like, I will speak to Wena 'Ahote of your wish, and he can speak to Taatawi, who will speak to the elders."

Another gust of wind caused him to replace his face cloth and turn away from the heavy dust. Though he could not look at her, he said, "I would like that very much. I have lived alone long enough, and you know that I have tried very hard to make up for my past transgressions."

Moon Fire laid her small hand on his arm and squeezed a little. "Palasiva, I will do what I can. In my mind you were never at fault, and I wonder how anyone as young as you were could ever know what to do."

He placed his calloused right hand on her shoulder, and said, "Little sister, there is one more mission I must accomplish, and one I must not speak of, for it may be more dangerous than any other."

"Is this last mission really necessary?" she asked.

"It may or may not be more important than any in my life, but shh. We must not discuss it. I will return when Moon Mother is in the same phase."

"That is good, Palasiva, for during the cold season, I would normally not be coming here, but I will promise you that, if I am permitted to do so, I will speak to the elders on your behalf."

Palasiva wrapped his hardened sinewy arms around Moon Fire in a warm embrace. He whispered softly, "I must go, little sister. I want you to know I care, and I would be there for you if I could. Perhaps someday . . ." His voice trailed into nothing.

Moon Fire's mind seized the precious moment, for only Awonawilona knew what might happen. "Please take special care of yourself. We will meet again soon."

"And you do the same," he exclaimed with a chuckle. "You have two to care for." He turned away from her quickly, and in no time at all, was out of sight.

Since she usually shared the last meal of the day with Wena 'Ahote, she found herself sitting on his mat when she had returned from her cave. This was their time to talk and go over all that had happened during each sun cycle. She felt quite nervous knowing she must tell him of the coming of their child. It was customary that there should be no discussion while eating a meal, so she had a short reprieve before they both finished, and he said, "Well, Little Fire, while you were away, Taatawi and I had a discussion about the seriousness of the drought, and how it is slowly killing our people. News arrived informing us that the Mayan-Toltec traders are ignoring us, and trading with our most northern outlier, which continues to grow. I am not sure what our people in the north are trading, but there is at least some trading going on. Taatawi says he feels completely ineffectual as sun priest. He faithfully charts Sun Father's path, and tries to advise the people when to plant, but Awonawilona has withheld the rain to nurture the corn, beans, and squash." He looked lovingly at Moon Fire and added, "But enough of what has been going on here. It's always the same. How was your visit to your cave? I would hope you got some much-needed rest."

"I did," she said anxiously. "Oh, I did." She wiped out their bowls with a soft cotton cloth, and hoped he would be satisfied with her response.

"You are not yourself, my love. Is there something you wish to tell me?"

She shook her head and took a deep breath. "Yes, there is something I must tell you." She decided to speak of Palasiva in order to put off the announcement of her pregnancy. "While I was out walking early in Sun Father's journey, I met Palasiva. He told me he had successfully done to the Mogollon village elders what he had done to the Hohokam elders. He hoped that with new elders the village would no longer trade their own people to the Mayan-Toltecs for slaves. I told him of the desire of our parents to reunite the family. He said there was nothing he would like more, and that he had lived alone too long. I promised I would speak to you with the hope that you might speak to Taatawi, and perhaps the elders on his behalf. If you wish, I will also speak on his behalf, for I know that his return would more than rejuvenate our parents."

"Taatawi is a just man. I am sure he will be no problem, but I feel certain that Ruupi would not hear of it. Of course it is not a decision for Ruupi to make, but he will probably not make it easy. Yes, my love, we will try. Perhaps a meeting can be arranged."

"Thank you. I knew you would support me." She bowed her head and remained silent.

Wena 'Ahote bent toward her and asked, "Is there something else you would have me know?"

She squeezed her eyes shut, then opened them. "Yes, my love, there is."

When she did not readily volunteer an answer to his question, he asked, "Why do you hesitate to speak. You know we have no secrets."

A tear escaped from each of her dark eyes as she looked up at him. Finally she said, "We are to be parents."

Wena 'Ahote was not sure he had heard her correctly. "We are what?"

She repeated, "We are to be parents. Oh, Wena 'Ahote, I took the medicine, but it did no good. I am pregnant. You are never with me when I first awake, so you could not know how nauseated I am. I have missed two womanly cycles. I went to the cave, hoping that I might have reason, but the only real reason was to meet Palasiva."

Wena 'Ahote shook his head and smiled. Then taking her into his arms, he lay on his back and molded her body on top of his. "Awonawilona has sent us the ultimate gift, my love. It may be untimely, but we will do what is necessary to bring this new life into a horribly unbalanced world. Now let me love you."

Tears of joy and relief ran unbidden down Moon Fire's cheeks as she welcomed his tender attention.

Palasiva left Moon Fire with a heavy heart. Since he strongly doubted that his people would take him back, he felt an urgency in his new mission. The reason he could not tell Moon Fire about it was because the telling of it might take away some of his power. For three sun cycles he traveled back over the mountains to the west of his people toward the camp of the raiders. He had been unable to get thoughts of Mina out of his mind. The raiders' way of life was so foreign to him that he wondered what they would do with her. She was so lovely with her sad dark brown eyes and full mouth. Her nose was not flat against her head as so many of the raiders displayed. It was softly pointed and unobtrusive. Her hair was long and thick with just a suggestion of red in it, and her bones were small and delicate. He could not help but wonder how her petite body had withstood the lashing that Teo had administered. In truth, she was the one person in his stay with the raiders who had reached out to him. Now he sensed she was in trouble, and he was motivated to move with relentless speed.

It was not long before he approached their camp. He circled around it and noticed his old lodge, which was removed from the rest of the village, and sensed it might be occupied. He was not certain that anyone was living there, so he lay down and waited in observation. The camp was nestled among piñon pines and junipers that completely hid it from anyone who might be approaching. He had arrived at his vantage point during Sun Father's zenith, and was not surprised that he saw no one at home. He had avoided the sentries by becoming his totem animal, and lay patiently in wait.

At last, very late in the sun cycle, he saw a small figure approaching the solitary lodge. He was unable to tell who it was until she was closer, and he knew it was Mina. Why, he wondered, was she living outside the village of her people. The customs of her people were so different from his own. He watched as she took the roots she had gathered and scraped the dirt and skin off to make them ready for cooking. Her worn buckskins could not hide her nearly emaciated body, but she maintained the feminine grace that he knew so well. It was obvious that no one was bringing her game, and that she had lived on whatever she could since he had left.

Sun Father disappeared beyond the horizon in the west, and Palasiva saw that no one approached or even seemed to be interested in Mina's lodge. He rejoiced, for this was the opportunity he had never imagined he would have. Darkness had set in, and he stealthily crept toward her lodge. Moon Mother was only a sliver in the sky, which shielded him from view of any guards.

Mina had just settled down for a vegetable stew, and was taken by surprise when Palasiva raised the skin that covered the door to the lodge that was now hers. "Praise the Creator, it is you. I never thought you would still be alive."

"Mina," he said, "I have come to ask you to be my wife. I suspect I know why you are living in my lodge as an outcast, but I would like to hear it from you." He kept his distance, for he still did not want to assume what her circumstances might be.

She looked at him shyly, then answered, "My future husband did not want anything to do with me when you left. My parents offered me no support, so I was left as an outcast. I live here because I feel your spirit. I do the best I can."

"But you are so thin. You are not the Mina I knew when I was here." He reached for her and she readily accepted his embrace.

"Will you join me for a root stew? It is all I have, and all I have had in a very long time."

"Do you think we should take the time to enjoy a meal, ever so meager as it may be, or would you pack up now and go with me. I have asked you to be my wife, and I would surely strive to serve you with at least some meat to accompany your stews."

She flashed him a wondrously warm smile and said, "Oh yes, I would be delighted. It will not take me long to pack what little I have."

After a warm hug, they left. Palasiva thanked Awonawilona for his good fortune as they disappeared into the darkness.

CHAPTER 21

A.D. *1137*

Wena 'Ahote hesitated when he entered Taatawi's quarters to chart the path of Sun Father. He knew he had two very difficult problems to present to him, and he was feeling very unsure of himself. He reminded himself that he had promised Moon Fire that he would speak on her brother's behalf. He spent time with Taatawi during almost every sunrise, and he thought that it might be best to speak of only one problem at a time. Either way, he was not particularly confident when he sat down beside the sun priest.

Taatawi sensed Wena 'Ahote's anxiety immediately. "You are not yourself. Do you wish to talk?" he inquired.

"You are indeed a highly sensitive person, and you are right. Let us do our observation first, then we will speak."

Taatawi said no more, but when they had completed their observation and noted the exact position as Sun Father arose, he sat on a mat, inviting Wena 'Ahote to join him. "Now, young priest, what is it that is bothering you?"

Ordinarily he would not have lashed out, but he retorted, "Please don't call me 'young priest'! Ruupi brings it up to me often enough."

Taatawi placed his hand over Wena 'Ahote's, saying, "Stop. I knew you were disturbed when you arrived, but I did not know to what extent."

Wena 'Ahote struggled to regain his composure, and was appreciative that Taatawi allowed him time to do so. After a short period of time, Wena 'Ahote said, "I am sorry, but this thing with Ruupi is an ongoing thing, and it eats at me. I am doing my best to contain my true feelings."

"That is perfectly understandable, but now can you tell me what is troubling you?"

Wena 'Ahote rubbed the bridge of his nose with his thumb and forefinger, then said, "Moon Fire's brother, Palasiva, has made every effort to reconcile himself with the people. You know much of the heroic things he has done to prevent our southerly neighbors from trading their own people into slavery. You also know how, without him, our own people might not have survived the invasion of the raiders. What you may not know is that he has accomplished with the Mogollon what he also accomplished with the Hohokam. Through Moon Fire he has asked to be reinstated with his people. His exile has been long and harsh, and he is now a hardened warrior who could teach us much about our neighbors with whom we trade. There! Now you have it, and you know what my problem is."

"I cannot explain why, but I think your problems are more than one. Let us deal with one at a time." Taatawi clasped his hands together, then ran them through his long flowing gray hair. "It will be no problem to run this by the elders, and others who govern us, but I am afraid Ruupi may be a problem. Of course you know that he always is, and ever shall be a most difficult person for many of us to handle, but rest assured, I will do all I can."

Wena 'Ahote looked at him gratefully, then hung his head, indicating that, as the sun priest had suspected, there was more.

Taatawi patiently waited, shook his head, and lit a pipe. He tamped the tobacco, then uttered a prayer as he blew smoke to the north, east, south, and west. At last he said, "What is it that hangs so heavily on your mind?"

"She is with child," he whispered.

"I am not surprised. Did she forget the medicine?"

Wena 'Ahote looked up with flashing eyes. "No, Revered One, she did not."

Taatawi chuckled. "Then you are a very potent male. Do you realize that?"

Wena 'Ahote did not appreciate the fact that his mentor was taking his confession so lightly. He stared at Taatawi as if he were a stranger. "How can you make light of such a situation? Priests are not supposed to be fathers. What will other people think?"

With a stern look, Taatawi said, "You and Moon Fire have been together for many season cycles. Our herbal means of contraception are not guaranteed. Awonawilona has made his wishes known, and we humans must accept what is meant to be."

"But I cannot hunt for our child. I am a priest. I am not supposed to have children."

"That is not so. There have always been priests who have had children, but it is the role of her family to care for her and the child. Have you told anyone else? Has she told her parents?"

"No, we have told no one, because I only recently was informed by her. Taatawi, I love her, and want to do all I can. Do you really think things might work out?"

Taatawi emptied the ashes out of his pipe and smiled. "Have her inform her parents. I promise you I will work on your first request, but you will have to handle the second one."

Wena 'Ahote gave an enormous sigh of relief. "Thank you, Revered Sun Priest. I will do the best I can." He began to climb the ladder to begin his other duties.

Taatawi murmured so softly that no one could have heard him, "And so shall I, and so shall I."

Moon Fire descended the ladder into her parents' home. She should have been extremely nervous, but found herself instead, feeling very steady and happy about her child who was a result of the love that she and Wena 'Ahote had shared for so long. She only hoped that her parents had truly gotten over their bitterness for her choice of Wena 'Ahote as a lifetime mate even though she could not marry him. She still debated in her mind whether to tell them of the efforts being made to reunite Palasiva with her family and her people. Both Tupkya and Sikyawa seemed ten season cycles younger since they had seen their children work together successfully for the good of the people, and she did not want to see their hopes dashed again.

Tupkya looked up from her grinding stone in surprise. "Ho, daughter. What brings you here? This is highly unusual."

Moon Fire giggled in response and replied, "I was sure you would say that, Mother, but at least you can never say that I make a nuisance of myself."

Tupkya chuckled. "You are so right. Come sit by my side." She rose, wiped her hands on her skirt, and rolled out a mat. The two of them sat cross-legged facing each other.

"I was hoping my father would be here. Perhaps I should come back at a time when I know you are both here."

"Your father is in the men's kiva and has been there for quite some time. He may return any time now. Why not wait?"

"I cannot wait long, I am afraid." Then looking at her mother, she asked, "It pleases me to see you and Father happy once again. I hope it will always be as it is now."

Just then they heard a heavy tread on the roof and watched as Sikyawa descended the ladder. He registered a look of surprise at finding the two women together. "Lovely daughter, to what do we owe this occasion?" He put down another mat close to them, stuck a stick in the cooking fire, and lit his pipe. The smell of sweet grass wafted around him.

Moon Fire took a deep breath. She had finally decided to tell them about Palasiva because she was sure that her father would hear of it very soon in one of his visits to the men's kiva, and she was certain that they both would be hurt if the news came to them in a roundabout way. At last she said, "I have been in contact with Palasiva and he is well. He has been successful in his mission involving the Mogollon elders who were responsible for trading their own people to the Mayan-Toltecs for slaves. He has truly become a hardened, skilled warrior. He asked me if I would speak on his behalf to the proper people to see if it might be possible for him to return to us. I have spoken to Wena 'Ahote who has also spoken to Taatawi. I would not want you to hear this from anyone else, and I only hope that Awonawilona will somehow stir the hearts of the elders to bring him back to us." She stopped speaking when she saw Tupkya dash tears from her eyes with the back of her hand.

Sikyawa's expression remained the same. Taking another long draw on his pipe, he said, "You are right, Moon Fire. We would not want to learn of this from anyone else. It is in my mind that we should not build our hopes too high. Some of those who spend time in the men's kiva with me would think that what Palasiva did to his own people is unpardonable. Yet there are others who understand that he was young and thought he had little choice."

Tupkya regained her composure and said, "We will spend extra time in prayer to Awonawilona." After an enormous sigh, she added, "It is in His hands. I am also grateful to hear such hopeful news from you."

Moon Fire looked down at her hands that rested in her lap. Softly she said, "There is more."

Both Tupkya and Sikyawa remained silent, knowing that she would speak when she was ready.

Squaring her shoulders, she looked up at both of them with an enormous smile, saying proudly, "I am with child."

Tupkya stared at her daughter in disbelief. Sikyawa simply took another draw on his pipe, then chuckled. "So I am to be a father again. Perhaps this child will be a girl to carry on the family clan name. As I see it, and since many of our cousins, aunts, and uncles have left the canyon in search of better living conditions, this child is a blessing."

Tupkya reached for Moon Fire's hands to draw her daughter's thin body close to her. "I, too, am happy to be a mother once more. I am only sorry that you cannot marry Wena 'Ahote, who should provide for you and the child. Times are hard and the world is terribly out of balance. Know in your heart that your father and I will do all we can for you and the child. I am sure that Lansa will also be more than happy to provide for you both when he can. Does Sihu or Lansa know of this?"

Moon Fire breathed a sigh of relief. "No, Mother, they do not know. I wanted you to be the first to know, though I am sure, by now, Wena 'Ahote has told Taatawi, who will inform those he feels should know."

"And what of your health?" Tupkya inquired. "The conditions in which we are living are unstable, if not deplorable, and food and water are scarce. You must see that you eat enough and drink enough water to sustain both you and the child."

"I appreciate your advice, and I am sure that with your help, and also Lansa's, the child and I will do very well. Thank you for being so understanding. I must go now." She rose from the mat and walked to the bottom of the ladder.

Sikyawa tamped his pipe, and said, "Would it not be better to say, 'We must go now'?"

With a giggle, Moon Fire turned and said, "I suppose you are right. For a while I must learn to speak of we, not I."

"She is *what*?" Ruupi shouted. "Tell me I did not hear you correctly."

"You heard me, Ruupi. I said she is with child. Under ordinary circumstances I would be happy for her and Wena 'Ahote, but a child growing within her womb needs proper nourishment, and . . ."

"I can't believe what I am hearing! You speak of concern and happiness that a child will be born. You speak of nourishment. Ha! You and I both know that a priest cannot marry, and should never be foolish enough to get a woman pregnant. What is *wrong* with you? You are crazy! Have you lost your senses?" Ruupi paced the floor and threw up his hands in disgust as he ranted.

"No, Ruupi, I have not. Our heritage speaks of priests occasionally being fathers, though you are right. They cannot marry or support the child."

Taatawi forced himself to maintain a calmness in his voice. "Her parents are aware of everything and have said that they, along with their son Lansa, would do all they can. Ruupi, I don't see what your problem is. We should be overjoyed that a child is to be born among us. Perhaps the little one will be as gifted as her mother."

"Moon Fire, gifted? Pah! She is a slut. She has been rutting with Wena 'Ahote for so long that it is no wonder she is finally pregnant. Wena 'Ahote is unfit for the priesthood." His bronze face took on a purple hue, and he shook with rage.

Taatawi had heard enough. "You have gone too far, Ruupi. It is not a pleasure to say this to you, but I must. I would remind you that you have 'rutted' with Leetayo for almost as long a time, and I am amazed that you have not impregnated her. Perhaps you are not man enough." He still did not raise his voice.

"Man enough? *Man enough?*" Ruupi's voice was becoming shrill and piercing. "You would speak about being a man, when you have never had a woman! It is you who are not *man enough!*"

Taatawi closed his eyes briefly and clamped his lips together in an effort to retain his composure. At last he said, "I have no time for women. I take my position as sun priest seriously. This conversation is out of balance, and in truth, is no conversation at all. I can only say that it is a shame you are obviously not in any mood for me to speak of any other important issues. If you will excuse me, I will return to my quarters." He wanted to add that, he would like to go anywhere rather than be around Ruupi, but kept such thoughts to himself. As he left their private corner in the plaza, he thought he heard Ruupi say, "It would not surprise me if you preferred the company of a man."

Ruupi found Tenyam in his quarters, which surprised him since Tenyam usually spent most of his time in the men's kiva. Due to his anger, he barely noticed Tenyam's wife, who labored over the metate as she ground corn. Ordinarily he would have offered her a greeting, but because of Taatawi's insults, he ignored any formalities, and waited for Tenyam to acknowledge him.

After a long draw on his pipe, he said, "To what do I owe the honor of your presence? This is highly unusual."

"I would speak with you privately, Tenyam."

Tenyam moved his old pained bones carefully as he came to a standing position. "I will follow you," he said.

Ruupi led the way up the ladder and into the plaza to a corner where they might not be heard by others who might be passing by. "Tenyam, Taatawi has informed me of Moon Fire's pregnancy. He seems to be taking it well, but I feel that Wena 'Ahote has gone too far, and is unfit for his priestly position."

Tenyam stood quietly while drawing his thumb and forefinger across his chin. "In the past there have been priests who have fathered children. Is this the only reason you feel Wena 'Ahote is unfit for his position?"

Ruupi was at his wits' end. "So you would take Taatawi's position? He says that there is no problem with the pregnancy."

"Yes, I am in agreement, for, in truth, I do not expect the baby to live under the present terrible circumstances. There are many more important issues at hand than this."

Ruupi stopped in his tracks and looked long and hard at Tenyam. "Taatawi refused to tell me of an important issue that has apparently come up very recently."

"Yes, Ruupi. If you had not been so hotheaded, he would have told you that Palasiva has asked to return to his people. It is true that he did us a horrible injustice, but he has worked hard to make all of his people aware that he had no choice. He has not only saved our people from the ever dangerous raiders, but has also freed the Mogollon and Hohokam from their elders who favored the slavery of their people."

Ruupi did not hear the last part of Tenyam's statement at all. He just looked at him incredulously and said, "You sound as though you are in favor of this twisted young man. What is wrong with you? Don't you realize that the young man and his entire family are out of touch with reality?"

"No, Ruupi, I am not sure I agree with you, but I will think on what you have said. I must admit that I am not particularly fond of Sikyawa's family, but I also know that Wena 'Ahote is descended from the family of the long-revered and now-deceased sun priest of long ago, and the one who was the lover of the female sun priestess who took over his position when he died."

"Then it would seem that we are of opposing opinions." Thrusting out his chest and clenching his fists, he proclaimed, "I think you should know that I will not support any action to reinstate Palasiva for I believe the whole family is evil. I believe Moon Fire, with her supposed gift, is evil, and I believe Palasiva is evil. What he has done once, he will do again. I also believe that Lansa is evil. He lives in his own world of trading, and has not lost weight as we all have. I am surprised that his wife would take him back."

Tenyam chuckled and said, "Why, then, have you not lost weight as everyone else has done? Where are you getting your nourishment? What is it that we don't know?"

Ruupi bristled and his face took on a deep purple hue. "You know it all. I just need less food than most people." Then taking his rage with him, he declared, "Just remember, I am fully convinced that the world is out of balance, and that Taatawi, Wena 'Ahote, and Moon Fire's family are evil. I had hoped to gain your support, but I can see that it is impossible. I go now, for there seems to be nothing more here that I can gain." He walked angrily away.

Tenyam remained in thought for some time, then finally turned toward the men's kiva.

Three sun cycles passed when Moon Fire learned of a council meeting that was to be held when Sun Father next made his descent. She had been told that she must be present, and she assumed and hoped that perhaps Palasiva's request might be considered. She had spoken to Lansa, who had heartily agreed to speak on behalf of his brother. She had also learned of Taatawi's and Ruupi's conflict of interests, and she wondered how many of the voting members Ruupi would court with his hatred and irrational thinking. In spite of herself, she had ominous feelings about the outcome of the meeting.

She prepared herself as well as she could, considering the lack of water. Since there was no water for cleanliness, she smoked her head and body by the fire once a sun cycle to repel lice and any other insects that still survived. She could not remember the last time she had truly felt clean. She donned a turkey feather cloak over her cotton shift that tied at one shoulder, pinched her cheeks for color, and walked to the kiva where the meeting was to take place.

She took her place next to Lansa, who anxiously awaited her arrival. Everyone who had the power to cast his opinion was present. Wena 'Ahote, Taatawi, and Ruupi were also in attendance, though they could not vote, due to the fact that they were priests. The tension was so thick that she felt even an obsidian knife would never have been able to cut it. The heat was almost unbearable, and the body odors were strong. The smoke from the fire wafted its way to the hole in the roof and out into the darkness. She glanced nervously at Wena 'Ahote, and felt his anxiety.

At last Tenyam, as usual, began the meeting. "There are some minor issues we must consider, but since we have guests among us, let us consider their issues first. It has come to our attention through Lansa and Moon Fire that their younger brother, Palasiva, has expressed an interest to once again become a part of the people. I would ask that before you draw any conclusion or opinion, you listen to Lansa, who would speak on his behalf." He returned to his place on the bench.

Awta, the construction supervisor, rose immediately, saying, "I see no reason why we should waste our time listening to his brother, who will no doubt defend actions that are unpardonable, and out of balance."

Tenyam quickly rose. "It is our duty to try to see things from all directions, for that is the way that Awonawilona has always advised us. If there are no other objections, let Lansa proceed."

A hush settled over the kiva. As Moon Fire looked from one face to another, she could feel the hostility as well as feelings of compassion. It was a strange mixture.

At last Lansa rose to his feet. He shut his eyes and clenched his fists, and began. "Elders and honored ones, I will try to make what I have to say as brief as possible. My brother was very young when he was exiled from our people. What he did was as wrong as anything Awonawilona has ever taught us. To that I will agree. He knew that he was in a no-win situation. He felt that if he told us the truth, the raiders would surely have come down upon us, promising him that they would kill Moon Fire, and he also knew that if he went along with the raiders, the death of his people would also be the result. I ask you to look at what happened through the eyes of a very young man who was naive.

"Since then, his conscience has worked on him, and he has tried to make amends by disrupting slave trade between the Mogollon and the Hohokam and the Mayan-Toltecs. He has also saved us, the people, by warning us, through Moon Fire, of possible total destruction. You know the rest since then. I would ask you to consider all the facts, and not rest on emotions. The world is already out of balance, and we must not make things worse. Let us have some compassion." He stopped as if he had run out of breath, and took his place next to his sister.

Moon Fire's heart filled with pride as she glanced at her brother, the brother who had always been a thorn in her side, and she in his. "Why?" she thought, "does it take a crisis to finally bring people together?" Her thoughts were brief, for what happened next, she was totally unprepared for.

Tenyam stood while all eyes turned toward him. "Life is full of decisions, some good, some bad. I have been deep in thought for three sun cycles, and have come to some conclusions. First, it is in my mind that people do not change. What someone does once, will happen again. We are dealing with a traitor among us, and are considering taking him back into our fold. A part of me wants to accept him, and another part signals a warning and says no. If I listen to my soul, I say that now is not the time to do this. What if he secretly still has connections with the raiders?"

Hoohu was quickly on his feet. "Wait! Don't you understand? If he secretly has connections with the raiders, then why did he become a traitor to them, and inform us of their intentions?"

Angwusi shot out of his seat on the bench. "Perhaps because this is all a masterminded plan. If he is reinstated, he can continue his informing and deception."

Maahu, the architect, rose and said, "None of you seem to see that the young man has grown and matured. He has lived a hard life, and dealt with his punishment, and miraculously survived. Not only that, but he is responsible for the death of the warrior leader of the raiders. How can you conceive of this as a masterminded plan? Is that not enough? Have you no compassion?"

"No, that is not enough. He has cost many lives of our people. Why should we be so readily forgiving?" Awta snarled.

Posaala, the building surveyor, was up immediately shouting, "Because that is what we, the people, are about! Awonawilona has instructed us to be forgiving. He has told us we are never to be a warlike people, yet here we are fighting among ourselves with some of us showing no mercy. I do not say much, but I agree, the world is terribly out of balance. I say, let us take a vote."

Moon Fire's heart felt sick, even though she knew she should expect no better. She closed her eyes and prayed to Awonawilona.

Tenyam heard no objection, so he called for a vote. Four of those able to vote were in favor, and four were against. Tenyam and Angwusi, who always stood together, were against, along with Eykita, who was always easily led, and of course, Awta. Hoohu was for Palasiva's cause along with Posaala, Maahu, and Iswungwa, the trade manager.

Moon Fire's disappointment made her feel as though her heart had landed on her stomach. She knew Ruupi had done his homework well. She stole a glance first at Wena 'Ahote, then at Lansa, who also looked as crestfallen as she. Though the decision had been made, she immediately wondered how she should inform Tupkya and Sikyawa. She decided she would ask Lansa to accompany her.

Tenyam stood hesitantly looking around the kiva, then his gaze came to rest on Wena 'Ahote. "It has come to our attention that there is to be a birth. If any of you who are present did not know, Moon Fire is with child." He waited, then hearing no response, continued. "In normal times, this would not be an issue, but you all know the conditions in which we are living. I would welcome any opinions."

Angwusi, of course, rose immediately, saying, "It is in my mind that our young priest is obsessed with Moon Fire. As Tenyam has said, these are trying times, and we need our young priest to devote all his attention to his people. We also need Moon Fire, whose counseling ability is very valuable, to give all her attention to her starving people. I feel, in this case, that there is a conflict of interest, and Wena 'Ahote should put her aside for the good of the people."

Moon Fire was horrified. She was already giving her all to counsel her people, and had little enough time to herself. The only time she had with Wena 'Ahote was during the evening repast, and occasional stolen moments that they might find together. She could not believe that her pregnancy could possibly make any difference in the quality of her work or his. It was common knowledge that other priests had fathered children, and as long as they were cared for, it was accepted among the people. Why, now, was there a problem? She put her thoughts aside as the meeting progressed.

Hoohu quickly stood. "There have been priests in the past who have fathered children. I see this as no problem of ours for, as I understand it, her parents and her brother have taken on the responsibility for her support, which will not effect Wena 'Ahote. They will both continue their duties as they have always done, with no change until time for the birth of the child. Who knows where we will be then?" He placed his forefinger and thumb along the side of his nose and closed his eyes. "Why, I ask, are we making this an issue?"

"Because there is a conflict of interest here!" shouted Tenyam. "The question is, are you interested in your woman, or are you interested in your people? That is the question. I cannot understand why anyone would see it any other way!"

Wena 'Ahote's heart shuddered as he took in what he had heard. Suddenly, as if spiritually guided, he stood, and said, "When the sacred act becomes debatable, it is time that something be done. It seems you all come here to judge my private life. It is true, and I will say it to all of you, I love Moon Fire. She has conceived a child, and I am the father. If this is more than you can deal with, I resign the priesthood. I want no part of a system that has no compassion. Both of us would continue our duties to the people, but with what I am hearing now, I cannot go on. I no longer belong to the priesthood. I will support my child and soon-to-be wife. It is not just this event that has brought on my decision, but many others in the past." He glared at Ruupi and added, "I also know who is responsible for it all. I cannot understand why you are so blind. Taatawi knows. I have nothing else to say."

Moon Fire was taken completely by surprise. Wena 'Ahote was giving up the priesthood for her and their unborn child. Guilt washed over her mixed with a deep feeling of honor due to the fact that he had placed their relationship above everything else. Tears ran down her cheeks as she made a valiant effort to show no emotion, tears that she dashed away with the palm of her hands.

A dark, wrenching silence pervaded the kiva. It was as if no one ever expected such an outcome except perhaps Ruupi, who showed no reaction at all. Taatawi was shaken to the bone. He knew that Wena 'Ahote was hated by Ruupi, but he never suspected how much. It was now becoming clear to him what Ruupi's motives really were and had been all along. With Wena 'Ahote out of the way, he was planning to be the next sun priest, and Taatawi realized he must guard himself well, both physically and politically. Ruupi had finally proved that he had not changed, and that his exile had done no good. He was now, more than ever, a dangerous and evil man.

At last Tenyam. broke the silence. "I must say that I never expected the response that we have all heard. I am fully aware that there have been other priests who have still fulfilled their duties even though they fathered children. Perhaps we have been hasty in our judgment, or maybe we have listened to other irrational opinions when we should have known better." He cast his angered eyes at Ruupi as he spoke. Then turning back to Wena 'Ahote, he asked, "Would you reconsider?"

"No, absolutely no. There is more political upheaval than I wish to deal with. There is no respect, and the world is out of balance. You have made my decision an easy one. I would ask that you excuse Moon Fire and me from this meeting." He strode quickly to her and took her hand.

"So it shall be," Tenyam said meekly.

As they left, Lansa also asked to be excused. After their consent, he also took his leave.

The meeting went no further.

When Moon Fire, Lansa, and Wena 'Ahote were far enough from everyone else, Wena 'Ahote took Moon Fire into his arms. As her head rested on his chest she could hear his heart pounding. She knew if he was not a man, he would be openly grieving. "My love," she said, "may I come to you after Lansa and I have given our parents the news?"

After nodding his consent, he released her and turned toward his own quarters. With shoulders slumped and head bowed, he turned back long enough to give her another wordless message. "Come as soon as you can," he seemed to be saying.

Moon Fire was filled with sorrow and wonder, for now she was fully aware of the depth of his love for her. She turned to find Lansa patiently waiting only a short distance away. "Come, my brother, we must do what we must do."

Together they walked to Tupkya and Sikyawa's quarters. At the top of the ladder, each took a deep breath before Lansa asked, "May we come down?"

"Of course. As family you need not ask." Tupkya's voice seemed to be pitched a bit higher than usual, indicating her anxious concern.

As soon as Moon Fire and Lansa reached the bottom of the ladder and turned to face their parents, they realized that Tupkya knew as she read the expression on her children's faces. Sikyawa sat in his usual corner, and looked at them only briefly, then drew in on his pipe. He said nothing, allowing Tupkya to speak for him.

Tupkya had stopped grinding corn, and wiped her hands on her skirt as she stood. "So, my children, it was not good."

"No, Mother, I gave it my best. I spoke on Palasiva's behalf, but even so, the vote was split four to four. There was no one to break the tie. Everyone knew that even if they asked Ruupi and Taatawi to vote, it would still have remained a tie." Lansa walked quickly to hold her, for she slumped so heavily that he was afraid her old bones would not support her. He felt her tears soak the cotton cloth of his shirt.

When she had regained her composure, she stepped back and said, "I guess I should not be surprised at the outcome. At least I have two of my three children, and perhaps one day, if it is the will of Awonawilona, I shall once again have all three."

Sikyawa grunted his consent, took another draw on his pipe, and asked, "Was there anything else of interest that took place in the meeting?"

Lansa deferred to Moon Fire, who said, "Yes, my father, oh yes. There were those in attendance who thought Wena 'Ahote's love for me was an obsession and a conflict of interest. To put it bluntly, they were asking him to stop seeing me, saying his priestly duties should come first." She sighed deeply and stared at the pots that were neatly stacked near the metate in another corner of the room.

"And?" Sikyawa coaxed.

"He said he wanted no part of the priesthood if it meant we could not acknowledge our love for each other. He said that there have been other priests in our past history who have had children even though they could not marry."

Sikyawa looked at his daughter through the smoke rings that surrounded him. "Let me guess. Those who were pushing this action were . . ." He paused, then continued. "Tenyam, yes Tenyam who is always a grouch and Angwusi who follows him in almost everything he does. Oh, yes, and Eykita. Eykita would have found the whole thing too much trouble, and would have been the third. Of course, little daughter, we common people know a lot more than many would think. The person at the bottom of this is our own crystal scrier whose name I need not mention. Am I right?"

Moon Fire stared at her father in amazement. "Would everyone see it as clearly as you do?"

"Yes, Moon Fire. The people know more than you think. It is still the consensus of opinion that our crystal scrier is evil, but what can we do about it?" He tamped the ashes of his pipe in a small bowl, and walked to his daughter's side. Placing his hands on her shoulders, he added, "It is my suggestion that you go to Wena 'Ahote immediately. He surely needs you."

Moon Fire looked up at Sikyawa with tears swimming in her eyes and love in her heart. "Thank you, Father, thank you." Giving her mother a quick hug, she hastily climbed the ladder, leaving Lansa to offer them further consolation.

She found Wena 'Ahote stretched out on his back on his mat, with eyes that seemed to stare into nowhere. She knelt down beside him and tenderly took his left hand into her own. She knew his heart must be crushed at the loss of his career and any possibility of becoming sun priest. Deep within her heart, she felt that part of his pain was her fault, and that perhaps her mother had been right so long ago, when she objected to their relationship. She was only thankful that Tupkya had not reminded her of it, for she already felt guilty enough. It was with these thoughts that she waited for Wena 'Ahote to respond.

At last he turned his head toward her and said, "Come, Little Fire, let me hold you."

Her heart sang as she stretched out beside him, laying her head on his shoulder and molding her body to his. "I hope you will always hold me," she whispered.

"You know it will be so. You are all I have now, and I'll never let you go. I just hope you never see fit to put me out."

She giggled and nibbled on his earlobe. "Then you must not give me any cause."

"Ha, I suppose I'll just have to be sure to behave myself. You know, as a child, I was forced to behave or I knew the spirit dancers would punish me publicly. Now, I must behave because my spirited woman might put me out and also punish me publicly. I just can't win." He cleared his throat and continued. "Of course there really is no danger since we are not yet married."

"That is true, my love, that is true."

"Moon Fire, I want you to know of my concerns. I am no hunter and will have to learn in order to be a husband to you. I am also worried about our unborn child. With as little as we have to eat, and a diet that is almost always lacking in meat, and greens, I am afraid for both of you."

Moon Fire's pulse accelerated as she said, "You do not have to be a hunter, for there are no animals to hunt." Then very softly she asked, "Are you saying you would be my husband if you could learn to hunt?"

"Ah ha! Of course I will marry you if that is what you want. You know I adore you, and would not want to live without you." He turned his head toward her and stole a kiss.

"My parents would be very happy if we were married. Many season cycles ago, before the time when they were not speaking to me, my mother made it very clear that she only objected to our relationship because we could not be united as one in the sight of Awonawilona, and there might never be a girl child to carry on the family name. She and my father are undoubtedly elated at the turn of events, however painful they may be to you and me." She wound her free hand in his long hair and held it tightly.

He groaned and stole another kiss. Huskily he whispered, "When we are united, I want things to be right. The world is so out of balance."

"On that we can both agree. Don't tell me. Let me guess. You are considering the ceremony, and the fact that there is no water for the mud fight, and no quantity of corn for me to grind as my gift to you. It would also be extravagant to use what little water we have for the washing of our hair."

"Yes, Little Fire, those are my thoughts, and I want everything right in the eyes of Awonawilona. Perhaps later . . ."

She heaved a deep sigh. "I may not like it, but I must agree. What does it matter when we are united? Awonawilona already knows that my heart is yours, and has even blessed us with a child to further tie the knot. We will wait, and if Mother asks any questions, I am sure she will understand. It may be that she has already had the very same thoughts."

"Then it is settled. Just let me love you."

"Yes, oh yes!" she moaned, as he pulled her on top of him. Later, she would recall that their lovemaking was more intense than any other had ever been.

Moon Mother had gone through one complete cycle when Moon Fire returned to her cave. This had been the time frame that she and Palasiva had agreed would be more than sufficient. She had left the canyon when Sun Father had first appeared, for the sun cycles were very short, and the air very cold and dry. She knew she must return by the time Sun Father sank beyond the western horizon or she might be bitten by the cold. There was no wind, and it seemed to Moon Fire that the world was truly dead.

She reached her cave at Sun Father's zenith and sat on a warm rock with her feet tucked under her. To her delight she found that there was no need to cover her face, so she lifted her eyes to the sky in search of Red Eagle. The sky was a beautiful brilliant turquoise color with a few clouds that resembled cotton puff balls. When she lowered her eyes to the horizon, she spotted two figures coming toward her. One was familiar, but the other was not. Why, she wondered, would Palasiva have someone with him? She waited patiently for them to draw near, and when they were close enough, she realized that the second figure was a woman.

When they were at last close enough to speak, Palasiva said, "Ho, little sister, it is I, and I bring a friend."

Moon Fire's curiosity was piqued as she took in the young woman's appearance. In some ways she found that looking at the young woman seemed to be like looking at herself, as she had done so many times when water was available for reflection.

At last Palasiva put his arms around her and said, "Is this woman who accompanies me not beautiful? Mina, this is my sister, Moon Fire. She has always been close to me. She has always trusted me, and is all that a woman should be."

Moon Fire was shaken by his words. "I am pleased to meet you, Mina, but no one is ever all that a woman should be."

Mina smiled as she said, "In that you are correct. I, too, am pleased to know you. I hope you will not hold it against me that I am descended from the 'mountain people.' "

"If you are a friend of my brother's, you are a friend of mine." Then turning curiously to Palasiva, she said, "I somehow feel that this lovely woman is more than a friend."

"Hehe, you are right. She is to be my wife when Awonawilona will permit such an occasion. For now we live alone as well as we can, but tell me, sister, what news do you bring?" He watched her expression change from light to dark, and he knew without any words from her what she would say.

"Palasiva, Ruupi did his work well. The vote was tied, and could not be broken. They are still afraid to trust you. Lansa pleaded for you, but to no avail."

"Ruupi is a hateful man," he declared.

"Not only is he hateful, but he is truly evil. If you will remember, it was Ruupi and Leetayo who tried to convince the council that Wena 'Ahote was the informer to the Mayan-Toltecs, and with your confession, they were exiled for two season cycles. The council thought that they might have time to change their evil ways, but that has not proven so. They are still together and are worse than ever. Ruupi states that our entire family is evil, and has made every effort to bring members of the council to support him. Palasiva, I don't know what else to say except that our people have surely reached the point that there must be some major changes. With the cold season closing in on us, we must wait, but with the season of greening, who knows?"

Palasiva threw his head back and groaned. At last he said, "Then know this, sister. Mina and I will wait. We will bide our time in the mountains to the west of the canyon. Somehow we will make it through the winter. Perhaps there will be changes." He embraced her and continued. "It is my feeling that at some point in time, Mina and I will be reunited with my people, and for that, I will have no choice but to trust in Awonawilona."

"I am proud to see that you are still an Anasazi at heart, my brother. I would like to stay and talk, for I am curious about you, Mina, but I know if I do not leave quickly, I will be arriving in the canyon when the cold becomes impossible. Know that I love you both, and that includes you, Mina. I will pray to Awonawilona that you both survive the cold season with no problems."

"I must say the same to you, Moon Fire." Palasiva squinted his eyes to prevent the tears that threatened to gather. "Give our parents my love, and take care of them."

Before she turned to go, she said, "It shall be done."

CHAPTER 22

A.D. *1138*

It was, as the sun priest had calculated, the season of greening, but the earth remained parched with very little rainfall.
Wena 'Ahote and Moon Fire's family had given as much of
their food and water as they could without hurting themselves
to sustain the child that had grown to maturity within her. The
cold season had been the hardest ever, and everyone, except
perhaps Ruupi and Leetayo, had lost even more weight. Most
of the people were nothing more than skin and bones.

Moon Fire bent double with a seizure of pain. Tupkya had
warned her that the first child was always the most painful, and
with each pain she wondered why she had doubted what her
mother had told her. The pains were far apart, and she breathed
deeply whenever they occurred, as she had been instructed.
Sihu was by her side since her time was near, and wanted to assist in the birthing process. Tupkya had told her not to be concerned until they began to be more frequent, and that there was
even such a thing as false labor. In her heart she knew this
could not be so, for it seemed like she had been pregnant forever.

The widely spaced pains continued for half a sun cycle, until
suddenly she felt a gush of water rush down her legs. Sihu rose
and ran to summon Tupkya along with another old woman who
was much experienced in birthing children. The old woman
scolded Moon Fire and Sihu for waiting so long to summon
her, but Moon Fire knew that these women who specialized in
this were really very kind of heart, and only scolded so that she

might fear them enough to obey them. Now she straddled the birthing stool, as so many women had done, with sweat pouring as the pains came with closer frequency.

The old woman asked her to look within her own body to see if everything was as it should be. She said that the child's head should be pressing hard at her opening, and that she would know if she really looked within. Between pains, she closed her eyes. Her middle was by its own volition squeezing down hard, so she did not have to think about pressing and pushing. She only knew she hurt everywhere, and that there was a protruding pressure and a twistedness inside her that was not normal. She told the old woman that the baby was not where it should be while sweat poured in rivulets over her whole body, much like a violent thundershower she remembered from when she was very young. Concentrating very hard, she wheezed "I think the child's elbow may be trying to come out first."

The three women lay her down on the floor where they raised her legs and hips high while Sihu stood between her legs, and grasped them firmly, rocking her from side to side. Tupkya and the old woman prodded and kneaded her belly in an effort to change the baby's position. She knew the old woman would not put her hands inside her unless there was no other choice, but many were very skilled at doing just that if necessary.

At last she felt herself being lifted once again to the birthing stool where the next great shove ripped through her middle while the heels of the old woman's hands continued to prod and massage her belly. She groaned when she felt an awful stretching that was followed by a huge sliding sensation that seemed like she might be losing all her insides. She felt so faint that only Sihu and Tupkya kept her from collapsing and falling off the stool.

When she opened her eyes, she saw the radiant smiles of all three women. "It's a girl," Tupkya whispered.

"Is she well?" Moon Fire murmured.

"She is fine," declared her mother.

The old woman placed some kind of crushed herb under her nose, and she sneezed. She sneezed and sneezed until finally the afterbirth had been expelled, after which she was bathed of her sweat and allowed to lie on a mat. She was dozing off from exhaustion when her mother lay the child on her bosom. She immediately put the child to her breast, feeling the little one suckle strongly at her nipple. She looked at the dark head of hair, the little miniature hands and little brown buttocks, as if it were all a dream. The old woman had tied a soft cotton cloth around the child's middle with herbs to make certain that the connection between mother and child would not become infected.

It was then that Wena 'Ahote was summoned. With four huge strides he was at her side. His face was radiant with joy, love, and devotion as he took Moon Fire's hand in his own. "Ho, Little Fire. So together we have made a beautiful little girl." He placed his forefinger in the tiny palm, and beamed with pride when the newborn lightly gripped his finger. "I only hope her delivery was not too painful, and that there were no complications."

Moon Fire smiled as the baby continued to suckle. "I must tell you it was not much fun, but I'm sure I will forget the pain in due time, for she will bring us much joy."

"Not only that," he whispered as he watched Tupkya busily cleaning supplies in the corner of the room, "but she will carry on your family name as your parents want so desperately to happen. Shall I summon your father?"

"Ask my mother. She may have already done so." Her eyelids suddenly seemed as heavy as stone and she struggled to remain awake.

Wena 'Ahote squeezed her hand and said, "Sleep, Little Fire. Your work is done for a while. Know that I love you." Then rising to his feet, he turned to Tupkya. Taking her elbow, he asked, "Has Sikyawa been summoned?"

Tupkya flashed him a radiant smile. "Yes, but he has been told she needs to rest, so I do not think he will arrive soon."

Wena 'Ahote nodded, then said, "Honored Mother, I do not recall ever having told you this, but I want to thank you for the blessed gift of your daughter. We have loved each other for many season cycles, and now with the arrival of a daughter, we are truly one."

Tupkya returned him a contented smile, then said very simply, "It is so, and it is as it should be."

* * *

Ruupi had declared to Taatawi that he needed time for introspection and to fast. When Taatawi had asked him how many sun cycles he might need to take, he remained vague, telling the sun priest he could not say. He had watched Taatawi's skeptical expression, but ignored it, refusing to go into any detail. It did not matter to him whether the sun priest believed him or not. He had also informed Leetayo that he would be away for a while, and had given her no details as to where he was going or the length of his stay. Packing very little, he left with the few things he needed in a basket on his back held in place by a tumpline across his forehead.

Sun Father warmed the land during his journey across the sky, but left the time of darkness very chilly. Ruupi was glad to have his turkey feather cape to warm him along with a blanket. As he traveled, he noticed that in several locations the ground was so parched that it was cracked with little pockmarks, indicating a sprinkling of rain. He ate very little and conserved his water supply until, at last, he was in the land of the Mogollon. Here he found what was left of a sizable river with only a small bit of water left in it as it wound itself around an arroyo. After replenishing his water supply, he continued on his journey. To some extent he had told the truth when he said he needed time for himself and to fast, but that was only part of it. He knew of his destination, and what he must do.

He journeyed for nearly a moon cycle through dry, rough terrain, and unmerciful heat complicated with brambles and cactus everywhere. At one point he stumbled upon some small button cactus that the people valued highly as a hallucinogenic, and after boiling them well, he partook of them and lost two sun cycles in the experience. Finally he shouldered his basket and continued on.

The trading center was a dot on the horizon, but Ruupi was overjoyed. He knew that before Sun Father set, he would reach his destination. As he had expected, it was not long before two well-armed Mayan-Toltec warriors appeared out of nowhere to escort him. Both wore their hair fringed with bangs over their foreheads and two fat braids in the back. Their bodies were painted red and black, indicating their warrior status. Both also

wore only breechcloths and single bone necklaces. Neither of
them intimidated Ruupi in any way, for they knew he was expected.

When they were close enough to begin to see the trading
center well, Ruupi observed massive plastered walls gleaming
under the heat of Sun Father. They entered through the south
side of a large plaza that resounded with the squawks and gobbles of caged turkeys, the barking of dogs, and the cheeps of a
large bird he did not recognize. He had also noticed a very large
ball court before they entered the plaza, and recalled the religious game the Mayan-Toltec played, where the losers lost
their heads. He hoped he might be lucky enough during his
short stay to see one of those ball games.

With hand signs one of the warriors told Ruupi to wait
where he was, then both warriors left him. While he waited he
noticed that the few who were in the shady spots of the plaza
were mostly older men who were undoubtedly traders. Their
dress reflected some amount of wealth since their white shifts
were cinched loosely around the waist with belts of glorious
color. They also wore broaches of topaz, opal, emerald, and
jade while each one of them boasted more of the same inserted
in the sides of their noses. Ruupi could not help but wonder
why, with so much wealth, the Mayan-Toltec coveted the
Anasazi turquoise so intensely. He only knew that it was to his
advantage that it was so.

His thoughts were interrupted suddenly by the arrival of two
Eagle Knights. Due to the heat, they were not dressed in their
full feather attire, but wore only their eagle helmets to indicate
their status. The helmets were complete with plumage with a
wide open beak, the top part of the beak being above the forehead and the bottom part under their chins. The eyes of the
eagle were of obsidian.

One of the knights removed his helmet. "Welcome," he said
in broken Anasazi. "My name is Tecpatl, which means 'flint
knife,' in our language. The knight who stands beside me is
called Chicauaztli, meaning 'rattle stick.' We offer you our hospitality."

Chicauaztli removed his helmet and said with hand signs
and some Anasazi words, "Our scouts have followed you for

many sun cycles, and informed us of the time you would arrive. We have been expecting you."

Ruupi replied, "It is my pleasure to be in your company. I am Ruupi Tuuhikya, which means 'crystal medicine man' in my language. Is it appropriate for us to do business here in the plaza?"

"It is normal for us to do so here or anywhere. What would you prefer?" Tecpatl asked.

"I would prefer the coolness and privacy of a room."

"Then come this way," said the knight.

They led Ruupi to a small room, which was somewhat dark until his eyes grew accustomed to the poor lighting. They motioned for him to sit on a low bench with a back attached. After taking his seat, he marveled that such a thing could be so comfortable. It was then that his eyes opened wide, for this room was filled with jade, opals, and emeralds as well as quartz crystal, obsidian, agate, and jasper. The colors were beautiful even in the dim light. To his delight, the one gem that seemed to be missing was turquoise.

When neither of the knights seemed willing to open conversation, Ruupi took the lead. "I have traveled far to have the honor of speaking with you. I would ask that what I have to say be kept in strict confidence, and be revealed to only those who would be necessary to implement any action."

Chicauaztli smiled, saying, "It shall be as you ask."

Gathering his thoughts, Ruupi began. "As you undoubtedly know, my people are starving and desperate due to the drought we have experienced for so many many season cycles. They are vulnerable and weak, as are the Mogollon, Hohokam, and even the raiders. I come to offer what I think is a reasonable exchange. I am aware of your constant need for prisoners for sacrifice to appease your gods. If you were to attack my people in the canyon in which I live, it would be easy for you at this time, and you could take many prisoners of all ages. I was sure this would be of interest to you."

Tecpatl raised his eyebrows, which arched over his crossed eyes. As was the custom among his people, his mother had dangled a beautiful bright stone on a string very close over his nose as a baby, which had resulted in what was considered a mark of beauty to his people. "You speak of an exchange. What do you expect in return?"

Ruupi had waited and hoped for this occasion for many seasons. Clearing his throat, he said, "As I have already told you, my people are desperate, and indeed, if I had not been occasionally secretly trading with you for food, I, too, would be skin and bones as they are. In addition to that, my people have turned against me, and there is no future for either me or them. I would ask that you permit me and my woman to come to live in Tula or Chichen Itza, where we can both escape the miserable conditions in which we are living. I would further ask that I be allowed to continue as a priest and a crystal scrier among your people. Of course my woman and I would be willing to learn your ways, and I could offer you my talents."

"You drive a hard bargain," replied Tecpatl. "It is in my mind that to grant you such favors, there should be more in the bargain for us." Looking around at the myriad of gems, he continued. "I am sure you have noticed that there is one gem that is not here, and one that my people covet. Turquoise is sacred to us as it is to you and your people, for in it is the color of the sky and water. We might be willing to seal the bargain if you could help to correct our shortage."

Ruupi's heart leaped with enthusiasm. "Revered Eagle Knights, you are the ones who drive a hard bargain. As if offering my people to you were not enough, you want even more. I must take some time to think on this."

Now Chicauaztli leaned forward, placing one elbow on his knee. "You must realize that to come to your canyon with a full army would be a long, exhausting, and expensive trip. If your drought is as you say it is, it would necessitate many more supplies than we would ordinarily need. Perhaps we should just drop the whole thing, and you can return to your people."

"I do not think you would really want to send me back to my people if you knew what I am about to disclose."

"Then speak, priest. We have no time to waste."

"If you will give me one moon cycle to return to my people, you may plan your attack soon thereafter. After the attack, to sweeten the bargain, I will lead you to one of our turquoise mines and make it available to you. This is as much as I can offer."

Tecpatl slammed his fist on his knee. "Done," he said. "Now come join us for our last meal of the day. We will put you up during the time of darkness, and you may depart when the sun rises."

All three men rose at once to enjoy the final meal of the day.

The fact that the knights had called it a meal was a dreadful understatement. Ruupi was amazed at the variety that was before him. There were large amounts of corn, two kinds of beans, chili peppers, tomatoes, roast turkey and dog, corn cakes, breads called atole, tortillas, and tamales. There was a stew made from beans, corn flour, ground tomatoes, and a curious green pear that he was told was called an avocado. But the most wonderful culinary treat was the drink made from cacao beans that was sweetened with honey.

When Ruupi finished he patted his distended belly with one final thought. He had completed his mission just as he had planned it.

Moon Fire had moved in with Wena 'Ahote soon after she had learned she was pregnant. Since there was no shortage of rooms, she maintained her own quarters for counseling purposes. Wena 'Ahote had become as good a provider as any man who yet remained in the village. There were many occasions when he and Sikyawa hunted together, but they seldom returned with anything to eat except for an occasional lizard. The northern outlier sent small quantities of corn, beans, and squash, but there was never enough. She could not remember the last time she had eaten a meal that was satisfying. Most of the time, the meal consisted of thin corn gruel with a few beans or squash and a tiny bit of lizard to give a meat flavor. The baby was frail, and often listless, and she found it necessary to put the child to her breast more frequently than was normal. As was the custom of her people, the baby would not be named until it was certain that she would live, and times were such that she wondered if her baby would ever have a name.

There was only a sliver of a moon in the sky. She finished nursing, and lay with her body molded to Wena 'Ahote's, and the baby's body next to her own. She found herself reveling in the heat of Wena 'Ahote's body, and at the same time worrying about their daughter. It was clear to anyone that the child was not well, and no one in the community had any answers. She lay awake with her stomach rumbling and a mind that refused to shut down. She knew Wena 'Ahote was asleep, for his breathing was even.

Suddenly she felt him twitch and moan in his sleep. According to the custom of her people, one should never try to awaken someone who might be dreaming, for the dream might be important. It was the same if someone was meditating. She only knew she must wait, and that it probably would not be long before he awakened.

Unexpectedly he moaned, gave a great lurch, and sat bolt upright on their sleeping mat. "The gods have deserted us! There are evil forces," he growled.

Not wanting to disturb their daughter, Moon Fire said, "I knew you were dreaming, my love, and I am awake. Our daughter is finally resting, and I am afraid to move."

He rose to stoke the fire that had died down to embers. Finally he said, "In my dream it all became clear."

She waited without responding, knowing he would tell it when he was ready. She watched him as he stared despondently at the wall that he had painted with stars.

At last he sat down beside her and took her hand in his. "Little Fire, in my dream, I was told there are evil forces who will soon overtake our people, or at least the people in our community. There is someone among us who is bent on destroying us, and it will not be long before a great tragedy will befall us. It is in my mind that we are being told to leave this canyon before it is too late."

"If what you say is true, then we must not waste any time. Do you have any idea what or who these evil forces might be?"

"Little wife, you and I know that Ruupi is up to no good. He has been gone too long to be on a fast or a vision quest. All I know is that things are not right, and time is crucial."

Moon Fire was thankful that the baby was sleeping rather peacefully. "I think it is essential that you speak to Taatawi of your dream. He will know what to do."

"I agree. In fact, I am sure he is awake, for it will not be long before Sun Father rises. I will go to him now."

"I am sure you would never be able to sleep, my love. Speak to Taatawi. When the dawn comes, I will take our daughter to Mother and see what I can find out."

He kissed her lightly, then moved quickly up the ladder. As he had anticipated, he found Taatawi awake, and surprised to see him.

"Ho," exclaimed Taatawi, "this is as the sun cycles of old. To what do I owe this honor?"

"I have had a dream, and one that I feel is important to the very security of our people who remain in the canyon."

Taatawi raised his whitened eyebrows, wrinkling his forehead. "Speak on. I am listening."

"Taatawi, Revered One, according to my dream, there are evil forces that are an immediate threat to the welfare of all of us, and not just one evil force. It is in my mind that we should leave, and that we should waste no time. Have you thought about the length of time that Ruupi has been gone? How could he have gone on a spirit quest for more than a moon cycle? There is nothing to eat or drink out there. He is the one. I am sure he is the one."

Taatawi gave him a troubled look, then said, "I must tell you that Ruupi's quest has also been on my mind. I will think on what you say."

Wena 'Ahote looked at him imploringly. "Do not take a lot of time, or we may be too late."

"It shall be so, my son. It shall be so."

Moon Fire left the baby with Tupkya and went out of the canyon. Fortunately there was no wind, but she took the precaution of tying a cloth around her wrist to shield her face in case the wind should change. It had been quite some time since she had had the opportunity to leave the canyon to communicate with Awonawilona's creatures great and small, and she hoped she would not have too long a wait before she found one. After seating herself on the ground and using the side of a large rock to support her back, she closed her eyes.

She had not long to wait. Something within her told her to

look to her left, and when she did she spotted a lizard with spines and crests down the center of its back. With a smile, she said, not in words, but in thoughts, "I am honored to share your space, and I am surprised that you are still here. You must know that if you are not careful, my people will eat you. Things are really bad when we humans must resort to eating insects and lizards."

The lizard's tongue darted in and out as he eyed her. "I will agree with you on that issue. Most of my fellow lizards have either left the canyon or been eaten by your people. As a matter of fact, I am leaving this dust bowl of a canyon as we speak."

"What can you tell me, lizard? Should we humans also leave the canyon? What do you know?" Moon Fire asked.

Once again the lizard's tongue darted in and out. "As you know, we lizards can sense vibrations through the ground. Our eyes can also detect the subtlest of movements, and we have extremely acute hearing. All this gives us the gift of seeing more than most. I would suggest that you and your people pay attention to your dreams."

Moon Fire was visibly shaken. Lizard was telling her that her people should pay special attention to Wena 'Ahote's dream. "What more can you tell me?" she asked.

Lizard moved himself into a more comfortable position as he absorbed the heat of Sun Father. "I am sure you are also aware that I am able to shed my tail. A predator may grab me, but I am often able to get away when I give up my tail, and then I will grow another. I am here to teach you humans that sometimes it is important to become more detached in life in order to survive. Sometimes it is important for us to know that we must separate ourselves from others in order to do the things we must do."

"Are you saying that we humans must leave the canyon?"

"You may stay if you wish, but there are times in life when one must break from the past. Perhaps your people should consider exploring new possibilities. You may need to follow your own impulses before what is happening swallows you up." Lizard blinked and his tongue darted once more, then he turned tail and ran.

Moon Fire's breasts were becoming increasingly sore as her

milk swelled. She remained where she was for only a short time before she knew she must quickly return to the canyon.

Together they decided to approach Taatawi. Wena 'Ahote held her hand tightly as they moved toward the sun priest's quarters. His face was a grim mask of concern, and his body tensed with the realization that time was of the essence. Though he had not said it in words to either Moon Fire or Taatawi, he knew Ruupi was bent on destroying those living in the canyon. He had no idea where Ruupi was, but he had very strong feelings that even in the next breath, mass destruction could be upon them. Since Ruupi had been gone so long, he surmised that the Mayan-Toltecs would be the ones who would attack. He had said nothing to Moon Fire, but he could not help but wonder if she was not mirroring his thoughts.

Taatawi must have heard their footsteps at the top of his ladder, for he said immediately, "I have been expecting you. Enter." When they reached the bottom of his ladder, he beckoned them to sit on a mat, and said to Moon Fire, "So you are as concerned as we are. What are your feelings?"

"I have just returned from a confrontation with Lizard. He said several things that I feel are important for us to consider, aside from the fact that he, too, is leaving the canyon. He said we should pay attention to dreams." She rearranged her cotton cloak, and continued. "He said that sometimes we must become detached in life in order to survive, and also that it is important to know that we must, on occasion, separate ourselves from others in order to do the things we must do. He also added that there are times when we must break from the past, and that we should follow our own impulses before something happens that might swallow us up."

Taatawi's jaw dropped in amazement. "He really said all that? Sometimes I believe that those who are not human know more than we do. We, who are so proud, have lost our gut feelings. Awonawilona, be praised, Moon Fire. Lizard may or may not have saved us." Then turning to Wena 'Ahote, he said very quietly, "We must move on. We have been in this canyon for many generations, but the signs are right. We must move on, and we must waste no time."

Wena 'Ahote cast him a grim smile. "I am fully convinced, and though I have not spoken of this even to Moon Fire, I would not be surprised if Ruupi were not gathering Mayan-Toltecs to destroy us, or at least take us all for slaves."

His words shook Moon Fire so soundly that she stared at him in disbelief, for these had also been her own thoughts for many, many sun cycles. She had not wanted to think about it, but now she knew that his thoughts had truly been hers. "Then we must warn the people," she said.

"That is so," Taatawi stated, "but there is something that must be done first. We must send a warrior to find out as much as possible about Ruupi's whereabouts. Then we will know. I will see that this is done. There is really nothing either of you can do until you hear from me."

"Then it is agreed that we should make ready to leave," exclaimed Wena 'Ahote.

"That is so. Now both of you go in peace, and nurture the daughter you and Awonawilona brought into this unbalanced world."

Wena 'Ahote anxiously took her hand, and they departed.

CHAPTER 23

A.D. *1138*

A warrior had returned, saying that Ruupi was, when the far-
thest of the relaying warriors saw him, about half a moon
cycle away. This meant due to the time it took the warriors to
return, he was now probably not more than ten sun cycles away
from the canyon. Taatawi informed Wena 'Ahote, who in turn
told Moon Fire. Together they decided that the people should
be informed as quickly as possible, but that Ruupi's name
should not be mentioned. Why, they thought, should it be necessary to strike too much fear into the people, when they would
all be using the last vestiges of strength to prepare to leave.
Since Sun Father had almost set in the west, they decided to
wait until he rose to begin informing the people.

Wena 'Ahote quietly spoke to Moon Fire of his concern that
the people would have enough faith in him, even though he was
no longer a priest, and would heed his words and respect his
dream. He also told her that he was unsure that their daughter
would be able to handle the harshness of the journey they all
would be making.

Moon Fire also admitted to him that she, too, was worried,
but that there was little they could do except to trust in Awonawilona. She nursed their little girl and they retired for a much-
needed rest.

Sleep eluded her. Her thoughts were full as she wondered
what her people would do and how they would respond when
asked to leave behind all they had known for so many generations. Most of those who lived in pit houses or small outliers in

and around the canyon had left a few at a time over the past several season cycles. Perhaps, she thought, they were smarter and braver than those who still clung to the canyon. She thought of her parents and all the other old people and how hard it would be for most of them. Tupkya had once told her, "You can transplant a sapling easily enough, but you can't transplant a fully matured tree." She had no idea how the elders would take to the idea, and so she spent some time in prayer to Awonawilona until at last she fell asleep with the baby nestled tightly against her and her back molded to the front of Wena 'Ahote's body.

She awoke with a start. The baby was still, very still, when she should have been ready to nurse. Moon Fire pulled the baby tightly against her, but the child did not respond. She checked the infant's pulse and there was none. She shook the child, awakening Wena 'Ahote.

"Are you all right, my love?" he mumbled.

"I'm . . . it's our little girl. I think she has crossed over," she said as she held the little one to her breast.

Wena 'Ahote sat up immediately. "Let me have her. Perhaps you are wrong." He took her from Moon Fire, putting his ear to the tiny chest. Staring at Moon Fire in disbelief, he said, "Awonawilona has taken her. She grows cold." Then placing the child on the mat, he took Moon Fire into his arms, blending his tears with hers. They clung to each other until, at last, Wena 'Ahote said, "I shall begin the preparations for her journey to the other side. I want you to go to your mother and father, because I don't want to leave you alone."

Looking at him as bravely as she could, she said, "I shall be fine. Leave the baby with me until such time as we must prepare her."

"Moon Fire, I usually give in to your wishes, but this one time I cannot. Come. We go. Now climb the ladder and I will hand our daughter to you."

She rose to her feet, feeling utterly beaten. She felt as though a piece of her had been ripped out of her and would never return. She walked in a daze as they crossed the plaza to the ladder of her parents' home. At a later time she would come to realize that she was in shock.

Wena 'Ahote tapped on the ladder several times before getting a response from Sikyawa. "Who is there in this time of darkness?"

"Father and Mother, we need you," he answered.

"Come then. What is wrong?" Sikyawa inquired.

When they reached the bottom of the ladder, Sikyawa needed no words to understand. He shook Tupkya, who awoke with a start. In less than three blinks of an eye she knew, and quickly hobbled over to Moon Fire to wrap her old arms around daughter and granddaughter.

Sikyawa and Wena 'Ahote also embraced until Wena 'Ahote said, "Father, will you assist me in making preparations for the crossing of our daughter? I would like to leave Moon Fire and the baby here with Mother. I do not think she should be alone."

"You need not have asked, my son. It is my duty."

Wena 'Ahote turned to Tupkya. "Watch over her, Mother. She is still in shock."

"Of course," she said. "It shall be so."

The two men slowly climbed the ladder to make the arrangements, arrangements that would be hasty due to the fact that many would be preparing for departure from the canyon.

Tupkya asked to hold her granddaughter, but Moon Fire held her baby fast as tears fell unbidden. Tupkya knew that grief was expressed differently by everyone, so she waited patiently until Moon Fire's tears were spent.

At last Moon Fire placed her daughter gently on a mat, and squared her shoulders to look at her mother. "Give me a knife," she rasped. "I must do what I must do."

"You may have the blade, daughter, but do not damage yourself more than is necessary. Your people need you now more than ever, and so does Wena 'Ahote." When she saw a glazed look in Moon Fire's eyes, she added, "Do you hear me, daughter?"

Moon Fire snatched the knife from her mother and hacked off one of the whorls over her ears. When she turned the knife toward her arms, Tupkya seized the weapon, saying firmly, "The time we live in is a time of change, and the change must be honored. There are rumors that we must leave the canyon quickly. Oh yes, your father has heard the rumblings. We have no time for deep external wounds, for we must be strong as a people. I know your internal wounds are raw and bleeding, and that is the way of it, but somehow you must get hold of yourself."

Moon Fire let her mother have the knife, then raked her fingernails down her upper arms to draw blood. "Let me have the knife, Mother. Let me have it!"

"No, no, and no! Hear me well. Are you listening? Our little daughter would not want you to consider her welfare above that of the people. She would look down from above and frown at your weakness. Her spirit knows you are needed, really needed by your people now. Will you let her spirit down?"

It was as though a cloud had been swept aside to reveal a rainbow. Moon Fire gazed at her child and then at her mother. A stillness almost as in death overtook her. She collapsed on the mat beside the baby, and shivered uncontrollably. She knew she must go on, and that her mother was right. Other women had survived the loss of a child, and gone on in life. Other women had had other children to help make them forget. She looked up at her mother with a tiny, brave, quivering smile of understanding.

Tupkya knelt behind Moon Fire to massage her shoulders and to let her know she would always be there for her, or at least until she, too, crossed over.

The infant was buried quickly and with little ceremony under the corner of Moon Fire's quarters. Sihu and Lansa had offered their support, as well as many others in the community. Wena 'Ahote's family had many season cycles ago left their outlier outside the canyon to find better living quarters, so they, of course, were not present. Moon Fire had never met them, but she hoped that Awonawilona might at some point in time allow such an occasion to happen.

The people were being rallied, and many of them were willing to follow Taatawi and Wena 'Ahote. Only a few said they would never leave, and those were the few who had always supported Ruupi, no matter what he did. Leetayo was among those who refused. Moon Fire was not surprised. She supposed

Leetayo would always be loyal to Ruupi. The plans were to leave when next Sun Father began his journey.

Moon Fire was walking toward Wena 'Ahote's quarters after counseling someone who was in doubt about leaving when it happened. It began as a low rumble almost as if the earth was moving, and seemed to be coming from behind the holy school. Though she could not see what was happening, she intuitively knelt down and covered her head. She noticed that there were several in the plaza who were doing the same. The rumblings turned to crashes that shook the walls of the rooms around her. The thought that Awonawilona might be destroying everything she loved made her stomach churn, and her heart palpitate. Her body broke out in a sweat as she wondered where Wena 'Ahote might be, and prayed that he was safe. She also prayed for the safety of her parents.

Then, almost as quickly as it began, it was over. The crashing became an occasional rumble, then a final enormous crash. Moon Fire rose and ran out the front of the plaza to the back of the complex. What she saw was unbelievable. The cliff behind the multistoried building had broken off, and tumbled into several small storage rooms that were not really a part of the complex. Now what she saw behind the complex was nothing but a huge pile of jumbled rocks that had completely obliterated the storage area. Much to her delight, Wena 'Ahote and Taatawi were not far behind.

"Awonawilona, help us!" cried Taatawi as he took in the destruction.

"I thank the gods you are safe," Wena 'Ahote gasped. He wrapped his arms around Moon Fire, and buried his head in her hair.

"But what of our parents?" she cried.

"They are fine. Their quarters are nowhere near the back of the building. They are fine," he assured her.

She trembled in the safety of his touch, then said to Taatawi, "Was anyone hurt?"

"I do not know, but time will tell. Let us say that this is surely a clear sign from Awonawilona that we must leave immediately. He has sent us an omen. Those who are here must be made to understand." He turned to the people who had gathered around with eyes wide in terror and disbelief. "Hear me well, my people. We have been sent a sign. Regardless of what has happened, we must somehow leave when Sun Father rises as planned. Go now, and make ready." He waited and watched as the people slowly returned to the plaza and to their quarters.

It was learned within only a short time that there were three who were buried beneath the pile of rocks. Only one could be found and once again, grief flooded the hearts of the people. The body that they had been able to recover was that of an old one, who was a cook, and was probably looking for what little, if any, corn, beans, or squash she might find in the storage rooms. She was buried hastily under a storage room, next to her own quarters, though she had no family to mourn her. The other two bodies were also older women, as was found out later. One of them had family members in the community, but the other did not. It was said that her family had also long since left the canyon, and that she had not, due to the fact that she thought herself too old to make a long journey.

With this turn of events, and the fact that Taatawi proclaimed the rock slide as a message for departure from Awonawilona, it was easy to convince the people that it was time to move on. Almost all of them diligently prepared to leave. Though many were physically weak, they had become psychologically strong, and they knew they had little time.

Sun Father was nearing the end of his journey. Moon Fire had already made her preparations for what little she needed to take with her, and was walking toward Wena 'Ahote's quarters when a figure approached her. She had not seen Leetayo for a long time, and even when she had, it was only briefly. Nevertheless, she watched her approach. She wished there was some way she could avoid her, but it seemed to be an impossibility.

Leetayo had matured physically over the season cycles. Her hair was still the same lustrous black that it had always been, but her face had filled out along with her body, indicating that she was not starving as were the people. Her hips swayed provocatively as she approached Moon Fire, and her foxy eyes sparkled through the fullness of her face. She stopped squarely in front of Moon Fire and with her hands on her hips planted her feet firmly on the ground. Then pointing her right forefinger in Moon Fire's face, she said, "You! I spit on you! You are the fool who is responsible for the ruin of our people. You, Taatawi, and that stupid husband of yours are splitting our people and making a mock of our greatness. Well, let me assure you, there are some who will not follow. There are some who are intelligent enough to await Ruupi's return, and who realize that he is the strong leader our people need. You and Wena 'Ahote have caused trouble ever since I can remember, and now you are the cause of the most heinous of crimes, that of dividing our people. Again I say, I spit on you!"

Moon Fire simply stared at her, for she knew there was really no response that would make any difference. Leetayo's mind was already made up, and she did not want to be confused with any new facts. Moon Fire's expression was as cold as ice and her lips remained sealed.

Leetayo became even more inflamed as she said, "So now you are not only stupid, but are also deaf and dumb. You are mocking me!" She dropped her hands from her hips and clenched her fists at her side.

Still Moon Fire remained silent. Leetayo was so irrational that she knew there was nothing she could say. What she did not realize was that, with her silence, she was fanning Leetayo's flames of anger. She noticed a couple of people who happened to be nearby stop to listen. Then one of them turned and made off hastily toward Taatawi's quarters.

Seething with fury, Leetayo seized the long side of Moon Fire's hair and pulled as she screeched. "You are an evil abomination! You were being punished with the loss of your child. Can't you see that Awonawilona does not approve of the witch that you are? Yes, you, who talk to the animals, are nothing more than an evil witch. Evil, I say! Evil!" She twisted and tightened Moon Fire's hair around her neck.

Panic surged throughout Moon Fire as she began to struggle to breathe, but she still made no sound, for she knew that if she did, it would be just what Leetayo wanted. Never, in her wildest imagination, would she have believed that Leetayo would stoop so low, and resort to violence. She had always known that Leetayo's hatred for her ran deep, but she had never expected that her hatred would consume her as it was doing now. Moon Fire was finding it harder and harder not to strike back.

Again Leetayo spat straight into Moon Fire's face, and the spittle ran down her cheek. "Look at you!" she hissed. "The proud Moon Fire, beloved among her people. You, with the six toes on each foot, and people believe you are gifted. You are surely gifted, but not for the good of the people. You are a witch!" Again she tightened the hair around Moon Fire's neck.

Moon Fire was gasping for breath when a figure stepped behind her laying a hand on the hand of Leetayo's that was clenching her hair. "Unhand her, Leetayo. Have you lost your senses?" Moon Fire recognized the voice of Taatawi, and regained her composure.

"Unhand her? *Unhand her?* She is a witch, a witch I say!" screeched Leetayo.

Another figure approached Leetayo from behind and seized her around the waist. "Unhand her!" the voice commanded. "Would you fight us all?" It was the voice of Tenyam, who, in spite of his age, was strong enough to hurt Leetayo if he so chose.

Still another voice exclaimed, "Let her go, Leetayo. She has done nothing to you."

Reluctantly, Leetayo loosened her grip on Moon Fire's hair. Suddenly she realized that she could not fight them all. She was convinced that Moon Fire, the witch, had their support, and that there was nothing she could do about it short of murdering her opponent. She knew that without Ruupi's assistance, it would never happen, and she had been a fool to think otherwise. She would await Ruupi's return. He had been gone too long, much too long, and she should not have tried to take things into her own hands. She dropped her hands to her side, stepped away from Moon Fire, and cast her eyes to the cracked dirt of the plaza floor.

Taatawi stepped in front of her and took her by her shoulders. "Leetayo, the world is out of balance. Would you kill her and have her blood on your hands and in your mind? Ruupi will return soon. Go now. Most of us will be gone soon."

Suddenly her failure and embarrassment was too much to

handle. She turned abruptly and ran, ran, ran as fast as she could to her and Ruupi's quarters.

When the time of darkness finally arrived, Tupkya and Sikyawa sat in the small part of the complex that they had called home for so long. Sikyawa had lit his pipe, and closed his eyes, though Tupkya knew he was not asleep. They had packed all that they could carry comfortably, and there was nothing to do but to rest. Tupkya was not certain how well she and Sikyawa would fare on such a journey as they were about to undertake due to their aching bones and of course their age. The whole idea had happened so quickly in her mind, and she felt deep sorrow with the thought that they would be leaving this wonderful canyon with its enormous buildings that had supported them for so many many generations. She looked at Sikyawa and said, "We go when next Sun Father rises. How do you feel about that?"

Sikyawa blew smoke rings in the air, and simply said, "Change is inevitable."

"How can you make it sound so simple?" she inquired.

"Only because it is so. I am only sorry that it did not become necessary when we were younger. The journey will be difficult."

Perhaps it *was* necessary when we were younger, and the children were younger, but the gods did not speak so clearly."

"You may be right, but what is in the past, is in the past. When we awaken, we go."

Tupkya remained silent for a while longer, then asked, "Are you not concerned for our children, and grandchildren, and how they will fare in such a journey? Our people are not accustomed to the wandering way of life."

Sikyawa looked at Tupkya lovingly as he laid down his pipe. "Yes, of course I am concerned. Life is always a gamble, but our people are hearty and spiritually strong, and they will find a way. Our children will find a way. They always have."

"You make it sound so simple. I wish I could think as you do."

"It is in my mind that we should get some sleep. It is always easier to deal with major problems when we are rested." Then taking her hand, he added, "Come, sweet wife. Let us enjoy what may be our last sleep of privacy."

She smiled as he led her to their mats.

Sun Father rose and so did the people. They assembled in the plaza. Everyone had been in agreement that they should leave immediately, but it was apparent that no one had given much thought as to which direction they should take. Some wanted to go toward the thriving northern outlier that was now the main distribution center of trade for their people due to the presence of at least some water in a river that ran nearby. Some wanted to go east, for there was also a great river far away that never ran dry. And some wanted to go west into the mountains and beyond, where there was abundant firewood, and a place to hide from the possibility of the approaching Mayan-Toltecs. It was also known that within the mountains due west of the community they were leaving, there were springs. None wanted to go south, for that would be the direction from which the Mayan-Toltecs would come.

At last it was agreed that each group would go in the direction that called them. And so they departed with tearful farewells.

CHAPTER 24

A.D. *1138*

Three sun cycles before the people had left the canyon several scouts had been sent out to the south in an effort to confirm the presence of the invading Mayan-Toltecs. There was much concern among Moon Fire's people that the scouts might not know where to find them since the dividing of the routes had not occurred when the scouts had set out. Taatawi assured them that their path was clear enough for any scout to follow, and that they would soon know the whereabouts of the Mayan-Toltecs if they were anywhere near.

The people had traveled west for three long sun cycles when a scout finally arrived. Taatawi, Wena 'Ahote, and Moon Fire conferred with the scout, who told them that indeed the Mayan-Toltecs were approaching from the south, and would probably be in the great canyon in three or perhaps four sun cycles.

Hoohu and his wife had decided to go westward with Moon Fire's people. He stood close by and overheard all that transpired. "I praise Awonawilona that we left the canyon when we did. I can find no joy in thinking of the fate of those who chose not to leave the canyon. It is in my mind that Ruupi has betrayed his own people, and for what reason, I cannot imagine. Can it be that Ruupi wishes to live among the Mayan-Toltecs? If that is so, then I say that he is more evil than any of us would ever have thought."

As everyone nodded in agreement, Wena 'Ahote said, "Something has come into my mind that I wish to share with you." He paused as if waiting for consent that he might go on.

"Then speak, brother," declared Taatawi.

"It is clear to me that Ruupi must have struck a bargain with the Toltecs. They will no doubt take those who are still in the canyon as slaves, but do you think that just slaves would be enough to entice the Toltec warriors to make such a lengthy journey? I think not." Again he paused to take in the thoughtful expressions of those around him.

"What do you think?" inquired Hoohu.

"What is the commodity we possess that the Mayan-Toltecs have always coveted?" Again he watched Hoohu and Taatawi as they dropped their jaws and raised their eyebrows in recognition of what they knew he was about to say. "Turquoise. They always demand turquoise. Ruupi knows the location of the mine that is hidden in these very mountains at the foot of which we now stand. It is my guess that he may have promised to guide them to the source of that mine. Perhaps we should take some precautions."

"Wena 'Ahote, I am glad you have such a brilliant head on your shoulders. You are right. You are very right. If no one disagrees, I think we should send some of our strongest men to close the mine immediately," exclaimed Taatawi.

Everyone grunted in agreement, and Taatawi with the help of Hoohu and Wena 'Ahote rounded up ten volunteers who were eager to be of assistance. They set out immediately while Taatawi informed the people what was being done and what the scout had said. Then, wasting no more time, they continued on their way into the heart of the mountain range.

The people trudged on for three more sun cycles, but at a much slower pace due to strenuous climbing and the challenge of crossing numerous canyons of various sizes. Two of the older men in the group knew of several springs in different locations within the mountains, and guided the people to the nearest one. Their knowledge was due to the fact that they recalled bringing huge logs out of the mountains for building purposes in the canyon many many season cycles ago. Much to everyone's delight, there was still a constant trickle of water, and in time they were all able to fill their water skins. On the second sun cycle one of their hunters brought down a young buck, and brought it back to share with everyone. Though it did not allow much meat per individual, it was relished by all.

Temporary shelters were erected with fire pits in each one. Though it was the season of growing and the season of rain showers, no one gave any thought to the possibility of rain. Due to the higher altitude, however, low-hanging clouds brought enough moisture to allow some wild greens to grow. The women also gathered juniper berries, which were normally not eaten, but now offered still another addition to their diet. In the higher altitude among the grandfather pines there were onions for spicing, wolf berries, wild currants, and yucca that grew occasionally here and there among rocks. In the lower altitude there was bear grass, rice grass, and goosefoot, whose seeds and grains could be used to thicken stews. These were only a few of the bounties that the mountain range had to offer. Here was where Moon Fire and her people had decided they would spend the cold season.

As she nestled close to Wena 'Ahote beneath their blankets, she said, "I am glad we are going no farther at least for a while. Our parents have done surprisingly well under the circumstances. By staying here through the cold season, our old people will gain strength enough to travel when the season of green arrives. We women will have time to gather and preserve food, and the men can hunt to provide us with at least some meat." She giggled and nudged him. "It's funny to think that we will not need as much food as most since our stomachs have become so small."

Wena 'Ahote lovingly traced her profile with his forefinger. "It's a good thing Ruupi is not with us if only because he would eat more than his share in order to sustain his robust appearance."

Again she laughed and said, "I would love to be there when Ruupi brings the Mayan-Toltecs to the mine. I would like to see the expressions and reactions when they see what our volunteers have done."

"I, too, Little Fire. I, too. Now let me love you in our new home. Perhaps we can make another child together."

"No, my love, not yet. If I conceive now, I would be delivering about the time we will leave when the green season arrives. Though you know I want us to make a child, I do not think it the proper time. Do you agree? I still have some of the herb that prevents conception, and I will use it at least as long as it lasts."

"Ah, my little woman. How is it you are always right? You won't believe how hard it is to live with such perfection."

"Ha," she said, "perfection I am not, but you are when you make love to me."

"Why are we wasting time with conversation then?" Without another word he began to caress her, turning their simple little hut into a world of ecstasy.

Ruupi had taken his time returning to the canyon. Twice he again indulged in the funny little cactus that gave him such delight. He had also stopped very briefly at a small Mogollon village to replenish his water and food supply. Now he was thinking of Leetayo, and the heat of her loins that awaited him. Relieving himself manually was no substitute for a woman.

He rounded a hill on the south side of the canyon and gazed at the holy school. For whatever reason, the entire canyon seemed eerily quiet. Of course the heat was almost intolerable due to the fact that Sun Father was at his zenith, but even as he stood and watched, he did not see a single figure. Immediately sensing that something was wrong, he rushed to Leetayo's quarters. Since his quarters were at times her quarters, and her quarters his, he did not tap on her ladder for permission to enter as was the custom.

He found her repairing a pair of sandals that were badly worn, and found it odd that she paid him no attention. "Leetayo?" he said. "Are you all right? What is wrong? I am back and I've missed you."

She put the sandals aside, and looked at him with saddened eyes. "Things are not the same. They have all gone."

Seating himself beside her, he asked, "What are you trying to tell me? What do you mean when you say they are all gone?"

She squinted her eyes, then bowed her head. "I mean there are only about forty of us left."

"What, in the name of Awonawilona, are you talking about?" Panic seized him as her meaning gradually began to dawn on him.

Looking at him with huge tears of desperation brimming in her eyes, she declared, "There are only forty of us left in the canyon. Only those who supported you are still here. Everyone else agreed with Taatawi, Wena 'Ahote, and Moon Fire, who said it was time to move on. I wanted you to return to me, but I dreaded it at the same time. Can you understand?"

He felt as though his stomach were being wrenched from his belly. A wave of sickness washed over him as he thought of the Mayan-Toltecs and what their reaction would be. He had not told Leetayo of his mission. Her temper was such that he was afraid she might betray him, and he had no desire to confide in her now. He only wanted to go away to nurse his misfortune. To learn the details of what had happened did not seem important to him, for the shock was too great.

Rising to his feet, he said, "Yes, I understand you well, but I must have time to think. I shall be in my quarters. If you need me, you know where I am." Then turning from her, he despondently climbed the ladder, hoping she would not need him, and that she would give him time alone.

When he had settled on his mat, he ruthlessly berated himself. The great priest and crystal scrier who would have been sun priest! How stupid to become so self-assured. He wanted to surprise Leetayo when he took her as his wife to live among the Mayan-Toltec, and had not told her of any of his plans, but it was also true that he did not entirely believe her capable of keeping his secrets. Now he was wondering how much he should tell her or if perhaps he should tell her nothing at all. The thing that pressed most heavily on his mind was the fact that he had told the Mayan-Toltec that there would be many many people, enough for an army, and now there were only forty. They would think he had been lying, and his punishment would be great. Suddenly he realized how smart he had been to throw the turquoise mine into the bargain. He only hoped that the mine would make up for the loss of slaves, and that they would be lenient with him.

He lay down on his mat with no thought of food, and tossed and turned, until he finally slept.

For two sun cycles she did not come to him and he did not go to her. There were questions he wanted to ask of her, yet he knew the answers were not important. If he was still successful when the Mayan-Toltec arrived, he would take her as his wife into their lands regardless of what may or may not have happened while he was away. There was still some food in the storage bins, and he commanded an acolyte who was loyal to him to cook for both of them. He could not remember ever living so close to the edge of life. Even when he had been exiled, they had sent him to an outlier where he knew he would live well, be fed, and even revered as a priest. Now, as so many had been saying, the world was truly out of balance, and there was nothing he could do about it but hope.

There was a tapping on his ladder, and a runner descended. Turning to him, the runner gasped, "They are coming. An army is coming! A Mayan-Toltec army of great size. Why, Revered Priest? Why are they coming here?"

"Have no fear. Thank you for the message." He watched as the runner fairly sprinted up the ladder.

"Yes, they are coming," he thought while he slowly climbed the ladder.

News had spread like lightning. There were people in the plaza whose curiosity had overcome their fear of the fierce army approaching. The tension was so high that it would have taken the finest obsidian knife to cut through it.

The army stopped at the entrance of the plaza. Tecpatl and Chicauaztli stood in front as commanders, assessing the holy school, and those who stared at them in the plaza. They seemed to be waiting for someone before they entered.

Ruupi easily made his way between the people to welcome the Mayan-Toltecs, though there were butterflies in his stomach. He swallowed hard as he assessed the army in front of him. All that he could see were dressed sparingly in breechcloths, due to the intense desert heat. Tecpatl and Chicauaztli were the only ones who carried headdresses, indicating their status as Eagle Knights, and obviously the commanders of the unit. What really concerned Ruupi was the variety of weapons they carried. Each warrior carried a bow and arrow, a javelin for fighting at close range, an atlatl, a long spear, and another extremely dangerous weapon which was called "the hunting wood." It was a flat hard wood stave the length of a man's arm and as wide as his hand. Above its handle on both edges of its length, large sharp pieces of obsidian had been inserted. Ruupi cringed to think of how lethal such a weapon could be.

At last Tecpatl spoke. "Greetings, Ruupi Tuuhikya. We are here as we promised to keep our part of the bargain. Will you also live up to your commitment?"

After nervously shifting his weight from one foot to another, Ruupi replied, "I shall honor my commitment to the best of my ability."

"Then bring on the prisoners," Tecpatl pompously declared.

"They are in front of you," murmured Ruupi.

Tecpatl's gaze scanned the plaza in disbelief that was rapidly turning to rage. Returning his attention through narrowed eyes to Ruupi, he said, "Surely I must not have heard you correctly. Did you say the prisoners are in front of me?"

Ruupi held his chin high and said, "Indeed you heard me correctly."

"Am I to understand that there are only about forty people in this canyon? How can that be? Where are you hiding the others? You spoke as though there would be many hundreds. Come now, what sort of dangerous game are you playing?"

"I am not playing any game, and I am not hiding the people. Leetayo, who is my woman, told me that they had all left several sun cycles before I returned to the canyon. Yes, there were many hundreds, but they split into three groups and left with only what they could carry on their backs. May our god Awonawilona strike me dead if I am not speaking the truth."

Tecpatl seethed inwardly as he once again looked over the small number of scrawny people who stood in the plaza. Most all of them wore fearful curious expressions except for one woman, who Tecpatl assumed must be Ruupi's woman. He struggled to fight the anger that was growing in intensity with every breath he took. With a raspy, hissing voice, he said, "You have betrayed us. By rights we should kill you all right now." He turned his back on Ruupi and raised his right hand as if to signal his warriors.

"Wait!"' Ruupi cried. "Have you forgotten the other part of the bargain? There is still the turquoise mine!"

Tecpatl spun to face him once more. "Ruupi Tuuhikya, crystal medicine man, you are no scrier. If you were what you say you are, you would have seen within your mind that your people were leaving!"

"And even if I had seen that they were leaving, was there anything I could have done when I was several sun cycles away from them? Come now, think clearly. There is still the turquoise mine that awaits you."

"This turquoise mine had better more than make up for the lack of prisoners we were promised or you may rest assured that you and your woman will also be taken prisoners. My men will surround this building and camp around its perimeter. When Sun Father begins his next journey across the sky, we will set out for the mine. Consider yourself lucky that you and your people are alive for at least one more sun cycle." Saying no more, he turned to his warriors and barked orders to them in a voice that shook with rage.

In no time at all, the Mayan-Toltecs had surrounded the holy school, and made themselves as comfortable as was possible. With a heavy heart, Ruupi turned to Leetayo. Together they walked to his quarters.

Ruupi slept very little. He had finally had to explain their predicament to Leetayo, much to his embarrassment, but she supported him, assuring him that there was nothing else he could have done. She also told him she was not particularly enthusiastic at the thought of living with the Mayan-Toltec, but that she would follow him if that was his wish. She also asked if she could go with him to the mine, but he refused her, saying that the journey was long and dangerous, and that one woman with so many warriors might be asking for trouble. She turned on her side and fell asleep, leaving him staring into the darkness.

Sun Father rose too soon. Though he did not often do so, Ruupi prayed to Awonawilona, asking for guidance and protection through the next few sun cycles. He knew Leetayo's confidence in him was complete, and for that he was grateful, but in truth, he had never felt so out of control. Even in that terrible time when his people had exiled him, it had been only temporary. He had known that he would return to his people and once again gain control. Now he had no such feelings. He could only hope that the mine would pacify the Mayan-Toltecs, and that they would still hold up their end of the bargain.

Leetayo helped him pack what few belongings he would need. They both climbed the ladder to the roof, then down another into the plaza. The people glowered angrily at him, for it was clear to them that they were being held prisoners and that somehow Ruupi had betrayed them. Ruupi tried not to make eye contact with any of them, but walked with Leetayo to the outside entrance. There he saw that Tecpatl and Chicauaztli had divided the warriors into two groups, one large group to stay back to guard the prisoners, and a smaller group to travel to the turquoise mine.

Chicauaztli turned to Ruupi, saying, "We go now."

Ruupi squeezed Leetayo's hand and said, "Guard yourself well. Because of your association with me, the people may turn on you. If it is the will of Awonawilona, I will return to you." Saying no more, he walked toward Chicauaztli, Tecpatl, and the accompanying warriors to begin the journey.

Most of the Mayan-Toltec warriors had stayed back in the canyon. The traveling party consisted of twenty warriors, Tecpatl, Chicauaztli, and of course Ruupi. It took three sun cycles for them to reach the foot of the mountain range that lay directly west of the canyon. The ground was so dry that dust rose with every footstep, and it became necessary to cover their faces with cloth to prevent breathing in the dust. Everyone squinted their eyes for the same reason. Few of the plants in the desert showed any sign of life, yet everyone knew that if the rains ever came, the plants would reseed themselves, and the desert would eventually come to life.

For three sun cycles no one had spoken to Ruupi, even around the campfires when Sun Father had set. They had given him just enough food to barely sustain him, yet they treated him as though he were already a dead man. Perhaps, he thought, he was as good as dead, for he had no idea whether the mine would please them or not. It had been a long time since he had visited it, and he knew that, due to the terrible drought conditions, his people had not worked the mine for some time. There were times when panic seized him, and he thought the only answer was to run, to escape. But then hard reality hit him as he realized that he was no hunter, and probably would not survive even if he did escape. He fought off a serious depression that threatened to overtake him.

At the end of the third sun cycle, as they all sat around the campfire, one of the warriors brought him a leg of a rabbit that one of the hunters had killed a short way into the mountains, along with a small corn cake. The warrior said nothing, sneered at him, and turned back to his companions. He ate in silence.

He bedded down before everyone else, partly because he knew there would be no conversation, and also that they would rise early, well before Sun Father rose, to begin their trek into the mountains. Although there was conversation all around him, he shut it out, and turned within his own mind and his own thoughts. He wondered how Leetayo was doing, and if she would truly realize what a dangerous situation she was in. He only hoped she would not try any of her feminine wiles on any of the Mayan-Toltec warriors. He wondered if the group of people who had chosen to go west might be within these mountains, and if so, could he escape and find them. Again despair engulfed him. First he realized he had absolutely no training as a tracker or a warrior, and secondly, there was always the possibility that the group who had traveled west were led by Moon Fire and Taatawi. He had not thought to ask Leetayo what she knew about the direction the groups might have taken.

He turned on his side to try to still his mind, but sleep

eluded him. He forced himself to close his eyes, yet in spite
of himself his mind remained alert. His mind began to flash
back over the events in his life and many things he had and
had not done. He remembered his childhood and his father,
who had been a revered powerful leader of his clan, his father, who had told him that to be a priest would make him
equally as powerful, and perhaps more so. His father had
controlled his clan with a temper like an erupting volcano,
and Ruupi had learned well.

Suddenly he sat bolt upright almost as if he were having a
vision. His thoughts turned to the constant gentleness of Moon
Mother, and the contrasting angry fire of Sun Father. He remembered one of his teachers saying, when he was preparing
to become a priest, that to be a balanced person, one should be
a combination of the traits of Moon Mother and Sun Father.
He now knew he had ignored that teaching due to his upbring-
ing. Despair washed over him with the thought that he only
knew the angry compulsion to control, and that he lacked the
traits of compassion and the willingness to help that were so
necessary to be a balanced person. Humility washed over him.
He knew now, that he would rather be starving with his people
and suffering with them, than to be in the precarious position
that he had brought upon himself. At long last sheer exhaustion overtook him, and he slept, feeling that he had been re-
born.

Scouts had returned informing Taatawi that the Mayan-
Toltecs and Ruupi were perhaps two sun cycles from the mine.
When Taatawi told Moon Fire and Wena 'Ahote, he watched
their eyes light up as they looked at each other. "What is it you
are thinking? What is it in your eyes?" he asked.

Wena 'Ahote smiled and said, "I cannot say, Revered One.
It is not important."

"What do you mean, it is not important? Such expressions
are usually meaningful, are they not?"

"Well, yes, of course. May I talk to you in private?"

"Come to my hut. I will listen."

Together they walked, leaving Moon Fire curiously watching. When Sun Father next rose Wena 'Ahote and Moon Fire headed east.

The Mayan-Toltec party had traveled another two sun cycles when Ruupi announced that they were drawing near to the mine. He told Tecpatl that it would be necessary to descend into a canyon very soon, and that the mine would be near the floor of the canyon. This, he told them, was the mine closest to the lands of the Anasazi, and the most prolific before the drought had caused vast numbers of people to evacuate the canyon. The result was that there were not enough men left to hunt and also work the mine.

They were at an altitude where piñon pine and juniper were prevalent along with several varieties of cactus. Much to their relief, the party was fortunate enough to happen upon a small spring, which enabled them to fill their water skins. One of their hunters even brought down a deer, which provided them with a delightful meal. They retired when Sun Father set with a full stomach.

They broke camp when Sun Father rose as the sky was turning pink and gold. Ruupi assured them that they would be at the site of the mine before Sun Father was at his zenith. The sky was a beautiful clear turquoise color, and the green of the pines and juniper seemed deeper than Ruupi had ever remembered. He was sure it was because he had not been in the mountains for a long time.

At last he said, "We are beginning to enter the canyon that contains the mine." No one responded.

As they began their descent, they climbed down for a short time, then rounded an outcropping of rocks. A scorpion skittered away from Ruupi's sandals, which caused sweat to bead his forehead. Since he was in the lead, he was the first to view the mine. His heart leaped into his throat when he saw the jumble of massive stones that covered the entrance of the mine. Anyone could see that it would take many men many days to even begin to clear the entrance. A wave of despair washed over him as he realized his people had outsmarted him. That emotion was followed by one of panic, for he knew he was a dead man. Clutching his robe around him, he dashed quickly away from the warriors in an attempt to gain his freedom. With every breath he took he expected any one of their weapons to strike him dead.

On he ran, jumping doggedly over rocks while trying to avoid the thorns and spikes of the cactus that littered the ground. He found himself becoming short of breath, and cursed the fact that he was a soft priest, and not a hardened warrior. A warrior would be able to run indefinitely, and might stand a chance to escape but he was paunchy and out of shape. Then as he rounded another turn he ran headlong into Tecpatl and three of his warriors.

"So," Tecpatl growled, "you have completely broken your end of the bargain." He held Ruupi tightly while one of his warriors bound his hands behind his back.

Ruupi fought the urge to kick and spit to vent his rage, but he knew that by doing so, things would only be the worse for him. "It is not I who betrays you. It is my people who have betrayed me."

Tecpatl laughed and said, "It is in my mind that your people did not betray you. They outsmarted you."

"Why did you not shoot me or club me?" he whined.

The Eagle Knight's eyes narrowed as he answered, "You are not worthy of being shot or struck. You are the scum of the earth. Can anyone who betrays his own people be worthy of respect? If we wounded you or killed you, you would never make the trip back to Tula with the rest of your people. You will be sacrificed to Tlaloc, our rain god, along with those who await our return in your canyon."

Ruupi bowed his head in humiliation and fear, knowing his disgrace would be complete when he faced Leetayo and those who had trusted him. His mission had failed miserably. He realized that his life had hit rock bottom, and that he had not appreciated the joy of being at the top. Awonawilona had seen fit to show him that he had grossly misplaced his priorities, and it would cost him his life. He knew his life was over.

Moon Fire and Wena 'Ahote had watched all that had happened from afar. From their vantage point, they could not hear what was being said, and were too far away to see facial expressions clearly. Even so, it was obvious that the volunteers, who had created the rock slide that covered the entrance to the mine, had done the job well. Neither of them spoke or dared to make a sound as they watched the events unfold. It was not until Ruupi and the warriors were completely out of sight that Wena 'Ahote said, "You know, Little Fire, he got what he deserved, but a part of me feels sorry for him. In spite of all the grief he gave me for so many season cycles, no one deserves the fate that will ultimately be his." He took her hand as they began the two-sun-cycle return trip to their camp.

Just before Sun Father dipped below the western horizon, they camped for the night beneath some piñon pines. Moon Fire gathered some pine nuts while Wena 'Ahote built a fire. He had killed three ground quail and plucked them, then skewered them to roast over the fire. When Moon Fire had completed her time-consuming task, she was delighted to find that Wena 'Ahote had fixed their meal. Her stomach growled at the smell of the succulent meat. Together they decided to take the precious nuts back to share with the people.

After finishing their meal, Wena 'Ahote rebuilt the fire to ward off animals and they settled into their blankets for some much-needed sleep.

Moon Fire turned on her side and molded her body against his. "My love," she said, "I know you are tired, but there is something I must say."

"Uh-huh, and what might that be, Little Fire?"

"I want you to know that the time we have shared alone together, just you and me, has been the loveliest time of my life. I hope we can do this more often."

After an enormous yawn, and a nuzzle on her neck, he said, "I must agree with you. Perhaps the raiders do not have it so bad after all as they wander from one place to another."

"Yes, but they travel together as a group, I suppose for safety. I like the privacy of just you and me alone. Please let us do this again."

"We will see, Little Fire. We will see. Now if you keep talking to me, I might not answer." He breathed deeply and yawned once again.

"Sleep then, my love. We will see what tomorrow brings."

They rose early, packed their belongings, and started on their way, hoping to make it back to their people by the time Sun Father was setting. For that reason, Wena 'Ahote did not hunt, for it would have only delayed their progress. They spoke very little as they made their way over rock formations and small gorges.

Sun Father had just passed his zenith when Wena 'Ahote gripped Moon Fire's arm and pressed his forefinger over her lips. Whispering in her ear, he said, "We are being followed."

She froze, then whispered in his ear, "How do you know?"

He said nothing, but mouthed the words, "I just know. I heard them." Then again he whispered in her ear, "Stay where you are. I will try to find them." He squeezed her hand and moved silently away.

Wena 'Ahote crept silently along a deer trail, moving toward the place where he had thought he had heard the enemy. Then it occurred to him that it might be one of their own hunters. With this realization, he decided to be extra cautious. He hid himself behind another pile of rocks that were covered with lichen and waited.

In only a short time, a man and a woman appeared, walking confidently toward him. Their appearance indicated that they were raiders, but if they were really raiders, why would they not be hiding? Wena 'Ahote raised his spear.

"Please do not shoot," the young man said in Anasazi.

Wena 'Ahote dropped his weapon in surprise. This couple were not raiders. They spoke his own language. There was a strange familiarity in the features and gestures of the young man. He was handsome, but thin and sinewy. She was quite lovely with long black hair and doe-shaped eyes. "Who are you?" he asked.

"You are Wena 'Ahote. Am I correct?" inquired the stranger.

"Yes, that is so, but again I ask, who are you?"

"You knew me as a young boy. Will you take me to my sister?"

Wena 'Ahote studied the man carefully until at last he knew. "Palasiva! Your sister is not far away. She will be delighted. Come." Then he turned to the woman at Palasiva's side. "And who is this lovely young woman?"

"She is my woman, and soon to be my bride. We have lived alone too long."

Wena 'Ahote beckoned them to follow him. After only a short walk, they found Moon Fire sitting in a hollow in the middle of a rock outcropping. She jumped to her feet and ran to her brother, throwing her arms around his neck. No words were said until at last Wena 'Ahote broke the silence. "Don't you think the little woman needs some attention too?"

"Oh, I am so sorry," she said as she broke away from Palasiva's embrace. Turning toward Mina, whose eyes were filled with tears, she embraced her. "Welcome, little sister. Palasiva, Mina, have you been following us for a long time?"

"We have been in this same mountain range that your people are now occupying for some time. As you know, Moon Fire, I promised to remain close to our people after I rescued Mina from her near slavery with her people. Do you suppose that there might be a chance that we could be reconciled with my family?"

Moon Fire broke into a huge smile as she said, "I see no reason why not. Oh, Palasiva, I cannot see why not."

Wena 'Ahote broke into the conversation. "Then let us speak no more, for we must not delay if we are to reach the people by the time Sun Father sets."

Everyone agreed as they set out with hopes held high in their hearts.

Just before they entered the camp, Wena 'Ahote placed his hand on Palasiva's arm. "You must stay by our side when we enter. We will walk straight to Taatawi's hut and ask him to handle your request."

Palasiva nodded his agreement as they walked into the camp. He took Mina's hand, and gave her a reassuring smile. He also looked around the camp for anyone he might recognize, but saw only a few women and children and a few old people. He assumed that the men must be out hunting and some of the women would also be out of the village gathering and digging.

They had barely arrived at Taatawi's hut, when, as if on cue, he lifted the blanket that covered his door, and stepped out. Seeing that Wena 'Ahote and Moon Fire had safely returned was foremost on his mind, and he welcomed them with a short embrace. He turned to Palasiva with his eyes narrowed and a tiny smile tugging at the corners of his mouth. "Can this be who I think it is? Moon Fire, where did you find him? And who is this lovely young woman? Did you find her with him?"

"Revered Sun Priest, if you fire any more questions at me, I'll never be able to sort them out in my mind. Yes, this is my 'not so little anymore' brother, Palasiva. We did not find him. He found us. This is his woman, Mina, and like us, they would like to marry whenever we are in such circumstances that we can be married properly."

Taatawi stroked his chin, then said, "I must assume that they both are asking to become accepted by this faction of the people. Am I correct?"

"In that you are correct," declared Wena 'Ahote.

"I suggest, then, that you bring Hoohu to my hut. He is our only elder now, and he must agree for this to happen. Moon Fire, you, Palasiva, and Mina remain here with me."

In a very short time, Wena 'Ahote returned with Hoohu, who looked curiously at the strangers who stood before him. At first he just stared, then suddenly his eyebrows shot up in recognition. "Palasiva?" he asked.

"You still recognize me. I am honored. It is my pleasure to introduce Mina, my betrothed."

"I can only assume since you are here that you wish to become part of the people once more." Then turning to Taatawi, he said, "May we speak in your hut?"

"By all means," said Taatawi as they both disappeared into the privacy of his meager living quarters.

It seemed to Moon Fire that she had taken only several breaths when the two men were at their side once again. Her heart skipped a beat when she saw their serious facial expressions.

Palasiva's eyes were focused on the ground in front of him as he held Mina's hand with a fierce grip. He, too, had noticed the extremely short time in which the two older men had conferred, and was uncertain whether it was good or bad.

Hoohu sucked in his breath, then exhaled. "We have decided to welcome you back to the people. We need you as a hardened warrior and hunter, and we also think you will be able to teach us some additional survival skills we may not already know." Then placing his right hand on Palasiva's left shoulder, he added, "We welcome you both. Perhaps you might like to visit your parents and older brother."

Palasiva could not believe his good fortune. As hardened a warrior as he had become, he was having trouble fighting the tears that threatened him. "I would like that very much, and I feel sure that I can be of great help to our people," he said in a quavering voice.

Moon Fire sensed his emotion, and quickly led Mina and Palasiva toward the direction of her parents' hut. At the entrance, she said, "Wait here. I will call you when it is time."

She found Tupkya wearily grinding rice grass on her stone metate. Sikyawa was busy blowing smoke rings into the air and up the ventilation hole in their hut. Both of them said to her, "Welcome, daughter." Then Sikyawa said, "To what do we owe this unexpected visit? We thought you and Wena 'Ahote were still out at the mines."

"No, we only just returned. There is someone outside your hut who would like permission to see you. Are you both feeling well?" Moon Fire asked that question only because her parents were slowly failing, and she wondered how any shock might affect them.

"We are fine. Why do you ask if we are feeling well? Welcome them to our hut," declared Sikyawa.

Moon Fire raised the blanket that covered their door, allowing Palasiva and Mina to enter. Wena 'Ahote had decided to stand quietly just inside the door in order to maintain a low profile.

Again Palasiva held Mina's hand as he faced his aged parents. He saw the shock of white hair on both of them along with the wrinkles, and wondered how much of it he had caused. Finally he said, "Mother. Father. Do you not know who I am?"

Tupkya's mano dropped on the dirt floor as she gasped. When she rose, her skirt swept the rice grass out of the metate all over the ground, but she never gave the loss any thought. "Tell me I am imagining," she exclaimed. "Tell me you are an apparition!"

Palasiva swept his mother into his arms. "No, Sweet Mother. Do I not feel like flesh and blood?"

Tears of happiness flowed as she whimpered, "Yes, and bones, too."

Sikyawa had been a little slower to rise, but at last he was at his son's side, and Palasiva turned to him for a long warm embrace. Suddenly Sikyawa's attention was drawn to the pretty young woman at his son's side. He disengaged himself and asked, "And who is this lovely young woman at your side?"

Palasiva made the introductions, then went on to say that he wanted to marry Mina whenever the conditions for a marriage according to the way of his people were right.

Sikyawa looked at him curiously, then asked, "From what I have just heard you say, my son, it sounds as though you may be here longer than for just a visit. Am I right?"

"In that you are correct," Palasiva answered as Tupkya took his hand in hers. "Taatawi and Hoohu have met, and decided that I am needed as a hunter and also as a seasoned warrior here in this village. We are here to stay."

"I want you to know, my son," declared Tupkya, "that with all your father's and my aches and pains, there have been times that I wished I could cross over. Now I am so glad Awona-wilona did not hear me, for never would I have wanted to miss this occasion. I truly feel whole once again with my three children around me. Now, if and when your father and I do cross over, we can do so with a smile."

"When Lansa returns from the hunt, we must all go together to inform him, Sihu, and his son, Palatala, and have a reunion," Sikyawa announced.

Palasiva turned to Wena 'Ahote, saying, "I know where we can find deer. In case Lansa returns empty-handed, we can still provide for the reunion."

Tupkya spoke up enthusiastically. "Very good. Moon Fire, Mina, let us go get Sihu. We women have much gathering and grinding to do to make ready for the occasion. Sikyawa, come with us to watch over Palatala while we are gone."

In no time, they arrived at Sihu's hut, where once again joy was abundant. Palasiva and Wena 'Ahote left for the hunt, the women departed for their gathering. Sikyawa took his grandson's hand in his own gnarled one, then sat him on his lap. With a huge wink, he said, "Since it is just you and me, let me tell you a story of long long ago . . ."

EPILOGUE

A.D. *1142*

During the next four sun cycles Moon Fire and the people moved several times in an attempt to find what they considered the perfect place, which would have all that they would need to survive for many generations. They continued to move in a westerly direction toward the mountain that belched fire and smoke, the same one that first exploded during the time so long ago when I, Chakwaina, was a little girl and the fabled Coyote Woman was in her power. The soil was fertile due to the ash from the spewing mountain, and was also in close proximity to the great canyon where all our young men went to gather spruce as a part of their initiation into manhood.

Shortly after their arrival, Taatawi discovered a hole in the ground that blew air from beneath the bowels of Earth Mother, indicating to him and everyone else that the ground was blessed with her sacred breath. They began building a great house once again, and planted their corn. The harvest of their crops was abundant, giving everyone a feeling of security that many of the people could never remember having.

It was after that first harvest that Moon Fire and Wena 'Ahote and Mina and Palasiva were married in a double wedding. Moon Fire had had a little girl child during the third season cycle of their wanderings, while Mina and Palasiva had had a little boy. Lansa and Sihu still only had Palatala, but vowed they would have another if Awonawilona granted their wish. Tupkya had come through the time of wandering quite well, and was very happy that her family was reunited, and that there would, at last, be a little girl to carry on the family clan name.

No one ever mentioned anyone they had known in the community before, for it was believed that the spirit of the dead person would be invoked if their name was spoken. In truth, many of those persons from the past had only caused pain in their lives, and negative thoughts were not accepted by Awonawilona.

Two moon cycles after their arrival in the new land that seemed so much like home, a star appeared in the sky with a tail brighter than anyone had ever heard of or seen. Taatawi declared it an omen, an omen of a new beginning for the people. Though he said it might not be the last, it still confirmed the fact that the people were being given a chance to put the world in balance once again.

Now, forgive me, but this old wandering soul needs a rest.

AUTHOR'S NOTE

When one visits the Southwest, one cannot help but be impressed by the thousands of ruins that still remain to attest to the existence of the peoples who built them and proudly lived in them. Archaeologists believe that many again may have been destroyed by bulldozing, the damming of rivers, and looting. They also believe that Chaco Canyon, with its glorious, enormous apartmentlike buildings, was the center, or mecca, of the Anasazi culture for at least one hundred fifty years. Arrow-straight roads chiseled in rock when necessary shot out in all four directions, leading to outliers, some small, and some large. Since they did not possess the wheel, it is my belief that the roads were used both for ceremonial and for trading purposes. It is now well known that the Anasazi were the ancestors of the Hopi, Zuni, and other Pueblo tribes living along the Rio Grande, and that their modern legends speak of one migration after another as they searched for the perfect place in this their fourth world.

Cultures rise and cultures crumble. Such has been the way for thousands of years, and the Anasazi were no different from others. They wrestled with the same problems of other sophisticated cultures who also declined or even completely disappeared. Like others, they fought with raiders and outside enemies, and struggled to survive through harsh weather conditions. But the most devastating problem for any culture is when that culture decays from within, as I have called it, "a world out of balance."

Today we also deal with the very same problems. It is my most fervent hope that we can awaken before it is too late, and learn from the past in an effort to resist making the same mistakes again.